# THE CHILDREN'S HEART SURGEON

## BY
## MEREDITH WEBBER

**Meredith Webber** says of herself, "Once I read an article which suggested that Mills & Boon were looking for new Medical Romance™ authors. I had one of those 'I can do that' moments, and gave it a try. What began as a challenge has become an obsession—though I do temper the 'butt on seat' career of writing with dirty but healthy outdoor pursuits, fossicking through the Australian Outback in search of gold or opals. Having had some success in all of these endeavours, I now consider I've found the perfect lifestyle."

# CHAPTER ONE

THE music followed Alex from the ballroom to the bar—deserted now the dancing had started. The band was the best, seducing even the most staid of attendees at the congress onto the floor, and as his feet moved to the beat he felt vague regret that he hadn't brought along a partner.

He gave a huff of self-mocking laughter as he ordered a brandy.

What partner? He couldn't remember the last time he'd had a girlfriend for long enough for her to qualify for the word.

His own fault, as his last non-partner had pointed out, but she had been wrong about the cause. Wrong to blame his focus on his work.

What he couldn't handle in a relationship was emotional dependency. Put that way he sounded cold, which he knew he wasn't. But what woman would understand that he carried so many emotional burdens and expectations in his work that he was looking for escape from them in his private life?

Impossible, his sister had told him. In any good relationship there has to be an element of dependence…

He shook his head in denial of his thoughts and sipped his brandy, moving his head in the action just enough to realise he wasn't alone at the bar. Way down the other end of the horseshoe, deep in shadow, he caught a glimpse of silvery hair, moving like a moonbeam on flowing water.

A woman swaying to the music, as alone as he was but feeling the lure of the beat in her body.

He hesitated a moment, aware that what he was about to do was totally out of character, then with great deliberation he put down his glass, stood up off the stool and moved towards her.

She was dressed all in black, which explained why he'd only seen her hair in the shadows, and still she swayed, unaware of his approach.

'The music's great. Would you like to dance?' He spoke quietly but knew he'd startled her, for she stopped abruptly and he could have sworn her pale skin turned even paler.

Behind him, he sensed the barman watching both of them—suspicious of him, protective of his female customer.

It was her turn to hesitate, but then she gave a smile so sad it hurt his heart.

'I'm not dressed for a ball, and I'm fresh out of fairy godmothers,' she said, holding out her arms to show him she was wearing black trousers and a high-necked black sweater.

'We can dance outside,' he said. 'On the terrace.'

Then he waited, willing her to say yes—willing her to dance with him because, for some unfathomable reason, it suddenly seemed important that she did.

He waited for ever, it seemed, until she gave a why-not, almost fatalistic kind of shrug and slipped off her stool.

He took her arm, tense as a steel rod, and led her out onto the terrace. Beyond it, manicured lawns led down to a large artificial lake, but the moonlight shining on the water was authentic, and the stars in the black night sky twinkled like fairy lights.

She was slim and lithe, and once she relaxed very light on her feet. In fact, she danced with a grace that made his dancing better—made him feel like someone from an old movie. Fred Astaire? Was that the dancing guy's name?

Her body fitted his so they moved as one, gliding across the terrace to the strains of the big band inside.

A moment out of time.

He was aware of that even as he held her in his arms, and an inner instinct told him to remember it, so he looked at her face, seeing a dusting of freckles across her pale skin and dark shadows beneath her eyes. He'd seen shadows like those under the eyes of his patients' parents. Shadows etched by emotional pain and physical exhaustion.

He held her closer, wanting to protect her, forgetting he needed to avoid emotional dependency.

Forgetting he didn't know her.

He was vaguely aware the real music had stopped, but he heard it playing in his head and danced on, knowing she, too, was hearing it—dancing to it. Then it started up again, a different tempo—slower, more seductive.

He felt her body stiffen beneath his hands, but he wasn't through dancing yet. Through holding her! Could he will her to open her eyes so he could see their colour? They'd looked dark in the shadows of the bar, but with her fair hair and pale skin, they could be light. Her lips were pinker than the skin around them, which wasn't saying much. No lipstick, but he could see their shape—their soft, ripe fullness.

Best he think about her eyes again, he told himself, but his feet had guided them to the darkest corner of the terrace and as the music slowed their feet stilled while their bodies kept swaying to the tune, as close as two people could be— two fully clothed people.

Seduced by music, and moonlight on water, and the feel of the woman in his arms, he bent his head and kissed her.

There was a long, indecisive moment as she again stiffened in his arms, then as suddenly relaxed against him. She didn't quite kiss him back, but didn't pull away or slap his face, indicating, he decided, by these two negatives that he could continue with this gentle, exploratory quest.

He could feel her heart beating against her ribs and sensed a tension in her, as if kissing a strange man was a very risky business even with two hundred congress delegates and their partners within screaming distance. And while he guessed she wasn't *not* enjoying it, she was also poised for flight.

Then suddenly she was with him, opening her lips to him, responding—whatever inhibitions had been holding her released.

Had they really kissed for an hour, or had they danced for longer than he'd thought they had? Afterwards he tried to work out the timing, but found he couldn't.

Unless they *had* kissed for an hour…

Could anyone kiss for an hour?

All he knew was that they'd kissed for a long time, demanding more and more of each other until it had seemed they'd known each other's blood.

Until he'd known they'd had to get off the terrace before they'd become a public spectacle!

'Can I walk you to your room?' he asked, voice husky with the passion kissing had aroused.

She leaned back in his arms, and looked up into his face. Dark eyes—brown or hazel, though he couldn't tell which in the shadows—scanned his face, while his own eyes were riveted on her bruised and swollen—well-kissed—lips.

'No,' she said, and pushed away from him, but as he released her he felt a shudder pass through her body, as if his suggestion had repelled her.

When she'd kissed him like she had?

Then she touched his hand and said gently, as if apologising for the shudder, 'My room's too far away.'

And with that she departed, not back into the bar where

the dancers were now gathering for nightcaps, but down the steps towards the lawn, vanishing into the night's shadows.

He'd find her again, he vowed as disappointment doused the fire within his body.

The congress ran for three more days, and the hotel was closed to all but congress attendees and their partners.

Partners? He hadn't seen her at any congress sessions. She was with someone?

Married?

But unhappy—he'd felt her unhappiness from the moment they'd met.

He'd find her. Find out about her.

Kiss her?

That would be up to her!

# CHAPTER TWO

'YOU know something, Henry,' Annie said, pouring milk over the cereal she'd piled in both their bowls, 'I hate the idea of starting this new job.'

Henry, far more interested in the preparation of his breakfast than in Annie's conversation, said nothing, prompting Annie to explain.

'I know I was excited about it back when it was first offered to me. Really excited. Well, all right, I was over the moon—but that was before I realised Dan Petersen was leaving. I thought Dan would be my boss.'

She lifted Henry's bowl and put it in front of him.

'Now I've got a new job *and* a new boss! And there's something dodgy about it, I know there is. I've been invited for little chats with just about every hospital executive, which, even when you consider it's a new unit, seems strange. And there've been looks between those pencil-pushers, and conversations that stop when I walk near them. Definitely dodgy.'

Henry gave a derisive huff, as if he didn't believe a word she was saying.

'Then there's the man himself—the new boss,' Annie continued, refusing to be put off by his lack of support. 'You know I don't listen to gossip—'

Henry's look of disbelief forced her to add, 'Well, I do listen, it's the lifeblood of the hospital, but I don't repeat it, except to you. And even if I didn't listen I couldn't have helped but hear the stories about him—they're legion. He may be a surgical genius but he's a tyrant both in Theatre

10

and in the ward, and the words they use about him. ''Ruthless'' seems to come up most often. Now ruthless, as you and I both know, usually implies a person who'll do anything to get ahead, so why's a ruthless top US surgeon with an international reputation coming here, to Jimmie's, to work? Working here, even setting up a new unit, isn't going to put four stars on his CV—not even one star, to tell the truth—so why? That's what I want to know.'

Soft brown eyes looked into hers, but Henry offered no comment. Instead, he turned away, scoffed his breakfast then, realising she hadn't started hers, looked hopefully at her.

'You're not getting it,' she told him, 'so don't sit there drooling all over the floor. Go outside and chase a cat. Bark at something. Wake the neighbours.'

He gave her a look that acknowledged her contrary mood but made no move to offer comfort by bumping his big head against her legs. You've only yourself to blame, he was telling her. Or maybe she was telling herself, only it seemed more definitive coming from Henry.

'That dog doesn't understand a word you say.' Her father propelled his wheelchair into the kitchen. 'They go on tone of voice. Listen.'

In the sweetest, kindest voice a gruff and unemotional man could muster, he called Henry all the harshest names under the sun, berating him without mercy, while the dog fawned at his feet—bumping his head against her *father's* knees in utter adoration.

'We all know that trick, Dad,' Annie grumbled, picking up her handbag and looping the strap over her shoulder. 'I'll leave you two here, bound in mutual admiration, and go to work to earn some money to keep us all.'

Her father grinned at her, while his hand, twisted and

gnarled by the rheumatoid arthritis which had also crippled his body, fondled Henry's head.

'Someone's got to do it,' he said, 'and Henry's got a full-time job taking care of me.'

Annie dropped a kiss on his head, patted the dog and left the pair of them in the sunny kitchen. Her going out to work to keep them all was an old joke between them, her father being well enough off to afford to pay for whatever care he might need and to keep her and Henry in relative comfort. But her father knew how much her work meant to her, so had encouraged her to continue her career.

'Or how much work used to mean to me,' she muttered to herself as she strode along the tree-lined street towards the hospital. 'Back when getting back to work was part of feeling normal, and having responsibilities in a job gave me a sense of being in control. Maybe it's the control thing that's making me edgy about the new position. Maybe I'm afraid this man will take that away from me. Maybe I'm not ready to lose control again…'

Two schoolboys steered a wide path around her, no doubt taking her for a nutter because she was talking to herself.

'A lot of people talk to themselves,' she said, turning to address the words to their departing backs.

The body she slammed into was solid enough to not only keep its balance but to stop her falling as well.

'Yes, but most of them look where they're going as they do it,' a male voice, enhanced by a rich British accent, said, and she looked up into the amused blue eyes of a handsome, well-built man, clad in an impeccable three-piece suit.

'Not necessarily,' she felt constrained to point out, backing hastily away from the suited chest. 'A lot of the ones around here keep their heads right down and mutter, mutter, mutter into their beards. If they have beards.'

She wasn't sure why she was arguing with a stranger over such a trivial matter.

Or talking to him at all!

She had to get to work. Start the new job. Meet the new boss.

'Being new around here, I wouldn't know,' he said, the blue eyes still smiling into hers in a disconcerting manner— a flirtatious manner.

'I've got to get to work,' she said, resorting to a mutter once again. Then she added 'Now!' because her feet hadn't started moving in that direction.

'Me, too,' blue eyes said cheerfully. 'I'm heading for the hospital, and you seem to be going in that general direction. Shall we walk together?'

She could hardly say no. He'd come out of a house only four doors up from hers—a house that had been on the market for so long she'd stopped looking at the sign, so had missed the 'Sold' banner she now saw slapped across it. That made him a neighbour and to say no would be downright unneighbourly.

'I guess so.' Still muttering, though this time it was un-graciously. Now she had a new job, new boss and a new neighbour, and she hated change.

They were walking together now, and she knew it was time for introductions, but couldn't bring herself to take the initiative, feeling that if she didn't know his name, she needn't count him as a neighbour. She'd make idle con-versation instead.

'You're going to the hospital? Visiting someone?'

It was early but the place allowed relatives in at just about any time.

'Going to work,' he said, surprising her, as she'd put him down as a lawyer.

'At the hospital?'

'I'm a doctor—a lot of us work at hospitals.'

She knew the eyes would be twinkling but refused to look as he turned sideways towards her and held out his hand.

'Phil Park. My father wanted to call me Albert or Centennial, but fortunately my mother's common sense prevailed.'

He dropped his hand when Annie failed to take it, and she could sense he was disappointed his little joke—which he'd probably told a million times—had fallen flat, but Annie was too busy absorbing his name to be smiling at weak jokes.

Phillip Park. His name was on the list of new staff—one of the doctors who had come along in the new boss's train. Paediatric surgery fellow? Anaesthetist? No, Annie was pretty sure the anaesthetist was a woman—Maggie Walsh.

Annie had personnel files of all the new appointees on her desk, but she'd purposely not read through them, deciding to meet the new staff without any preconceived ideas. Now she was sorry she hadn't checked. She'd known Alexander Attwood was American, but had assumed the other staff would be Australians from Melbourne, where Dr Attwood had been working for six months.

'And you are?' Phil was saying politely.

'Annie Talbot, former sister in charge of the neonatal special care unit at St James's Hospital and, from today, manager of the new paediatric surgical unit. Great way to start a working relationship—running headlong into you.'

Phil Park's hand clasped hers, warm fingers engulfing her palm, holding her hand just a fraction too long.

She withdrew hers carefully and moved a little further

away from him, guessing he was a toucher, and not wanting to be the touchee.

'But that's great!' he said. 'We'll be working together, and neighbours as well for a while. At least I assume we'll be neighbours—or are you a health nut, and had covered several kilometres before you bumped into me?'

'No, we'll be neighbours,' Annie told him, though she didn't share his enthusiasm. Because, with the smiling eyes and hand held too long, she was sure he was flirting with her?

Or because the smiling eyes and hand held too long reminded her of Dennis?

'Manager of the new surgical unit, eh?' he asked, not in the least put out by her lack of enthusiasm. 'How do you feel about that—coming from hands-on nursing in the PICU? That is what your special care unit is, isn't it? A paediatric intensive care unit? And don't most unit managers come from a secretarial or management background rather than a nursing one?'

Annie breathed easier. He might rattle on but she'd followed his thoughts and talking work was much better than considering flirtatious new neighbours.

Or Dennis.

'I've mixed feelings about the shift from nursing,' she told him, 'but the new job's a challenge. The new unit is a challenge—I imagine that's why someone like your boss has come on board. Shifting to Jimmie's isn't like taking up a post at one of the renowned children's hospitals. We're just starting up. Neurologists and cardiologists—all the specialists, in fact—are still going to refer patients to the bigger hospitals.'

'Not for paediatric cardiac surgery—not with Alexander the Great on board,' he said.

'You call Dr Attwood Alexander the Great?' Annie was

awed by such daring. Everything she'd heard or read about the man had instilled her with enormous respect for him.

Not to mention apprehension about the 'ruthless' part.

'Not to his face.' Phil retreated. 'But all of us—Maggie, Kurt, Rachel—use the title when we're talking about him. He's come here because of the opportunity to start a small specialised unit that he hopes will be used as a model for other small units. Other hospitals have paediatric surgical units, but they're not specialised to the extent we'd like to be. They do some congenital heart defects, which is our specialty, but they also do other congenital defects and things like brain tumours, gut obstructions, kidney and liver transplants—the lot.'

He glanced at her as if to see if she was listening, and as she was—and was fascinated as well—she encouraged him with a smile and a quiet, 'Go on.'

'Well, Alex hopes that if a small cardiac surgical unit can be made to work, physically, medically and financially, he'll have a model to set up similar units in city hospitals across the US. At the moment, over there, they have places like Boston Children's and Cleveland Clinic, maybe ten large hospitals with elite paediatric surgery units, but that means seriously ill babies, often newborn, with complex heart problems requiring surgery, have to travel huge distances for treatment, which not only puts extra stress on them but also disrupts family life and support systems.'

Annie took it all in—even felt a skip of excitement for the vision in her own heart—but at the same time his words puzzled her.

'Does anyone else know of this plan of Dr Attwood's? Is the hospital CEO on side? Does the board know? The government? After all, most of our funds come from them.'

She glanced towards Phil and for the first time saw his smile replaced by a frown. She hurried to dispel it.

'I'm only asking because, as unit manager, I hadn't heard any of this,' she explained. 'I thought we were going to be just another paediatric surgical unit like the ones you've mentioned.'

Her voice trailed away as she wondered if she'd missed something in the job description and in the interviews that had followed her application. Although that might explain the 'little talks' and her feeling that something 'dodgy' was going on!

'A number of people know,' Phil said, then he must have realised he'd spoken abruptly, for he found his smile again and favoured her with a particularly warm and teasing version of it. 'Though I've just committed the cardinal sin in Alex's book and blabbed about it to a virtual stranger before he's held his briefing.'

A pause, then he grasped her arm and added, 'You won't give me away, will you? You'll look suitably surprised and then delighted when he tells everyone at the staff meeting?'

They were walking through the hospital gates and up the paved path towards the main staff entrance as Phil made this plea. Annie studied him for a moment, wondering why an attractive, self-assured man should be worrying over such a minor indiscretion as telling a colleague something she'd hear very shortly anyway.

The word 'ruthless' echoed in her head. Was the gossip even half-right? Was the new boss tyrannical enough to cause his colleague such alarm?

She patted Phil's hand, still resting on her arm, to reassure him and led the way through the doors, nodding at other staff arriving early for their shift.

'Trust you to find a beautiful woman before you've even entered the hospital,' a deep voice said, and Annie turned to see another immaculate three-piece suit standing just inside the entrance. Inside it was a tall, rangy man, with a craggy face and the coolest, clearest grey eyes she'd ever seen.

Her heart stopped beating, stuttered back to life, then raced out of control. It couldn't be…

Yet she knew it was.

Had known it was from the moment she'd heard his voice…

'Do I know you?' He reached out a hand towards her as he asked the question, and Annie stepped back.

He sounded perplexed and when she glanced at him again she saw the untidy brows drawn together in a frown as if perplexed wasn't an emotion he enjoyed.

'No!' she said, far too loudly in the small space, then wondered if something less definite—a vague *I don't think so*—might have been more believable.

'This is Annie Talbot,' Phil said to the suit. 'She's our neighbour *and* our new unit manager. She bumped into me—literally—outside our gate. Your gate. Annie, this is Alex Attwood.'

*This cannot be happening.* That was Annie's first thought.

*But it is,* was her second.

The third suggested it wouldn't matter. *Might* not matter. Especially if she stuck to her denial. She'd just go through to her office, sit down and think things through.

After which she could find out about jobs in Botswana or Tibet or somewhere.

Except she didn't have a passport—not a real one…

'Dr Attwood,' she said coolly, gaining some control over her panic and finally responding to Philip's introduction. 'Welcome to St James's. Phil, I'll see you later.'

She strode away.

Alex watched her long slim legs eating up the yards

down the corridor, saw her head move as she acknowledged colleagues and her hand lift to give a slight wave to others.

It was her. He would swear it was. The hair was different—but women were always changing their hair. He knew it was her from the way she moved. He'd watched her stride away from him once before.

And from her voice—low register, somewhat husky…

But he would also swear there'd been no Annie Talbot on the list he'd kept for the last five years. The most likely name, he'd eventually decided, after three days of detective work and straight-out gossip at the congress, had been Rowena Drake, wife of an Australian cardiologist called Dennis Drake. The fact that she was married should have stopped him thinking about her right then and there but, like the prince with the glass slipper, he'd wanted to know for certain who his mystery woman was.

Since coming to Australia six months ago, Alex had tried to find Dennis Drake, but though records of his training existed it appeared he was no longer practicing in Australia. Probably still working in the US, where he'd been five years ago, Alex had decided, and he'd put the matter to rest once again.

Now here she was!

Alex shook his head. He didn't know that. And she'd said they hadn't met. The odds of Annie Talbot being Rowena Drake—being his mystery woman—were a million to one, probably even higher than that, given the population of the country and the percentage of women in the figure.

Yet he'd felt that connection, and he would swear she'd felt it, too.

'Are you listening to me?'

Phil's question made Alex realise how deeply he'd lost himself in his memories of the past.

'Not really,' he told Phil, certain all he'd been delivering had been gossip about their colleague. Although learning more about her might help him…

'I was saying Maggie phoned just after you left the house. She wanted to know when you hoped to start operating. A colleague has asked her to stand in with him in a liver transplant later tomorrow, but she doesn't want to say yes until she's spoken to you.'

'We won't be starting tomorrow,' Alex replied, feeling better now he could focus back on work. 'I kept the week clear for checking equipment, staff training, talking to local cardiologists, reviewing files of possible patients and generally settling in. I'll be seeing Maggie at the meeting, we can talk about it then.'

He'd be seeing Annie Talbot at the meeting, too. Seeing a lot of her, in fact. But if it *was* her, and she'd lied about meeting him before, what kind of base was that for a working relationship?

'Who are you waiting for?' Phil had broken the silence again.

'Waiting for?'

'We're standing here in the staff entranceway, which, in case you haven't noticed, is becoming increasingly congested. You were standing here when I arrived. I assumed you were waiting for someone.'

'Oh! No! Well, I might have been waiting for you. Actually, I came in, then wondered about exits and entrances—not knowing the hospital—and went back outside to look around. I'd just come back in and was looking at the fire evacuation plan on the wall when you walked in.'

'You were checking out the fire exit plan?'

Phil's disbelief was evident and Alex wasn't surprised but, having seen the plan on the wall, it had seemed like a good excuse. He could hardly admit he'd seen Phil come through the gates with the woman, and something about her—the way she'd moved—the way her hair had swung to her shoulders, though it was dark, not fair as moonlight—had caused a hitch in his breathing and held him rooted to the spot.

'Let's go,' he said, refusing to be drawn any further into a totally pointless conversation. 'There's a small lecture room included in the space the hospital has allotted us. It's not ideal for staff meetings as I'd rather we were all on one level, but with space at a premium in all hospitals we were lucky to get it. Nine o'clock, we're on show. That's if your pretty woman has organised things for us.'

'She *is* pretty, isn't she? And she struck me as an efficient type—power suit and all. Though she told me she was head of the PICU before she took this job. Did you know that? Do you know of many hands-on nurses who've gone into admin positions?'

Alex felt his forehead tightening and realised he was frowning, though he tried hard to control this facial expression, knowing it made him look especially grim and therefore intimidating to the families of his patients.

'No, I didn't know, but I don't think it matters as long as she's efficient at her job. I did ask to be involved in choosing the manager—after all, she'll be acting as my personal assistant as well—but I was told in no uncertain terms they already had someone for the job.'

'You didn't do too badly, getting to bring your own fellow, anaesthetist, perfusionist and head theatre nurse.'

'It was a condition of my employment,' Alex said briefly, his mind, now they'd reached the fourth floor where the unit would be situated, on what lay ahead. He may have brought key figures with him, people who'd worked with him during his time in Melbourne, but for the unit to succeed it had to be a team effort. An image of Annie Talbot flashed through his mind. She would be both the hands-on team leader and his liaison with the powers that be within the hospital. The second element was as important as the first—in fact, it could be the key to success.

So he had to get over his reaction to her. Even if she *was* the woman on the terrace, she didn't want to remember it. Didn't want him to remember it.

Well, he'd tried darned hard not to, yet for five years his subconscious had measured all women against her.

Against a ghost.

A wraith.

A woman he didn't know!

Annie slumped down at her desk and buried her face in her hands. This couldn't be happening.

It was!

OK, so did it matter?

She took a deep breath and thought about that one.

In some ways yes, because it had physically hurt her to deny they'd met before, when it had been that night—that small experience of dancing with that man and kissing him—which had freed her from her living hell.

Kissing Alex Attwood, although she'd had no idea at the time who he was, had shattered the chain that had bound her to Dennis. Kissing Alex Attwood had made her turn away from the hotel room where her husband had slept, knocked out by a drug he'd been given for seafood poisoning, and keep walking until she'd reached the nearest town, where she'd gone into the police station and asked the sleepy man on duty if she could phone Australia.

Heavens! She should be down on her knees kissing Alex's feet, not denying she'd ever met him, but the denial had been instinctive, and now, she knew, on so many levels, it had been the right thing to do.

And, given that cardiologists and cardiac surgeons, even

in a place the size of the US, moved in the same small world, it was also the only safe thing to do.

Having sorted that out, she raised her head and looked at the clock. Five minutes to the staff meeting and she hadn't checked the room. Hadn't done anything but panic since she'd seen him.

Again she felt the jolt of recognition that had shaken her body when she'd looked at the man. Could one body know another so instinctively?

After so short a time?

After one dance?

One kiss?

She shook her head. *Forget it. Get moving. You're here to work, and you're Annie Talbot, not Rowena Drake.*

Dragging air into her lungs, willing the deep breaths to calm her nerves, she entered the small lecture room, crossing to the table on the raised dais, checking there was a jug of water and sufficient glasses for those who would be sitting there—her new acquaintance, Phil; the big boss and the rest of his retinue; Col Bennett, hospital CEO; and herself. Col would introduce the newcomers, then hand over to her to introduce the staff members who would be fixtures in the unit—the unit secretary, two paediatric special care sisters, two sisters from the paediatric surgical ward and two theatre sisters. Other staff would be rostered through the unit once operations were under way.

She was using efficiency to block off any other thoughts. If Phil was right about Alex's plans for the unit, she'd need to focus completely on what lay ahead workwise.

'All ready?'

She recognised the voice and turned to see Alex Attwood, frowning grimly, apparently at her. Then, as if he'd suddenly become aware of his fierce expression, he adjusted his features into a smile. The expression shifted the planes of his craggy face so he looked not exactly hand-some but very close to it.

Though it wasn't just the look, but a kind of power she felt emanating from him as he came towards her, that made her realise he was an attractive man. Not conventionally good-looking as Phil was, but attractive nonetheless.

Not that she'd considered attractiveness five years ago when he'd asked her to dance. She'd been too caught up in the music and in an illicit feeling of freedom to take much notice of him as anything more than a dance partner.

Until he'd kissed her…

And by then he'd been too close for her to really see much of him.

'I think so,' she said, wishing she could press her hands to her overheated cheeks but knowing that would just draw attention to them.

He was looking at the table on the dais, as if checking off who would sit where. Maybe he hadn't noticed her scarlet cheeks.

'I'm sorry we didn't get a chance to get together before today,' he said. 'I'd intended getting over on Friday, but a friend asked me to assist at the Children's Hospital—an emergency admission. Three-month-old brought in from the country with an undiagnosed PDA.'

Mentally, Annie translated the initials into patent ductus arteriosis. The foetal duct between the pulmonary artery and the aorta hadn't closed, so oxygen-rich blood was still flowing from the aorta back into the pulmonary artery and the lungs. It occurred more often in premmie babies and usually closed spontaneously, but if it didn't, it could lead to a number of problems for the infant or growing child.

It was a relatively common operation now, with good success rates. The best ever achieved in Australia had been during the time Alex Attwood had been in Melbourne.

'The baby OK?' she asked, and saw her new boss smile again—though this time with a warmth that had been absent when he'd used a smile to reassure her earlier.

'Doing great,' he said, still smiling. 'Just great.'

Annie heard genuine satisfaction in his voice and some of her apprehension faded. She had enormous respect for doctors who cared deeply about their patients. So with respect, and with admiration for his ability as a surgeon, she could shut that tiny moment in time when their paths had crossed back where it belonged, in a far corner of her memory, and get on with the job she'd been appointed to do. She was so pleased with this discovery she forgot her promise to Phil.

'Phil was saying you're hoping to make this unit a specialised paediatric cardiac surgery unit—a model for small units that could work in other hospitals across the world. Does everyone know this? I mean, the hospital CEO, the board. I'm only asking because no one mentioned it to me...'

Too late, the echo of the words she'd used to Phil reminded her she wasn't supposed to know, and the return of the frown to Alex's face suggested he was less than pleased with both her and his offsider.

'Quite a number of people know.'

The voice she remembered, even with the memory tucked away, hardened.

'And a high percentage of them are influential in both medical and government circles, but—what are you? Thirty-one? Thirty-two?—you must know how political medicine is. Hospitals have to fight each other for the best funding deals, fight for corporate sponsorship. If news of this unit had leaked out, there'd have been a furore about funds being diverted from other places. We needed it to be a *fait accompli* before making any announcement.'

He strode across the dais then propped his elbows on the lectern and turned to look back at her, as if prepared to lecture his audience of one.

'You'll hear all of this very shortly—and after that the word will spread and the fun and fighting will begin. But believe me, Annie Talbot, this unit will not only come into being, it will eventually be the best in the country. *And* the model that I want it to be.'

Annie, at first affronted by his quite accurate guess at her age, heard the fire of dedication in his voice. It made her study him more closely—the craggy face, with a straight sharp nose, firm chin, untidy eyebrows over stern grey eyes—and what she saw—and sensed in him—stirred a feeling of true elation. Forget jolts of recognition and kisses in the past! If what he was saying was true, then this was going to be the job of her dreams, not just, as she'd thought when she'd applied for it, a stepping stone to something special. This was going to be the something special she'd always hoped was out there for her. The something special to which she could dedicate her life!

Alex watched a whole array of expressions flash across his companion's face. Used to reading faces—how else could babies tell you how they felt?—he saw puzzlement, then surprise, then something that looked very like excitement. Whatever it was, it brought a glow to her pale skin, making the brush of freckles—a familiar brush of freckles, he was sure—across her nose and cheeks appear luminous. Then clear hazel eyes lifted to meet his, and her smile lit up the dreary lecture room.

'This, Dr Alex Attwood, is what I've been waiting for for ever, it seems. Yes, I know about hospital fighting and it won't only be hospital against hospital, there'll be in-house battles as well as other departments fighting to keep money or claim money they feel is being siphoned off to your unit.'

'Our unit,' he corrected, but he doubted she'd heard him, so intent was she on what lay ahead of both of them.

'But we'll fight and we'll win,' she continued, as if driven by some inner force. 'Because you're good—the best, most people say—at what you do, and because I'll be the best damn unit manager ever put on earth.'

She smiled at him again, triumph already shining in her eyes.

'You have no idea just how much this means to me,' she said. 'Thank you.'

Then, almost under her breath, he thought he heard her add, 'Again.'

Puzzled by the strength of her reaction, he forgot the puzzle of 'again' and considered where they stood. He was pleased to hear the commitment in her words and voice, but to be thanking him?

Did she not realise just how hard and dirty the fight ahead of them was likely to be? Didn't she realise she should be running for her life, not thanking him with such delight?

And why would any woman so obviously welcome the challenge the unit would provide? Most women he knew would back away—say thanks but, no, thanks.

Maybe she saw only the glory at the end—the image of herself as manager of an elite unit. But she looked far too sensible—and if she'd managed the PICU she was far too experienced—not to know how dirty hospital fights could get.

'To the best of our ability we'll ignore the politics,' she said—not 'we should' but 'we will'! 'We'll make our name on results. Of course, to get results you need the best staff, and that usually requires money, but if we have to work with what we have, then we've got to make them the best.'

'Hey, we haven't had the staff briefing yet, and already you're into staff training.'

She swung her head to look at him again, and the way her hair moved reminded him of moonlight on a lake, although her hair was dark and shiny, not pale as the silk he'd spun off silkworm cocoons when he was a child.

'Aren't you?' she challenged, and it took him a moment to think what they'd been talking about.

Of course he was. He'd thought of nothing else for weeks. Every free moment had been given over to working out how he could bring the unit staff to the level of expertise he'd require from them. But he wasn't sure he wanted to admit that to this woman just yet.

In fact, he felt a little put out—as if she'd taken some of his dream away from him, as if she was already sharing it.

Which was good, he reminded himself. The entire staff needed to share the dream—to be committed to it. And it wasn't that he wasn't ready to share, he just hadn't expected anyone to take it on board so wholeheartedly—so immediately.

Noises outside suggested other staff were arriving.

He glared at Phil as he wandered in, greeting Annie as if they'd been friends for years, putting his arm around her waist to draw her forward so he could introduce her to Maggie and Kurt and Rachel.

For one brief, irrational moment Alex was sorry he'd brought Phil to St James, then he remembered that Phil, for all his flirtatious ways and womanising, was one of the best surgeons he'd ever worked with. He needed Phil here—the unit needed him.

Besides, Annie Talbot had drawn away from his arm, positioning herself out of touching distance of Phil.

# CHAPTER THREE

'YOU'D like them, Henry. All of them. Even the boss,'
Annie said, as they breakfasted the following day.
'Maggie's an Australian, from Melbourne, Kurt and Rachel
are Americans—they came out to Melbourne with
Alexander the Great.'

As Henry was the recipient of this information, she
didn't have to explain that the title his staff had given him
had stuck in her brain. That was the nice thing about talking
to Henry. She didn't have to explain.

'Phil, although he's originally from England, came with
them from the States as well, because he's learning under
you know who for five years. Phil's a flirt with a predilec-
tion for blondes, I suspect. He's been chatting up Becky,
the unit secretary, and she's blonde, and I saw him in the
canteen with one of the unit nursing staff—another blonde.'

Annie reached up and pushed her hair back behind her
ears, then she rubbed Henry's head.

'Good thing I've had a dye job, isn't it, Henry?'

But although she spoke lightly, her heart was heavy, and
though the new job seemed to hold the promise that all her
dreams could come true, she was edgy and apprehensive
about working with 'the Great'.

She'd spent a restless night hovering in the no man's
land between sleep and waking, trying desperately to ra-
tionalise this uneasiness, finally deciding that in part it was
to do with her denial—that their work relationship had
started off on the wrong foot because of that one word.
Because of a lie!

But she couldn't have said yes—couldn't have admitted they'd met before then gone through the 'where and when' questions which would inevitably have followed. It was unlikely Alex even remembered dancing with a stranger one night five years ago, and to say 'I'm the woman you kissed on the terrace at Traders Rest' would have been too humiliating for words. Especially with Phil standing there, all ears.

And, she feared, it would have been too dangerous as well, for it would tie her to the congress, to the delegates—maybe even to Dennis…

Annie stood up, hoping physical movement would shake off the hungover feeling that was the legacy of her sleepless night. She patted the dog, called goodbye to her father and walked briskly out the door.

Today she wouldn't talk to herself, would look where she was going, would not bump into anyone and would not tell any lies. Even small ones. Even small self-protective ones.

'Good morning!'

Not Phil's cheerful cut-glass accent, but a slow, deep, American drawl. Alex was emerging from the front gate of the house four doors down.

'Good morning,' Annie managed, mentally noting that was lie number one and her resolution was already shot to pieces because there was nothing remotely good about having to walk to work with Alex.

'The meeting went well. The staff seemed enthused. You met with the nursing staff later—are you confident we'll have them all on side, even when things get tough?'

Annie should have felt relief that the walk to work was going to be nothing more than a business meeting with added exercise, but relief wasn't happening. What was happening was a hot flush. Premature menopause it must be, because just walking next to this man couldn't make her feel hot all over.

*Very* hot all over.

'Are you all right?'

Annie stopped walking and turned to glare at the questioner.

'Why wouldn't I be?' It *must* be early menopause—menopause made you snappy!

'You're a little flushed and you didn't hear my question.'

Alex Attwood was now frowning at her—so much for good mornings!—but it seemed more an enquiring kind of frown than an angry one, then he reached up and touched a finger to her cheek.

'You're not sickening for something?'

*Only love.*

The thought came from nowhere, and so horrified Annie she knew whatever colour had been in her cheeks was now gone as all the heat drained from her body, leaving her deadly cold.

'I might be,' she told him, 'and it might be catching.' She turned away to keep walking. *Think premature menopause, not love.* Although menopause itself wasn't contagious—and not really a sickness, either, though she was reasonably certain premature menopause could be classed as such. And as she'd now come up with a third symptom, fuzzy thinking—why else would love have popped into her head?—she was willing to believe that's what she had. Especially since she also had mood swings and she'd felt like crying when he'd touched her cheek.

'Annie!'

She'd been striding determinedly along the footpath, but something in the way he said her name made her look at him again. She read confusion on his face, yet he seemed to have nothing more to say.

Alex cursed his ineptitude with words. It had always been this way. As a child he'd made things with his hands, fixed things—found making a gift for his mother easier than saying he loved her.

Oh, he could talk about his work, to a certain extent. Though even there he preferred to do it—to operate—and to let the results do his talking.

But at some stage he had to talk to Annie, really talk to her. Find out if there was any validity in the way his thoughts kept imposing a fair-haired ghost over her features. Because if there wasn't, then he might be going mad. He might, as his sister had so kindly suggested when she'd visited him in Melbourne, be suffering the effects of living upside down for six months—mental muddle-headedness, she'd called it.

Though she'd only accused him of that because he'd refused to laugh at her absurd jokes and failed to accompany her on an umpteenth shopping expedition.

She'd walked on—Annie, not his sister—and had stopped at the lights on the busy intersection opposite the hospital. He took her arm as the green man indicated they should cross, and though he felt her soft muscle go tense she didn't pull away, accepting the touch as nothing more than a courtesy.

Not knowing that he'd *had* to touch her, *had* to feel her flesh and the hardness of bone beneath it. Closer to madness than mental muddle-headedness. He sent the thought-wave to his sister, now back in North Carolina with the rest of his family, then, the crossing safely negotiated, dropped Annie's arm and turned his thoughts to work.

'The staff are really keen. It was a good idea to negotiate to have our own staff treating our patients even once they leave the special care unit for the ward.'

'I'll be observing in Theatre Three today—adult patient but an intricate aorta repair.'

They spoke in unison, then Annie gave a laugh and said, 'As I was answering a question you asked ages ago, it seems only fair you continue.'

Though equally willing to talk about the nursing staff—anything to get his mind off the physical manifestations of Annie's close proximity—Alex continued.

'It was torn in a MVA, repaired at the time, but now the cardiologist feels there must be adhesions slowing the flow of blood through the vessel. The echo shows some kind of blockage but it's where the aorta's tucked away behind the pulmonary artery and it's hard to get a clear picture of the problem. Even the MRI doesn't show much.'

'Sounds tricky,' Annie said, though he guessed from the relaxation in her voice that she was relieved by the topic. 'I'm assuming that's this morning. You've a couple of patients booked for consultations this afternoon.'

They were inside the staff entrance, in the small alcove where he'd waited for them yesterday, and she turned and smiled at him.

'To think I doubted you'd get referrals. I know Phil laughed at me when I said as much yesterday, but I wondered if paediatric cardiologists here would prefer to continue to use the surgeons they knew.'

He found himself smiling back.

'I knew I could always take cases from the waiting list at Children's. That was part of the deal, but referrals? I had a few doubts about them myself,' he admitted, still smiling, because Annie's smile had brightened up his day.

He sent a new thought-wave to his sister. Total muddle-headedness!

Annie wondered if it was because they were in the hospital—on her home ground, so to speak—that she felt able to relax. Back there, when he'd said her name, even premature menopause couldn't explain away the quiver of excitement that had ricocheted through her body. But now they were talking work, and she was so relieved she smiled at him. A real smile, not a pretend one, so the score on small lies for the day remained at one.

And he was smiling back—which made her confidence on being on home ground waver slightly. But she held firm and asked about the operation, and somehow they made it to the office without any further manifestations of her condition.

Manifestations of something else, perhaps, when they'd bumped together in the lift, but it certainly wasn't love, she assured herself. Attraction, maybe. And why not? He was an attractive man.

That thought alone was enough to make her seek refuge in her work. It had been so long since she'd considered the attractiveness or otherwise of men, this time she felt a shiver, not a quiver, and the shiver was more fear than attraction.

'Come on, the unit can't afford too much overtime. We're all heading for that pub up the road for a drink to celebrate day two safely over.'

Phil had poked his head around the door and, looking at him, Annie suspected he hadn't poked more of his body into the office because the rest of it was attached to Becky.

'Maybe later. If you're still there.' Second small lie of the day as she had no intention of going near the pub. But it was only a self-preservation-type lie so surely that didn't count! 'Right now I have to finish some requisitions or the Great will have my hide.'

Phil rolled his eyes. 'Forty-eight hours into the job and he's got you bluffed already. Believe me, his bark is far worse than his bite—not that he barks all that often. Come and see the man relax—learn for yourself he's human.'

For some reason Annie's mind flashed to the kiss, and though she didn't tell Phil, she was willing to admit to herself that she knew for sure he was human.

'Maybe later,' she repeated, pulling a sheaf of paper across the desk to let him know she was serious about working.

He shrugged good-naturedly and walked away, but what seemed like only minutes later her diligence was again interrupted.

'Phil says you're not coming for a drink. He's blaming me—says I'm a slavedriver. Is there really so much work for you to do?'

Annie considered lie number three, then shook her head.

'Not really. I do want to check these letters going out to possible corporate sponsors. You mentioning that cardiac units can generate more money than most hospital divisions started me thinking. It won't take long, but I don't feel like going out tonight anyway. I've not let anyone know I'd be later than usual, so I'd prefer to go straight home.'

Was that a lie? *I'd prefer not to spend avoidable time with you* would be closer to the truth, but that could be translated into going straight home.

'There are people at home you have to let know?'

He asked the question softly, as if he didn't want it to sound like prying.

'Of course,' she said, answering the question yet knowing it wasn't an entire answer.

Knowing immediately from his silence he was waiting for the rest of it.

'Dad and Henry. Both at home. Waiting.'

The silence that followed this less than explicit explanation seemed to hover in the room like a third person,

then Alex nodded briefly, said, 'Goodnight, then,' and
walked away.

'If he'd asked, I'd have told him Henry was a dog,'
Annie told the door which had closed behind him.

'Plege on!' Alex said, the order crisp.

Who outside this room could guess it meant a cocktail
of chemicals and nutrients, in the main a potassium solution—poison—would flow into the baby's heart?

The tiny heart stopped beating. It was pale and floppy-
looking, clearly visible to Annie where she stood on a stool
behind the heart-lung machine that was oxygenating the
baby's blood while the intricate surgery took place.

She held her breath, knowing every second Baby Ross
was on the machine increased the risk of long-term damage
to his frail body. Alex had explained exactly what would
happen at every stage of the operation. He'd called all unit
staff, including the sisters from the special care unit, together and drawn diagrams on a whiteboard, but nothing
had prepared Annie for how small and totally vulnerable
Baby Ross would look on the operating table, or how desperately sad it would be to see the still, lifeless little heart.

She reminded herself his heart would start beating again
within minutes. That Alex was the best at what he did. She
swallowed the lump of fear for Baby Ross that had lodged
in her throat, and concentrated on what was happening now.

The switch, they called it. Baby Ross had been born with
TGA, or transposition of the great arteries, which in effect
meant that oxygen-rich blood from his lungs, instead of
being pumped around his body, was being pumped back
into his lungs, while oxygen-depleted blood was recirculated through the rest of his body.

Baby Ross was unlucky to be born with TGA, but his
lucky break had been being born in St James's—Jimmie's

as the staff called it—not just at any time but three days after Alex and his team had begun work there.

Annie studied the man they called 'the Great'.

Cool. Detached.

Ruthless?

She wasn't sure about the last, although both the other words would describe her impressions of the man. Having worked with critically ill children for the last five years of her career, Annie knew both the children and their parents needed very special characteristics from their doctors and nurses—characteristics like warmth, compassion, understanding.

Yet the parents she'd seen with Alex in consultations in his rooms didn't seem bothered by his attitude. In fact, some of them—the fathers in particular—seemed to appreciate the forthright way he described their child's condition, and the deliberate way he warned them that all surgery had potential dangers for the patient, who could die or be brain damaged for life.

The first time Alex had said this in Annie's hearing, she was sure she'd reeled from the shock, but in retrospect had decided it was only fair the parents knew the risk, although Alex had quickly followed up his warning with statistics proving how unlikely such an outcome was.

Her thoughts were wandering but her eyes followed every move of the surgeons' hands. Alex, Phil and a surgical registrar Annie didn't know were all working on this one small mortal, while Rachel passed instruments and Kurt Reynolds operated the heart-lung machine, making sure the flow of blood was just right for tiny fragile arteries and veins. Maggie Walsh gave blood-gas readings and oxygen perfusion rates in a calm, relaxed voice.

Maggie, a petite brunette, oozed confidence, a great asset in an operating theatre where things could so easily go wrong. Even when Baby Ross had arrested earlier, she'd remained calm, giving Alex the information he'd needed, easing everyone's tension with her quiet calls of pressure and blood gas.

Was she involved with Alex?

Annie wasn't sure why the thought entered her head, but once it lodged there she looked from Maggie to Alex, considering the idea. Almost wishing she'd gone to drinks with them on Tuesday evening so she could have seen them together socially.

She gave an impatient shake of her head and turned her attention to the tiny form on the table, although she was sure she felt a frown gathering on her forehead and there was a definite squeamishness in her stomach.

Nonsense!

She concentrated on the operation, watching the glove-sheathed fingers of the surgeon sew with thread so fine she couldn't see it. The clock on the heart-lung machine ticked off the seconds. Baby Ross had already been dependent on it for over an hour. Below the clock, another set of digital numbers—the baby's core temperature. Baby Ross's blood had been slowly cooled as it had gone through the machine so when the machine was stopped for the final stages of repair, he wouldn't suffer brain or other organ damage.

All this Annie knew in theory—theory she'd brushed up on before the hour the staff had spent in front of the white-board—but her own heart thudded with tension as the operation continued. How much could this tiny baby take?

She looked at Alex again, and saw the precision with which he moved, the teamwork between himself, Phil and Rachel. They made it look easy—a symphony of hands moving in concert—and though one small slip could mean the baby died, Annie couldn't feel any tension emanating from the group.

A little of her own tension eased, as if their confidence was transferring itself to her, but when the heart was stimulated and cannulae to and from the heart-lung machine were removed, the tension built again, until the little heart pumped on its own and the repairs to the big vessels held.

A faint cheer from Phil, while Alex nodded his satisfaction, stepping back from the table and pausing there while the circulating nurse unplugged his light.

Annie glanced at the clock and saw the operation must have proceeded according to plan, for Alex's estimation of the time of completion of the major work had been spot-on.

He would now leave Phil and the registrar to close.

Annie remained where she was. She hadn't done much theatre work in recent years, but she knew from her work in paediatric special care units that every stage of an operation was important. OK, if Phil slipped up and didn't insert his stitches into Baby Ross's chest just so, it might not make a difference to the final outcome of the operation, but regularly spaced stitches put equal pressure on the fine new skin, so the wound healed more quickly and left less scarring.

She gave a nod of satisfaction as she saw Phil's work. He might be a light-hearted flirt outside the theatre, but in here he was as meticulous as his boss.

Alex, still trailing the cord from his light, stripped off his gloves and gown and dumped them in a bin. The design of the new theatre meant all the electrical equipment was contained in one central column so there was no tripping over leads and having no room to move because of bulky equipment. Even the echocardiogram machine was fitted into the column, with screens around the walls of the theatre so everyone could see what the machine found.

In this case, as Kurt, who was working it, had run the

sensor over Baby Ross's chest, it had showed blood flowing sweetly through the switched vessels, and now the camera in the column was focussed on Phil's hands as he closed.

Alex sighed, awed as ever by the insults such small mortals could take to their bodies and yet survive. Behind him, an increase in the chat level signalled the operation was nearly at an end. Normally, he'd be operating again within an hour, but he'd deliberately not scheduled anything for this week, wanting to get the unit organised to his satisfaction first. Baby Ross had been an emergency admission—and in some ways it was good to get that first op out of the way.

Annie had said as much when he'd called the staff together for a pre-op briefing, and he'd wondered if she'd been as nervous as he had been about this first case in the new unit.

Annie, or Rowena?

He shook his head, unable to figure out why he couldn't let it go. OK, so he'd looked for his ghost on and off for years, trawling through the names at medical conventions, checking lists of hospital employees. Not all the time—not obsessively—not *quite* obsessively…

She didn't give much away—the woman everyone knew as Annie Talbot. Very self-contained. Very cool. Utterly charming to everyone she met, yet detached somehow.

He smiled to himself—knowing that was exactly how people described him. But he had his reasons for avoiding emotional involvement. Although he rarely admitted it, his job made huge demands on his emotions. To hold the life of a newborn infant in your hands—to hold the dreams of the infant's parents—this was where his emotion was spent.

So where did Annie spend hers?

On Henry?

Was he a boyfriend? Lover? Partner?

He turned as he remembered she was here in the theatre. Remembered telling her he wanted her to observe the operation. She was still perched on the stool, and he saw her give a nod as if approving Phil's handiwork.

'Can I help you down?' he said, then clutched at her waist as she wobbled precariously.

'Sorry, you startled me,' she said, her soft throaty voice made huskier by the mask she was wearing, although she was beyond the vital 'clean zone' of the theatre. 'Yes, I could do with a hand to get down.'

Eyes he'd thought green earlier today but which now seemed blue looked down into his then slid away as if embarrassed by his closeness, while beneath his hands he could feel her body contracting—drawing away from his touch.

Drawing away as it had once before…

What rot! his brain scoffed as he lifted her easily and set her down on her feet. But the speed with which she stepped back made him wonder if it had been rot, or if she had indeed flinched from his impersonal touch.

Not that it mattered one way or the other. Now she'd seen something of his work, there'd be no further need for her to be lifted off the stool by himself or anyone else.

Especially not Phil, who'd taken the liberty of lifting her up there!

'That was unbelievable,' she said. 'I'm glad you suggested I watch.'

She'd moved to the wall and was watching the screen that showed the registrar, under Phil's instructions, securing the drains, catheters and pacemaker wires on the baby's body.

'That's the pacemaker,' Alex explained as she peered closer to see Phil adjust the wires. 'It's there in case Baby Ross's heartbeats need regulating over the next few days.

A heart that's suffered the trauma that one did during the op might not work perfectly as it heals. We give dopamine as well, to keep it beating.'

Alex saw Annie nod at his explanation but her eyes remained on the screen as she watched the final stages of the operation. She lifted her hands to untie her mask, undoing the top strings and letting it dangle, revealing a slight smile hovering on her pale, curved lips.

'You must have done so many, to be so sure in all your actions.'

The words, and possibly the smile, were meant for him, but her eyes, and, he thought, her attention were still on the screen.

'What now?'

'For Baby Ross?' Alex said, coming closer so he could check the tubes and wires were all positioned as he liked them. 'He'll go back to the PICU on the respirator, and we'll see how he is when he wakes up tomorrow. Sometimes babies are strong enough to breathe on their own after twenty-four hours, but this little chap was so young, we'll just have to wait and see.'

He paused then touched her lightly on the shoulder.

'Good to have the first one over?'

'I was thinking that myself,' she said, 'though it seems unfair to be pleased about something when that little fellow has been through so much—and will go through more before he can be discharged.'

'We should always be pleased when things go right,' Alex told her. 'Things go wrong all too often, so it's right to rejoice in successes.'

She studied him for a moment, then nodded and smiled.

'OK, I'll rejoice without the guilt,' she said, and walked out of the theatre.

Alex followed, pausing at a cupboard outside the theatre

to pack his loupe into its special wooden case, then he did the same with the fibre-optic light. Tools of his trade, he thought, as he often did. More important for the delicate and intricate work he did than the needles and thread. Well, maybe not more important, but as important. Weird conversation to be having with himself, but a successful operation invariably left everyone on a high, and his high, since he'd lifted Annie off the stool—felt his fingers span her tiny waistline—seemed to be taking off in an unexpectedly sexual direction, so it was better to think about loupes and lights.

At least she'd walked away now, so his physical awareness of her had lessened.

Was it because she reminded him of the ghost that he felt this?

Because she might be the woman who'd featured, on and off, in his dreams for the last five years?

He shook the thoughts away.

It wasn't that he was against involvement with work colleagues, although personally he did his best to avoid it, but Annie gave off vibes that would put off any but the most determined of suitors. There wasn't much of her—above medium height but slim, almost willowy, yet she generated an enormous amount of 'don't mess with me' attitude. Even Phil had backed off his usual flirtatious approach.

Though knowing Phil, he was probably planning to come at her from a different angle. Alex caught his finger in the catch on the box and cursed softly. At least he told himself it was the catch that had made him swear.

Why Phil felt that every pretty woman he met presented him with a challenge, Alex didn't know. Though to be fair to Phil, he usually went for blondes so maybe Annie would be safe from his attentions.

She'd better be, he grumbled to himself as he changed,

but the possibility that Phil might consider a darker-haired woman as fair game rumbled within him as he made his way to the office.

Annie looked up from some paperwork as he walked in.

'I saw Baby Ross's parents on my way here,' she said, 'and told them everything had gone well. I said you'd probably see them in the special care unit later. Coffee and sandwiches should be here any minute.'

Alex's scraggly brows drew together in a frown.

Had she come on too strong? Made herself sound too businesslike?

Should she not have spoken to the Rosses?

She was about to apologise when the frown cleared and he smiled. At least, she thought it was a smile. It wasn't exactly radiating warmth and sunshine, but it stretched his lips and even pressed the hint of a dimple into his left cheek. Something she hadn't noticed before.

'I'm sorry, I was still thinking about the procedure.'

His excuse sounded lame, but Annie could hardly accuse him of lying to her about his frown. As if it mattered, she scolded herself crossly, watching him settle his rangy frame into the comfortable chair on the other side of her desk, then reach for the sheaf of mail she had waiting for him.

But somewhere deep inside her was a niggling feeling that it did matter. She could tell herself it was because this new work relationship was the most important one in her career thus far. That this was her dream job, and she wanted to get it right from the very beginning. But she didn't think she'd believe it...

An aide came in with a tray holding a big pot of coffee—Annie was getting used to Alex's coffee addiction now—two mugs and a plate of sandwiches. She lifted the plastic wrap off the sandwiches and pushed the plate towards him, then poured his coffee, glad to have something to do while her mind teased at the niggle she was feeling.

OK, so there were some small hitches. The long shadow thrown from the past for a start, but if she kept denying they'd met before—not that he'd ever mentioned it again— surely they'd get past that.

And then her attraction to him—she'd get past that as well.

And as long as she was here and Dennis was in the US, then any tenuous link between him and Alex wouldn't matter.

Maybe—eventually—when Alex went back to the States, it would be different. Maybe then there'd be some danger. Maybe, just before he left, she'd have to tell the truth…

Satisfied with this decision, she reached out for a sandwich, mistiming the movement so her hand brushed his. He looked up from the letter he was perusing, the movement so quick she knew he'd felt the same jolt she'd experienced. More electrical than sexual, like a mild shock.

'Dry air?' His eyebrows lifted and his lips half smiled as he asked the question, but Annie, mesmerised by that half-smile, couldn't answer. She looked away, while heat again surged into her cheeks.

'It must be,' she said, released from the spell and using her hands to hide her colour. Then, after checking his hands were nowhere near the sandwiches, she reached out again.

Alex tried to concentrate on the letter he was reading, but knew he'd have to read it again later. In another room. Away from Annie and the strange effect she was having on him.

He glanced at her, head bent as she ate her sandwich, pretending to be reading the file in front of her. He knew she was pretending, because he was as well. Silky dark hair fell forward on either side of her face so all he saw was the curve of her cheek, pale as cream, enhanced rather than marred by that light scattering of freckles bridging her neat, straight nose.

A slim, neat, self-contained person, he guessed, but super-efficient, according to Col Bennett, the CEO.

He remembered the way his hands had almost spanned her waist and the feeling of lightness as he'd lifted her off the stool. Remembered the same feeling of lightness as he'd danced with his ghost. Was he still in post-op euphoria that he couldn't concentrate on business matters? That he was distracted by this woman?

Post-op euphoria was common, although, generally speaking, he didn't get it after a straightforward operation like Baby Ross's. Different hospital, new theatre—either could explain it. But did the euphoria usually take the form of distraction?

Not women-type distraction, he was sure.

In fact, a lot of his ability to focus so strongly on the job stemmed from his deliberate decision to avoid women-type distraction. Not avoiding women as such, just any distraction associated with them.

Avoiding emotional dependency.

The woman he was pretty sure wasn't distracting him gave a little cough and he realised he'd been miles away, lost in his thoughts—distracted!—instead of checking his mail and giving her answers to any questions she'd written on it.

'What if I take it all through to my office and rough out some answers for you?' he suggested.

'No way,' she said, then, perhaps noticing his surprise, she added, 'I've worked with doctors for years. That mail will go into your office and not be seen again for months. No, Dr Attwood, today's the day. There's nothing difficult, and if we work through it together we should be finished by the time you've eaten your lunch.'

'Slavedriver,' he muttered at her, and heard her laugh.

The sound, so clear and fresh and light-hearted, startled him, and he looked across at her again and decided maybe he was wrong about her being his ghost. His ghost had had dark, bruised shadows under her eyes, and had carried a weight of sadness he had felt as he'd danced with her.

Annie Talbot of the carefree laugh was exactly who she said she was, a super-efficient, career-driven woman who would help him make his dream a reality.

She leaned forward again, jotting a note on the file, and he saw a line of pale hair along her parting. The sight jolted him nearly as much as her touch had earlier. She was either prematurely grey, or dyed her blonde hair dark. And didn't women usually go the other way—go blonder rather than darker?

# CHAPTER FOUR

ANNIE heard the hum and beep of the machines that guarded Baby Ross's life, but they were no more than background noise, a kind of counterpoint to her thoughts. It was late evening, but she'd been unable to go home without seeing him again, and now she was sitting by his bed, her forefinger gently stroking his skin, and wondering about fate.

A sound outside, beyond the glass, made her look up. How appropriate—here was fate himself.

The door opened, and Alex walked in.

'He's doing well—better than I'd expected,' he said, and Annie nodded.

'I know. I'm not here because I'm worried, but because Madeleine—Mrs Ross—needed to sleep and she wasn't happy about leaving him on his own.'

Alex smiled.

'Then you'll be pleased to know the cavalry's arrived. I've just been talking to Ben, Madeleine's husband. He's come down from the country with a tribe of relatives—a brace of grandparents, several aunts and the odd cousin, if I got the introductions right.'

'I'm glad they're here,' Annie told him, ignoring the squelchy feeling of regret she'd felt as Alex had spoken of family. She, too, had a brace of grandparents, several aunts and various cousins—relatives she no longer saw, who no longer knew where she was, or even who she was. 'Madeleine's been strong, but she's still only, what, three days post-partum, and she needs to look after herself as well. With family support she should be able to do that.'

The door opened again and Madeleine Ross returned, with a tall, suntanned man she introduced as Ben. As she moved to the bed to introduce her husband to their son, Annie slipped away.

She assumed Alex had stayed to answer any questions Ben might have, so was startled when he joined her in the lift.

'Are you heading home?' he asked, no doubt finding the conclusion easy as she had her handbag slung across her shoulder.

She nodded confirmation and edged slightly away, although there wasn't much room for manoeuvring in a lift crammed with end-of-visiting-hours commuters.

'I'll walk you there,' he announced, leaving no room for manoeuvre at all.

She could hardly say there was no need when he lived only four doors up the road, and they could hardly make the walk—if he was going to his place—ignoring each other.

So they left the building and walked through the soft autumn night, cutting down the side street away from the hospital traffic and along the tree-lined avenue where they both lived.

'I flew up a month ago to look for a place to rent then I saw these old houses and knew I wanted one,' Alex remarked. 'They're like something out of a fairytale.'

They were. It was exactly what Annie had loved about them, but walking with Alex in the lamplit darkness had filled her with too much emotion for speech so she made do with a nod of agreement.

Until they passed his house.

'You've missed your gate,' she told him, stopping on the pavement outside his place. He smiled at her.

'I'm walking you home, remember?'

'It's only four doors. I hardly need an escort.'

'No, but I'll escort you anyway,' he said, and waited patiently until she began walking again. 'See you safely home to Henry and your father.'

Already confused—by the walk, his presence, her own reactions to it—she was even more fazed by his mention of the dog. Suddenly letting him believe Henry was a person seemed unfair and yet...

Surely it was OK if she was doing it for protection?

Protecting herself against herself?

They reached her gate and he leaned over to open it. A low, gruff bark woke the night's stillness, and as Alex straightened he smiled.

'Henry?'

Then, without acknowledging her reluctant nod of agreement, he put his hand behind her back and guided her down the path, up onto the little porch with its gingerbread decorations and into the shadows cast by the huge camellia bush that grew beside the fence.

And Annie went, propelled by something beyond the pressure of his hand on her back. Guided by the acceptance of fate.

He turned her, slid his hands behind her back and drew her close, then he bent his head and kissed her.

Annie stood there, held not by the light clasp of his hands on her back but by memories, then, as the gentle, questing exploration continued, she kissed him back, losing herself in sensations she'd forgotten existed because five years ago she'd been too frightened to enjoy them.

The kiss went on for ever—nothing hasty or half-hearted in Alex Attwood's kisses—but just when Annie knew her

knees were going to give way beneath the emotional onslaught, he raised his head and looked into her eyes.
Another long moment, then he said, 'I had to know!' And
walked away.

Annie slumped against the wall and watched him. Up the
path, out of the gate, along the street, in through his gate—
then he disappeared behind the shrubbery in his front yard.

Thoughts and feelings battered at her, so strongly felt
she rubbed her arms as if to stop them bruising. Clearest
of all was the knowledge that Alex knew exactly who she
was—maybe not her old name, but certainly that she was
the woman on the terrace.

Annie was certain of this because, although she'd have
scoffed if someone had suggested to her that all kisses were
different, she'd certainly have recognised Alex by that kiss.

So, he'd left the ball in her court. It was up to her to
admit they'd met before, or to carry on the charade. Thank
heaven it was Friday and she had two whole days before
she had to see him again.

Before she had to sort out the muddle in her mind...

'I know I don't *have* to go to work, Henry, and I know
going up there carries a risk of running into Alex, but it's
early—barely six-thirty—and not many people will be out
of bed, and I want to see for myself how Baby Ross is
doing. Maybe they've even decided on a name for him. I'll
just slip up there, then come back and take you for a walk.'

Lacking a waggable tail, Henry made do with wiggling
his hindquarters on the floor at the sound of his favourite
word, but he obviously hadn't taken much notice of the
first part of the conversation because the moment Annie
stood up, he fetched his lead and stood hopefully beside
her.

'Put it down before it goes all mushy,' she told him, then

added, 'Later,' knowing it was one word he did understand. Food, walk, later, fetch—he had quite a vocabulary.

She walked to the hospital, adding words to her list of Henry's vocabulary, deliberately not peering towards the front of the house where Phil and Alex resided.

Fancy buying a house when you were only here for twelve months! Although houses in this area were a good investment…

Thinking about the house was better than thinking about the man, or thinking about the situation the two of them were now in, so she mused on why someone might buy a house for a short-term stay all the way to the hospital and up to the fourth floor.

'I'm sure he's more alert than he was,' Madeleine Ross greeted her when she walked into the room.

The sister on duty had reported a quiet night, and assured Annie all the monitor results were positive.

'It was weird, working in here on my own and with only one baby,' she'd added. 'Though staff from the special care unit next door, your old stamping ground, kept popping in to see me.'

'Make the most of the quiet time,' Annie warned her. 'You know how hectic it can get, and I have a feeling that will happen sooner rather than later.'

'Once word gets out Dr Attwood is operating here, you mean?'

Annie nodded. She'd had her doubts but referrals were coming thick and fast, from as far afield as Indonesia and the Middle East.

She sat with Madeleine until Ben returned with coffee and a doughnut for their breakfast, and was about to leave when Ben asked her to stay.

'We want to ask you something,' he said. 'About the baby, but not about his health. About his name.'

Annie waited.

'It's like this,' he said, so slowly she wondered if he was having trouble finding even simple words. 'We had names picked out, but now they don't seem right…' There was a long pause, then Ben looked at his wife as if he didn't know how to continue.

Annie came to his rescue.

'They were names for a healthy baby—a different baby you'd pictured in your mind.'

She smiled at both of them, and touched her hand to Madeleine's shoulder.

'It's OK to feel that way. In fact, it's healthy to grieve for that baby you didn't have. It's natural for you to have a sense of loss.'

'It's not that I don't love him,' Madeleine hastened to assure her, touching the still arm of the little mortal on the bed.

'I know that,' Annie said. 'Of course you do. You probably love him more because he needs so much help. But you can change your mind about his name—call him something different.'

'We'd like to call him Alexander, after Dr Attwood,' Madeleine said shyly, and Annie smiled, wondering how many little tots with congenital heart disease were trotting around America, proudly bearing the same name.

'I'm sure he'd be honoured,' she said, and heard a voice say, 'Who'd be honoured, and by what?'

He was there again—as if she was able to conjure him up just thinking or talking of him. Like a genie in a bottle. Not a good thing when most of the genie-in-a-bottle stories she'd heard had terrible endings!

'I'll let Madeleine tell you,' Annie said, and she slipped away.

It had been stupid to come up here. She'd *needed* two

whole days—two months? Two years?—to work out how to tackle the recognition thing. *And* the kiss! Now here he was, back within touching distance again. Or he had been until she'd fled the room.

Determined to head straight home and thus avoid any chance of having to walk with him, she was leaving the ward when the sister called to her. A different sister, seven o'clock change of shifts having taken place while she was in Baby Ross's room.

'We've a new admission coming in. Sixteen-month-old baby, Amy Carter, shunt put in to deliver blood to her lungs at birth, but now something's gone wrong. Dr Attwood's called in all the theatre staff. He's briefing them in half an hour.'

The information upset Annie. She should have been the first one called so she could contact the necessary staff. She'd been at home until half an hour ago. She had her pager.

She touched her hand to her hip and realised she didn't have it! How could she have been so careless?

She didn't like to think about the answer to that, because she knew it involved distraction, and the reason for the distraction was so close.

But she was here now—she could be involved.

Alex came out of Baby Ross's room—Alexander's room?—at that moment and she turned to him, ready to confess her mistake, but he did little more than nod at her before entering the next room where, Annie guessed, Amy Carter would be nursed.

Annie followed him, and saw him peering at the X-rays in the light cabinet on the wall.

'You've heard we've an urgent referral on the way?'

He didn't wait for an answer, but pointed to a small tube clearly visible in the cloudy murk of the X-ray.

'The cardiologist sent these on ahead. I believe in shunts—I use them myself in a lot of cases. You can insert them through a thoracotomy, rather than cracking open the chest, which is far less traumatic for the infant, and by putting in a shunt you give the baby time to grow, and give the heart muscle time to firm up so it's not like sewing mousse.'

He had his finger on the shunt, as if he could feel the small plastic tube itself rather than the image of it.

'The other school of thought, of course, is to do all the repairs as early as possible—do a switch like we did on Baby Ross within days of discovering the problem. That saves the baby another operation later, and is possibly easier on the parents in the long run, but to me it's still a huge insult to a newborn infant and the softness of the tissues can lead to complications. Stitches not holding, that kind of thing.'

He was frowning as he spoke, voicing a debate that must often rage in his head, but when he'd switched off the light he turned and smiled at Annie.

'I'm operating in an hour. As you're here, do you want to watch? I didn't call or page you because I felt you deserved a day off, and you've seen one switch. This will be similar.'

'I'd like to watch.' Mental apology to Henry—did he understand 'later' was a very indefinite concept?

'Good.'

Alex walked away, leaving Annie wondering just where things stood between them. This was *not* the post-second-kiss conversation she'd expected to have. Had he forgotten what he'd said last night?

Or did he have no wish to pursue it—now he knew she'd lied to him?

Or—duh!—maybe he was just better than she was at separating work from personal matters.

Whatever, it didn't matter. Alex was working and she was here to see it all went smoothly. Theatre first.

Rachel was supervising the scrub nurse setting out what the surgeons would need, telling the nurse, a lanky six-footer called Ned, what would be happening.

'I saw him at work in an adult cardiac operation the other day,' Rachel said, following Annie out of the theatre. 'I think he's good and I'd like to think we can keep him.'

'If you want him, he's yours,' Annie promised her. If he was equally popular with the adult cardiac surgeons she might have a battle, but she was willing to fight for whatever they needed to make the unit work. She was good friends with the director of nursing and would speak to her first thing Monday.

'Saturday morning—I was going sailing on the harbour with some mates from the UK, and what happens? The slavedriver drags us all into work.'

When Annie went in, Phil was sitting in the office, drinking a cup of coffee from the machine she'd had installed to feed Alex's habit. She smiled at Phil's grumble, made a note about phoning the DON, then asked who else was coming.

'Not Maggie. She had the good sense to get out of town for the weekend. Alex has got some hospital anaesthetist—with paediatric experience—so we should be OK.'

'And Kurt?'

'Yes, he'll be here. As a matter of fact, I think Kurt sleeps with his machine, and as it's now fitted in Theatre here, he was probably asleep beside it when the call came.'

Phil was still grumbling when they moved to the little lecture room, where Alex had already drawn a diagram of Amy Carter's heart on the whiteboard. With simple words, and an economy of description, he outlined what he intended doing, pointed to the spots where trouble could be expected then asked for questions.

'I saw the X-rays,' Phil said, surprising Annie, who thought he'd been mooching in her office since his arrival. 'There seemed to be a lot of scarring on the heart—far more than there should be if the duct was inserted through a thoracotomy.'

Alex sighed.

'You're right. I looked at it with Annie, and hoped I was wrong, but I've just received another file—fortunately, her parents had kept a comprehensive one as they moved from hospital to hospital. She's had two operations already. The first tube became compromised and they opened up her chest. We're going to be going through a lot of scar tissue, both outside and inside.'

'So we don't really know what we'll find in there,' the registrar suggested, and Alex agreed.

'Expect the worst in these situations,' he said, 'then if things aren't as bad, you're pleasantly surprised.'

'And if it is the worst?' Ned asked.

'You have to remember that this little girl will die without the operation,' Alex said carefully. 'She may still die with it. I've just told her parents that. She could die on the table and we might not be able to save her. But we go into every operation confident of a positive outcome. If I didn't feel that way, I wouldn't do it.'

This operation was different. Annie felt it in the tension that vibrated around the room, and heard it in the quiet swear words Alex and Phil were both muttering into their masks.

She could see for herself the difference between Alexander Ross's heart and the scarred, gristly organ little Amy was carrying inside her chest.

Alex, no doubt conscious of the registrar and his need to learn and understand, explained things as he went—explained what should be happening, and how little Amy's tiny heart should be configured, cursing only when he found too many anomalies.

'The problem is the heart has compensated for its weakness. The coronary arteries, feeding blood to the heart muscle, were compromised when the shunt was put in, so the body has grown new vessels and now we've this bizarre network and can't be sure what we can safely touch.'

He bent his head to his work again, then added, 'Touch none of them is the rule in these cases. If you don't know what it is, don't touch it.'

Four hours later Alex thanked them all and left the theatre. Ned helped Annie down from her stool, and she followed Alex out, passing him as he packed away his loupe and light just outside the door.

'Annie!'

She stopped and turned towards him. The equipment he'd been wearing had left parts of his face reddened and his cheeks were drawn. He looked exhausted.

'Are you doing anything now?'

'Right now? Going to my office.'

'After that—are you busy?'

He paused and rubbed at the red marks on his face as if they bothered him.

'I know you have a life, and you have no obligations to me, but…' Another hesitation, then he said, 'I don't know the area. I have to shop or Phil and I will starve to death over the weekend. I need a guide to help me get my bearings.'

Annie's turn to hesitate.

It wasn't much to ask, but it would put her in his company for the rest of the day.

'I've promised Henry a walk,' she said, and saw Alex smile.

'But that's great. Minnie needs a walk as well, and though I've seen the park down the road, I don't know where dogs can or can't go. We'll walk them both and then we'll shop, grab some lunch somewhere along the way. I'll change, see Amy's parents, then collect you from the office and we can go home together.'

Go home together! The three words rang in Annie's ears, prompting a surge of loneliness.

But she wasn't going to be seduced by words or loneliness. This was a business proposition. They'd walk their dogs—presuming Minnie was a dog—then shop, and that was it.

'I'm worried about that baby.'

Alex's opening remark as they left the office reassured Annie. The business side of things had been confirmed.

'She's been through so much,' he continued, putting his hand behind Annie's back to steer her into the lift. 'And she was really down when she came in. Can a child in such a debilitated state survive another major operation?'

'But you must have seen so many children like Amy. There must be plenty of cases where you've been called in after a previous operation hasn't worked.'

He nodded, and escorted her out of the lift.

'Of course, but I still worry every time. It's one of the reasons I'd like to see more trained paediatric cardiac surgeries, and units set up specifically to handle congenital heart disease. CHD is the most common of all congenital conditions and the long-term survival rate of children who have surgery is excellent. It's not a question of allocating blame in an operation that's gone wrong. I understand the difficulties a cardiac surgeon who operates on adults ninety-nine per cent of the time must face when he sees a neonatal heart. But it needn't happen—he wouldn't be forced to operate—if there was a paediatric cardiac surgeon within reach.'

'But would that have made a difference to Amy? Having someone more skilled to do the op?'

They were outside the hospital now, walking towards the crossing, and Alex paused and looked down at Annie.

'Are you really interested or just making conversation?' His voice made a demand of the question and she frowned at him.

'Of course I'm interested. What are you thinking? That I'm asking questions so I'll *sound* interested in your job? That it's a way of showing interest in you? As if!' Scorn poured like hot oil over the words. 'I'd like to remind you that it's my unit, too, but I can't run it effectively if I don't know as much as I possibly can about it.'

Alex saw her anger reflected in her eyes, and wondered how an intelligent man like himself could always find the wrong thing to say to a woman.

But walking with Annie—talking about work—had made him feel great—comfortable, relaxed and at ease with the world. Then his pessimism had surfaced, and with it memories of women who'd shown interest in his work early on in a relationship, then had blamed his job for the breakdown of the same relationship.

Not that this was a relationship. Other than purely work-related...

Not yet, hope suggested.

Maybe not ever, pessimism reminded him, giving an extra nudge with a reminder that she'd lied about not having met him before.

Unless she really didn't remember…

Damn his pessimism! Right now he had to make amends to his colleague.

'I'm sorry. I don't know why I said that. Of course you're interested.'

They resumed their walk, but he'd lost the conversation. It was being with Annie that was the problem—being with his ghost. The kiss, if it had done nothing else, had confirmed that.

But it *had* done something else. It had stirred his blood and not a little lust, so he'd walked home determined to get to know her better. Actually, he'd walked home with phrases like 'woo her and win her' running through his mind, but in the sober light of day he had modified these aims.

In the sober light of day he'd also found his tattered list of the delegates at the congress, and had gone through it once again, searching among delegates and partners for an Anne, or Annie, even Joanna and Annabel—any name that might conceivably be shortened to Annie.

He hadn't found one, and couldn't help but wonder just who she was.

Get to know her first, he'd decided, yet now here he was, treating a simple question with suspicion.

'So, are you going to answer me, or shall we continue this walk in silence?'

'What was the question?'

'I asked about Amy. Would it have made a difference if she'd had a paediatric cardiac surgeon do the first two ops?'

Alex set aside thoughts of stirred blood and lust and concentrated on his reply.

'I couldn't say that. So much can go wrong. There are risks involved in all operations. But I firmly believe we can cut down on the percentage of risks with more specialists and specialist units.'

They'd reached his gate and Annie stopped.

'I want a shower, and need time to write a shopping list if we're shopping straight after we drop off the dogs. Say half an hour? You'll be going past my gate to get to the park so I'll wait for you there.'

'*You'll* wait for me?' he teased, eager to rebuild the relaxed atmosphere they'd shared early in the walk.

'Yes, I'll wait for you. I don't subscribe to the ''women are always late'' theory. I find, in fact, that women are more likely to be on time than men.'

She walked away from him, leaving him wondering just where things stood between them.

Not relaxed and easy, that was for sure! Her pert retort had underscored that point.

## CHAPTER FIVE

ANNIE managed to stay angry with Alex until she saw him emerge from his front gate twenty-five minutes later. Though it wasn't Alex emerging from the gate that made her laugh, but the little black bundle of curls trailing along behind him on the end of a lead.

Alex Attwood had a *spoodle*! A designer-bred spaniel-poodle cross, clearly still a puppy as it was the size of a large guineapig. The little thing cavorted along behind him like a curly black wig caught up on a rat on speed.

'I hope you're not laughing at my dog,' Alex said, though the corners of his mouth were twitching as if he understood her mirth. 'And you know the old joke about a little dog killing a big dog. Tell your Henry he'll choke to death if he tries to swallow Minnie.'

But Annie didn't have to tell Henry anything. He was sitting at her feet, forty kilograms of Rottweiler muscle and bone, gazing at the little spoodle with love-struck eyes, while she yipped and yapped about his feet, and explored him as if he were a new kind of doggie toy.

'She's gorgeous,' Annie said, kneeling down to pat the excitable little creature. She covered Henry's ears with her hands and added, 'I fell in love with these dogs at the pet shop, but really needed something big and fierce.'

Loyalty made her add, 'Not that Henry's all that fierce, it's just his size that frightens people.'

'I can see he's not that fierce,' Alex said gravely, and she looked down to see Henry was now lying down, so the little dog could lick his face and climb across his back.

'He's supposed to frighten people, not other dogs,' Annie said defensively, then realised this conversation was veering dangerously close to places she did not want to go, so she called to Henry and started walking towards the park.

'There's a dog-walker who walks Henry and other dogs in this area every weekday,' she told Alex, pleased they had the dogs to talk about. 'Mayarma, her name is. If Minnie stays inside while you're at work, you'd have to leave a key. She collects Henry and his lead from my dad, but other dogs she picks up straight from the yard. Are you interested?'

'Very,' Alex told her. 'If someone could walk Minnie during the week, I wouldn't feel guilty about not walking her at weekends, and as perfect strangers react to seeing me walking her as you did—with hysterical laughter—I'd as soon skip the park sessions. At least with you beside me, people might assume she's yours and we've just swapped leads.'

Annie listened to the grumble but guessed he was far too self-assured to care what other people thought about his dog. But the conversation did raise a question.

'If you're embarrassed walking a wig on legs, why buy a spoodle?' she asked.

'Buy a spoodle? Do you seriously think a man my height would buy a dog this size? That I wouldn't have considered the aesthetics of the situation?'

'A girlfriend's dog?' Annie guessed, although the idea of a girlfriend brought a stab of jealousy in its train.

'My sister's idea of an ideal companion for me,' Alex told her, gloom deepening his voice. 'My sister has despaired of me ever having a long-term relationship with a woman, so when she was visiting me in Melbourne a month or so ago she bought me the most curly, frilly, impossible sort of dog she could find. To keep me in touch with my feminine side, would you believe?'

Annie was laughing so hard she had to stop walking, although Henry, determined to stay close to his new friend, was dragging on his lead.

'She *is* all woman,' she conceded. 'That's if dogs can be classed that way. Look at how she's vamping Henry.'

They were entering the park, and as dogs were allowed off their leads in this part of it, she bent to unclip Henry's.

'Will she come when you call?'

Alex looked at his small responsibility.

'Who knows?' he said. 'She's been to puppy school, but seemed to think it was a place she went to flirt and play with other dogs. How seriously she took the lessons I don't know, because sometimes she'll obey all the commands she knows, but at others she's totally deaf.'

'Maybe Henry will teach her some sense,' Annie suggested, although the way he was behaving made her wonder.

But Alex unclipped Minnie's lead anyway, and the two dogs, so absurd together, gambolled across the grass, Henry using his huge paws with gentle insistence to guide the smaller dog around the trees and bushes.

'I usually sit over there,' Annie said, pointing to a comfortable seat beneath a shady tree. Since meeting Minnie and laughing at Alex's story of her advent into his life, she'd relaxed. He'd made no move that could be indicative that she was anything other than a colleague, so she could put the kiss down to him wanting to prove something to himself.

Or to both of them.

And from now on, colleagues were all they'd be, so when he said things like 'walk home together' and she felt prickles of excitement, or when he put his hand on her back to guide her into a lift and she felt tremors of attraction, she had to pretend it hadn't happened, and act like the efficient, dedicated, focussed unit manager he wanted her to be.

It's what you want to be as well, she reminded herself.

Alex could feel the woman's presence on the bench beside him—feel it like a magnet drawing him towards her. But he didn't move.

He thought instead about the conversation they'd had earlier—about one snippet of it. About her needing a dog that was big and fierce.

Because she was a woman living alone?

But she wasn't—her father lived with her.

He remembered the bruised shadows under her eyes, the vulnerability he'd sensed in her five years ago. He thought about her change of name, and anger coiled like a waking serpent in his gut.

No, he was letting his imagination run away with him. There could be any number of reasons for a woman to change her name. Marriage was the obvious one. Attractive woman—she could easily have been separated and married and separated again in five years.

He glanced towards her, doubting that scenario. It didn't fit with the sensible woman he was coming to know—a sensible woman now smiling at the antics of the dogs, then laughing as Henry toppled Minnie with his paw, then rolled around on the grass so the little dog could climb all over him.

Once again Alex heard the joy and light-heartedness in the sound and saw a glimpse of the warm and vibrant woman inside her efficient, work-focussed façade. But she'd laughed earlier, when he'd told her about Minnie coming into his life, then she'd shut that woman away and become a colleague again, as if that was all she wanted to be to him.

Yet last night, when he'd kissed her, there'd been more. He was sure of that. As sure of it as he was that she was his ghost.

As sure of it as he was that he wanted to know more of Annie Talbot.

As sure of it as he was that he wanted to kiss her again.

'Are you doing anything tonight? Hot date?'

His thoughts must have prompted his subconscious to ask the question because it was out before he'd had time to think it through. Or consider how Annie might react to it.

She turned towards him, and studied his face for a moment, a slight frown replacing the smile in her lovely eyes.

'Why do you ask?'

He shrugged—tried to make less of the question than there was.

'I thought as we're shopping, I might get the ingredients for a curry. I do a mean curry but it's hardly worth making it for one person and, knowing Phil, he won't be home on a Saturday night.'

'You're asking me to have dinner with you tonight?'

She spoke the words carefully, as if she needed to make sure there was no misunderstanding.

He answered just as carefully.

'Yes.'

A long silence, until Alex realised he was holding his breath. He let it out as silently as he could—a sigh might have made him sound impatient.

'I don't date,' she said at last, which wasn't an answer but was ambiguous enough to give him hope.

'It needn't be a date,' he told her. 'Just a couple of colleagues sharing a meal.'

She studied his face again, as if trying to read his thoughts behind the words, and her frown deepened.

Then *she* sighed.

'I don't know, Alex,' she said softly. 'I don't think it's such a good idea.'

He sensed her backing off—felt her retreat—and moved to stop it.

'Sharing a curry? What harm can come of that?'

Another pause, so long this time he *had* to breathe.

Then she said, almost to herself, 'Who knows?' and shrugged her shoulders.

There was something so pathetic in the words—so vulnerable in the gesture—it took all the restraint Alex could muster not to pull her into his arms and promise to protect her from whatever it was she feared. Because fear was certainly there. It was in her eyes, and in the quietly spoken words.

In the big fierce dog.

And still she hadn't answered.

She looked away and whistled to her dog, and as he came gambolling back towards her, Minnie herded in front of him, she straightened her back, squared her shoulders and turned to smile at Alex.

'Oh, what the hell!' she said. 'Yes, I'd like to share a curry with you, Dr Attwood!'

Henry brought Minnie safely to their feet, received a pat and a 'good dog' from his mistress, then as she clipped on his lead and stood up, she said to Alex, 'They were once herding dogs, you know, Rottweilers. They followed the Roman armies across Europe, herding the animals they kept for meat. Apparently some instinct still remains in Henry.'

Alex heard the words. He was even interested in the content. What he couldn't follow was the switch in the woman who was now walking on ahead of him, back towards their respective houses. Had she reverted to this 'unit manager' persona so he wouldn't be under any misapprehension that their dinner together tonight was in any way a date?

He didn't know, but he did know that the more he got to know Annie Talbot, the less he really knew of her!

Anxious about Amy's condition, they called at the hospital before hitting the mall. The little girl was stable—which was as much as Alex felt he could expect at this stage. After talking to her parents for a while, he climbed back into Annie's car, a big, comfortable SUV, and they drove the short distance to the shops. As he had been in Melbourne, Alex was surprised by how familiar the mall seemed, although Annie called it a shopping centre.

He was also surprised at how many things *he* considered staples went into Annie's shopping trolley. The same brand of pancake mix he used at home, pretzels, sourdough bread and even tart green pickles.

Well, since last night he'd known she was the woman on the terrace, so she'd been in the US then. If she *was* Rowena Drake—or had been in the past—then she'd lived over there for some years. He knew enough of Dennis Drake's history to know that—even knew he'd been married when he'd first arrive to work in St Louis.

But a number of her purchases were unusual. OK, the amount of dog food was explained by Henry's size, but so many cans of soda and packets of crisps?

'My dad's a writer—he says munching helps him think,' she said, as they pushed their trolleys towards the checkout.

'A writer? What does he write?'

She smiled at him.

'Mysteries. Detective stories. They've only just started

being published in North America so even if you read mysteries, you probably haven't heard of him.'

'I do read them—all the time. They're my relaxation. What name does he write under?'

A beat of excitement in his heart. Would he learn Annie's maiden name if her father wrote under it?

Would that help him get to know more about her?

Probably not.

He realised he'd missed her answer, and blamed it on untangling his trolley from the woman in the queue beside him.

'Sorry—what name? His own?'

'Yes. Rod Talbot,' Annie said, and Alex felt relief.

So she'd left Drake for whatever reason and had reverted to her own name. And her real first name could well be Rowena, with Annie a family nickname, and she'd reverted to that as well.

And he'd had her with serial marriages!

Then the name she'd said sparked recognition in his brain.

'But I've read his books! Or some of them. They're set right here in Sydney, aren't they? A friend, knowing I was coming here, lent me a couple, then while I was in Melbourne I tracked down a few more.'

He was genuinely excited, having enjoyed the fast, racy read Rod Talbot provided. And to think he was Annie's father!

She was unpacking her trolley onto the checkout counter at this stage and he wondered if he should ask her father to dinner as well. There was obviously no Mrs Talbot in the picture, and if this *was* just a neighbourly, colleague type dinner, then asking her father would be the right thing to do.

But in some uncharted territory of his heart, he was

aware that this wasn't just a neighbourly dinner—or a colleague-with-colleague one. He wasn't sure what it was, maybe a first small step towards something, but, whatever, he wasn't going to invite a third party to partake of his curry. Not tonight.

Annie, refusing his offer of help to unload her groceries from the car, dropped Alex and his shopping off at his front gate, then drove around the block and down the lane behind the row of houses, into the garage behind her house.

She turned off the engine, opened the door but didn't get out. Instead, she slumped across the steering wheel in relief. Shopping with Alex had been far too intimate an experience for her to ever want to repeat it.

'Intimate?' she muttered to herself, as the thought registered in her brain. 'Shopping?'

But she couldn't find another word for the confusion of symptoms she'd displayed as they'd pushed their respective trolleys up and down the aisles. No premature menopause this time, for which, she supposed, she should be grateful.

But empathy, togetherness, bonding stuff had happened, and when they'd both reached for Aunt Jemima's pancake mix at the same time, and they'd turned towards each other and laughed, a heap of other emotions had fluttered in her heart. Emotions she didn't want to think about.

'It was pancake mix, for Pete's sake,' she said to Henry, who'd come out to the garage to see why she was so slow at bringing in his food supplies. 'You can't get all squishy and romantic over pancake mix. Especially when the other pancake-mix purchaser would have been considering his stomach, not his heart.'

Henry gave her his 'don't take it out on me' look and sat, willing, if necessary, to wait by the open car door for ever.

'I'm coming,' Annie told him, reaching over the back of the seat to pick up her first load of supplies. 'At least now he knows where the shops are, so there'll be no excuse for the two of us to ever shop together again.'

She hauled the bags out and started towards the house, arms getting longer by the second as innumerable cans of dog food weighed them down.

'Which reminds me, Henry. That dog of Alex's eats about one hundredth of what you do. Shopping would have been a lot easier if I'd got a spoodle.'

Henry was unperturbed by her rant, even helping out by nudging the back door open for her.

But Henry was no help at all as she dressed for a curry dinner with a colleague. Her black jeans were fine, but what top? The T-shirt with a pattern and a few sequins to make it sparkle wasn't dressy but might be considered so for a casual dinner, yet a plain T looked *too* plain, and her white shirt looked like work, while the green one—a favourite— had developed a nasty habit of popping the top button, re- vealing too much cleavage for a curry with the boss.

'If he hadn't been with me, I could have ducked into that new shop at the mall,' she grumbled at Henry, who was watching her fling tops on and off with a tolerant expres- sion on his face.

In the end she settled on the white shirt, but tied a lacy, emerald green scarf around her neck.

'Life's all about compromise,' she told the dog. 'And, no, you weren't invited. Which is just as well because if Minnie saw you drooling near a dinner table she'd go right off you.'

Her father was out, so she said goodbye to Henry and walked up the road, with each step regretting her decision a little more.

It wasn't that she didn't want to see Alex, or try his

curry, just that the thought of an evening alone with him—any time alone with him—filled her with a cocktail of contradictory emotions.

So she was enormously relieved when it was Phil, not Alex, who opened the door to her.

'I never disturb the chef when he's creating,' he told her, welcoming her with a huge smile and an only slightly less huge hug. 'Come on in. See our place. Is it very different to yours?'

Annie looked around. It was furnished very differently—a man's abode—but the house plan was the same and a sense of familiarity made her feel instantly at home.

Phil was explaining how his date had stood him up, and was ushering Annie in, arm around her waist, when Minnie came hurtling from the kitchen to greet the new arrival.

Annie scooped up the little dog, using the movement to move away a little from Phil. She held the black bundle of delight close to her chest and pressed kisses on its soft, curly head, then glanced up to see Alex watching from the kitchen door.

Watching and frowning.

'What? I'm not allowed to kiss her? But she's adorable!'

The frown disappeared, replaced by a smile.

'Kiss away,' he said easily, but Annie had to wonder what he'd been thinking to prompt the frown. 'Phil's told you he's joining us?'

Annie nodded, still cuddling the dog.

'I did offer to go out rather than play gooseberry,' Phil said. 'But Alex assured me it was only a neighbourly, colleague type dinner and I didn't feel so bad.'

Annie had been thinking of saying much the same thing to him—hadn't she spent the short walk convincing herself that was all it was?—yet she felt put out that Alex had been so quick to label it that way.

*That's all it is*, she reminded herself as she set Minnie back on the floor, but as she straightened she saw Alex give a little shrug, and wondered if he'd felt the same disappointment.

'You might offer our guest a drink,' Alex said, then he disappeared back into the kitchen.

'Is he the kind of chef who hates having an audience as he works, or could we join him in the kitchen?' Annie said, holding the light beer Phil had poured her. 'It seems kind of antisocial to be drinking out here while he's slaving in the kitchen.'

'I wouldn't venture in there,' Phil said. 'You've heard him swear when things go wrong in Theatre. Well, he's twice as bad in the kitchen.'

*But if you weren't here, surely I'd have been invited to join him*, Annie thought, but she didn't say it, wondering if Alex had regretted his decision to ask her to dinner and persuaded Phil to stay.

Then Alex announced the meal was ready, and Phil escorted Annie into the big kitchen where the table was set with an array of condiments and sambals, and the tantalising scent of curry spices filled the air.

'After living with him in Melbourne, I know the deal with the little dishes. These are all cooling ones,' Phil said, pointing to cucumber in yoghurt, and sliced fruits, 'while the chutneys will make it hotter. Don't touch this one, potent chilli, unless you like eating fire.'

Annie glanced at Alex, wondering if he minded Phil taking over the host's role, and saw the real host smile, sharing her amusement at Phil's behaviour.

'I don't mind a bit of fire,' Annie said as Alex sat down and put a little of the chilli on the side of his plate.

Again Alex smiled at her, and a warmth that had nothing

to do with curry, or the chilli sambal, or even premature menopause, spread through her.

Forgetting to feel apprehensive about whatever was happening between herself and Alex, she relaxed, settling down to enjoy the food and the conversation, pleased to be sharing talk and laughter with these two men.

The phone rang as they were finishing their second helpings, and Alex, who was closest to the kitchen extension, reached out to answer it.

He was on his feet within seconds, assuring someone he'd be right there.

'It's Amy. Her temperature's going up and her blood count down—could be a haemorrhage somewhere.'

'I'll go,' Phil offered, but Alex shook his head.

'No, it's my job to see it through. Let Annie finish dinner and you see her home. You can come up then if I'm not back.'

Phil's behaviour was exemplary, and when he put his arm around her as they walked back to her place, she accepted it, knowing he was a toucher, and telling herself they'd be working together for a year and she'd better get used to it. But having Phil walk her home wasn't the same as having Alex do the short trip, and she felt a surge of regret that he'd been called away.

A totally uncalled-for surge of regret, given how adamant she'd been about their dinner together not being a date.

Phil saw her safely to her door, said goodnight, took a couple of steps towards the gate, then turned.

'I'm sorry it was Alex called away, not me,' he said. 'He doesn't do much relaxing and I think an evening with you would have been just what the doctor ordered for him.'

He grinned at her, then added, 'Just what this doctor would have ordered, anyway.'

He hesitated, as if expecting her to say something, and when she didn't, he spoke again.

'Are you interested? In Alex?'

Another pause during which he maybe realised he'd overstepped some invisible boundary.

'Not that it's any of my business,' he added quickly. 'But I kind of like the chap and I'd like to see him happy. Not that he's not happy. Lives for his work. But that's hardly a balanced life.'

Annie beat down the excitement this conversation had generated, and said quietly but firmly, 'I don't think we should be discussing Alex behind his back.'

Phil seemed surprised, but he took it well, shrugging his shoulders and repeating his goodnight. Then he walked off up the road, not turning in at his gate but going on to the hospital.

Where little Amy was fighting for her life!

Annie wanted to call Phil—tell him she'd go with him—but there was nothing she could do up there, and Amy was in the best possible hands.

But knowing that didn't help her sleep, and at five she gave up, got out of bed, showered and dressed and walked up to the hospital.

The first person she saw in the ward was Alex. An exhausted, unshaven-looking Alex, who greeted her with a tired smile.

'You know, you're admin staff now and don't have to be here all the time,' he teased, and she was pleased to hear the words, certain he wouldn't be making light-hearted comments if Amy hadn't survived the night.

'She's all right?' Annie asked, needing the verbal confirmation.

'She's one tough little lady,' Alex said. 'It's an infection, not a haemorrhage—thank heaven.'

Then he rubbed his hands across his face.

'Fancy thanking heaven for an infection in so frail a child, but I doubt she'd have survived another operation. We've done a culture and now have gram specific antibiotics running into her, and she's slowly improving. I'm worried about fluid retention. The kidneys are susceptible to damage when a patient's on bypass, and I hate to think we've added kidney problems to her other burdens.'

'Catheter OK?' Annie asked, remembering a child she'd nursed who'd had every test imaginable for bladder and kidney problems, and in the end the trouble had been with his catheter.

'I like your thinking,' Alex told her. 'They're such tiny tubes for infants, they could easily block or kink. I'll check that now.'

Annie stayed and talked to Amy's father, who came out of the room while Alex watched the intensivist on duty remove the old bladder catheter and insert a new one.

'He's been here all night,' Mr Carter told her, nodding towards the glass-enclosed room where they could see Alex bending over the bed. 'I doubt my wife would have gone away to have a rest if he hadn't persuaded her *and* promised he'd stay himself until she got back. You don't get many specialists like that.'

'No, you don't,' Annie agreed, feeling ashamed she'd regretted him being called away, though it had hardly been a date with Phil there. Then she wondered just when Mrs Carter *would* get back. Alex, too, needed to sleep.

Annie went into the next room, where small Alexander Ross was now off the ventilator. An older woman—one of the brace of grandparents, no doubt—was dozing in the chair beside his bed.

'He's doing well enough to be going to the ward tomorrow.'

Annie swung towards the speaker, and then regretted it, because she wanted nothing more than to run her hands across his face, smoothing away the lines of tiredness.

'That's wonderful,' she said instead. 'His recovery's going far better than we'd expected, isn't it?'

Alex nodded then led her out of the room.

'Far better,' he confirmed. 'Are you going back home now you've checked on your two patients?'

'I suppose so,' Annie said, 'though Dad will still be in bed so I thought I might stop at the canteen for breakfast. They do a wicked big breakfast here.'

'I obviously didn't feed you enough last night,' Alex said mournfully. 'But now you mention it, a big breakfast might just hit the spot. Mrs Carter is back with Amy so, come, let me escort you to the canteen.'

He bent his arm and held it towards her and Annie could hardly refuse to tuck her hand into the crook of his elbow. What did surprise her, though, was the way Alex then drew her hand close to her body and, in so doing, drew her body close to his.

'Story of my life,' he said conversationally as they walked along the corridor to the far lift that would take them directly down to the canteen. 'Phil and I entertaining a beautiful lady, and he gets to take her home.'

He was holding her too firmly for Annie to pull away, and she hoped he didn't feel the blush that spread through her body.

'Beautiful lady, indeed!' she scoffed, as they reached the foyer and were waiting for the lift. 'Look at me! Straight out of bed into jeans and trainers—slept-in hair and no make-up.'

But if he heard the last part he gave no sign of it, saying only, 'I do look at you, Annie,' in a voice that made her toes curl in the tips of the maligned trainers. 'All the time.'

# CHAPTER SIX

'WHAT do you mean?'

Her voice seemed to come from a long way off, and it wavered slightly, but she got the question asked.

Alex looked down at her and a smile shifted the lines in his tired face.

'Just that,' he said. 'I find myself looking at you—or looking for you if you're not around. Part of it's to do with a ghost who's haunted me for the past five years, but more to do with the flesh-and-blood woman who came into my life less than a week ago. Crazy, isn't it?'

The lift arrived and they squeezed in, Alex still holding her close. The lift was full of staff heading for breakfast, and various acquaintances greeted Annie. Hospital gossip being what it was, she was glad she was working in the unit now and not out on a ward where she'd have been teased unmercifully about such blatant behaviour as standing arm in arm with her boss.

But the press of bodies also saved her answering Alex—had she had an answer—and they travelled in silence, then discussed food options as they stood in the queue, everything so back to normal that Annie thought they were safely past the conversation until, once seated at a table in a quiet corner of the room, Alex reintroduced it.

'You must think I'm crazy, and maybe I am. If this conversation embarrasses you, please write it off as lack of sleep, but yesterday in the park I spent so much time assuring you that dinner would just be a colleague-with-colleague thing—emphasising the casualness of it—and then I had to leave you with Phil last night. Phil with his charm and his good looks and his success with women! I was caught up with Amy and there you were with Phil—that's when I realised.'

He stopped, perhaps realising now that he wasn't making a lot of sense, and looked across the table at Annie. Then he shook his head, and this time his smile was tiredly rueful.

'What I'm trying to say in my inadequate way is that I like you, Annie Talbot. I'm attracted to you, and if it's OK with you, I'd like to get to know you better.'

Excitement vied with apprehension, but beneath both these emotions was a longing so deep Annie was shaken by it.

It was a longing for love in the biggest, widest, most wonderful sense of the word. A longing to be part of a couple—to share a little of another person's life, to give and take support, to have someone to laugh and cry and rejoice with, to have someone to hug, or to give a hug to when a hug was needed.

'What really rocks me is that I thought I'd got over wanting someone in my life,' she said, looking at Alex as she spoke, knowing he probably wouldn't understand, as she was no better with words than he had been. 'I've built my life as a single person and, truly, Alex, I've enjoyed it. I *do* enjoy it. I have company when I need it, a job I love, I'm career-focussed and happy that way.'

Alex watched her carefully choosing words and putting them together. He listened to them and though they didn't spell it out, he was reasonably certain she was telling him she was no longer quite as happy with her chosen path, which, as far as he was concerned, was tantamount to admitting she was as attracted to him as he was to her.

'Eat your breakfast before it gets totally cold,' he told

her, though he smiled so she would know it wasn't an order.

She smiled back and a little of his tiredness lifted. Somehow they'd muddled through a very awkward conversation and reached a place where he was pretty sure they could go forward.

Together.

On a kind of trial basis.

He felt an insane urge to shout or clap or otherwise celebrate this breakthrough in the Annie-Alex relationship, but then he remembered other relationships he'd had and the dismal hash he'd made of them. He watched Annie cut a piece of bacon then spear it on her fork, and more doubts assailed him.

Not doubts about Annie and wanting to get to know her better, but doubts about his ability to make her happy—to chase away the shadows he sometimes saw in her eyes.

Was he, with his antipathy to and avoidance of emotional dependency, the right kind of a man for Annie? Could he give her the kind of unconditional love she would need to heal whatever wounds she carried from the past? And wouldn't wrapping Annie in the kind of love she needed mean unwrapping the protective barriers he'd erected around himself? How else could he bring her close?

And had she actually said she was happy to get to know him better? No, she hadn't. She'd waffled on as badly as he had, and hadn't really said anything at all when you got right down to it.

Because she wasn't sure?

Wasn't sure about exposing herself to love and perhaps to whatever hurt it had brought to her before?

So he'd have to be mighty careful! Mighty sure that nothing he did would put her in more emotional jeopardy.

'Aren't you going to eat yours?' she asked, drawing his wandering thoughts back to the here and now.

'I'd better, hadn't I?' he said. 'Or I won't have the strength to walk you home.'

He watched her as he spoke and saw the shadows he'd been thinking of chase across her face, and he felt a steely resolve to do whatever he could to chase those shadows away.

'It's not commitment, Annie,' he said quickly, not wanting to lose her before the relationship had begun. 'Just a ''getting to know you'' kind of relationship. A ''let's see where it goes'' experiment.'

The shadows cleared and she smiled at him.

'In the interests of science, of course,' she teased, and Alex felt the tension drain out of his body. Yes!

He didn't punch the air, not physically, but in his head he saw his fingers clench and his hand go up in triumph.

Because she'd tentatively agreed to get to know him better?

*Come on, man!*

But he couldn't curb his inner excitement, though he hoped it wasn't showing on the outside.

He attacked his breakfast, barely noticing it was less appetising than it would have been if eaten hot, but before he'd finished his pessimism had surfaced again, reminding him he was a stranger in a foreign land, in a city he didn't know. Where was he going to take Annie for a first date? First dates should be special.

'What are you worrying about now?' she asked, reminding him he had company at the table.

'How do you know I'm worrying?'

'Your eyebrows knit together.' She softened the blow with another smile. 'And your lips go tight.'

He tried loosening his tight lips with an only slightly tight smile, and admitted his dilemma.

'I don't know where to take you. For our first date.'

He'd expected understanding, but not laughter. She laughed and laughed, the sound so joyous he couldn't help but enjoy it, though he was a little disgruntled that he could cause such mirth.

'It's not a cardiac operation,' she said when she'd controlled herself enough to speak. 'It doesn't have to be planned to the nth degree. We can go to the beach—or for a walk around the harbour foreshore. We can eat at the Thai restaurant down the road from where we live, or at the little Italian place on the other side of the park.'

*And why are you suggesting places to go with this man when you know full well you shouldn't be seeing him at all?* Annie's head asked her, but the longing had won out over caution, and already she was excited about going to the beach or walking the foreshore with Alex.

If he ever had any time off, she amended as a buzzing sound had them both reaching for their pagers.

'It's mine,' he said, pushing back his chair and standing up. 'It's the ward. I'll phone from over there...' He nodded towards the house phone on the wall. 'But if it's the unit, I'll have to go.'

He hesitated for a fraction of a second, then reached out and touched his hand to her hair.

'May I call and see you later? When I've slept and showered and shaved?'

Big moment this, but Annie barely hesitated.

'I'd like that,' she said, then she looked up into his face. 'But if you don't make it, I'll understand. You need to catch up on your sleep. That's far more important than visiting me.'

Alex smiled at her.

'I wouldn't be too sure about that,' he said, then he lifted a strand of hair and gave a gentle tug. 'See you later, Annie Talbot!'

Annie Talbot! If only she *was* Annie Talbot! Annie Talbot could certainly have a 'getting to know you' relationship with Alex. Or run with a 'see where it goes' experiment.

After all, the man was returning to the US in a year. It wouldn't be a for ever and ever kind of relationship.

She worried about it all the way home.

'So, what do you think, Dad?'

Her father was breakfasting with Henry in the kitchen, and as he had so willingly gone into exile with her—had, in fact, arranged a lot of it—she'd had to share this new development with him.

'You like him?'

'I do,' she admitted, then she took a deep breath. 'But there's more to it than liking and more complications than a quick romance with a nice man. Remember I told you about dancing with the man on the terrace at the hotel? The night I left Dennis? The night I phoned home?'

'I remember too much about that night,' her father growled. 'Too bloody much!'

Annie reached out and squeezed his shoulder.

'It's all behind us, Dad,' she said. 'We've moved on. Anyway, he's the man. Alex is. He's the man I danced with that night.'

'Then I should like to shake his hand,' her father said, not seeing the point Annie was trying to make.

'You will, and maybe soon, but you won't say anything. That's the problem, Dad. Don't you see? He moves in the same circles as Dennis. You've done so much to hide me from him and his private investigators, and by getting close to Alex I could wreck all that.'

'If he's a decent man, there's no way he'd betray you to that—that animal!'

'He *is* a decent man, and that's what worries me. I'll be going into a relationship with him, however casual, under false pretences—knowing it can never go anywhere, that I could never marry him. Oh, I know I'm looking too far ahead, and we might never get that far in our relationship, but if we do…'

She broke off, unable to put into words the uncertainty she felt.

'What if you enjoy the present and let the future take care of itself, love?' her father suggested, covering her hand with his and giving her fingers a squeeze. 'You had precious little happiness in your life with Dennis, for all your insistence he wasn't always the way he turned out. You deserve all the love that comes your way. Go for it, and we'll sort out what needs to be sorted out when and if it happens.'

Annie felt her heart lift at her father's assurance, though some doubts remained. Plenty of doubts!

Alex was as good as his word, arriving early evening, freshly showered and shaven and slightly less tired-looking, wearing black jeans and a charcoal polo shirt and looking so—so manly that Annie felt her heart skip with excitement, the way it had when she'd been a teenager on one of her very first dates.

'You'd better come in and meet the author,' Annie suggested, when they'd both stood awkwardly on the doorstep for far too long.

'I'd like that,' Alex replied, and Annie relaxed. For a moment there she'd thought it was all going to fall apart—her with her skipping heart, dry mouth and brain that refused to function, and Alex thinking who knew what about the dummy who'd opened the door.

Primed to say nothing about the past, Rod Talbot greeted Alex easily, but Annie knew his sharp eyes were taking in the man, and his writer's mind would store all the conversation for perusal later.

'Annie tells me you've read some of my books. I hope they haven't had you cursing over the author's ineptitude.'

'On the contrary,' Alex said. 'I've found them good fast reads. Totally engrossing. And though I don't as yet know Sydney, you paint a picture of a fascinating city.'

'It is that!' Rod said, and Annie smiled to herself, remembering the hours she and her father had spent exploring the city when he'd first decided to set his mysteries here.

She watched Alex as he chatted to her father, bringing up scenes from the books he'd read, asking questions about writing.

'Can you type or do you use a voice-activated programme on a computer?'

Her father held up his hands.

'Tactful way to ask the question,' he answered. 'Rheumatoid arthritis—terrible disease. Started out thinking I'd save my hands—had knuckle replacements and all, but no good came of them. No, the voice programme works for me. You have to train them, you know, to your own voice and words, but Katy—I call mine Katy—makes me feel as if I've got a secretary. Katy knows me nearly as well as Annie does.'

'Dad also runs a tape recorder, so if something happens to the computer version of the story, he's got it on tape.'

'But what about changing things—going back over to take something out or put something in? I have to do that all the time just writing a paper, so that must be hard.'

'I have a real secretary for that,' Rod explained. 'She

comes for three hours every afternoon and we tidy things up. I can type a bit so I do some of that part as well.'

'And you're fairly mobile? Able to transfer yourself? Do you drive?'

Annie smiled to herself. She'd heard Alex ask the parents of his patients personal questions that seemed unrelated to their child's condition, but knew he liked a whole picture of the family, saying it helped him see what stresses might arise later when they were responsible for caring for their convalescing child.

Her father seemed untroubled by Alex's interest, explaining he could take care of himself, just used the chair for mobility because his hip joints made walking both painful and risky. But, yes, he drove—had a lift on the car to put his wheelchair on the top of it, and used hand controls fixed to the steering wheel.

'It's the very latest system. Would you like to see it?'

'I would,' Alex said, and Annie started planning dinner. Her father was enjoying Alex's company and Annie knew Alex was genuinely interested, not just trying to make a good first impression. In fact, she doubted it would occur to Alex that he *was* making a good impression.

'We may as well eat here,' she said, when they returned an hour later—her father having taken Alex for a drive to show him how the car worked.

Alex began to protest, but Annie shook her head.

'We can go for a walk after dinner,' she told him. 'After all, you cooked for me last night—why shouldn't I cook for you?'

Henry, who'd greeted Alex earlier, sniffed around him, looking for Minnie, and not finding her had gone to bed, now heard the magic word 'walk' and appeared from the laundry where he slept.

'Not you,' Annie told him.

'Best you take the dog,' her father said, but Annie ignored the comment, instead instructing the men to sit down and asking Alex what he'd like to drink.

'Dad and I will both have red wine. Would you like a glass or would you prefer something else?'

'A glass of red would be great,' he said, and went on to mention some of the Australian red wines that had become his favourites.

'Lucky you,' Annie told him, showing him the bottle before she poured. It was on the top of his list!

'So we've similar tastes in red wine at least,' he said, smiling at her, though with a rueful look in his eyes as if to apologise about this 'first date'.

But the evening, for Annie, was just perfect. Alex seemed right at home, discussing books and wine and making them laugh at the things he'd found hard to understand when he'd first arrived in Australia.

'Just because we speak the same language, we assume we understand each other,' Annie said, about to recount an anecdote about her early days in the US then remembering she shouldn't. She changed the conversation to pronunciation differences, talking about New Zealanders and South Africans rather than Americans, but she guessed Alex had caught the conversational shift.

It was impossible, she decided. She couldn't go out with Alex, not if it meant pretending she'd never lived in the US. Not if it meant never acknowledging she was the woman he'd danced with on the terrace. How could they ever be at ease if that knowledge lay unspoken between them, yet how could she explain—tell him about that night—without telling him more?

She looked at him, his craggy face alive with intelligence and good humour as he explained the intricacies of American football to her father. Everything she knew of

Alex indicated he was a good man—firm and demanding of his staff but quick to praise their efforts. Honest in his dealings with his patients' parents, yet empathetic as well, so they trusted their children's lives to him and knew he'd do his best.

But he wouldn't tolerate sloppy work, or anyone doing less than their best. She also knew, instinctively, he wouldn't tolerate deception, and what else would a relationship between them be?

She cleared away the dishes while Alex drew a diagram of a football field in the notebook her father always carried, and talked about offensive plays and touchdowns. By the time her father had learnt all he needed to know to enjoy the American football games he watched on cable television, Annie had stacked the dishwasher and put a plate of cheese, fruit and biscuits on the table.

'No more food!' Alex protested. 'In fact, I think it's time I walked off some of that delicious dinner.'

He turned to Annie.

'You mentioned the beach, and I know it's not far away. Shall we go there for our walk? I'm happy to drive if you direct me.'

Annie hesitated.

'You go,' her father said, no doubt aware of all the machinations of her mind.

Annie nodded, thinking the beach would be as good a place as any to tell Alex what she had to tell him. To tell him she didn't think even a getting-to-know-each-other relationship would work.

'I'll just get a jacket. I can duck up the back lane and meet you at your car,' she said, but Alex shook his head.

'I'll wait for you. We'll go together. We'll sneak away without our respective dogs knowing what we're up to.'

Annie slipped upstairs, heart again skipping with excitement although she kept telling it this was the end, not the beginning.

Alex drove easily, and in one of life's little miracles they found a parking space not far from the wide concrete steps that led down to the beach. It was after eleven and only a few people wandered along the broad strip of sand, although a scattering of couples and groups, drawn to the soothing sounds of the surf, were walking on the promenade.

Annie breathed deeply, drawing the damp, salt-laden air into her lungs.

'I love standing by the Pacific and thinking the next big lump of land it hits is America. I love the idea that the water in a wave I'm watching here might one day, depending on the currents, wash across a beach in California.'

Alex put his arm around her shoulders and pulled her body closer to his.

'Should we talk about the big lump of land that is America? About North America in particular?'

Annie sighed.

'We should, Alex,' she said, relishing his warmth and closeness, wishing with all her heart this could be a real 'first date' so they were coming together with nothing but expectations of fun and pleasure—with no baggage from the past. 'But I'm not sure that I can. Or ought to…'

She couldn't go on, couldn't come right out and say, *I'm living a lie*.

'Then we'll walk,' he said, his voice strained. 'But one day, Annie, I hope you'll feel you can trust me well enough to talk.'

His disappointment in her was so obvious, it cut into Annie like a scalpel.

'Maybe we shouldn't even walk,' she muttered, but Alex

was already guiding her towards the smooth wet sand where the waves finished their journey across the Pacific. He released her for a moment to slip off his shoes and turn up the bottoms of his jeans, and she bent and took off her sandals. Then, with his arm around her shoulders once again, they paddled through the shallows to where the beach ended in a high tumble of rocks that stretched, like the humped back of some fossilised sea creature out into the waves.

And in the shadow of the rocks he turned her towards him and drew her body close to his, then bent his head and kissed her with a mastery his previous kisses had ensured.

Annie was surprised at how familiar his body felt, how at home she felt in his arms. And the kiss. It was a different kind of magic—sweet, gentle and seductively addictive.

Until the first easy exploratory moves were done! Then the attraction she felt for Alex fired a need so deep and filled with longing she couldn't pretend, even to herself, that this was just a casual, first-date kind of kiss. This was a kiss that sent tendrils of desire spreading through her body, seeking out the deep-hidden places and bringing nerves and flesh to life with a tingling, trembling, pleading anticipation.

Somewhere there was noise. Loud noise. Annie hoped it wasn't her making it—whooping and crying out as her body delighted in Alex's embrace. Then Alex gently put her from him.

'Someone's in trouble,' he said, sounding as breathless as she felt. At that moment Annie saw the source of the noise, a young man standing on one of the humps of rock, calling for help.

'Someone swept off the rocks,' she guessed. 'Fishermen usually.'

They were both scrabbling towards the lad who was still

yelling for help but not offering any more information until Alex reached him.

'It's Dad. He slipped and backwash carried him out. I can see him in the surf but I can't reach him.'

Other beach-walkers were gathering on the sand at the base of the rocks.

'I've called triple O,' one said.

'My wife's run back to the lifesavers' clubhouse. There's usually someone there.'

Alex had pulled on his shoes and was accompanying the youth back to where his father had disappeared. Annie followed more slowly, barefoot, because her sandals would be worse than useless on the rocks.

'I can see him,' Alex told her, 'but he's being buffeted by the waves and hitting against the rocks. He needs to swim out beyond where the waves break and wait for rescue there.'

Alex called to the man, telling him to swim away from the rocks, but he either couldn't hear or had already been injured and the best he could do was stay afloat. Before Annie realised what was happening, Alex was stripping off his clothes, thrusting first his shoes, then his trousers and shirt at Annie, telling her to hold them.

Then he walked out to a high, dry rock and was about to dive when Annie yelled at him.

'Jump, don't dive. It might be shallower than you think.'

So he jumped, while Annie held her breath, first until he surfaced then again until he reached the man and together they swam beyond the curling breakers. She refused to think about the sharks that cruised these shores, or of the way a freak wave could lift the pair and throw them up onto the rocks. Her mind concentrated on willing them both to stay alive.

Then she heard the roar of the jet skis and knew help

was on the way, but she still watched tensely as the first jet ski stopped, the driver dropping a flotation device to Alex then lifting the fisherman onto the back of the seat. The driver of the second jet ski helped Alex aboard, and the two machines roared off towards the beach.

Annie followed more slowly, having to pick her way across the rocks, clutching Alex's clothing to her chest. They smelt of him, she realised as she drew warmth and comfort from objects as mundane as a pair of jeans and a shirt. Then she shivered as her body lit again with excitement, imagining enjoying the scent of the man himself just as intimately.

*Get real, girl! It's not going to happen. It can't happen. Can't it?*

The mental argument took her to the clubhouse where Alex, wrapped in a blanket, was waiting for her.

'Much quicker to get a ride back,' he teased as she passed over his clothes. And seeing him there, alive and well and teasing, made her remember the clench of terror she'd felt when he'd gone into the water, and she had to bite back an urge to yell at him for being so foolhardy.

'I'm OK,' he said gently, taking her hand and pulling her close enough to drop a kiss on her hair. 'I'm a strong swimmer and could see the safe way to approach the man, or I would never have gone in.'

'OK,' Annie conceded, but he wasn't completely off the hook. 'But don't go doing that kind of hero stuff again! Not when I'm around anyway.'

She thought about it for a moment, then added, 'No, not even when I'm not around. You're far too important to too many people to be putting yourself in danger. And don't bother telling me there was no danger. I was there. I saw it.'

He touched his hand to her shoulder.

'I'll grab a quick shower and get dressed. The lifesavers offered coffee. Do you want a cup?'

Annie shook her head. The words she'd just spoken about Alex putting himself into danger were echoing in her head, together with an insistent little voice suggesting she might be doing it herself—putting Alex into danger by associating with him.

Dennis dangerous?

To her, most probably, but to someone else?

She didn't know.

Yet acts in their past and his persistence in trying to find her suggested it was a possibility. It certainly wasn't to finalise divorce proceedings, because she'd started them herself and through a string of different lawyers, all protecting her confidentiality, had had papers served on him.

But all that had done had been to increase the pressure of the private investigators on the family she and her father had left behind.

'Stop frowning. I'm fine!'

Alex's return brought her back to the present.

'Yes,' Annie said, vowing inside herself that she'd have to keep things that way.

This resolution weakened somewhat when he drove his car into the garage behind his house then walked her home down the back lane, no doubt aware of the privacy its dark seclusion offered.

And when he kissed her, which he did at intervals all the way along the lane, Annie's resolve weakened, and she found herself arguing, mentally, that everything would be all right.

# CHAPTER SEVEN

ALEX could sense resistance in his companion as they made their way, with frequent stops, towards her house. Not resistance to his kisses—she was too honest and wholehearted in her response! No, it was to do with the past, and whatever it was it haunted Annie as she had haunted him.

They reached her place and he took her to the back door and waited while she unlocked it, calling to Henry to quieten him.

'Would you like a coffee now?' she asked, but lack of sleep and an evening swim had taken their toll and Alex shook his head.

'I'll say goodnight,' he said, and took her in his arms again, kissing her thoroughly, winning sweet, hot kisses in return. But although his body hungered to take things further, his head decreed caution, and he knew it was the right decision at this stage of their relationship.

Especially if Annie was, as he suspected, trying to work out how to tell him it was over before it had begun.

He said goodnight and walked home up the lane, wondering if he was at the two steps forward or one step back part of this relationship. He also found time to wonder why he, with his aversion to emotional dependency, wanted so badly to find out about Annie's past. Wanted so badly to make things right for her.

Wasn't he better off just accepting the Annie of the present, enjoying a relationship with her and letting the past remain where it was—in the past?

Yes was the answer to that question, but he knew that wasn't going to happen. If he had a relationship with Annie then it was already tied to the past.

'Give it up,' he told himself, letting himself in through his back door and bending to lift a delighted Minnie and hush her excited yapping. 'Think about work!'

He dialled the hospital, remembering as the phone rang at the other end that he hadn't told Annie that Amy's new catheter had worked and her kidneys were functioning if not perfectly then well.

The report from the PICU was all good, and he went off to bed thinking of work, but with a twist of Annie, because he'd be seeing her there in the morning.

'So you see my dilemma, Henry,' Annie said, when she'd filled him in on the Alex situation over a very early breakfast the next morning.

'Just tell the man about Dennis,' her father said, coming in on the tail end of the one-way discussion. 'For Pete's sake, it doesn't reflect badly on you.'

Annie looked at her father. He'd been a policeman for over thirty years, yet he still had no real understanding of how victims of the crimes he'd fought—and now wrote about—felt. This wasn't the first time she'd tried to explain it to him, and it probably wouldn't be the last, but still she tried.

'Dad, you and I were closer than most fathers and daughters are—far closer—but it still took me four years to lift that phone and call you.'

Four years and a stranger's kiss, she amended silently.

'I've known Alex for a week. I *can't* talk to him about it, and even if I could, don't you think he'd run a mile? What sane sensible man would want a woman with so much baggage?'

'A man who loved you, that's who,' her father growled, then he wheeled himself away, not, Annie knew, because he was angry with her but because he, too, still found it hard to cope with what had happened.

Annie said goodbye to her two protectors and walked to work, pleased not to have company because, after a weekend of emotional upheaval, she wanted to get her mind focussed back on the job. Especially as this would be the first week of full-time surgery, the patient first up this morning a young girl Alex had seen last week. Jamie Hutchins was a six-year-old with a previously undiagnosed atrial septal defect, or, in medical shorthand, an ASD, and Alex had scheduled a staff briefing for eight with the operation to start at nine. And because she wanted to be at the briefing, wanted to learn all she could about the work Alex did, here she was heading for work before seven.

And beating Alex, she found when she checked in at the special care unit and learned both patients had enjoyed a peaceful night. But she wasn't the first on duty. As she pushed open the door that led to the suite of open-plan 'offices' she and the doctors used, she saw the light was on, and though her heart skipped an anticipatory beat it was Maggie, not Alex, already at a desk.

'You want a coffee?' Maggie used the question as a greeting. She looked and sounded tired, which puzzled Annie, given the status of their patients.

Annie said yes to coffee and watched Maggie as she poured, seeing tiredness in her actions as well.

'Are you OK?' she asked, and Maggie gave a weary smile.

'When Alex offered me the job up here, I thought it would be a good chance to catch up with my sister, who shifted up here when she married, and get to know her family a bit better. So I asked if I could stay with them until I found somewhere to live.'

'Not a good idea?' Annie sugared her coffee and stirred it.

'A terrible idea,' Maggie told her. 'She's got a spaced-out family—I mean in ages, although Pete, the eldest, is definitely spaced out in other ways. Pete's fifteen and we go down through an eleven-year-old I swear has ADD and twins going through the delightful Terrible Twos.'

'Not much peace and quiet?'

'None!'

'Do you have to stay?'

Maggie shook her head.

'Not really. I think I'm probably as disruptive for them as they are for me. But finding somewhere else isn't all that easy. I don't know the city at all, and have no idea of where to start looking. Somewhere near the hospital, I suppose.'

Annie thought of the house she and her father shared. It had been converted before they'd bought it, so there was a self-contained suite for him downstairs with three bedrooms and two bathrooms upstairs. More than enough room for an extra person.

Yet she felt reluctant to make the offer, and knew the reluctance was tied up with Alex and the relationship they didn't yet have, and might never have, and really, when she thought about it, should never have.

Then she remembered the size of the hearts Alex operated on, and the skill he required from his anaesthetist.

Would an exhausted anaesthetist exhibit the same skill?

How could she *not* offer?

'We've plenty of room at our place and it's just down the road—you can walk to and from work. You don't have to stay for the whole year, but at least it would be handy while you looked around. You can pop down and check the place out during your break between ops and meet my father, and if you like it, I can drive you to your sister's after work and bring you and your gear back home.'

Maggie stared at her.

'You don't know me,' she pointed out, and Annie grinned at her.

'I know you're an excellent anaesthetist and this unit needs one of those, so anything I can do to make your job easier, it's yours.'

Maggie got up from where she'd been slumped behind a desk and came across to give Annie a big hug.

'It needn't be for the whole year,' she assured Annie. 'Just until I get my bearings in Sydney and find somewhere for myself.'

'Whatever suits you,' Annie said, though a sinking feeling in the pit of her stomach told her she'd have a boarder for a year. Where else would Maggie find so ideal a situation?

Maggie was chattering on, so obviously delighted by this change in fortune Annie had to feel happy for her.

'You don't need to drive me. I've got my own car. I'll check out your place at lunchtime then go back to my sister's for tonight to say goodbye to them all, pack my stuff into the car and bring it all over tomorrow.'

'Bring what all over where tomorrow?'

Annie turned at the sound of Alex's voice. Inside, her stomach turned as well, a happy little flip-type somersault.

She smiled at him—a unit co-ordinator greeting the main man smile—and saw a bit more warmth in the smile he gave her back. Although the warmth faded, and the smile grew forced as Maggie happily explained the situation.

'Maggie's coming to live with you?' Alex asked, when Maggie had left the suite to check her new patient.

He sounded hurt, and puzzled, and Annie understood both reactions.

'It might only be temporary,' she said, then remembered why she'd offered.

'Personally, it might not be ideal,' she said, standing up so she could look Alex in the eye, 'but professionally—do you really want a sleep-deprived, twitchy anaesthetist working with you on a child? What else could I do but offer?'

His smile improved, though it was still a wry effort.

'I wish I'd been here. I could have offered to have her at my place. With Phil there already, it wouldn't have mattered and we'd still have had some privacy from work colleagues at your place.'

He brightened considerably.

'We could still do that! I'll offer to have her at my place. She'll be with Jamie. I'll go now.'

He touched Annie on the shoulder and breezed away, obviously delighted with his own brilliance.

But his face was glum again when Annie saw him at the briefing, and he looked far from happy as he explained Jamie's problem, where a hole in the wall between the heart's two upper chambers, the atria, hadn't closed, so blood shunted between the two chambers.

'It causes increased pressure in the right atrium and ventricle, and too much blood flowing into the lungs. Usually the patient suffers few symptoms—a bit of breathlessness and fatigue from time to time. In Jamie's case these didn't become obvious until she started at Little Athletics. Echocardiography has confirmed the hole is there, and her cardiologist has done a cardiac catheterisation as well to determine just where the hole is.'

Alex pointed to his diagram on the whiteboard.

'New technology is being tried for holes in the centre of the atrial wall, and holes are being successfully closed using transcatheter management—inserting wires through a catheter. But Jamie's hole is higher up and the new technique doesn't work, hence the need for an operation.'

'If she's been OK up until now, and is only breathless after running or jumping at Little Athletics, is it worth the risk involved in any operation—particularly open heart where she'll be on a bypass machine for some of it?'

One of the sisters from the special care unit asked the question, and Annie was pleased. For one thing, she'd wondered about it herself, and for another, it meant all the unit staff were becoming increasingly involved in all stages of their patients' operations.

'There's a twenty-five per cent risk of early mortality through pulmonary vascular obstructive disease if it's not repaired and a less than five per cent—in fact, I feel less than one per cent—risk with the operation itself.'

Alex turned back to the board and sketched a small chest.

'We make a much smaller incision than we do for a PDA, only...' He paused, then smiled at them all. 'I have to convert inches to centimetres...say eighty to a hundred centimetres. Then the defect is fixed with either a patch or stitches, depending on what we find. As you said, the child has to go on the heart-lung machine as soon as we open the pericardium, then once the aorta is clamped, we stop the heart beating with cardioplegia, open it up, fix the hole and Jamie's back in business again. Within weeks she should be back at Little Athletics.'

'The results are really good,' Phil added, turning to smile at the sister who'd asked the question. 'You probably won't have her more than a few hours in the PICU, then she'll be moved to the ward.'

'Which reminds me,' Alex said, directing his question to the two nurses present who had been specially selected to work with his patients once they reached the children's post-surgical ward. 'How do you think you'll go, working with our patients exclusively when they're back in the ward with the others?'

'I love the idea of it,' one of them said, while the other nodded agreement. 'It means you can really get to know the children and their families, and there's something special about being chosen as part of the team that's working to make them well again.'

Whatever gloom Alex had shown earlier disappeared, and he beamed at the pair, one male and one female.

'That's great to hear, and don't forget, if you run into administrative trouble at any stage, see Annie and she'll sort it out.'

Annie's turn to smile. Alex could so easily have said to see him, but he had enough faith in her to know she'd handle it.

She just hoped his faith would never prove to be misplaced.

The briefing over, the operating crew headed off for the theatre, the nursing staff back to their places and Annie returned to the office. Alex's prediction that there'd be hospital infighting was already coming true. She had a meeting with the CEO and other surgical co-ordinators at nine-thirty, and guessed pressure would be applied for other surgical services to have equal access to the new theatre.

Not this week they wouldn't, as Alex was booked to operate twice and sometimes three times a day right through until Friday.

'Adult cardiac surgery brings in more dollars than CHD,' the administrator of the adult cardiac programme yelled at her less than an hour later, confirming Annie's prediction.

'But it requires more outlays as well,' Annie shot back, determined to remain calm. 'And takes more hospital resources as patients are hospitalised for longer. Plus, you have to realise that if we operate on infants and children with CHD, it means these children won't need cardiac surgery as adults.'

As soon as the words were out of her mouth, she realised she'd made a mistake. The adult cardiac administrator was a money person through and through, and telling him there'd be fewer patients for him in the future was a challenge to his job security.

'Surely people matter more than dollars!' she stormed at Alex much later when he was foolish enough to ask her how the meeting had gone. 'Surely it's more important to offer children with CHD an opportunity to lead a normal life than to keep up the numbers of adult cardiac patients?'

Alex smiled at her vehemence.

'Of course it is, but you'll find very few administrators within a hospital system—or any system, I suppose—who aren't bent on defending their territory.'

Another smile, and if the first had soothed some of her anger, this second one warmed bits of her left cold from the other man's attitude.

'Weren't you doing just that?' he asked, and the warmth turned to heat.

'No, I wasn't. I was talking people, not numbers or money. I was talking about infants and kids like Jamie who'll go back and run the legs off the others in her age group at Little Athletics. I won't talk numbers and money—I'll keep the figures and use them to prove our worth, but the children and their families will always be my prime concern. And if that's going to make me a bad unit manager then you'd better sack me right now.'

She glared defiantly at him, though she knew a lot of her rage was leftover frustration from the morning's meeting.

'I don't think I could sack you,' he said, another smile,

gentle this time, playing around his lips. 'The CEO was most insistent that the job was yours, right from the start. I could ask for just about anything else I wanted, but you were a given. The powers that be in this place have a very high opinion of you.'

'You make it sound as if you didn't want me here!'

He sounded so tired she almost let him off the hook, but if the man this morning had made her angry, this man was making her doubly so, with his assumption that she might not be up to the job. Because she was a woman?

'Were you against me, or against having a woman in the job? Was this a gender issue?'

'Not at all. Actually, I wanted my old administrator, Karen. Annie, are we arguing?'

'Yes,' she told him, then she relented. 'Not arguing precisely, but I'd like to know more about it. It's not exactly confidence-building to think you'd have preferred someone else in this job.'

'Can we talk over dinner?' he suggested hopefully. 'Did you say there was an Italian restaurant near the park? Could we go and argue there? I'm famished, and if I caught the drift of all the arrangements you and Maggie made—I did ask her to stay at my place, by the way, but she refused— this might be my last opportunity for a proper first date.'

'Oh, Alex,' Annie sighed, then, because the longing was still there—strong and hot and insistent—she nodded. 'OK. I'll just phone Dad, because it's closer to walk straight there, then we can cut across the park to come home. It's well lit at night.'

'That's a shame, though there are sure to be shadows. No rocks and fishermen?' Alex said, and Annie smiled at him, knowing he was remembering the interrupted kiss.

'No rocks or fishermen,' she promised.

*     *     *

Definitely two steps forward and one back in this relationship, and right now he was at the back stage, Alex thought as he had a wash before leaving the hospital.

Hell's bells, he hadn't had a date with the woman yet, and he was thinking relationship longevity. And she was as uncertain as a woman could be about *any* relationship— let alone one with him.

And prickly!

Because she'd been hurt before?

He was as certain of that as he was of his own name. If he wasn't careful, he'd blow this before it had even begun, and every instinct told him that would be a very bad thing. A disastrous thing! Muddle-headed he might be, but one thing he was quite clear on—both physically and emotionally he wanted Annie Talbot, and he was pretty sure it wasn't because she was his ghost.

Well, he hoped it wasn't, because he knew from experience that flesh-and-blood women were a lot more bother than ghosts, but in Annie's case he was certain…he smiled to himself…she was worth the effort.

'You don't have to talk about the administrator issue,' Annie said as they left the hospital and she guided him along a path that led around the perimeter of the park. 'It's really none of my business if you wanted to bring her out here.'

Alex was more than happy to accede to this request, but a tightness in Annie's voice suggested he'd better get it settled or he'd be eight steps back.

'Karen Ritchie, my old—no, ex—administrator, is a single mother who has worked sometimes at two or three jobs for the past ten years since her husband left her, to keep her kids and get them through college. They were old enough to be left on their own for a year, with relatives keeping an eye on them, and I thought the year out here, as well as being hard work, would be a treat for Karen.'

'Oh!' Annie said, in a very small voice. 'Yes, she'd have enjoyed it, I'm sure.'

'But, in case you're now feeling bad about Karen, I can see it would have been impossible for her to function efficiently in such a different work environment. I discovered that in Melbourne when I needed administrative help to find my way around the workings of the hospital, and without you in the job here we wouldn't be nearly as far along as we are. So stop worrying about it and let's just go out and eat together and enjoy it.'

Now they were safely over that issue, Alex wondered what they should talk about.

Annie solved that problem.

'I phoned Mayarma, the dog-walker I told you about, and she's more than happy to add Minnie to her mob. She'd like to take her out on her own first to see how she behaves, but I assured her Henry would look after her—Minnie, not Mayarma—if she joins the group.'

'And what do I have to do? How do I arrange things? And what is this wonderful service going to cost me?'

Annie explained the various ways owners left their dogs to be collected, and then named a sum that seemed ridiculously low to Alex.

'That's all she asks?'

Annie nodded.

'It's cash. She's from the Philippines, married to an Australian, and she loves dogs but can't have one as her husband's getting on and could be knocked over by a big dog or trip over a small one. I'll give you her phone number and you can speak to her direct about the arrangements.'

Which sorted out the dogs. Alex wondered if he could

turn the subject to more personal matters, but Annie fore-stalled him with a question.

'Did Maggie tell you why she didn't want to stay with you?'

'No, though I guess it could be something to do with sharing with two men. She might have imagined she'd have to do all the cooking and housework.'

'Mmm.'

Alex waited for an explanation and when none was forth-coming asked, 'That's it? Mmm?'

'It was a considering kind of mmm,' Annie explained. 'An ''I'm not sure enough to say anything'' kind of mmm.'

'About what?' Alex persisted, realising Annie's conver-sation, first about the dogs and now about something to do with Maggie, was actually relaxing him quite nicely. It seemed so normal somehow, to be walking like this with Annie and talking trivia.

'About Maggie,' Annie now said, and Alex found he was intrigued. He liked Maggie and greatly appreciated the con-tribution she made to his work. A good anaesthetist was essential in all operations—but even more critical when working on hearts that could be as small as plums.

But they'd reached the restaurant, and his first whiff of the garlic-scented air turned his thoughts from staff to food.

And once again he made Annie laugh, his indecision over what sauce to have with his *penne* delighting her. Her laughter filled his heart with a heady gladness that went beyond the attraction he felt for her, and filled his mind with a resolve to continue this rather strange courtship.

'It's all very well for you,' he grumbled. 'You probably cook delicious sauces every day of the week. Once I'm past curry, it's steak or steak. Not that you don't have great steak out here in Australia, but it gets a bit boring after a while.'

'You can buy prepared sauces then all you have to do is boil the pasta and heat the sauce and *voilà*, an Italian meal.'

'*Voilà*'s French,' he said, still grumbling, but now because Annie had slipped off the jacket of her suit, revealing a dark green blouse that made her eyes seem greener. And just as he was comparing the colour of the eyes to her blouse the top button popped, revealing a glimpse of a deep shadow between her breasts, so lust replaced the gladness in his heart, while an inner voice—a mean-spirited voice, sharp with jealousy—wondered if she'd had her jacket on or off at the meeting that morning.

'The waitress asked if you'd decided,' Annie said, indicating a young woman who'd materialised by his side.

'I'll have the Matriciana,' he said, and silently congratulated himself on his recovery.

'It's about the only pasta sauce not on the menu. How about you try the Alfredo?'

Annie was just being helpful, but he glowered at her anyway, knowing he couldn't ask what she'd had on at the meeting, suspecting he might be seriously love-struck to be thinking this way, and, as the wine waiter approached, wondering if it would be totally improper behaviour if he reached across the table and did up the wayward button.

He didn't, asking Annie instead if she had a preference in wine, and when she settled on a glass of the house Chianti, he told the waiter he'd have the same. Thankfully, the man departed.

Which left him with Annie, and the revealing neckline of her shirt, which kept drawing his attention as surely as seagulls were drawn to fries at a picnic.

His silence must have stretched a fraction too long.

'You're frowning again. Is it Jamie, or are you still worried about Amy?'

Annie's question—so work-oriented when his mind had been so far away—made him smile.

'If I confess I was thinking of seagulls...' not entirely true but close enough '...would you think I was totally mad?'

'Not totally,' she said, a smile lighting up her face and twinkling in her green-today eyes.

She sat back, obviously waiting for him to explain, but of course he couldn't. Neither could he think of any logical thoughts he might have been having about seagulls.

Apart from them liking fries!

'Jamie came through really well,' he said, reverting to work as an escape from dangerous territory. 'It's hard to tell how older children will react. I think because they understand the concept of an operation, and have some knowledge of what's happening to them, they can be more fearful. I don't know of any studies that have been done to see how that affects recovery, but it would be interesting to test the theory. I had a teenage patient once, and though he was used to having catheters stuck up an artery or vein from his groin, and knew all the process, and watched the screen to see the tube travel to his heart, he told me, years later, how much he'd hated it and how he'd far rather have been knocked out before the procedure took place.'

'Why wasn't it an option?' Annie asked, and Alex smiled to himself. He'd mentioned the case as a diversionary tactic but Annie was so eager to know things he enjoyed these discussions nearly as much as—

Boy! He'd nearly thought 'the popped button' and pulled himself up just in time.

'A lot of older children enjoy being part of their treatment, and we'd assumed that was the case with this youth. However, him telling me how much he hated it was a wake-up call for me, because I'd made an assumption on his behalf. Early on, we did all catheterisations for testing and small ops while the patient was sedated slightly but not out of it, mainly because we didn't have the mild, short-acting anaesthesia we have today. And though we knock the infants out, we'd continued doing the older children with just sedation.'

'Until someone protested?'

Alex nodded. 'Bad medicine, that!' he recalled. 'We should have asked. I always do now, and I make sure the cardiologists—they do most of the caths these days—know how I feel about it. I even gave a paper on it once.'

And as he said the words he remembered where and when he'd given that paper. At the congress at Traders Rest five years ago...

# CHAPTER EIGHT

ANNIE knew from the way he looked at her exactly where and when he'd given that paper. And suddenly it was the right time to say something. Not a lot, but enough for Alex to decide if he wanted to keep seeing her or not.

Though it shouldn't be his choice. *She* should decide. And she knew what that decision should be!

But her heart longed for the love she felt might be on offer, while her mind reached out for companionship and her body—well, her body just plain lusted after his!

So she had to say *something*!

She reached out and placed her hand over his, so they both rested on the table. Gave his fingers a squeeze because this could well be the last time she touched him.

Then she withdrew her hand and used it to grip her other one—tightly—in her lap beneath the table so no one could see them twisting anxiously.

She looked at Alex, at the grey eyes that seemed to see right into her soul, and with a heavy heart blurted out the words that needed to be said.

'You've probably guessed I was with someone at the congress. My husband. I left him that night. I haven't seen him since. I started divorce proceedings eighteen months ago, but as I haven't heard from the lawyers I don't know if it's gone through so I could, technically, still be married.'

Alex seemed to be waiting for more, his eyes fixed on her face, then he smiled.

'Are you telling me this in case I have strong feelings about dating married women? Believe me, Annie, if you

111

haven't lived with the guy for five years, I don't think you count as married any more, so you can't escape me that way.'

The teasing tone in his voice warmed all the cold places in her body that thinking about Dennis had produced, but as she replayed all the words—both hers and his—in her head, she realised she was still a long way from explaining exactly where things now stood between her and Dennis.

Not that she knew for certain…

Alex was talking again and she shut away the sudden tremor of fear.

'Annie,' he said gently, 'you must know there are plenty of places in the States where divorce is cheap and easy. Maybe he's divorced you.'

'Maybe,' she said, though she doubted it. When the first of the private investigators had called her father—only two days after she'd left Traders Rest—her father had said Annie was in the US and as far as he knew still with Dennis. Her father had also supplied the man with the name and contact details of the family's solicitors and asked that all contact be made through the firm, which meant there'd always been an address available for the service of papers or for information about a 'quickie' divorce.

'Well, as I said, it doesn't matter,' Alex reiterated. 'Now, would you like to put your hand back on the table? I think on a first date, even in Australia, we'd be allowed to hold hands.'

Annie smiled at the weak joke, but as her fingers were now icy from remembering, she was happy to rest her hand back on the table, appreciating the warmth of his when he placed it on top of hers.

He gave her fingers a squeeze, thanked the waiter who'd brought their wine and then said, 'My mother always said to show interest in one's companions—ask about their jobs and so on. But I know all about your job and you know about mine, and we've already talked about the pets and the food, so I guess we might be up to families. Is it just you and your father in yours? Having had my sister visit last year, I can only see that as a blessing, although I suppose it's been fun having her around. She was an afterthought, my sister. Three boys, then when the youngest was eight along came Frances. I was thirteen, old enough to understand the basic sex education we'd had at school, so you can imagine how horrified I was to realise my mother and father must have done *that* to have produced Frances! Totally grossed me out for a long time!'

Annie laughed.

'I can imagine!' she said, but though her laughter sounded genuine, Alex could still read strain in her face, and the cold fingers nestling beneath his suggested that telling him even the bare bones of her story had upset her.

She lifted her other hand up to pick up her wineglass, tilting it towards him in a toast.

'To the new unit!' she said.

Alex lifted his own glass and clinked it against hers, although he'd always thought the gesture corny.

'Not to the new unit, Annie, but to us!' He raised it higher, then moved it to his lips and took a sip. 'This is a date, remember.'

A slight smile trembled on her lips.

'I'm out of practice at dating,' she said. 'This is the first in a very long time, and I've already probably blown it with a confession about my dubious marital status, and now I'm feeling envious of you, growing up in a family with four kids. You asked if it was just Dad and me in our family, and it is. My mother died when I was eleven, so he and I are closer than most fathers and daughters.'

'Nothing to feel envious about,' Alex assured her, although he felt sorry for anyone who hadn't experienced the kind of upbringing he'd had, and he couldn't imagine not having the close connections he'd retained with his siblings. 'After three boys my mother had always prayed for a girl so she'd have female support within the family, but when Frances came along Mom swore she was more trouble than the three of us put together.'

He could feel Annie's fingers growing warmer and could see the tension draining out of her face. His imagination had provided him with a vivid image of her travelling to the US with her husband, separated from her father—the only close family she had—by an ocean. No mom at home to phone when things were difficult, no supportive letters like the ones he still received from members of his family—though now they were emailed, not posted.

The waitress set their meals on the table. Annie thanked her then took back her hand so she could handle her fork and spoon for some spaghetti-twirling.

'I always order pasta in pieces because I've never mastered that art,' Alex confessed, after admiring her expertise for some time.

'Student meals!' she said. 'I trained in—in a city and Dad was posted in the country at the time, so I shared a flat with three other students. I think we lived on spaghetti for four years. When we were flush we had sauce on it, other times olive oil and garlic.'

She paused then grinned at him.

'Come to think of it, I didn't have many dates back then either!'

Alex knew she was doing her best to keep the conversation light, but her hesitation in mentioning a particular city struck him as off-key and he remembered other times she'd caught herself in conversation.

Were things not finished between herself and her husband in other ways—apart from the divorce? Was she fearful of him finding her?

Mental headshake. OK, so some men did get hung up on ex-wives or ex-partners—you read about it every day in the paper—but Annie had been at the congress with her husband—a congress of cardiologists and cardiac surgeons. Yes, there were ancillary services represented, and a clutch of representatives from drug companies, but to think of any of these people as...

Dangerous?

Annie was talking, about the food and some place at the beach that sold fresh pasta and a variety of sauces.

'It's really delicious, and well worth the drive.'

'We could go together on Saturday—if all's well at work,' Alex suggested, then knew from the arrested look in Annie's eyes that she'd mentioned the place as offhand conversation. And he knew, in her mind, this wasn't just a first date. It was a final one as well.

But why? He tried to get inside her head. To work out what might have happened to make her so determined not to get involved with him when it was equally obvious she liked him.

*And*, from her response to his kisses, felt an attraction towards him.

She'd had a bad experience with marriage—that was obvious—but that wasn't at all rare these days. People he knew had been married three or four times and had very few hang-ups about it. He didn't think that kind of short-term arrangement would suit him, but still...

He considered how things must have been. Marrying fairly young then travelling to the US where her husband had been her sole support—probably, if she hadn't worked, her sole contact with the outside world. If things had been difficult between them, she'd have been truly isolated.

Living in the most civilised country in the world, yet so alone she may as well have been on the moon.

The waiter appeared to ask if he'd like more wine, and he realised he'd been sipping at his glass, emptying it, as he thought. He thanked the man and was about to wave him away when he realised Annie's glass was also empty.

'Would *you* like another glass of wine? Don't stop because I did. I'm always aware I could be called in, so I usually stop at one—on rare occasions two.'

She shook her head and the waiter went away, then she smiled the slightly mischievous smile that made her eyes sparkle.

'Just because I didn't have a mother, it doesn't mean I wasn't warned about drinking too much on a first date. I think my father, having been on the other side of the dating game, probably knew more about it than any woman ever would. He typed up lists of warnings he not only read out to me before I went out the door but also taped all over the place.'

Alex chuckled at the image of fatherly concern.

'How did it start? Boys are only after one thing?'

Annie relaxed for the first time since they'd sat down and Alex had mentioned the paper he'd given at the congress.

'That was the first, fourth, sixth, eighth and eleventh, if I remember rightly. It was something he repeated with such regularity it confused me more than it helped. To begin with, I thought the ''one thing'' was a kiss, so for my first three years at high school, on the rare dates friends arranged for me, I refused to let any of the boys kiss me. Then the story went around that I had some terrible lip disease—far worse than herpes—and I didn't have to worry about saying no because no one ever asked me.'

Alex laughed, and Annie felt absurdly pleased that she could make him laugh.

'Did your father spread the rumour?' he asked, and Annie joined in his laughter.

'I often wondered,' she admitted, and with the tension eased between them they finished their meals, refused coffee and set out to walk home through the park.

'Terrible lip disease all cleared up now?' Alex asked, slowing their pace as they drew near a patch of shadow beneath a spreading, leafy tree.

'I think so,' Annie said, allowing him to turn her in his arms, wanting his kiss so badly she refused to think past the here and now. 'And if it isn't,' she added softly, moving closer so he'd know she wanted to be kissed, 'you've already been contaminated.'

He bent his head until only a breath of air separated them.

'Not contaminated, Annie,' he whispered into that tiny space. 'Addicted.'

Annie's lips responded first, remembering delight imprinted on them from the previous kisses, then her body warmed and heat glowed within it, and the longing grew so strong she knew there was no way she could resist a second date and then a third and whatever all of this was leading to.

And though doubt and guilt still existed in her head, what was happening in other parts of her enabled her to ignore them, offering up feeble excuses about Alex only being here for a year, and wasn't it time she got some pleasure out of life, and why shouldn't she enjoy his company for a while?

'Ah,' Alex said, a long time later, lifting his head and taking a deep breath. 'I thought I'd lost you there for a while, but once you put your mind to a kiss, Annie Talbot, I can only say you do a first-rate job.'

He smoothed her hair back from her face, cupped his hand around her jaw and cheek and looked into her eyes, though she knew it was too dark for him to see more than a blurred outline of her face.

'I've stopped kissing you and I'm making this ridiculous light conversation, because if that kiss had gone on for much longer, I'd have had to ravish you right here beneath this tree. And while I don't know about Australian customs, public exhibitions of lovemaking are not looked on kindly by the police in most places where I've lived.'

'No,' she said, though not sure if it should have been a yes. Not that Alex seemed to care because he took it as an invitation to kiss her again, this time on the forehead, and temple, and on her eyelids now she'd closed them to enjoy the sensation of his lips against her skin.

'So, where do we go from here? And I'm not talking about tonight, I'm talking about our dating, which, as I pointed out to you this morning, is going to get more complicated once Maggie moves in.'

His statement reminded Annie of his reaction to the news that morning, although what difference having Maggie in the house would make she wasn't sure.

Unless, as Annie had once suspected, Maggie was interested in Alex. And why wouldn't she be? He was good-looking, a top surgeon and, as far as Annie could make out, very nice. No signs of ruthlessness so far!

He was also a man, and he'd been in Melbourne for six months and busy at the hospital so most of the women he'd met would have been at or through work. Had he dated Maggie?

If he had, it could certainly get awkward!

'Why will it get more complicated?' Annie asked, thinking a direct question was the most tactful way of sorting things out.

Because she was still wrapped in his arms she felt rather than saw Alex's shrug.

'I don't know exactly, except that relationships between colleagues can sometimes turn sour, then that leads to disharmony in the team.'

'But if it's things turning sour that worries you, then you and I shouldn't be seeing each other at all, and Maggie living at my place makes no difference whatsoever.'

'No, I put that badly.' Alex pulled her closer. 'I've worked with too many husband-and-wife teams that work perfectly to ever denigrate them. And, anyway, it was just an excuse—a stupid, thoughtless excuse. My bad reaction to the news was a man thing—the thing your father wrote so often on your list. It's not all I want from you, Annie, you must know that, but, yes, one day I would hope our relationship progresses to a sexual one and, being a man, I think in practical terms of where that will take place.'

'And you've got Phil at your place, so my place was the obvious answer, but now I'll have Maggie at my place and it will be awkward.'

Annie put his thoughts together in the only way that seemed logical, but there were still holes large enough to drive a bus through.

'But I have Dad at my place anyway,' she began, then light dawned and she drew away from him.

'You don't mind Dad knowing you're staying over at my place, but you don't want other members of the team to know we're seeing each other? Or is it that you don't want them knowing we're having sex?'

Alex tried to draw her close again, but when she stiffened he immediately released her.

'Annie, it isn't that. Well, I guess it is, but I was thinking of you as well as myself. I was wondering how you'd feel about me emerging from your bedroom and running into Maggie in the bathroom.'

'I have my own bathroom,' Annie snapped, angry with him but also understanding the problem and angry with herself for causing it.

But she couldn't have not offered Maggie a place to stay!

'Well, in the hall, or anywhere, just as it could be awkward for you running into Phil at my place. It's an embarrassment factor, nothing else.'

He put his hands on her shoulders and applied just enough pressure to let her know he wanted to hold her. And this time she let him draw her close again.

'I do understand,' she muttered. 'I'm just cranky that it's all so muddled.'

She snuggled against his body.

'Anyway, it might never happen. I like you, Alex—a lot—but for all kinds of reasons, including the bathroom scenario, this should be a first and last date. I'm really not a datable person. Too much baggage, too many secrets, and if there's one thing I've carried with me from my father's lists of behaviour, it's the one about not having secrets in a relationship. I'm not talking little secrets, like being scared of snakes, but big secrets.'

She sighed, so happy in his arms, so sorry it couldn't be for ever—or even for a year—but knowing it couldn't.

Shouldn't!

'Apart from snakes, I doubt there's much you're scared of, Annie Talbot,' he murmured, pressing kisses against her hair and her ear, teasing at the lobe, making Annie's body squirm with delight.

But hearing the name that wasn't her name—hearing the gentle way he spoke the words 'Annie Talbot'—reminded her that what she'd said was right, and this relationship shouldn't—couldn't—be.

Until he kissed her lips again, seducing not only her body but her common sense as well.

It took a long time to walk home, and even longer to say goodnight in the shadows of the camellia bush.

'I really must go,' Alex said at last. 'I want to slip up to the hospital. I know they'd page me if they needed me, but in a new situation, with staff that don't know me and might worry about disturbing me, I like to check things for myself.'

'Like whether the tubes and wires are all in the right place,' Annie teased, knowing how insistent Alex was about the particulars of patient care.

'Exactly,' he said, lifting her hair and finding a new place to kiss, just beneath her ear, where the nerves must be connected directly to her nipples as they peaked in an exquisite agony of delight.

'Go,' she said, 'or we'll be embarrassing ourselves on my front porch.'

'I could come back,' he suggested, his voice hoarse with need, but without much expectation.

'Best not,' Annie said. 'My father's list didn't exactly say "don't put out on a first date" but I'm sure it was implied somewhere there.'

She spoke lightly, hoping Alex would accept it as a joke, but in her heart of hearts she knew that if she took this relationship with him any further she'd be lost—so under his spell, or the spell of the attraction between them, she'd never be able to push him away.

Alex grunted and kissed her once more on the lips, then touched his hand to her cheek again and said goodnight.

Annie leaned against the porch railing and watched until he disappeared into the shadows at the end of the road.

Her body ached with frustration while her mind churned with doubts and questions to which she had no answers.

Eventually, she unlocked the door and went inside. Seeing the light on in the kitchen, she found her father reading at the big table, Henry asleep across his feet.

'Do you think Dennis is dangerous?' she asked, the biggest question in the churn popping straight out.

Her father looked at her for a long moment, then he shook his head.

'You worried about what you might be getting that fellow into?'

Annie nodded.

'I think you've got reason to be,' her father said, then he sighed. 'Though I don't know for sure, Annie. We've never known for certain why Dennis has been so keen to find you, but my experience and that of other people on the force, and people I've spoken to in Social Services who deal with this stuff—it all points to someone as persistent in trying to find you as Dennis has been, being at least borderline dangerous. What he's done, with his private investigators roaming around the country, is tantamount to stalking. Stalking by proxy but still stalking. You took nothing from him—no money, clothes, passport, nothing—so it's not as if he's looking for you to get something back.'

'Is he still looking do you think? Has Uncle Joe said anything?'

Her father looked surprised.

'Why mention Uncle Joe?'

Annie smiled—a sad effort but a smile nonetheless.

'Dad, did you think I wouldn't figure out why you go off on your solo jaunts once or twice a month? Why you drive up to the Gold Coast or fly down to Melbourne? Why would you do it, if not to contact Uncle Joe from somewhere out of Sydney to find out how everyone is?'

'Think you're clever, I suppose,' her father growled. 'I assumed you'd think I'd headed off for a naughty weekend. But you're right, I do keep in touch with Joe. I let him know we're OK and find out what's happening over in the west. I phone him at work—no way all the calls to the internal investigations division in Perth could be traced—but I phone from other cities just in case.'

He sighed.

'Dennis is still looking. One of those PIs visited your grandmother just last week. A different firm this time. Your gran asked him to leave his card and whether his firm had contacts in the US because she hadn't heard from you for a long time and she thought she might hire someone to find you.'

'Good old Gran. I'm glad she knows we're OK,' Annie said, thinking of the tears she'd shed over not being able to contact her grandmother.

But right from the start, when a private investigator rather than Dennis himself had contacted her father, two days after she'd left the hotel, he'd been insistent she shouldn't see or talk to anyone from her past. She'd been cared for by the wife of the policeman she'd first spoken to and then passed on to an organisation that miraculously looked after women in her situation.

Through them and, she was pretty sure, illegally, she'd eventually flown back to Australia, or rather Annie Talbot had flown back. Then a similar though much smaller organisation in Australia had helped her father disappear—though as a policeman he'd needed less help—to re-emerge in Sydney as Rod Talbot, and take up the writing he'd played at for years, scoring a hit with his first published novel.

'But we're off the subject. Am I putting Alex in danger by seeing him?'

She sat down on the floor by her father's chair and rested her head on his knee.

'I like him so much,' she confessed quietly, 'that I couldn't bear for harm to come to him through me.'

Her father stroked her hair and Henry, perhaps sensing her deep need, moved so he could put his big head on her lap.

'I can understand that, love,' her father said. 'But maybe it's not your decision to make. Maybe you have to tell him all about it, and let him decide for himself.'

Annie thought about that for a while then shook her head.

'That's not going to work, Dad, because if we're not absolutely certain there's a risk to us, why would he think there'd be one to him? We don't *know* Dennis means us harm, and most men, I would think, confronted with my pathetic tale, would go all macho and protective, when in reality they should run for their lives.'

'Perhaps literally,' her father said, his voice sober with the gravity of the situation as he knew it.

Annie sat for a while longer, enjoying the closeness with her father but reliving the regrets she still felt that he'd given up so much for her.

'I'm happy, love,' he said, reading her thoughts in the deep sigh she gave. 'Happier than I would have been if I was still in the force—not that they'd have wanted to keep a broken-down old crock like me. I've discovered writing, and I love it. I lead a full life—you know that. My jaunts away aren't purely to phone your uncle!'

Annie chuckled, comforted by the words, but her laughter died when she reminded herself she was no closer to finding a solution to the Alex dilemma than she had been when she'd kissed him goodnight.

# CHAPTER NINE

LOOKING back, Alex wondered if he'd angered the gods in some way the night he'd eaten at the Italian restaurant with Annie. The week turned into a nightmare, beginning with little Amy's condition deteriorating to the extent where he had to admit her abused little heart just hadn't been able to cope with the most recent operation.

First thing Tuesday morning he met with her parents, and together they decided to put her on the list for a donor heart.

'Will you arrange it?' he said to Annie later. 'It will have to be a very small heart—she's such a tiny thing.'

'I can arrange the listing but, because patients from Jimmie's who required transplants were sent across to the Children's, I've never had much to do with the donor programme. How often would very small donor hearts become available?'

She'd zeroed on the heart of his despair.

'Not once while I was in Melbourne. I don't know the Australian figures but, I imagine, given the small population, donor programmes are struggling for organs. For that matter, so are the programmes in the US. The wait can be months or even years.'

'And Amy won't last years and possibly not even months,' Annie said softly. 'Look, leave it with me. I'll find out about priorities and what kind of waiting list there is and get back to you later today.'

Alex touched her shoulder by way of thanks—how could he not touch her when they were so close?—but his mind remained on work as they went through his schedule for the week.

'I'll see you later,' he said, leaving the office to meet the staff before the first op of the day. But in fact, though he did see her during that day and the next three, there was little time for social talk and no time at all for even thinking about dating.

'I'm whacked,' Maggie said to Annie, coming into the office early on Friday evening and finding Annie still at her desk. 'I was going to offer to cook dinner for you and Rod tonight as between you you've been feeding me all week, but I haven't the strength to pick up a stirring spoon, let alone a knife to slice anything, so how about I take the two of you out? Rod was telling me about a Thai restaurant nearby.'

Annie hesitated for a moment, then, realising she couldn't say, *I was rather hoping Alex might ask me out*, and as Alex himself had been conspicuous by his absence, she nodded.

'Sounds like a plan,' she said, ignoring the crunch of disappointment inside her chest and telling herself it was for the best.

Maggie left to check the special care unit where her patients from the three ops they'd done that day were under the care of the intensivist, and Annie stared at the wall for a while, wondering just where Alex was. They'd barely seen each other all week. No, that wasn't true—she saw him a dozen times a day, but it was always rushed and there were work-related issues to be discussed and reviewed.

'Wondering where to eat tonight?' Phil's voice made her turn. 'Come out with me. Rumour has it there's a first-class

Thai restaurant nearby and, as the local, it's your duty to lead me to it.'

Annie grinned at him, pleased as ever to see Phil, who could lighten up the dreariest day with a joke and a wink of his blue eyes.

'I'm leading Maggie to it tonight,' she told Phil. 'And my dad. Why don't you join us?'

She'd have liked to have included Alex in the invitation but didn't want to hear Phil tell her Alex had other plans—which he must have if Phil was at a loose end.

Though Phil at a loose end seemed strange as well.

'Join you and Maggie and your father? That's hardly a date!'

'No, that's why I suggested it,' Annie told him. 'Come on, it'll be fun, and we'll eat early so you can go gallivanting off later if you want to.'

'Can't,' Phil said gloomily. 'The boss has me on duty all weekend. I don't know for sure, but I suspect he has "plans".'

Phil used his fingers to give the word inverted commas, and the clench Annie had felt in her heart earlier became a gut-wrench.

'Good for him,' she managed, though she didn't mean a word of it. Betrayal, that's what it was! So what if she'd said Monday night might have been a first and last date—he didn't have to take it literally.

'You're looking at the wall again,' Phil said, and she turned and forced a smile to her lips.

'Helps me think,' she said, 'and right now I need to think because I've got to check a few things out before I leave the office and if I don't get on with it, we'll never eat.'

She looked at her watch. It was already close to seven.

'Shall we say eight o'clock at my place? We can walk from there. I'll phone and make a booking for eight-thirty.'

Maggie returned and waited while Annie finished what she was doing, then they walked home together.

'No word on a heart for Amy?' Maggie asked as they left the hospital.

'No, but she's only been listed for a few days. I speak to the donor programme manager at the Children's every day. I'm working on the squeaky wheel principle, but Amy's not top of the list. There's a little boy who's been waiting over a month for a heart and lungs.'

'But that's come up,' Maggie told her. 'This afternoon. Alex got a call while we were in Theatre, and when he called back it was a surgeon asking Alex if he'd assist. A team was flying out to some place in western New South Wales to harvest the organs and bring them back, and Alex is already over at the Children's, going through the op with the other surgeons. If Amy's next on the list, that's good, isn't it?'

It was, but Annie was too busy considering the other information. No wonder Alex hadn't asked her out to dinner! How pathetic was she to be getting uptight about it?

'But if the phone call came while Alex was operating, why doesn't Phil know about it? He was complaining that Alex had him on call all weekend, and hinting Alex had a big social weekend planned.'

They were nearly home now. In fact, they were passing Alex's house, and Maggie turned to look at it.

'Phil wasn't in Theatre for the last op. Alex had one of the residents there for experience.' Her voice was distracted and once again Annie wondered if Maggie harboured tender feelings towards their boss. 'And I think Alex did have plans for the weekend, but now he'll probably spend the two days over at Children's. He's always on edge when his patients are post-op and he feels better when he's close to them.'

*He has post-op patients here, too*, Annie wanted to say, but she knew today's list had all been minor repairs and replacements and all their patients, with the exception of Amy, were stable. She was just feeling peevish because she'd seen so little of him that week. Now a whole weekend stretched ahead of her, with no gleam of hope that they might somehow get together.

Maggie was talking about her experiences working with Alex in Melbourne, and how much she'd learned through being part of his team.

'I'd love to work in the US or in England, and this experience has been so advantageous for me.'

'Is work all you want out of life?' Annie asked, because Maggie sounded so sure and enthusiastic and because, although she herself had thought a career was all she wanted, lately she'd been aware it wasn't enough. Not nearly enough.

Although as things stood, it was all she could have...

'No, of course not. I want marriage, and children, but that won't stop me working. I think I'd make a terrible stay-at-home mother, and you can get such good nannies these days, I really don't see the point of giving up a career I love. That's the good thing about anaesthetics. I can keep working almost up until I have the baby, then take say two months' maternity leave to feed the little scrap when it arrives, then back to work. Actually, if I can time the feeds right, and the hospital has child-care facilities, I can keep right on breastfeeding for months.'

Annie considered this juggling of priorities and while she was aware it could work—and probably would for the efficient and determined Maggie—she wasn't sure it was the way she'd go if she decided to have a family.

She shook her head as she followed Maggie up the path to her house. For five years marriage and a family had been the furthest thing from her mind. Her career had been the be-all and end-all of her existence. Now, suddenly, she was going mushy over getting married and having babies— something she knew wasn't possible. The getting-married part anyway—she wasn't sure if having babies was or wasn't possible—but it certainly wasn't an option.

Henry, having greeted Maggie, now came gambolling towards her.

'Not an option for you either, is it boy?' she said, rubbing her hand over his head and scratching behind his ears.

Inside, she could hear her father laughing with Maggie, and knew she should be happy with the way things were going. The job was great, the unit was working success- fully, although with so many of their post-op patients now on the ward she wanted to go up there later and see how the night staff were handling things.

Everything should be rosy—and would have been if a stupid emotion called love hadn't come along and tapped her on the shoulder, reminding her she was a flesh-and- blood woman as well as an efficient administrator.

Maybe Alex was right, and he should have brought his own administrator, then all this would never have hap- pened.

Phil arrived while she was upstairs, showering and changing, and she came downstairs to find him sitting with Maggie and her father, discussing ways to kill off unwanted relations.

'Not me, I hope,' she said to her father, who grinned at her.

'No, Phil's dotty grandfather who has gone to live with his mother and is, in Phil's opinion, sending his mother to an early grave.'

'They're after me for info on undetectable drugs,'

Maggie offered, 'but I'm keeping my secrets in case I ever need to knock off a surgical fellow or two.'

She smiled at Rod, not at Phil, as she said it, but something in her tone made Annie wonder if perhaps Phil, not Alex, was the object of Maggie's affections. The idea gave her something to ponder as they walked down the road towards the restaurant, Maggie walking beside Rod's electric wheelchair, Phil beside Annie.

I'll make sure it's the other way around as we come home, Annie decided, pleased to have someone else's relationship to think about, but as they ate their way through a sumptuous feast, she began to wonder if she'd got it right. Maggie seemed to be flirting more with Rod than Phil, while Phil was close to embarrassing Annie with his attentions.

'So, shall we go on to a night spot? I'm on call so I'm not drinking, but there's no embargo on dancing,' Phil said, when Maggie had insisting on settling the bill and they were about to leave. He turned to Rod. 'Can that machine dance? Having seen wheelchair athletes playing basketball, I never assume there's anything a person can't do.'

'Damn, I didn't bring my dancing chair tonight,' Rod told him. 'But that's OK. I've a deadline to meet and should have been working anyway. You young folk go ahead.'

Maggie seemed eager, which suited Annie just fine.

'You two go. There are a couple of good nightclubs over at Bondi, which is closer than going into the city. But count me out. I want to go up to the hospital to see how the night shift are handling the kids we have on the ward. It's the first time they'll have had a full caseload.'

Phil protested, but by now Maggie had offered to drive so he could hardly pull out. They all walked home together, then Maggie led Phil through to the back yard where she kept her car in a paved area next to the garage. Annie watched them go, wondering why Phil had been at a loose end that evening—and whether his preference for blondes would stop him seeing what a nice person Maggie was.

Saturday was well and truly started by the time Alex, exhausted after a six-hour operation that had taken place after an already busy day, drove carefully home. Not wanting to leave until he knew the little boy they'd operated on was OK, he'd slept for a couple of hours in an on-duty room at the Children's but, as ever, the short sleep had made him feel worse than no sleep at all.

Minnie greeted him with hysterical delight and, knowing he wouldn't sleep again immediately and needing some exercise and fresh air, he clipped on her lead and led her outside, heading for the park. He paused only momentarily outside Annie's gate, though why she'd be up at six in the morning on a Saturday, he didn't know.

Minnie dragged him on, stopping to sniff at every second fence post but never deviating far from the path to the park.

Alex smiled at her antics—and at his thoughts. One of the adult cardiac surgeons had told him about a hideaway not far from Sydney in an area called the Blue Mountains, where one could rent luxury cabins for a weekend. Gourmet meals were delivered, the cabins had full facilities, including a glass-walled spa that looked out over great views, and in his mind he'd begun planning to take Annie there this weekend.

It was rushing things, he knew, but he'd sensed she was drawing away from him and he felt a need to rush. A weekend away would get them from first date to fifth or sixth and they'd both have the opportunity to relax far from the pressures of work.

He'd even booked—tempting fate, he knew—because

Annie could so easily have said no when he sprang it on her late Friday afternoon.

But instead of springing anything on Annie, he'd been asked to assist at Children's and known he couldn't say no.

They'd reached the park and he bent to let Minnie off her lead, wondering, as he did it, if this was wise. Without Henry to bring her back, would she come?

Excited yipping from his dog and a gruff, deep bark from behind some bushes solved his problem. Henry was here! Was Annie with him or did Rod sometimes walk the dog?

He followed the path and his questions were answered. Annie was sitting on the seat they'd sat on last week, her head tipped back so the early morning rays of the sun gave her skin the subtle sheen of gold.

Alex stood and looked at her for a moment. He was too far away to see the freckles on her nose, but his imagination painted them in for him. And suddenly, tired as he was, he wanted to kiss those freckles—to kiss Annie—here in the park, in the sunshine.

Had his thoughts arrowed across the space between them and disturbed her? He hoped not, because she might not welcome kisses in the park at the break of day. But, for whatever cause, she straightened and turned to look around, seeing him coming towards her and smiling a greeting.

Maybe she wouldn't mind kisses in the park at daybreak!

'Alex! How are you? How's your patient with the new heart and lungs? Did everything go all right?'

She stood up to meet him and put out her hand, so it seemed only natural to use it to pull her towards him so he could try the kiss option.

No sign of her minding, although Henry's bark suggested he thought it bad form to be behaving in this manner in his park.

Annie pulled away from him, but he kept his arm around her as they sat down on the seat.

'And how did you know about the heart-lung saga?' He was studying her as he asked the question and saw lines of weariness in her face, as if she, too, had had little sleep.

'Phil,' she said succinctly, then explained they'd all had dinner together.

Alex felt a tightening in his gut, but refused to accept he might be jealous of Phil having dinner with Annie, even as part of a group.

'It went well?'

Annie's repetition of the question reminded him he hadn't answered, so he told her all about the operation and that they were tentatively hopeful it would have a great result.

'Great result? That's wonderful! Far better than a good result?'

Tired as he was, Alex had to smile at her enthusiasm.

'It is,' he said, still smiling, because sitting in the sun with Annie was just about as good as life could get. Right now, that was. Later, he was sure, it could get a whole lot better. He even began to wonder if the cabin in the mountains might still be available.

'So I think they might be having second thoughts.'

'Who might be having second thoughts about what?' he demanded, as the scrap of conversation he had heard brought him back from thoughts of sharing a spa bath with Annie while enjoying views over the mountains.

'The Carters,' Annie explained, then she turned to look at him. 'Have you had any sleep? Did I wake you up just then? I was telling you I went up to the hospital after dinner, just to see how the staff were coping with our patients on the ward, and ended up spending the night with Amy's mother. She's distressed about Amy's condition—not about her not getting better but whether keeping her alive in the hope we'll get a heart for her is the right thing to do.'

Annie paused, because she understood the deeper implications behind Mrs Carter's doubts but wasn't sure how to explain them to Alex.

'It happens,' he said tiredly. 'We tell parents all we can, we see they get whatever help and counselling they need, but it's still up to them. And honestly, Annie, it tears at my heart to see a child like Amy deteriorating daily. I don't know what's the right thing to do—I don't even know what I'd decide for my own child, because I don't have a child. So when a parent asks me what I'd do, I'm only guessing.'

He drew her closer, and she relished the feel of his body against hers and stayed close while she tried to tell him more.

'What's really upsetting Mrs Carter is the thought that another child has to die for Amy to get a heart. She's having strong ethical doubts about the rightness of it.'

Annie sighed and snuggled closer, although the last thing she should be doing was snuggling close to Alex.

'What makes it worse is I can understand where she's coming from, Alex, so I wasn't the right person to be helping her. It's not a religious doubt, but something that sits a little uneasily with me. Not transplants in general—I'm a registered organ donor and should I suddenly drop dead, I'd be happy for surgeons to use whatever bits of me they can—but to be waiting for a baby to die somewhere—to think about the parents of that baby—yes, I can see why Amy's mother is having doubts.'

Alex stroked her hair, a gentle, soothing caress that eased her tension and her tiredness.

'We all think of that—think of the other baby,' he said slowly, 'and each of us, in our own way, has to come to terms with it. Like so many things in life, Annie, there's

no absolute right or wrong. No rules to guide us in deci-
sion-making. Oh, there are ethical considerations and laws
that govern the use of human organs, but it comes down to
personal decisions every time.'

'Personal decisions,' Annie echoed. 'That makes it sound
so easy, but aren't personal decisions often the hardest ones
to make?'

Alex sensed they were no longer talking about Amy
Carter, or even transplants, and once again he cursed the
fate that had ordained he'd needed to operate last night.

He was about to suggest they go to the mountains anyway—now, today—but reality intruded and in a not-so-
difficult personal decision he knew he'd be useless if he
didn't get some sleep. And before he could do that he
would have to go up to the hospital and see the Carters
once again.

Annie must have guessed their tryst was over for she
whistled Henry, who brought Minnie with him as he came.

'If I don't go home right now, I'll fall asleep on this seat
and be arrested for vagrancy,' she said, turning towards him
and resting her palm against his cheek. 'And you need sleep
as well. Not that you'll go weakly home and fall into bed.
You'll go and see the Carters, won't you? I shouldn't have
told you until later. Or I could have told Phil—let him talk
to them.'

He turned his head so he could kiss her palm.

'Phil's good but it's me who should be there for them,'
he told her.

Annie nodded, and he realised she understood exactly
how he felt. Would always understand...

He walked her home, suggested maybe they could get
together later in the day and read her refusal in her face
before she shook her head.

'I promised Maggie I'd take her into town to show her

where the best shops are. She suggested we stay there and catch a show.'

Annie didn't sound all that certain about these arrangements, but Alex didn't press the point. The way things were going, he probably wouldn't get to bed until the afternoon and might then, with any luck, sleep right through. But he wasn't going to give up on the entire weekend.

'Tomorrow?' he asked hopefully, and Annie smiled.

'Maybe tomorrow,' she said. 'One thing I'm learning with this unit—and that's to count on the unexpected.'

Alex had to accept that, then, aware the day was getting older and people were around, he dropped a quick kiss on her lips and took himself and Minnie home.

'All right for you,' he grumbled at the little dog when she had a drink of water then collapsed on her bed in the kitchen. 'I've got to go to work before I can have a sleep.'

He went upstairs to freshen up with a shower, passing Phil's closed door on his way to his bedroom.

'All right for Phil, too,' he muttered to himself. 'Dining out with my girl then sleeping in next morning.'

But the 'my girl' thought lifted his spirits somewhat, and before he had a shower he sat down at the computer and shot off an email to his former administrator, still working at the hospital where he'd worked previously. If anyone could dig out some details on the current life and whereabouts of Dennis Drake, Karen could. Do it discreetly, he warned her, not wanting to stir up any trouble for Annie with his enquiries.

# CHAPTER TEN

ANNIE went home, had breakfast with Henry and her father, then took herself off to bed. Maggie's door was shut but a note on her bed told her she had cried off the shopping expedition, the only explanation being, 'Late night, need sleep.'

Which meant Annie *could* have got together with Alex after all!

But while her mind grumbled over this change of plans, her body told her it was a good idea. She needed sleep more than she needed a shopping trip or a 'maybe' date with Alex.

She woke to evening darkness—she'd slept all day?— and the smell of something delicious cooking downstairs, and lay for a few minutes, savouring the exotic and unfamiliar aromas. Spices certainly, and a sweet smell—honey?

Tantalised tastebuds drove her out of bed and into the shower. She pulled on sweatpants and an old T-shirt and headed downstairs to find out what was cooking—literally.

The noise level from the kitchen suggested more than one person was involved in producing the tempting meal, but if for one moment she'd imagined Alex was one of those present, she'd have shot back upstairs and changed. Dating or not, a girl had some pride!

But Alex's voice didn't reach her above the hubbub and she wandered in to find him and Phil sitting at the table with her father, Alex with his single glass of red wine in front of him, Phil and her father each with a light beer, while a flushed, and very pretty-looking, Maggie wove some magic spell around the stove.

'This kitchen has never smelled so good,' she said, trying to still the heart flutters finding Alex there had caused.

'Ours never looks so good,' Phil added, looking from her to Maggie. Was he flirting with both of them?

'What smells so delicious?' Annie asked, moving closer to where Maggie was stirring something in an earthenware pot that certainly wasn't out of Annie's kitchen.

'It's a *tagine*—a Moroccan dish. Actually the name of the pot is a *tagine* and that's where the dish gets its name. It's made with lamb and apricots and prunes and spices, and I serve it with couscous.'

'It smells delicious and I can see it's drawn some of the neighbours in. I just can't imagine why the whole street isn't here to enjoy it.'

'I was invited,' Phil said. 'Saw your father earlier and he asked me over. Alex just came along.'

Annie was aware Alex was watching her, but the whole situation had got beyond her. She opened the fridge door, found a bottle of white wine and waved it in the air, asking Maggie to join her in a glass.

'Not me,' Maggie said. 'I had my weekly quota of wine last night.'

Her voice sounded tense, but as Annie knew *she'd* be more than tense if she was trying to cook something complicated in front of an audience—particularly this audience—she thought nothing of it.

The meal was as delicious as it had smelt, the subtle blend of flavours perfectly complemented by the bland grain. But for Annie it was spoilt by the company—or, more truthfully, by the behaviour of the company.

Because, with the exception of her father, they were all colleagues, she asked Alex about his talk with the Carters, but he dodged the question, talking instead to Maggie about the recipe for the *tagine*.

Phil, also, had no intention of turning this into a work night, flirting with Annie right through the meal and making her feel uncomfortable and embarrassed. Making her also the target of strange looks from both Maggie and Alex.

Surely Alex must know Phil well enough to realise he was joking—that it was just Phil being Phil.

The looks from Maggie were even more puzzling for, as the evening went on, Maggie grew quieter and quieter in spite of the praise heaped on her for her meal. In the end she stood up.

'I cooked so someone else washes up,' she announced, and she walked out of the room.

Phil and Alex both turned to watch her go, while Annie tried to work out when the mood around the table had changed from light-hearted fun to uneasy silences and sideways glances.

'Us men will stack the dishwasher. Alex and Phil can clear away and rinse and pass things to me—I'm at a better level for stacking.' Rod made the suggestion and with a slight movement of his head suggested Annie should, unobtrusively, leave the room and follow Maggie. Find out what was wrong!

Annie waited for a few minutes then as Alex stood up to clear the table, she headed upstairs. She tapped on Maggie's door, and when Maggie didn't answer Annie opened it, just a crack, and asked if she could come in.

A huge sigh from inside, where Maggie was face down on the bed.

'What's up? That was a fantastic meal, so it can't be that. What's happened?'

Maggie sat up, sighed again and rubbed her hands across her cheeks. She hadn't, as far as Annie could tell, been crying, but her expression—her whole attitude—told of despair.

'Phil's happened—that's what!' Maggie said bitterly. 'Oh, Annie, why are we women such fools? Damn it, I'm thirty-two, old enough to know better, but, no, I've been attracted to Phil from the first day we met, and as far as he's concerned I could be wallpaper.'

She sat up straighter and ran her fingers through her hair.

'The bloody man flirts with every female he comes across and has done since I first met him, but me—no! Wallpaper, you see.'

She sighed again before continuing.

'So what happens last night? We end up clubbing together. I *knew* he'd asked you out last night—that's how come he was in the party in the first place—but, no, we go off together and, because he's Phil, of course he puts the hard word on me at the end of the evening, and because I've been so attracted to him for so long—and probably because a couple of glasses of wine blurred what little common sense I've got where he's concerned—what do I do? Say yes, of course. Not only say yes but invite him back here, and, of course, he wasn't called out during the night. We both slept in, and the first person he sees as he wanders downstairs is your father.'

Maggie gave Annie a despairing look.

'I've been here less than a week and I'm bringing men home, so how do you think I felt about facing Rod again? But somehow—mainly thanks to your father's wonderful temperament and social skills—we muddled past all that, your father invites him back to dinner and I think maybe it's going to be OK, and then what happens?'

'He flirts with me all through the meal,' Annie said glumly, not knowing how to make things right for Maggie. 'He's got to be amoral—is that the word? Sleeps with women but refuses to get emotionally involved. A no-strings playboy.'

Annie couldn't think of anything more to say, so she put her arm around Maggie and gave her a hug.

'What are you going to do?'

Another sigh came up from somewhere near Maggie's toes.

'Do?' she said, the word squeaky and the laugh that accompanied it just slightly hysterical. 'What can I do but go on as I did before? Pretend it never happened, that's what I have to do. If Phil Park can do it, so can I!'

She straightened out of Annie's embrace.

'In fact, I should have been stronger downstairs. Shouldn't have let him get to me. Come on, we'll go back down and brazen it out. No, better still, let's get dolled up and go out ourselves. Go clubbing.'

Never having enjoyed the dark atmosphere of nightclubs, Annie was underwhelmed by this idea, but this wasn't about the outing, it was about sisterhood and solidarity. She understood that part.

'I'm really tired,' she said, knowing she sounded pathetically weak but not willing to take sisterhood too far. 'Can we get dressed up and pretend to go out? Leave the house and drive across to the beach then come back in a little while when they've gone?'

Maggie looked a bit disappointed but in the end agreed that she was also tired. Another sigh, this one regretful.

'He really was the most wonderful lover,' she said softly, then she shook off this momentary weakness and headed for her bathroom, poking her head back out the door to add, 'Wear something that will knock both their socks off.'

Annie trudged down the short corridor to her room. She wasn't against knocking Alex's socks off, just upset he was here, because doing this, in the name of solidarity and sisterhood, would make it look as if she preferred an evening out with Maggie to spending some time with him.

Maybe it was for the best. If he decided she was a frivolous, uncaring pleasure-seeker he might lose all interest in her and she could put a stop to all the futile arguments going on in her head.

She opened her wardrobe doors and looked inside.

'Knock their socks off?'

She echoed Maggie's words with despair. There was nothing in her wardrobe that could squeeze, even by the smallest margin, into that description. During her time with Dennis she'd worn nothing but high-necked, long-sleeved sweaters or shirts, and when she'd finally reached Sydney and gone shopping for new clothes, habit had had her doing the same thing.

One dress—bought to wear to work functions she couldn't avoid—also had the requisite high neckline. But it was in the dark green colour she liked wearing, was well cut and the fine fabric clung to her figure like a second skin. She loved it and felt good in it—but it was hardly a sock-knocking-off creation.

It would have to do.

Maggie, in a bright red miniskirt, lacy top and shiny red boots, took one look at her and dragged her into her bedroom.

'I don't have any knock-their-socks off clothes,' Annie explained, not liking the note of apology in her voice. Here she was doing Maggie a favour and apologising for how she looked!

Maggie slid open her wardrobe and looked from it to Annie.

'You have black trousers or jeans?'

Maggie nodded.

'OK, slip into them, and put on this top. Black boots?'

Maggie shook her head and Annie rummaged through a collection of shoes that would had done Imelda Marcos proud, and produced a pair of pointy-toed black boots with heels so high Annie was sure she'd fall over in them.

She was about to protest when she remembered solidarity again—and how upset Maggie had been over Phil's behaviour!—so she took the top and boots and went glumly back to her room.

Maybe if she took long enough, their two visitors would have gone, but Maggie didn't let her dither, following her with a serious-looking make-up case.

'You can't go out without eye shadow,' she announced, waiting only until Annie had slipped off her dress and pulled on the top before sitting her down and applying various potions and powders to Annie's face.

Ten minutes later Maggie pronounced herself satisfied, though she added rather bitterly, 'Though why I'm making sure you look stunning when Phil already fancies you, I don't know.'

'He doesn't fancy me at all,' Annie assured her, wondering how any woman could wear a top cut so low without spending the entire evening blushing and tugging it upward. 'He just flirts with any woman not yet certified dead.'

She made her way cautiously downstairs, heart leaping around in her chest when she heard voices in the kitchen and knew her prayer that the visitors might have departed hadn't been answered.

The boots had to be two sizes too small, but all she had to do was get through the kitchen and out to the car, where she could kick them off.

'I'll go first,' Maggie said, when they reached the bottom. 'Now, the rule here is "never explain"! We'll just sashay through, say "goodnight, boys" and keep going.'

That suited Annie just fine, although she usually gave

her father more particular information about her where-abouts.

'We'd better say where to,' she whispered to Maggie, who looked surprised, and then quite pleased.

'Good idea—that way they can follow us!'

'We're not really going there,' Annie reminded her, and Maggie looked disappointed.

'We're all dressed up—we may as well,' she said, and Maggie realised she should never had let thoughts of solidarity and sisterhood guide her path. If she was doing anything this evening, it should be with Alex.

No, it shouldn't!

Well, maybe not, but if she couldn't be with Alex she didn't want to be with anyone else.

Alex heard footsteps tapping towards the kitchen. High-heeled footsteps from the sound of them. He'd watched Maggie depart from the dinner table, then Annie follow, and wondered just what was going on.

Apart from Phil flirting with Annie all through dinner! What was happening there? Annie certainly hadn't encouraged him but, then, she hadn't singled him, Alex, out for attention either. She'd eaten her meal with desperate concentration, as if wishing she could be teleported to some other place.

The good thing was, her single-minded attack on the delicious meal had allowed him to study her—unobtrusively, he hoped. She wasn't the most beautiful woman he'd ever met, and she did very little to make the most of her striking eyes and neat, straight features. Not wanting to attract attention?

Male attention?

So why had she attracted his?

Why did he feel—and had felt from the beginning—that

there was something special about this woman? That she was—or should be—his?

The tapping footsteps drew closer, and he had to revise all his assumptions about Annie not wanting to attract attention. Next to Maggie in her bright red miniskirt and red boots, Annie, all in black, should have been invisible, yet Alex was stunned by her beauty.

'We're off out,' Maggie said, grabbing Annie's arm and all but dragging her across the room.

'Not without an escort you're not,' Phil said, leaping to his feet so quickly his chair tipped over. 'Come on, Alex. We've got our pagers. You can't let these two beauties out on their own. Who knows who they'll pick up?'

Alex looked at Annie for guidance but found she was looking at Phil.

'Who knows?' she repeated in a voice so dry it scratched.

Then she looked at Alex, and he thought he detected a plea in her eyes, but was it a 'come along and save me' plea, or a plea that he stay out of whatever was going on?

That something was going on, he had no doubt. And that it affected Maggie more than Annie, he was also certain. Annie might look stunningly beautiful, but the way she held herself was reminiscent of paintings he'd seen of aristocratic women being dragged off to the guillotine. Whatever was going on, Annie was a far from willing participant, and this fact alone had him rising to his feet.

'I guess a little gallantry on a Saturday night wouldn't hurt,' he said. 'But I need to change out of trainers and we should go in my car anyway. You're not drinking, Phil, so you can drive.'

And all I have to do is manoeuvre Annie into the back seat and this might turn out OK after all!

He winked at Annie, but she didn't seem as delighted— or even as relieved—as he'd expected.

And now he'd missed his opportunity to start the man-oeuvring, as Phil had moved closer to her and was ushering her towards the door.

Any moment now the situation would be lost.

Then Annie turned towards him—just a despairing glance his way—and the Galahad within him finally awoke.

'No way, Phil,' he said, elbowing his colleague aside. 'If we're making a foursome, then Annie's my date.'

He put his arm possessively around her waist—so small—and tried to draw her close, but he'd obviously mis-read the glance for she pushed away.

'No one's anyone's date,' she snapped. 'Maggie and I decided we wanted to go out. If you guys want to come that's fine, but you're tagging along, nothing more. Maggie and I might both meet our soul mates tonight, so we don't want our opportunities spoiled by you two behaving as if this is a date.'

If he'd been stunned before, he was doubly so this time, and though Annie now shot him a look that he *could* read as apologetic, he'd been wrong about reading the look she'd shot him just before, so he could easily be wrong again.

'Come on,' she was saying to Maggie, who looked as utterly miserable as someone dressed in red could possibly look, 'let's go.'

Annie hooked her arm through Maggie's and practically dragged her through the front door.

'You got us into this and now you're going to have to go through with it. And stop looking sorry for yourself,' she muttered fiercely. 'My feet are killing me in these boots, and on top of that I'm going to stretch them and have to fork out huge amounts of money to replace them for you.'

Maggie relaxed enough to give a very small giggle, but

Annie had to continue to force her to move—out the front door and up the road towards Alex's house—the conversation of the two men following them.

'It's all backfired,' Maggie whispered.

'I know it has,' Annie told her. 'But who knows? Maybe something good will come out of it. Maybe you'll meet some gorgeous guy who makes you forget all about Phil.'

Maggie didn't seem to believe her but thinking about Maggie's problems, Annie decided, was better than considering where she now stood with Alex. Maybe after this performance he'd forget about this obsession he had for dating her, which would be the best thing for both of them, even if her heart ached at the thought and her mind chided her for the way she'd spoken to him earlier.

Alex had been too good to her—considerate, understanding, great kisser… Forget the kisses.

Anyway, it had been a terrible way to treat him when all he'd done had been to come to her rescue so she wouldn't have to keep avoiding Phil's hands. But Maggie would have been miserable with a situation where Phil was forced into being her date. She wanted Phil to want her for herself, not as someone to make up the numbers.

Annie tried to sort through the problem in her head. As Phil was driving, maybe she could slip into the back seat with Alex and whisper that she'd explain about it later.

Only she couldn't explain much—not without breaking Maggie's confidence!

Damn!

They'd reached Alex's house, and Minnie was yapping excitedly from behind the front door. She turned somersaults of delight at seeing Alex and Phil, then showed nearly as much excitement when she recognised Annie.

Annie bent and picked her up, and was letting the little dog nuzzle her chin when Maggie said, 'I'm glad she's black. That way people won't notice the dog hairs on my best top.'

Alex and Phil were on their way up the stairs to change, and Annie heard Alex's footsteps falter at the comment.

'Don't you like dogs?' she asked Maggie, who sighed for about the fortieth time that evening.

'I love them. I have one at home that I had to leave with my parents. I'm just feeling bitchy and you know why.'

Alex had disappeared but Annie sensed he'd heard at least part of the conversation. She hoped he'd heard enough to realise there were things going on here that were beyond her control.

Also beyond her control were the seating arrangements in the car, for Maggie took over, climbing into the back seat while Alex held the door, dragging Annie in behind her.

'Great date, this,' Phil said, glancing at a silent Alex in the seat beside him.

'It's not a date,' Maggie snapped. 'You two asked yourselves along on an outing, that's all!'

Annie decided silence was the best option—that way she shouldn't get herself into any more trouble. But she hadn't figured Alex's determination into the equation. They were no sooner inside the club, Maggie heading with some resolve towards the bar, than Alex caught Annie's arm and nodded towards the small dance floor where a few couples shuffled to the music of a four-piece group.

And being in his arms, dancing with him again, she was in more trouble than she could ever have imagined, because this felt like bliss. It felt as if this was how things were meant to be.

It felt like heaven…

'For all her finery, Maggie doesn't look happy.'

Thoughts of heaven vanished. Alex had only asked her

to dance to question her. She wasn't surprised he wanted to know what was going on, so why had she thought this dance was something more?

Something special?

'She's not, but she'll get over it,' Annie said, then realised she sounded snappy. 'I assume,' she added, hoping that made her sound more sympathetic towards their colleague.

'I certainly hope so. I hate bad feelings between members of the team.'

You might have to put up with it, Annie thought as she became increasingly cross with him for pursuing the conversation and not enjoying the dance as she was.

For five years she'd had memories of being held in this man's arms—dancing with him—now here she was and he was grumbling about people not getting on at work.

Maybe if she edged a little closer…

'I've always thought Maggie fancied Phil, though why any woman would be interested in a man who flirts with every female on the planet I don't know.'

So much for moving closer!

'I think it's an inherited disposition in Phil's case. Apparently his father was a noted philanderer.'

Realising they were on different planes as far as mood was concerned, Annie reluctantly joined the conversation.

'Phil told you that? Boasted about his father's proclivities?'

'No, my mother told me.'

The evening, which had begun badly when Annie had come downstairs in her scruffy state, now deteriorated to the farcical stage.

'Your mother knew Phil's father?'

Alex laughed. 'Biblically, you mean?' he said, and laughed again. 'No, she read his autobiography. No, maybe it wasn't auto, maybe it was just a biography because if he'd written it, he might not have boasted about his sexual exploits—not an Englishman.'

'Phil's an Englishman and his behaviour doesn't indicate any delicacy where relationships with women are concerned,' Annie said, although she was more intrigued by Phil's father having had a biography written about him. 'Was he someone famous?' she asked. 'Phil's father?'

'More notorious, my mother said,' Alex explained. 'One of those upper-class Englishmen who had too much money and not enough to do with their time, so he played—all over the world, apparently. Drove fast cars and even faster boats and did daring, adventurous things, but in the end he must have got bored with playing and actually got interested in Antarctica and did a lot of the modern-day exploration down there.'

'Which wouldn't have brought him any closer to his children, one would think,' Annie said.

'No, it didn't,' Alex agreed, finally tightening his hold on Annie as if he'd realised they were dancing, not holding a conversation standing up. 'That's about the only thing Phil's ever said about his father—that he rarely saw him and barely knew him. Phil and his brother and sister grew up in the family home in the country, in the north somewhere, cared for by nannies and servants, while his mother grieved—Phil's word—for the husband who was gone but not dead.'

'That's so sad,' Annie said, and nestled closer to Alex's strong body.

His arms tightened a little more so he could hold her close, and finally she was reliving her dream, dancing with Alex, feeling as light as thistledown because of the magic of being in his arms.

'If I kiss you, am I breaking the ''it's not a date'' embargo?' he whispered against her hair a little later.

'Probably, but it doesn't matter—it's been lifted. I've done my duty to the sisterhood and from now on the night is mine.'

She knew Alex wouldn't have a clue what she was talking about, but she didn't care, allowing him to draw her into the darkest, most shadowed corner of the dance floor and bend his head to kiss her on the lips.

'Ah!'

She heard her own murmur of pleasure and relief, and imagined she heard a similar sound escape him, then they were kissing as if they'd just discovered how to, exploring their senses through lips alone.

'Not particularly good form, kissing on a dance floor,' a cool voice said, and Annie jerked away from Alex to see Phil, his arms around a blonde, dancing very close to where they stood.

'Where's Maggie?' she demanded, no doubt startling Alex with her vehemence. But if Maggie had seen Phil ask the blonde to dance, and had been left, deserted at the bar, who knew what she might do? Annie looked frantically around, but they were in a corner and she couldn't see the bar.

'Relax,' Phil said easily, nuzzling his lips to the blonde's neck and making Annie want to belt him. 'She's on the floor with some Neanderthal lifesaver type, dancing so close you couldn't slip a tissue between them.'

'Oh, dear,' Annie muttered to herself, as Phil steered his partner away from them. 'This isn't working out at all as it should have!'

'No?' Alex said, slipping his arm around her shoulders. 'I'd say it's working perfectly. Phil and Maggie are both above the age of consent—they both have partners for this dance if not for the night—so let's you and I slip out of here, get a cab home and kiss each other somewhere more private than this corner.'

Tempting though the offer was, Annie dithered. Kissing Alex somewhere private would be blissful, but deserting Maggie?

'I can't go,' she told Alex. 'At least, not until I've talked to Maggie. I can tell her the boots are killing me, which is true. I just didn't notice it while we were kissing.'

But Alex had already drawn away.

'What's going on, Annie?' he asked, and she knew he wanted a straight answer.

There was only one to give.

'I can't tell you,' she said, then watched him walk away, not back to the bar but past it and out of the door.

'It's for the best,' she told herself, making her own way back to the bar, where she found a stool, ordered a mineral water and rested her pinched and tortured feet, while fending off offers to dance, to drink, or to go home with various hopeful men.

## CHAPTER ELEVEN

ANNIE woke very early on Sunday morning to a sense of great misgiving. She'd stayed on at the nightclub for another hour, then, because the offers from men she didn't know had been getting more drunken and insistent, she'd tried to persuade Maggie to leave.

But Maggie had been having a wonderful time and had been happy for Annie to go on home, though she had insisted on phoning a cab from the club to make sure Annie was safe.

Where Phil had disappeared to, neither of them knew, though Annie sensed he was still somewhere around—no doubt with the blonde and her friends.

Where things now stood, with Phil and Maggie or with herself and Alex, she had no idea, but she'd been worrying more about the Carters during the night and regretted not asking Alex about the latest news on their decision.

One way to find out. She'd pull on some clothes and go up to the hospital.

Mrs Carter was in Amy's room, and Annie marvelled at the woman's patience and dedication as she sat beside her failing daughter, talking softly to her and rubbing one finger across the little girl's skin. Up and down her arm, around drip tubes and monitor wires, down her cheek, across her head.

If loving touch could heal, Amy would be better.

Annie sidled into the room and was greeted with a smile.

'Did Dr Attwood talk to you yesterday?' she asked quietly.

Amy's mother nodded.

'He's a wonderful man—stayed with us all morning and some of the afternoon as well.'

No wonder Alex hadn't wanted to stay at the club! Annie thought, then Mrs Carter was talking again.

'He talked us through all the pros and cons and let us ask questions, and just sat because he said the more we thought about things, the more questions we'd come up with. And we did.'

Realising the woman was so much more relaxed than when Annie had last seen her, Annie guessed the family had reached some kind of decision and were happy with it.

Should she ask?

Was it her place?

She'd need to know, but Alex would eventually fill her in.

She was still mentally debating her position when Amy's mother continued.

'We decided while she's still stable—and Dr Attwood says she is. He showed us how the monitors tell him things, and said her condition wasn't deteriorating. He said sometimes babies get so sick with other things they can't do a transplant, but Amy's not like that so that's why we decided.'

Mrs Carter gave a little laugh.

'I still didn't tell you, did I? We're going to wait. He said to take each day as it comes and not to hope too hard, but to believe that if Amy's well enough for them to do a transplant when one becomes available, we'll go ahead. If she starts to slip or gets an infection or we feel she's suffering, we'll think again and maybe turn off the machines supporting her.'

Annie reached for the woman's free hand and gave it a squeeze. She was too choked up to speak, knowing just how hard this decision had been. Yet Mrs Carter was far more settled now than she'd been the previous morning after Annie had spent the night with her.

All because of Alex who, no doubt in his precise way, had made it all sound so rational and easy, divorcing the huge emotional content of the decision from the medical one and letting Amy's parents see a way through their dilemma.

'Have you slept at all?' Annie asked when she'd swallowed her own emotional reaction. 'I could sit with Amy if you like.'

Mrs Carter turned to her with a smile.

'I slept all night. Bill sat with Amy and he's gone off to sleep now. We're so thankful for the accommodation provided by organisations so we can stay close to our darling all the time.'

Annie chuckled, genuinely delighted to see the woman so positive. Annie had known from the first operation she'd seen him perform that Alex could work miracles inside the chests of tiny babies, but apparently he was just as good with miracles outside the theatre, too.

She was still smiling as she made her way to the office, thinking she'd catch up on some paperwork while she was there, but she was barely through the door when her pager chirped and her heart accelerated.

As unit manager, she was the one who would receive first news of an available heart, and though, on another day, a page might mean Becky contacting her from the office, on a Sunday the sound brought hope.

She knew by heart the plan Alex had given her. She had to find out the details, organise a retrieval flight, have planes and ambulances for the retrieval team standing by at each end of the journey. Or just an ambulance on alert, if the heart was in the city. A member of the surgical team,

Phil preferably, would go with either Kurt or a nurse on the retrieval flight.

Annie ticked off this information as she dialled the number. It *was* the donor programme co-ordinator. A heart that might be suitable for Amy had become available in Brisbane. Did they want it?

'Yes,' Annie said, and got contact details of the hospital and attending paediatrician so Alex could talk direct to him. She paged Alex, then phoned the number she had for the Flying Marvels, a group of men and women who owned their own planes and volunteered to fly sick children to the city for treatment. They'd been used before for organ retrieval flights, and Annie was delighted when the man she spoke to said he could organise a flight to Brisbane and back and could have a plane and pilot waiting at the airport within forty minutes. Annie told him she'd phone him back to confirm it as soon as possible.

Alex phoned and once again Annie explained, giving him the Brisbane number and telling him she had a plane standing by.

'Who do you want to go?' she asked him, and he didn't hesitate.

'Phil—I'll wake him—and Kurt if you can get hold of him. He knows how to bring it back. But if you can't get hold of him, get Rachel—she's done retrievals before.'

'They both have pagers. I'll get one of them,' Annie assured him.

Alex hung up before she could ask if she should speak to the Carters or wait for him. Theirs would be the final decision—whether to put Amy through another operation, knowing that transplants could fail.

Annie looked at her hands and saw they were shaking, but there was so much still to do—people to call, arrangements to be confirmed.

Alex came into the office half an hour later, and Annie was able to tell him everyone was standing by.

'I'll talk to the Carters,' he said, and left the room, returning five minutes later.

'We're on,' he said. 'Can you give me a time frame for retrieval?'

'One hour and twenty minutes to Brisbane in the light plane, same for return trip, though one way is usually shorter than the other because of wind factors. Ambulance from here to the airfield, Sunday morning and not much traffic, twenty-five minutes, in Brisbane fifteen minutes. How long does Phil need?'

Alex looked at the ceiling for a moment.

'Thirty—maybe forty minutes.'

Annie was on the phone as they had this conversation, first confirming with the donor organisation that, yes, they'd take the heart, then speaking to the Flying Marvels man, getting details of where the team should meet the pilot and explaining where they were going.

'We have a cooler?'

Annie, dialling Kurt's number, looked up.

'A cooler?'

Alex made a gesture with his hands, outlining the shape of a small box.

'For drinks!'

And it dawned on Annie that in this day and age of such sophisticated medical technology, they carried hearts for transplant around in a drinks cooler.

'Pathology has heaps of them,' she said, then told Kurt that Phil would collect him in twenty minutes. Alex disappeared and she phoned the ambulance, asking them to pick up Phil from the hospital and to be standing by for a return trip from the airport in a little over three hours.

Alex returned with a cooler and Phil. Annie joined them

and the three walked together to the ambulance bay. Not running, but certainly striding out as suddenly every minute counted.

'That's why we go by ambulance,' Alex said to her as the vehicle sped away, siren wailing. 'Whatever minutes we save are minutes we can add to Amy's life.'

He slid an arm around Annie's shoulders and led her back inside, and for a moment she thought he was going to talk about the previous evening.

Silly thought. The arm was nothing more than a teamly gesture—his mind was totally involved with what lay ahead.

'I'll need Rachel, and if you can get that male nurse—'

'Ned?' Annie suggested, and Alex nodded.

'That's the one, and Maggie. No hurry, but I'll open Amy up as soon as we know the plane has landed back here in Sydney. It's all a matter of timing now.'

Annie made her way back to the office, ready to field phone calls if anything went wrong. All the team had pagers, the flight people had her number, the hospital in Brisbane had her number. What could go wrong? The weather was perfect, flying conditions would be great.

Alex came in and dropped a piece of paper on her desk.

'That's the number of the sister on duty at the PICU in Brisbane. Could you phone her and get some more details on the baby?'

Annie looked up at him, knowing she was frowning.

'Didn't you do that when you spoke to the paediatrician?'

'I asked medical questions, Annie,' Alex said gently. 'We don't need to know names and addresses—in fact, confidentiality is key in these cases—but Amy's family will ask questions about the donor, and if we can answer them, everyone will feel more at ease.'

Annie knew what he was saying must be true because Alex had been involved in these situations before, but in this position would she want to know more about a baby that had died to give her child life?

She wasn't sure and her uncertainty must have showed for Alex leaned across the desk and touched her lightly on the shoulder.

'Believe me,' he said, 'the questions will come. Maybe not right away, but soon, and it's best for us to be prepared.'

He sat down in the chair across the desk from her, and she could see the understanding in his eyes. Understanding that she was still coming to grips with the situation. Oh, she'd coped with the physical side of it, organising and arranging, but emotionally? Yes, she was at a loss.

'Knowing a little about the donor makes it more personal—which you'd think might be a bad thing, but it isn't. It makes it less like a shopping trip—I'll take those shoes, and if you have a very small heart, I'd like one of them as well.'

Alex smiled, but Annie felt more like crying, grieving for the owner of that very small heart, and for the owner's parents and siblings, and all the relations.

She blinked away a tear, and said, 'OK, I'll take your word for it and find out more, but I think I'd prefer the shopping trip. That way I could pretend it was just a heart, not something that had once been part of a living, breathing baby.'

'No, you couldn't,' Alex argued. 'You might be able to pretend to others, but inside yourself you'd know the truth. You're too courageous for pretence to be part of your life.'

Annie looked at him and shook her head, knowing they were no longer talking about the baby but about her own life. Had Alex guessed it was all pretence, that he was saying this? Was he pushing her to be honest with him?

Heaven knew, she wanted to, but the thought that in doing so she might put him within reach of even the remotest possibility of danger had made her hold her tongue.

She shook her head, and said sadly, 'No, Alex, that's wrong. My entire adult life seems to have been about pretence. You're so open and honest—with parents, staff, everyone—that you can't imagine that other people aren't.'

Alex heard the words, even took them in, but looking at Annie—knowing what he did of her—he couldn't accept what she was saying. Annie and deceit? The equation didn't gel.

'We'll talk later,' he said, more determined than ever to find out what lay behind some of the things Annie had said.

He needed to find out what lay behind last night's outing, too. That it was something to do with Maggie, he knew—but what? And why had Annie not come home with him?

That was the question that had tormented him during his cab ride home, but once there he'd put the entire evening into the 'too hard basket' and had gone straight to bed. He'd had two hours' sleep in the past thirty-six and had needed to catch up. Fortunately for him—and Amy—he did sleep well.

Maggie was in Amy's room when he returned there, taking blood for testing and making notes to herself about the medications Amy had been on since the operation.

She followed Alex out and they discussed what would happen in Theatre and the drugs they'd need for different stages of the operation. Amy's blood would be cooled to minimise organ damage during the changeover, and she'd need drugs to thin her blood while she was on the bypass machine. Once the new heart was in place, a lot of the actions of the drugs would have to be reversed. It was important to get blood into the coronary arteries as soon as possible so they could feed the muscle of the new heart.

So many details—so much to anticipate. If this went wrong, what would they need? If that happened, did they have the equipment on hand to make it right?

'Flight's landed in Brisbane and the boys are on their way to the hospital,' Annie reported, poking her head around the door of the theatre anteroom where Maggie and Alex were talking.

'Keep us posted,' Alex told her, then Rachel and Ned arrived, and Alex included them in the discussion they were having, explaining the operation step by step, though he knew Rachel had been through this with him before.

'What theatre staff do we have?' Rachel asked, and Alex shook his head.

'Don't know, but for sure Annie's dug up the best she can find.'

'Blood?'

'Already on hand,' Maggie told Ned.

'So, you guys set up, I'm going to phone a friend. I stood in as a spare pair of hands for him on Friday night, now I'll wreck his weekend by asking him to do the same for me.'

He phoned from the anteroom, and when his colleague agreed to come, Alex felt excitement begin to build within him. A lot of the operations he did on children were more complex and risky than a heart transplant, but this was life-giving.

'Aren't all of them life-giving?' Annie asked, coming in a little later to tell him the plane was in the air on the return flight.

'Yes,' he agreed, 'insofar as the child could die if he or she isn't operated on, but they're different somehow.'

Annie wasn't sure she understood, but she nodded anyway, then was surprised when Alex put his arms around her and drew her close.

'You've found out more about the other baby,' he said gently—a statement, not a question.

She nodded against his shoulder.

'We didn't make that baby die, or even will its death, Annie,' Alex continued, 'but through the sadness of his death, we can offer hope for Amy. Can you not find some solace in that?'

'I suppose so,' she said, her voice muffled by his shirt. 'In fact, I know so, but just not yet.'

He kissed her lightly on the top of her head, and she knew it was a signal for her to leave the comfort of his arms. It was work time and every second counted.

Annie went back to her office. She ran through the procedure schedule Alex had given her when the unit had first opened. Every item had been ticked off. Pathologists were on standby, drugs available, extra staff on hand in case the operation took longer than expected and the special care unit staff primed for what to expect when Amy returned to them.

Which left the Carters, but Annie, knowing phone calls could be coming in, couldn't leave the office to talk to them. Once Amy was in Theatre, she could sit with them, and though part of her really wanted to see this operation, another part of her felt she would be more useful waiting with the parents.

Alex phoned as she made this decision. 'We're taking Amy into Theatre now,' he said, 'so when you hear anything, let us know in there.'

Annie was about to hang up when Alex added, 'Aren't you going to wish us luck?'

'You don't need luck—you're the best there is,' she told

him, though she did add a soft 'Good luck!' before she put the phone down.

Now all she could do was sit and will the plane to land and the ambulance to make good time to the hospital. Once there, Phil and Kurt would have to scrub before taking their places in Theatre—Kurt already had a stand-in, a perfusionist from Children's, in Theatre, ready to operate the machine as soon as Amy was anaesthetised.

Looking back later, it seemed to Annie that everything had happened at once. The phone had rung to say the plane had come in and the ambulance was already on its way back to the hospital. The surgeon from Children's had arrived and Annie had taken him through to Theatre, then Phil and Kurt had arrived back, Phil holding the cooler with the heart as casually as he might have taken some cans of beer to a football game. Annie had watched him slide it through the theatre door, calling to Alex, 'It's just the best little heart. Behaved beautifully as we took it out. Be with you all shortly.'

Then he went to change and Annie sought out the Carters, sitting tensely in the family room off the special care unit.

'It's here?' they asked in unison, and Annie nodded, then Mrs Carter reached out for her hand.

'Tell me this is the right thing to do,' she pleaded, and Annie led her back to the settee and sat her down, sitting beside her and putting her arm around her shoulders.

'It seems to me,' she said carefully, 'that this is how things were meant to be. I mean, you'd decided to wait and see what happened—whether a heart became available while Amy was still relatively stable. The chances were so small really. I know Alex told you that. Yet it happened, and so quickly, and everything else fell into place, so don't you have to think it was meant to be?'

Mrs Carter considered this for a moment, then she nodded, while her husband, holding tightly to her hand now she was sitting down again, said, 'Makes you believe there's someone or something on our side. We wondered, when Amy was born with so much wrong and was so sick, whether it was our fault this had happened. But it's fate, isn't it? It's all about fate!'

He put his arm around his wife and Annie moved away, shifting to the armchair so the pair could share some physical comfort on the settee.

It seemed an interminable time but finally the door opened and Alex came in. He looked exhausted and Annie feared the worst, but he summoned up a smile for the Carters and said, 'All well so far. Her new heart is beating beautifully.'

They rose as one, Mr Carter gripping Alex's hand, Mrs Carter throwing herself against him and hugging him tightly.

Alex waited a moment, then said, 'She's not out of the woods yet, remember. Her body could reject it, or she could react badly to the drugs we have to give her to guard against rejection. Then there are other organs that might have been affected by the length of time she was on bypass.'

Annie listened, amazed as ever that Alex could list so many negatives yet still keep hope alive in his listeners. It wasn't that he told anything but the plain, unvarnished truth, yet people heard it with hope in their hearts and trusted him enough to believe those bad things wouldn't happen.

She studied him, wondering how the faith others had in him must affect him, physically and emotionally, when the bad things he spoke of did happen. For a moment superstition replaced faith and fate, and she crossed her fingers.

Not for Amy, she prayed silently. Don't let the bad things happen for her.

Alex left the room but Annie lingered in case the Carters wanted to ask questions, but they were so excited and delighted she might as well not have been there so she walked back to the office where Alex was slumped at his desk.

'What's wrong?' she demanded, frightened by this sight of a dejected Alex. 'Did things not go as well as you made out?'

He lifted his head and gave her a tired smile.

'Afterburn!' he said. 'At least, that's what I call it. It's a kind of exhaustion that comes with the let-down of tension when an op like that is done. I always feel totally wrung out. Phil's different, he gets a high, and I understand that because I feel like that after a good switch, or something regular, but for some reason I can't feel that euphoria after a transplant. For all my brave words to you and to the Carters, I still feel as if I'm meddling with fate, and on some atavistic level it scares the hell out of me.'

'Oh, Alex,' Annie said gently, walking towards him so she could perch on the desk and lean forward to massage his shoulders and neck, 'you give so much confidence, and talk such common sense to other people, can't you spare some for yourself?'

He smiled again and took her hand, resting it against her cheek.

'Later, I'll be able to,' he promised, 'especially if Amy pulls through the next few days. If that happens, I'll take it as a sign that fate didn't mind me meddling. Maybe even approved of it.'

He pressed a kiss into her palm, then gave her back her hand, and she knew he needed to be alone to work through his let-down in the way that best suited him.

Other members of the team drifted in, most of them, as Alex had foretold, on a high.

'Come on, late lunch in the canteen. The tab's on me,' Phil said, and even Alex stood up and joined the others trooping out. He turned back and waved to Annie, but she shook her head. Phil had put his arm around Maggie as he'd made the suggestion, and there was no way she was going to rain on whatever small parade Maggie might be enjoying.

'I've some phone calls to make. I told the Flying Marvels I'd let them know how things went, and I need to call a few other people who've been involved.'

Alex didn't argue but followed the others out, and though Annie told herself he had to go because the lunch would serve as a debrief after the operation, she was still disappointed.

'Stupidly disappointed!' she muttered to herself. 'Get over it!'

She didn't get over it, but she did get through the day, and then the week, and even into the next week. Amy had thrown up every complication Alex had predicted and then some, and he'd been all but living at the hospital, returning home at weird times to grab clean clothes but otherwise making the on-duty room off the special care unit his home.

Annie told herself this was good because, although she still saw him any number of times a day, and still had regular conferences with him over his consulting appointments and operating programme, work was always on both their minds, if not to the exclusion of all else, at least blotting out most of the manifestations of their attraction. The team might be operating normally, but every member of it was emotionally caught up in Amy's roller-coaster ride.

'Her condition's turned,' Alex finally announced the following Thursday. He'd called the team together, and Annie had found herself hoping it wasn't to say he was going to put Amy back on the list for a transplant.

His words elicited a rough cheer from the group and Alex smiled, his tired, drawn face lightening so imperceptibly that Annie felt her heart tug with pity for him.

'Days off all round! We've no ops scheduled for tomorrow so, the medical team, you're off for three days—four if Annie can juggle Monday's list and fit the ops in later in the week. Nursing staff, again, see Annie. We've enough experienced people who've been working with our patients on the ward to maybe bump some of them to the PICU and give you lot from there a few days off as well.'

He turned expectantly to Annie.

'Annie?'

She wasn't sure she had *that* many nurses at her disposal, but it was so good to see Alex starting to relax that she smiled at him and said, 'Can do, boss!'

She'd do it, even if it meant taking a nursing shift herself. The PICU was still a very familiar environment to her.

Alex went on to detail why he felt Amy was showing more stable improvement and why he didn't expect her condition to deteriorate again, then ran through what they'd be doing the following week and sent everyone home.

Everyone but Annie, who had to check the nursing rosters and see how she could juggle staff, and also to see the intensivist on duty at the PICU—how much easier to call it that as Alex and Phil did, than the special care unit—and make sure he knew the surgeons wouldn't be quite as available to him in emergencies as they had been twenty-four hours a day since Amy's operation.

She was pencilling her name into the altered nursing roster—she could work Saturday and Sunday nights—when

Alex walked into the office, a bunch of flowers in his hand and a much better smile on his face.

'These are for the best unit manager in the country, and I've more ordered for my best girl. They'll be waiting for you at a little cabin in the mountains where I'm taking you first thing tomorrow.'

# CHAPTER TWELVE

ALEX looked at his unit manager and best girl and wondered why flowers and promises of a weekend escape had made her look so unhappy.

He put the flowers on the desk between them and sat down across from her.

It was the cabin idea—it had to be. He'd got so carried away with advancing their relationship with a weekend away, he hadn't considered Annie's feelings.

'It's a two-bedroom cabin, Annie. I won't rush you into anything.'

She smiled but it was such a sad effort he felt his heart sink.

'A cabin in the mountains sounds blissful,' she said, then she pushed a piece of paper across the desk towards him and pointed to a couple of squares. 'But you were right about our special nursing staff being due a few days off, and the only way I can work it for them is by doing a couple of shifts myself.'

'Nursing?'

The idea was bizarre.

'I am a nurse, and I'm a good one,' she reminded him, 'and honestly, Alex, the very last thing I expected was for you to come up with the idea of a weekend away. The last few weeks—'

'We haven't had any personal time,' he finished for her. 'But you know why that's happened. We haven't had a spare moment.'

She reached out and took his hand, removing the pen

he'd been using to doodle triangles around her name on the roster.

'That isn't what I was going to say,' she told him. 'I was going to say I thought maybe you'd accepted there couldn't be anything between us.'

Alex could feel anger building inside him. For a moment he thought about fighting it but, damn it all, there was something special between him and Annie and no way was he going to let her hang-ups destroy that.

'Because of some rubbish about your past? About pretence? Do you think I care what happened in your marriage? Do you think I care that you might not be who you say you are? I know *you*, the person. That's who I fell in love with—not with a name, whether it's Annie Talbot or Rowena Drake.'

He knew immediately he'd made a mistake, but he hadn't counted on Annie's reaction. Sheet-white—there was no other way to describe her colour. Alex leapt to his feet and rushed around to grab her before she fainted. He eased her head down onto the desk and knelt beside her.

'Annie, it was just a guess—well, more than a guess because I went through the congress lists five years ago to try to work it out. It doesn't matter—that's what I was trying to say. I don't give two hoots who you are because it's a person I love, not a name.'

She lifted her head and looked at him, and he cursed himself because he knew he was responsible for the shadows of fear he saw in her eyes.

'Does anyone—?' she began, but the ringing of the phone cut her off. She lifted the receiver, said her name and listened, then sighed and shook her head.

'It's OK, Dad, Alex is here. We'll come right home and drive out together to pick them up.'

'Pick who up?' Alex asked, as Annie stood up, still pale but obviously in control of herself now.

'Henry and Minnie. Apparently Mayarma was knocked down by a car on her way home from the park and, although she's not badly injured, she was taken to hospital. The dogs were collected by the council dog-catcher and Dad's just had a phone call from the pound to ask if we could, please, collect our dogs.'

Alex knew Annie was worrying about Henry now, but he guessed she was also pleased that this small crisis had diverted them from the conversation they'd been having.

So much for plans for the weekend! he thought grimly, following her out of the office then out of the hospital.

'We could take my car,' he suggested when they were close to his place.

'Henry in your precious BMW? I don't think so. But I've got my car keys so we can cut through your place and down the lane to my garage. Do you want to come or will I collect Minnie for you as well? There'll be a fine to pay, even though it was an unavoidable circumstance.'

'I'll come with you,' Alex insisted, taking her arm as they walked through his gate, wondering if maybe they were past whatever had shocked her earlier. Wondering also if they could get another nurse to take Annie's place on that damn roster.

Annie drove, refusing to think of anything but Henry. Well, part of her mind was on Alex's revelation that he knew her real name, and that part was mentally arguing that it couldn't possibly hurt, but most of her mind was on Henry and how he was handling incarceration.

'I'd hate anything to happen to Henry.' She blurted out the words, only realising, once they were said, that more of her mind than she'd thought must still be on Rowena Drake.

And Alex was looking at her strangely, so something of her sudden surge of fear must have sounded in her words.

'They don't shoot dogs in the pound, you know. Well, not in pounds back home. They give the owners time to come pick them up. Plenty of time. More than a few hours.'

But Annie hardly heard the last sentences, the 'they don't shoot dogs' hammering so loudly in her ears it blotted out everything else.

'Why would you say that?' she whispered, driving up the track that led to the animal shelter and stopping the car so she could turn and look at Alex.

He was frowning at her.

'About having time to pick up your dog?'

Annie shook her head. She could feel her lips trembling.

'About shooting dogs.'

The words were little more than a murmur carried on a halting breath of air, but Annie was once again sheet-white. Alex leaned towards her and drew her close.

'I'm sorry. It was a figure of speech. Nothing more. A joke, Annie, if in poor taste.'

He held her close and kissed her head, his hands stroking her back, knowing he had to offer what comfort he could, knowing also that there was more than just a name change in Annie Talbot's past.

'OK,' he said, when the tremors in her body had eased and she was relaxed against him. 'Let's get these dogs then go back to my place or your place or somewhere private and have a long talk about all of this, because no matter who you are, I love you, and there's no way you're going to push me out of your life.'

Annie lifted her head and looked at him. He read surprise, and hope, and what he thought might even be love in her eyes.

'Oh, Alex!' she whispered, then she kissed him on the lips.

Kiss-deprived for so long, he drank in the taste of her, but she moved away.

'The pound will close. They were staying open an extra hour to try to sort out Mayarma's dogs, but the hour must be almost up.'

She moved away from him, opening the door on her side and climbing out. He joined her and put his arm around her as they walked towards the office.

'Henry Talbot,' Annie said, when asked for the dog's name. 'He's a Rottweiler.'

'Ah, Henry, yes,' the woman behind the desk said. 'You own the little spoodle, too. You really should change the Melbourne address on her tag.'

'The spoodle's not mine,' Annie said. 'She belongs to Alex.'

She turned to indicate Alex, who gave the woman a brave smile.

'Oh,' the woman said. 'We thought they must belong to the same owner. We couldn't separate them.'

'Henry's protective of her,' Annie explained, and Alex realised that's exactly how he felt towards Annie. He loved her, he was certain of that, but the protective issue was something new. He'd never felt like this about any other woman—and had always believed protection was associated with emotional dependency. Now here he was, *wanting* Annie to be emotionally dependent on him.

To a certain degree!

'It's forty dollars.'

The way Annie said the words suggested she was repeating them, but they still didn't make sense to Alex.

'For the fine,' the woman explained. 'I know it sounds

silly when they were brought in because the walker had an accident, but we have to follow the rules.'

Alex caught up with the conversation and paid Minnie's fine, then, with the woman leading the way, they walked around to the wire runs at the back of the office building.

Henry's bulk made him immediately obvious, but his demeanour was in such contrast to Minnie's delighted hysteria when she saw her rescuers that Alex had to laugh.

'He's got his "what took you so long" look on his face,' Annie said, and Alex put his arm around her shoulders.

'If he had a wristwatch, he'd be looking at it,' he said, enjoying both dogs' behaviour and pleased they had the dogs to talk about and laugh about so some of the tension of the previous conversation could drain away.

Enough tension for him to once again raise the subject of a weekend away?

They talked of the dogs most of the way home, and then, because he was anxious to know if it might be possible, Alex gambled.

'We still haven't talked about the weekend,' he said.

Annie glanced his way then concentrated on turning into their back lane. There'd be other weekends for both of them, she was suddenly sure of it, but she wanted to let Alex down gently.

'Why don't you come home with me and we'll talk about it?' she said, then, knowing it was time, she added, 'We can talk about a lot of things.'

'Great, but can we stop at my place? I'll drop Minnie home. I think she's a little dog who's had enough excitement for one day.'

He indicated the scrap of black curls sleeping soundly on his knee.

Annie pulled up outside his back gate, and Alex turned and kissed her on the lips.

'You go on home. I'll feed Minnie and see she's got fresh water, then walk down.'

'Come the back way—we'll be in the kitchen,' Annie said, and with the feel of his kiss still lingering on her lips she drove slowly the short distance to her home.

'Home again, boy,' she said to Henry as she slid out of the car, but poor Henry wasn't released as easily. The clip on the short lead that held him to a safety harness in the back seat was stiff, and she fumbled with it for a few minutes before finally getting it free. She could have released it from Henry's collar, but he had the idea the back lane was a place of dog magic and took off down it whenever he had the chance, so she always kept the lead on until they were well inside the yard.

'You've had your burst of freedom for today,' she reminded him, holding him in check as they came out the garage door. She saw her father waiting in his wheelchair in the doorway, a shadowy figure she thought might be Phil in the kitchen behind him.

'Why haven't you got the kitchen light on?' she called, then the world went mad. The shadowy figure yelled something so unbelievable she couldn't take it in, her father hurtled towards her in the chair, Henry started barking furiously and leaping against his lead so it was all she could do to hold him. Then Alex came flying over the fence between her place and next door, grabbed her father's wheelchair and sent it spinning off the path.

Annie was still trying to assimilate this and come to grips with who was in the doorway when shots rang out and Henry collapsed, dragging her down on top of him, her body deathly cold, her mind wondering how Dennis could possibly have found them.

Alex raced to Annie and knelt over her, easing her off Henry's body but unable to tell which blood was hers and which was Henry's. Annie had a pulse, and from the way blood was spurting from the dog, he, too was alive. Then Rod was there.

'He's dead—Dennis. Shot himself. And an ambulance is on the way—I had my mobile with me. Annie?'

Rod's voice shook as he asked the question.

'She's going to be OK,' Alex told him, and heard a quaver in his own voice. 'I think Henry took the first bullet. Annie's only wound seems to be high up in her shoulder. Maybe lung involvement, but even that's not too bad if they get her straight to A and E.'

He ripped off his shirt, then tore it to strips with his teeth and was binding a pad over the bleeding wound as he spoke. Annie was unconscious, but his heart kept telling him she'd make it. *Had* to make it.

Rod was talking to him again—something about the dog—and Alex forced his attention away from Annie's milk-white face to concentrate on what Rod was saying.

'Have to get him to the vet. Take Annie's car, there's a spare set of keys beside the phone. The vet's number's there as well.'

'I can't leave her to take the dog to the vet,' Alex said. Although he knew there was nothing more he could do for Annie here, there was no way he was moving from her side.

Then Rod grasped his shoulder and tugged at him so Alex had to turn.

'Listen to me,' he roared. 'You get that dog to the vet and you damn well make sure you save him. Get a heart transplant for him if necessary, but I'm telling you, if you've a scrap of feeling for Annie you'll keep that dog alive.'

He paused, then in a ragged voice muttered, 'She didn't

tell me for a long time after she came home, but he shot her other dog. The only damn friend she had in America.'

And Alex understood. He turned Henry gently, found the wound and used the rest of his shirt to make a pad which he pushed into place. Nothing to hold it there until Rod passed him his belt.

With the bleeding stopped, Alex paused only long enough to touch Annie's cheek then sprinted to the house, found the phone, the vet's number and Annie's keys, got directions on how to get to the surgery and returned to find the ambulancemen already bent over Annie.

'Give me a hand with the dog,' he said to one of them. 'It's important he lives.'

'I'll say it is,' another voice said, and Alex turned to find a policeman standing there. 'Damn monster, shooting at a harmless dog.'

It took three of them to lift Henry into the back of Annie's car, then the policeman asked which vet, and when Alex told him, the man said, 'Follow me.'

He went out to the back lane where a motorbike leaned against the fence, strapped on his helmet, and when Alex started Annie's car the policeman took off, siren wailing, leading Alex on a hectic race through the streets to the vet's surgery.

'Dogs were used a lot for experimental heart surgery,' Alex said three hours later, sinking into a chair beside Rod, who was keeping vigil at Annie's bedside.

Rod turned towards him and nodded, understanding that Alex had stayed for the operation on Henry.

'He's all right?' Rod asked.

'He will be,' Alex told him. 'He'd lost a lot of blood and the bullet has damaged his right shoulder joint. It'll be a while before he can move freely again and he'll probably develop arthritis in the joint.'

'Bastard!' Rod muttered, then he reached out and touched his daughter's cheek.

She lay so still Alex had wondered if she'd slipped back into unconsciousness, but the anaesthetist he'd spoken to had told him she'd come out of the anaesthetic well, and this was just a deep, healing sleep.

'She never told me a thing,' Rod continued. 'Not even about the dog. Not till a long time after she came home. The night she left him—walked out of that fancy hotel in the middle of nowhere and walked all the way to the local police station—she asked the man on duty to phone me, and when he put her on the phone, she just said, "He hits me, Dad." I thought my heart would burst with anger, that she'd been all the way over there and had been putting up with that kind of abuse. I'd have killed him myself if he'd been near. It was the kind of thing I'd seen time and time again in my working life, but for it to be happening to my own daughter...'

Rod paused as if the magnitude of his thoughts was too great to put into words. Alex understood, for his own insides were knotted with rage—made worse because it was futile to rage over something in the past.

'The best thing—apart from her finally leaving the sod— was that she found the right person to talk to in Jed McCabe. That's the policeman, and when you go back home, you might visit him for me and shake his hand. That Jed and his wife, they believed her, you see. Not all coppers do, and most hate domestics more than murder. But Jed had seen domestic violence firsthand in his wife's family and he brought his wife straight in. She took Annie somewhere private and made her take off her clothes, and she took pictures so there'd be proof if there was trouble. The bastard never touched her face, and hadn't hit her at the hotel, but old bruises were still there—yellow and purple, and thick places on her chest where broken ribs had healed. Anyway, Jed's wife, she got in touch with some mob over there who look after women like Annie—see, I call her that all the time now, that's who she is to me—and this mob made all the arrangements for her to start a new life.'

Rod's voice cracked again, but he steadied himself.

'I sent money—to Jed—and a month later Annie Talbot flew into Sydney. And you know what, Dennis never once contacted me—not in that month while I was at home. Two days after she phoned, a private investigator called me, and they've come ever since. Dennis never gave up. For five years the people he pays have been visiting and phoning our family back in West Australia, but we cut ourselves off from everyone. That was hard on Annie, losing her cousins and especially her gran, who'd helped to bring her up.'

Alex swallowed a lump that had made its way into his throat and shook his head in disbelief at what human beings could do to each other. He thought of the dead body he'd done no more than glance at in the doorway of Annie's house, and at the same moment heard Rod's question.

'What I can't understand is how the devil he found us now. After five years. What brought him here of all places? Right to our house?'

Alex felt his insides turn to lead, a sinking feeling spreading through his body. Two weeks ago he'd asked his old administrator to find out what she could about Dennis Drake, and although she hadn't come up with much more than his current employment at a hospital in San Diego, Alex knew for certain that somehow Dennis had found out about the questions.

And once he'd known who was enquiring, it would be

an easy step to find out where he, Alex, was working. Take time off, fly out to Sydney—

Alex's reconstruction stopped dead at that point, as another thought demanded attention. In the canteen—the whole group had been there—and, like a familiar face glimpsed in a crowd, Alex had noticed someone he'd thought he knew, or recognised from somewhere—but they'd all been talking and he'd thought no more about it.

Had Dennis Drake been in the canteen?

Where better to see most of the workers in the hospital than where they ate?

So, he'd recognised Alex…

'Excuse me,' he said to Rod, knowing he'd be tortured about this until he found out.

He went down to the front desk, but the night staff didn't know if anyone had been asking for him.

'Have you checked your pigeonhole?' one woman asked, and though he doubted Dennis Drake would have left him a message, he did check.

No note, but why would there be?

He was making his way back to Annie's room when he passed one of the sisters from the PICU in civvies, as if she'd already left the hospital and come back for something.

'Did a cardiologist from San Diego catch up with you?' she asked. 'He came by this afternoon and was really interested in the unit. Says they need one where he works over there. He took that little newsletter Becky did when the unit started—the one with the photo of all the staff.'

Somehow Alex found the strength to thank her, but this confirmation that he had indeed led Dennis Drake to Annie had shattered him. He remembered Annie protesting when Becky had taken the photo, but they'd all insisted she be included. Her name, Annie Talbot, was under her photo—

all the staff were mentioned by name—and Alex knew Dennis would only have to flash his credentials and say he was an old friend for someone on the admin staff to break the rules and part with Annie's address.

He could have killed her! Dennis may have fired the gun but he, Alex, had put her in danger—hadn't heeded the signs he'd known had been there and had stubbornly ploughed ahead in his own determined way, destroying all the safeguards she and her father had built up at such cost to their own lives.

He returned to Annie's room.

'It was my fault,' he said to Rod. 'My own stupid determination to find out more about her.'

He explained what he'd done, feeling more wretched every moment.

Rod said nothing for a while, then shook his head.

'Annie was worried she was putting *you* in danger,' he said. 'Thought she shouldn't go on seeing you because she was worried what would happen if Dennis ever found out.'

They sat in silence for a while, then Rod turned to Alex.

'Don't be so hard on yourself. Look at it this way. Annie's going to get better and we're finally rid of the black shadow Dennis cast over both our lives. Annie can still be Annie Talbot if she wants, but she can go visit her gran and get back with her family and never live in fear again. On top of that, you saved my life. He said he'd shoot me if I tried to warn Annie, and he meant it. If you hadn't come from nowhere and grabbed the chair, I'd be dead. We should be thanking you.'

'You can't possibly thank me for putting both of you in such danger,' Alex said hoarsely. 'And neither will she!'

He got up and left the room, wanting more than anything to be with Annie when she woke but feeling he'd forfeited the right. He went up to the unit and phoned the vet to learn that Henry was doing as well as could be expected, though it was still touch and go. Shock could do terrible things to a dog.

If Henry died…

No, Alex couldn't think about that. Surely he had enough guilt on his plate.

He wandered the corridors of the hospital for a while, unable to face the thought of going home, then eventually he made his way to the on-duty room where he'd spent so much time lately and lay down on the bed.

He had four days to get past this—to get his head together and be ready to face work again, face questions about what had happened to Annie. He'd have to talk to Rod again to work out how best to protect her. Probably have to talk to the police as well. He should do that now— see Rod first to discuss damage control. There was no way Annie would want details of her past plastered across the newspapers.

He got up off the bed and headed back to the second-floor room, where he and Rod made up a story they thought would be accepted.

'I've contacts in the police force over here,' Rod said. 'I'll make some phone calls, you stay here.'

'I can't stay here. She's never going to want to see me again when she learns what's happened.'

'She mightn't if you slink away like some lousy coward,' Rod said, 'but tell her face to face—that's different. And while I'm not a doctor, I don't think this is the time to say anything. Just let her get a bit better. Wait until she asks. You go blurting out a confession while she's still weak and confused, you'll make a hash of things for sure.'

He wheeled himself away and Alex was left standing sentinel beside the bed of the woman he loved.

'Sit down, you're in the way,' a nurse said minutes later, coming in to check on Annie's condition.

He sat, and when the nurse departed he took Annie's hand in his and started to tell her all the things he hadn't said about falling in love with her that night in Traders Rest and searching for her ever after, unable to believe his luck when he'd found her again.

He talked of love, and courage, and spread his dreams about the future out in front of her, knowing she couldn't hear him and that there might not be a future.

'And Henry's holding his own,' he said, when he'd un-burdened all the secrets of his heart.

The fingers he held in his stirred, and a sleepy voice said, 'Henry?'

Alex could have cheered, but knew he'd wake the entire ward so contented himself with quiet reassurances.

'He's OK—he's at the vet's. I stayed for the operation and phoned just minutes ago. He's lost a lot of blood,' he added, because even a bullet-weakened Annie wasn't one to be taken in by false assurances. 'But the vet says he's holding his own.'

'And Dad?' Annie asked, her fingers turning to grip Alex's.

'He wasn't hurt. He's here at the hospital—he just left your side. Had to speak to some people.'

Annie opened her eyes and turned her head to look at Alex.

'Dad's unhurt because of you. I remember that part. You jumped the fence and pushed him away just before Dennis fired the gun. He'd have shot Dad—could have shot you.'

Tears welled in her eyes and she shook her head.

'I knew it couldn't be, Alex. Knew I was putting you in danger just by knowing you. I tried to tell you, but I loved you and couldn't push you away—not hard or far enough to keep you safe.'

The tears were spilling on the pillow and breaking Alex's heart.

'Annie, darling, it wasn't you who put me in danger, but me who did this to you. Please, don't blame yourself. Please, don't cry. I'm not worthy of your tears.'

She sniffed and brushed her free hand across her cheek.

'Not worthy—that's nonsense. If anyone's not worthy, it's me.'

Then her eyes widened and she looked apprehensively towards the door.

'Dennis?' she whispered, so hoarsely fearful Alex himself turned to make sure there wasn't a dead man standing in the doorway.

'He killed himself, Annie. He's dead.'

Alex watched the emotions chase each other across her face—disbelief, amazement, a little sadness and finally relief.

'I wouldn't have wished him dead,' she said quietly. 'But it's for the best.'

Then she closed her eyes and Alex let her rest, knowing she had many memories of the past to finally put to rest—knowing she had to become used to not living in fear.

# CHAPTER THIRTEEN

ANNIE lay in the spa, looking out through the trees to the view of cliffs and gullies. The water bubbled around her, relaxing tired muscles and warming her body. It had been a long month, recuperating and getting Henry better. Then there'd been so much red tape to be sorted and often cut through. But they'd managed and yesterday Rowena Drake had married Alex Attwood, though it was Annie Talbot—no, Annie Attwood—who lay in the spa, waiting for her husband of a little over twenty-four hours to join her.

'OK?' he asked, as he dropped his robe and slid into the water, settling beside her and putting his arm around her shoulders.

'OK doesn't come near it, Alex,' she said, resting her head against his shoulder and nuzzling a kiss into his neck. 'OK isn't on the same continent as the way I'm feeling.'

'So tell me,' he suggested.

Annie shook her head, but because he'd come to know her so well he persisted.

'Come on—we're talkers, you and I. We tell each other things. That's the rule!'

'Your rule—and you just made it up.'

'I did,' Alex said smugly, 'but we're newlyweds, we can make up whatever rules we like for our marriage. I've thought of another one. Twenty kisses before breakfast—every day for the rest of our lives.'

Annie laughed.

'The way we kiss, it'd be dinnertime before we ate.'

She turned to kiss him to prove her point, and it was a long time before either of them spoke.

But one thing she'd learned about Alex was his persistence so, although his voice showed a fair degree of breathlessness from the kiss, he repeated his earlier demand.

'Tell me!'

Annie watched the tops of the trees that grew in the gully beneath the cabin sway in the breeze and saw the way the patterns of sky changed as the leaves moved.

'I feel new—reborn. I know that sounds silly, but I can't help feeling Annie Attwood is such a different person from the other people I've been.'

She turned and looked into the serious grey eyes of the man she loved.

'I have no fear, Alex. None at all. I was lying here in the spa, testing out all the bits of my body, and, no, there's no sign of it anywhere. And it's not just because Dennis is dead, but because of you. You've offered me a whole new life, and the thought of the two of us being together, of what we can do, the fun we can have, the joy we can share—it's blotted out the past completely.'

'No shadows?' Alex asked, tracing his thumb across her cheek, stroking the freckles he seemed so fascinated by.

'Not a one,' she assured him, and kissed him again to prove it.

Alex held her close. It had taken a while to get his Annie to the cabin in the mountains, but they'd finally made it. Made it in the most glorious way—in celebration of their marriage. And now Annie was truly his, in every way.

He drew her closer, feeling the softness of her body against his, feeling love in such overwhelming abundance he knew it would keep them both safe for ever.

'I love you, Annie Attwood,' he whispered, and kissed her once again, thinking how wide an arc they'd travelled since the first kiss they'd shared.

# THE HEART
# SURGEON'S PROPOSAL

BY
MEREDITH WEBBER

# CHAPTER ONE

PHILIP PARK, paediatric surgical fellow of some standing and reputation, folded himself into the seat in the small, dingy space behind the pilot. The stuffiness in his head told him he'd spent far too long breathing recycled cigarette smoke in a club the previous evening, having refused to leave before a certain miniskirted colleague had departed. And gritty eyes reminded him of the mostly sleepless night he'd spent wondering why this same colleague had accepted a lift home with one of those big bronzed Aussies that seemed to hang around all the beaches, and not with neat, clean, though fairly white-skinned, very English Phil!

So now he felt gnarly and out of sorts and totally irritated at being called out at the crack of dawn on a Sunday morning.

Added to which, he hated flying, hated small planes, hated retrievals—in fact, right now, he couldn't think of anything much he didn't hate.

He didn't hate his job. In fact, his job excited him more than any woman ever had.

Didn't really hate retrievals…

'You all saddled up back there?' the pilot asked. He was one of a group that called themselves, unbelievably, the Flying Marvels. They offered the planes and services as pilots, free of charge, to fly sick children from country areas to the city for treatment. They also donated their planes, time and piloting skills when or-

5

gans became available for transplants and no government plane was available.

But in spite of the man's worthiness, Phil found himself scowling at the back of the man's head. Top of his hate list were cheery pilots! This one would probably say 'Up, up and away' as he took off.

'Up, up and away,' the pilot said minutes later, and Phil had to laugh, amusement easing his grumpiness, though not the tension knotting his stomach—tension in part due to the flight but also, he knew, building up because of what lay ahead.

Think of something else, he told himself, and almost as if he'd snapped a switch an image of a petite brunette slipped onto a screen in his mind.

Maggie Walsh!

Because thinking about Maggie was infinitely preferable to thinking about sudden death if this flying sardine can plummeted to earth, or thinking about the task awaiting him if they survived the journey, he trawled through his mind for the moment when taking Maggie Walsh to bed had seemed like an excellent idea.

He'd taken little enough notice of her—as a woman, not a doctor—six months ago when she'd been appointed as the anaesthetist on their team. She was a calm, quiet, very professional anaesthetist, so focussed on her work that although his male mind had registered the additional words 'attractive brunette', he had ignored them.

Then, a couple of times, when the surgical team had spent social time together, he'd seen another side of Maggie. Freed of the restraints of Theatre—and of 'hospital' clothes—she'd metamorphosed into a sexy, boot-wearing party girl. Not a drinker, or outrageous in her social behaviour, just a woman who enjoyed going out and dancing the night away.

In truth, the change had kind of spooked him and he'd found himself studying her more closely in Theatre and around the hospital, wondering which was the real Maggie Walsh.

That had been OK. It hadn't affected his work or anything, and he didn't think Maggie had known he was puzzled—attracted?—by her other self.

Until two nights ago, when something had happened between them—something so totally unexpected he was still finding it hard to believe. It hadn't been entirely his fault because late that night, in the privacy of her bedroom, Maggie's hands had been as desperate in stripping his clothes off as his had been stripping hers!

But it was the aftermath of that encounter—could mind-blowing sex be described baldly as an *encounter*?—that needed consideration.

Firstly, there was the weird feeling he'd had when he'd woken in the night to find Maggie's small but curvy body tucked up against his. Protective: that was how he'd felt, the sensation so alien to his usual feelings and moods he'd searched his mind for another description.

But, no, *protective* stuck.

Then, maybe because of the protective sensation, he'd reacted badly, retreating from further intimacy with her by flirting outrageously with Annie the following night—last night.

Not that Maggie had seemed to mind, giving him the impression that what had happened between them had meant nothing to her either.

Another image of Maggie flashed into his mind. Not the quiet, efficient anaesthetist he saw every day in

Theatre, but a pocket-siren in a red miniskirt, black lacy top and shiny red boots!

Maggie dressed to go out last night…

He must have groaned for both Kurt and the Flying Marvel turned.

'You OK?' the Flying Marvel asked. 'Sick bag in the pocket on the back of my seat.'

Phil glared at the pilot then reminded himself they were in his hands, so he couldn't wish any bad luck on the man. Seeking diversion from his Maggie thoughts, he looked at Kurt, sitting beside the pilot, his attention now refocussed on the Western he was reading. The man was one of the best operators Phil had ever seen on a heart-lung bypass machine, but as a conversationalist—well, one might as well talk to one of the machines he operated.

But thinking of the heart-lung machine reminded him of why they were flying from Sydney to Brisbane—reminded him of work.

Enough avoidance tactics! Time to seriously consider what lay ahead.

Waiting for them up in Brisbane was a SIDS baby—an infant who had died from sudden infant death syndrome.

Phil's heart went out to the parents of this unknown infant, grieving for a beloved baby, yet still finding in their hearts the ultimate generosity to donate the baby's organs so other infants might have a chance to live full and useful lives.

He would be but one surgeon in Theatre tonight—he and Kurt working together to take the baby's heart for a little girl who would otherwise die. Then, with the precious organ packed in a slush of ice, they'd fly back with it to Sydney.

Think of the procedure, he told himself, and a picture of a small healthy infant heart came up in his mind. Mentally he rehearsed how he'd operate to remove it with the aortic arch intact, so he and Alex Attwood, his boss and team leader at the new cardiac surgery unit at St James's Hospital, could attach it to the vessels in Amy Carter's tiny chest.

'It's your heart, you do it!'

Back at Jimmie's in Sydney some hours later, Phil heard the words but at first didn't understand them. He'd only been in Theatre a matter of minutes, moving into the first assistant's position to help Alex as he carefully removed Amy's defective heart.

Now adrenalin surged through him.

'Me? Do it? Do the transplant?'

'Come on, man, we don't want her on bypass any longer than necessary!'

Alex's order was curt, as well it might have been, and Phil responded as much to the tone of voice as to the words. He changed places with Alex, moving in beside Rachel, the American theatre sister they'd brought, with Kurt, from the States, and his hands went through a routine he'd seen a dozen times but had never done as the lead surgeon in an operation.

'Sats are good,' Maggie said, and her presence and quiet voice gave him added confidence. This was just another op, only he, not Alex, was the lead.

His fingers working surely in the cooled body, he inserted tiny stitches, sewing Amy's arteries and veins into place in the new heart. Each stitch had to be spaced with care, so the pressure of blood being pumped through her body wouldn't force them apart. Kurt counted off the time since Amy's heart had been removed and Maggie's regular reports reminded him how long she'd been unconscious, and how her body was standing up to the bypass machine. Blood values told them Amy was OK, but the real test would come after the operation.

Then the new heart was stimulated with drugs and the silence in Theatre became absolute as they all waited to see if it would beat—and if the carefully stitched veins and arteries would hold.

'Yay!'

The cheer went up from Rachel, the first to see the rhythmic movement of the heart muscles as they squeezed blood from the atria to the ventricles and out into the arteries.

'Well done,' Alex said quietly, and Phil felt his knees turn to jelly with relief, though as he'd worked he hadn't been aware of the terrible tension building up in his body. He glanced involuntarily towards Maggie. Hoping for her praise as well?

Whatever!

It didn't happen. She was watching the screen of the monitor, oblivious to his presence—or his need for re-assurance.

Forget Maggie and concentrate on Amy!

'Should I close her chest or use a patch?' he asked Alex, knowing there was a likelihood of the new heart swelling in protest to the trauma it had undergone.

'She's got such a small thoracic cavity I'd use the patch,' Alex said, and Rachel nodded to the circulating nurse to pass over one of the sealed envelopes, each holding a fine silicone rubber patch.

Across from him, Alex was explaining to Scott Douglas, the surgical registrar assisting, that the patch would keep the wound sterile while maximising the space inside Amy's chest.

'In a couple of days,' Alex added, as Phil sewed the thin filmy material meticulously into place, 'we'll operate again to remove the patch and close Amy's chest.'

Inserting the final stitch, overseeing the taping of the drains and tubes and wires attached to Amy's tiny body—it all took time, but finally they were done.

'I'll take her into the PICU,' Maggie said, and Phil, who was feeling so elated to have successfully completed the op, wondered how she could possibly be so calm.

'Because I have to be,' she told him later, when, with an intensivist watching their charge, he persuaded her to go down to the canteen for lunch—a colleague-with-colleague lunch. 'I know you and Alex are exceptional surgeons, but even with you two there, things can go wrong, and while everyone else is cursing and swearing—and don't bother telling me you don't—someone has to remain calm.'

Her lips teased into a smile, and he remembered how that same teasing smile had set him on fire as they'd danced at the club.

It still set him on fire, although a hospital corridor was a most inappropriate place to be feeling lusty heat for a colleague. Not that he intended acting on it. He avoided relationships with close colleagues—too much fall-out when things ended!

He put his arm behind her back to guide her into the lift and looked at her, a small, pretty woman, with dark hair and even darker eyes, velvety dark—night sky in a hospital lift...

'First transplant I've been part of so the first time

I've seen a skin patch used on a baby. Do you always use one in transplants?'

As he usually had a post-op high himself, he understood why she'd be thinking about Amy, but he still felt a twinge of disappointment that the matter in the forefront of his mind right now—the night they'd spent together—had no place at all in hers.

He shook his head, hoping to clear it of wayward thoughts, and the velvet brown eyes looked puzzled.

'You don't know? But you worked so surely, and confidently, and calmly, and competently in there, I thought you must have done plenty of transplants. I was terrified—shaking like a leaf—although I kept telling myself it was just another op. It seems so—so omnipotent somehow!'

Phil smiled at her choice of words.

'Don't go saying things like that to Alexander the Great,' he teased. 'He's already given god-like status by most of his patients' parents.'

He paused, gathering his thoughts, telling himself it was good to be with Maggie, even if they were only talking work.

'It's not omnipotence, just good surgical work. If you think of the advances in medicine in the last century—especially in your field—you realise it's the researchers who should get all the praise. The people who made anaesthesia safer, or who went before us in surgical fields, developing techniques, working out how to keep a patient alive on a bypass machine—these are the ones who need the praise. We're just good technicians, following paths others forged for us.'

The lift had stopped, but before stepping out Maggie smiled at him.

'Super-duper technicians,' she said, and Phil felt a little hitch in the region of his heart.

It must be post-op excitement kicking in.

Couldn't possibly be to do with Maggie's smile.

He didn't do heart hitches where women were concerned.

# CHAPTER TWO

*Six weeks later*

'So, YOU see, Min, given what happened between Maggie and me that one night, it's going to be awkward to say the least with her living here.'

So much had happened in the interim. Amy, the little girl on whom Phil had done the transplant, had thrown up every complication known to man, and some not known ones as well; then Annie, their unit manager, had been shot, leading to the revelation that Alex, his boss and landlord, was madly in love with her, and the two were getting married. With the drama and wedding preparations on top of their usual heavy workload, there'd been no time for socialising for any members of the team.

'It's been chaotic, Min.'

He scratched the tummy of the little bundle of black curls nestled on his lap and smiled at the sympathetic glance the soft brown eyes of Alex's dog cast his way. Though maybe the look was a 'keep scratching' look, not one of sympathy, as Minnie was now pushing one paw against his hand in a 'don't stop now' kind of way.

'I have to stop,' Phil told her, setting her back down on the floor. 'That was a car pulling up out the back and I've got to do the right thing and welcome Maggie to her new home. Carry suitcases, act the part of the genial host.'

Phil stood up, straightened his shoulders and rehearsed his best welcoming smile. Even without a mirror in the room, he knew it was a poor effort. He'd never felt less welcoming.

'This is ridiculous,' he muttered as he made his way through the house towards the back door. 'I'm thirty-four years old, a surgical fellow to one of the best paediatric heart surgeons in the world, a noted wooer and winner of women, housebroken to the extent I can clean and cook, well off, a good catch, as they say, and a little snip of an anaesthetist has got me flummoxed.'

Minnie, capering gaily around his feet, probably didn't understand the word 'flummoxed', and she certainly didn't understand that while they were intending to be politely welcoming, they weren't going to exhibit any signs of hysterical delight over Maggie moving in.

The moment Phil opened the door she was racing across the back yard to leap and cavort around Maggie's feet—literally dancing with excitement at the arrival of the new housemate.

'I'll get the rest,' Phil offered, as Maggie, with a backpack slung across one shoulder, towed a medium-sized red suitcase along the path to the back door.

'There is no rest,' she said.

'No rest? You've fitted *all* your clothes and four pairs of boots into that case? And don't tell me you don't have four pairs of boots, I've seen you in at least that many. The black ones you wore to the wedding yesterday, a brown pair you had on one weekend when I saw you at the hospital, another pair that look like snakeskin you were wearing when you went out with that juvenile intensivist in Melbourne, and the red ones you wore to the nightclub with Annie!'

Maggie stopped wheeling and laughed, little lines crinkling the corners of her usually serious dark eyes.

'Philip Park! Do you have a shoe fetish that you remember all my boots?' She shifted her attention from him to the dog. 'Oh, dear, Minnie, what have I got myself into here?'

See! Phil wanted to say to the same dog. See what I have to put up with from her! But Minnie had obviously gone all female and would undoubtedly side with Maggie.

'Actually, I shifted the rest of my stuff in before Alex and Annie's wedding,' Maggie continued, moving again, the suitcase *and* the dog now following her. 'Alex cleared all his things out of his room so I could start unpacking. Last weekend. Alex insisted you take time off and you flew up to the Gold Coast with Becky, didn't you?'

'I flew up to the Gold Coast, but not, if you must know, with Becky,' Phil muttered, wondering why things this woman said pushed his buttons when someone else saying them wouldn't affect him at all.

'Some other blonde, then?' Maggie said blithely, reaching the kitchen and snapping the towing handle of her case back into place, then bending to lift it.

Fuming over the 'blonde' dig, but not forgetful of his manners, Phil reached to take it from her and nearly knocked her over, recovering quickly enough to grab her arm to steady her.

'Sorry! Don't usually send new housemates flying as a way of introduction.'

*And don't touch her again*, he added to himself, as the awareness he was trying to keep at bay flared through his body.

Maggie looked into his blue eyes, wondering where the smile that usually lurked there had gone.

Just as well it had. Living with Phil was going to be

bad enough, but it would be infinitely harder if he'd kept smiling and twinkling those devastating eyes in her direction.

Why on earth had she agreed to this crazy scheme?

So the newlyweds Alex and Annie could have some privacy at Annie's place—that was why, she reminded herself.

'I'll carry this upstairs for you,' Phil said, and Maggie stepped back, determined not to have any more physical contact between them, no matter how accidental it might be.

'Thanks.'

She followed him up the stairs, her eyes taking note of the set of his shoulders, of the lithe way he moved, her body remembering other movements, her head repeating a sharp refrain—*madness, madness, madness*—because that's what moving in with Phil was. Total and utter madness!

Especially now.

Especially with what was in the case he carried, though she knew taking a second pregnancy test was useless. It would show exactly what the first one had—that she was carrying Phil's baby.

Some of the cocktail of fear, despair, excitement, trepidation and confusion inside her must have escaped in an involuntary cry, for Phil reached the top of the stairs and turned.

'You OK?'

'Fine, just fine,' she said, and indeed she was.

Physically fine.

Mentally she was almost deranged with thinking about it. About being pregnant!

Again!

Would it be all right this time?

She tamped down the now-familiar flutter of fear, and told herself fretting over how it had happened when Phil had used protection was pointless.

It *had* happened but, given her previous miscarriages—back when she'd been married to Jack—was she likely to keep it? Have a live baby?

And if she did, could she juggle work and a baby?

Time enough to decide what to do—and how to tell Phil—when she'd carried it safely for three months.

Tell Phil? Hell and damnation—how *had* it happened?

'There. Is there anything else you need brought up? Do you want time to unpack? We should sit down and talk about household things some time, I suppose. What you like to eat, cooking rosters, shopping, all that stuff. Alex and I did what suited us—if there was no food in the house and I was here, I shopped. It worked most of the time, but you might like something more structured. Mrs Hobbs, the cleaning lady, comes on Thursdays, and she puts on loads of washing and comes back Friday mornings to iron.'

Phil was looking over Maggie's shoulder, out through the front window, as he imparted this information and Maggie realised he probably felt as awkward about the night they'd spent together as she did.

Well, not quite as awkward, given the baby, but perhaps she should clear the air.

She took a deep breath and started right in.

'Look, Phil, with Annie being shot, Alex going out of his mind with worry and the resulting pressure of extra work at the hospital, we haven't had much chance to talk to each other about that night. But we can't go on pretending what happened didn't happen. It did, and I enjoyed it and have no regrets—' well, maybe one which he didn't need to know about—yet! '—but we're going to be living together and we need to move on.'

'That's it?' he said. 'We need to *move on*? That's all it meant to you?' He was practically yelling the words at her.

Oh, dear! Now she'd hurt his ego, or whatever part of a man's mental make-up was attached to his sexual prowess. But she could hardly tell him that it had been like all her dreams coming true, that she'd been attracted to him from the first time they'd met six months ago—not when he had no idea how she felt about him and when he certainly wasn't even part way to falling in love with her.

Not when he usually took no more notice of her than he did of the furniture in their suite of rooms at work.

'Phil, we went out to dinner in a group, went on from there to a club and danced, got worked up and, being consenting adults, fell lustily into bed together. What was it meant to mean?'

Huge frown from Phil.

'Something more than it did to you, obviously,' he growled, adding under his breath, 'Fell lustily into bed! Move on!'

'But you can't make it more than it was,' she protested. 'It wasn't as if you'd been chasing me around the hospital corridors since we first met, or that we'd been dating and it was the next step in a relationship. It happened, that's all.'

'That's all!' he muttered, echoing her words but not the placating way she'd said them. Then he stalked out of her bedroom and clumped down the stairs, apparently meeting Minnie on the way for she heard him grumbling away to someone.

Realising her legs had become a little shaky, Maggie made her way to the bed and sank down on it.

Had she made a mistake, bringing up the subject at all? Or was it her minimising it—surely the only option, considering they'd be living together—that had upset Phil?

No answer to either question sprang to mind, so she stood up and crossed to her suitcase, unpacking it, putting clothes away, finding the new packet from the chemist and setting it down in the *en suite* bathroom. Then, because she wanted to leave it another week before she did a second test, and remembering the cleaning lady, she put it in the cupboard under the basin.

Another deep breath and it was time to go downstairs and join him. Time to discuss shopping and cooking, and pretend this was a normal house-sharing arrangement between two colleagues.

Yeah, right!

Phil heard the floor creak as she moved about upstairs, and reminded himself that at least she wasn't wearing boots. His libido was already running amok where Maggie was concerned, but had she been wearing the red numbers, he'd find it even harder to restrain himself from ravishing her right here on the kitchen table.

Though why he still wanted to, he had no idea.

Cool as a cucumber, she'd brushed him off. About the only thing she hadn't said to destroy his self-confidence had been that the sex had been forgettable. Although 'enjoyed it' was hardly high praise.

Probably next to forgettable, come to think about it.

'Pathetic, that's what it is, Minnie,' he complained to the dog who, missing Alex, had once again found her way onto his lap. 'It's not as if my self-worth and self-confidence are tied to my sexual prowess!'

Footsteps on the stairs—get a grip! They were house-sharing colleagues.

She breezed in and bent to pat Minnie, who'd leapt off his knee to greet her then settled at the other side of the table, though not far enough away for him to avoid the faint hint of perfume that seemed the only thing common to the two Maggies.

'Lilacs!' he said, and knew from her questioning glance she had no idea what he was talking about.

'The perfume you wear. I've been wondering for months what it reminded me of and it just struck me. Lilacs flowering in the garden at home. You notice the perfume most at night when it seems to scent the air all over the property.'

'Do you miss home?'

The question startled him, but not nearly as much as the look of genuine interest and concern on Maggie's face.

If she but knew!

'Not really,' he said, then something prompted him to add, 'I'm not quite sure where home is—in a permanent sense.'

'But home is where you grew up, surely!' A puzzled frown accompanied the words. 'I haven't lived at home for years, not in the house where I grew up, but it will always be home to me. Though I guess home is more a concept—a ''whole-of-family'' kind of thing.'

'Yes, well, family's nearly as alien to me as home.' Phil stood up and moved to fill the kettle, hoping his curt tone and his movement would be enough to signal the conversation was at an end.

'Alien? In what way?'

Persistence in a small package!

He could ignore her, but he had a feeling she'd just keep asking, so he sighed, rested his hands on the sink and looked out the kitchen window as he replied.

'I'm not sure about the concept of home, Mags, because I grew up in a house. It might have had beautiful gardens and lilacs that bloomed in spring, nannies, servants, horses, dogs and cats, but it was a house, not a home. I had a brother, a sister, a mother and a father—I have all but the father still, though his death made little difference, he was never there—and even now, when my mother writes dutifully once a week, she says things like, "Your brother has a new car, your grandfather kicked the cat." No one has a name and surely in homes, people have names.'

'Mags! I like that,' Maggie managed to say, though her chest was filled to overflowing with pity for the man who stood, turned away from her, shoulders bent as he revealed the poverty of his wealthy upbringing. She longed to go to him—to press her body against his back and put her arms around his waist, holding him in silent empathy. But something told her Phil hadn't shared this information with many people, and was probably already regretting having told her.

She'd have to be very careful how she treated it.

And him.

Especially him. No way could she let pity intrude into her determination to keep him at arm's length. Her body might shimmy with delight at even the most casual of touches, but embarking on a physical relationship with Phil would make things even more complex than they already were.

Especially when it would mean nothing more to him than physical pleasure…

'Coffee?'

Maggie breathed easily again, aware they'd negotiated a very delicate situation and got things back to normal.

'Black, two sugars,' she said, thinking about her relief, not the content of what she'd said, so she was surprised when he spun towards her.

'Two sugars? You? I know you're always drinking coffee so, with all the sugar, why don't you put on weight?'

His eyes were scanning her body to see where sixteen teaspoons of sugar per day might be showing themselves in unsightly bulges.

'I dance it off,' she told him. 'That's why I'm crazy about going out to clubs where there's dancing. I tried a gym membership at one time, and did one session. It was the most boring, tedious hour of my life and, believe me, as an anaesthetist I know about boring and tedious. From then on I stuck with dancing.'

Phil wished with all his heart she hadn't said that, because it brought back the night they'd danced and danced together, the music and the contact, and though a lot of it had been little more than occasional touches, it had primed them both for love.

He remembered how she'd felt in his arms—small, and warm, and cuddly in the final, slower dance—and his body, which had been on full alert since Maggie had entered the house, now went into demand mode.

He concentrated on making coffee, stirred the two spoons of sugar—heaped, so she'd need to dance again—into it, then brought both cups over to the table.

'We'll put sugar on the shopping list,' he joked, and wasn't at all surprised to hear his voice come out exceedingly croaky.

'Do we need a shopping list? Should we shop today?'

Once again, Phil felt relief. So far things weren't going too badly. Maggie seemed to have the ability to sail right over the awkward bits, which meant she was either totally insensitive or very adept at putting her fellow man at ease.

Whichever it was, long may it continue while he was the fellow man in question!

'We should. What with Alex spending most of the last month down at Annie's place, then the wedding preparations, we've done very little shopping and the pantry's almost bare.'

Maggie got up and crossed to it, familiar with the layout of the kitchen as she'd been living four doors down in Annie's house, which had a similar floor plan.

'You're right,' she told him, 'though Minnie either eats an inordinate amount for such a small dog, or every time either of you shopped you bought food for her.'

Minnie, hearing her name, got up from beneath the table and trotted across to look hopefully up at Maggie.

'Don't try that soft brown begging eyes stuff on me,' Maggie said sternly. 'I bet you have regular mealtimes and a proper amount of food at each. You go begging for food and you'll get as fat as a fool because you can't dance it off.'

The conversation eased a lot of Phil's tension and by the time he'd explained Minnie's routine and they'd made out a shopping list, he could almost believe this 'nothing-more-than-colleagues-sharing-a-house' pretence he'd engaged in might work.

'I love cooking, so I'm happy to cook if I'm home,' Maggie offered, and Phil smiled at her.

'Which means I get to stack the dishwasher—I'm good at that.'

'And unstack it,' she reminded him. 'That's part and parcel of the dishwasher job!'

They were arguing amiably about how to stack dishwashers and whether they'd shop before or after lunch when first his and then Maggie's pager buzzed.

'Hospital,' he said, getting up and moving to phone in.

'I'll change my shoes and be right down,' Maggie told him. 'You can fill me in on what's happening as we walk up the road.'

She will *not* be changing into boots, Phil told himself as he rinsed the coffee cups and stacked them on the top shelf—his choice of placement, not Maggie's—of the dishwasher.

# CHAPTER THREE

'IT's a newborn—male—with aortic stenosis,' Phil began as they walked the short distance to the hospital.

'Narrowing or failure of the aortic valve showing as
congestive heart failure and shock?' Maggie queried,
thinking of the symptoms and trying not to think of the
wee infant suffering them, or his desperately anxious
parents. 'Did they have pre-warning something was
wrong, and what are they doing for him now?'

'Apparently they had no pre-warning. No recent
scans to show something might be amiss. The baby was
born in a small birthing unit in an outer suburb, and
the midwife heard a heart murmur and had the mother
and child transferred straight to Jimmie's. The paediatrician called in a cardiologist, who's done scans which
show the valve problem. He tried a balloon valvulo-
plasty to open the valves, but it didn't work.'

'There are probably associated problems,' Maggie
muttered, shaking her head of the enormity of what the
little baby was going through. 'Don't you usually find
ventricular dysfunction—often left ventricle insufficiency—in these cases?'

'Yes, and the real problem is that surgery to correct
aortic valves—'

He stopped, and Maggie, sensing something big lay
beyond the beginning of the sentence, didn't press for
more while he was thinking things through, but she
wondered just what he hadn't said.

She found out a little later, as he argued with the cardiologist.

'I know from what you tell me the case is urgent, but every study done on AS in neonates shows a far greater chance of success with open surgery for valve repair in infants over one month. Even catheterisation repairs are more effective and last longer if the infant is a little older.'

'I've told the parents you can operate,' the cardiologist, someone Maggie hadn't met before, told Phil.

'Before I saw the child? You had no right to do that!'

'No? Seems to me it was the right thing to do, the way you're acting. I don't want you near the child at all if all you're going to do is cause problems.'

Maggie could sense Phil stiffening, and hear his determination to do the right thing in the way his voice became far more 'English', but he was still trying to placate the specialist.

'Look, we can use supportive management on the little chap until he's older. Prostaglandin to keep the ductus arteriosis open. The right ventricle in a neonate can keep blood flowing adequately through the whole body and newborns can tolerate less oxygen in their blood.'

'I have problems with prolonged use of prostaglandin,' the cardiologist said in a pompous voice bound to rile his listeners, 'but if you don't feel capable of doing the operation, then I suppose we'll have to try it. At least until your boss returns.'

He certainly riled Maggie.

'Excuse me!' she burst out, able to stand the man's snooty attitude no longer. 'I've been in Theatre when both Dr Attwood and Dr Park have been operating, and if you just watch their hands you could not tell which is which. Both are excellent surgeons with the figures from their successes to back this up. If Dr Park thinks this baby is too young for the surgery you want to inflict on him, he'll have solid statistics to prove it. You want to give him some figures, Phil?'

Phil smiled at her, but once again there was no smile lurking in his eyes, and she guessed the man's slur about waiting for Alex had bitten deep.

'I don't think there's any need for that. There are other paediatric cardiac surgeons in town. Dr Ellis might want to consult one of them.'

'I will!' The angry cardiologist spat the words at them, and strode away.

'Should we see the baby? The parents?' Maggie asked, watching Phil watch the man disappear, and wanting desperately to wipe the look of anguish from his face.

'We can't just barge in. The little chap's not our patient,' Phil reminded her. 'Ellis made that perfectly clear.'

'Yet you're desperately worried about him,' Maggie said, reading the expression on his face with ease.

'Because I know Dave Edwards, Alex's mate at Children's, is out of town for the weekend, and he's the only other surgeon I know here who'd be capable of doing the operation if the decision is made to go ahead.'

The full import of this struck home, and unconsciously Maggie's hand strayed to her own belly, where an embryo the size of a bean was currently producing its first organ—a heart!

'You think someone who might not have done one before—someone with less skill than you—will do it?'

'If Ellis can talk them into it!'

He rubbed his hands across his face and threaded his fingers through his hair, a gesture she'd never seen before but so redolent of despair her heart ached for him.

'Hell, Maggie, what do I decide? Is it the parents' choice? The cardiologist's? Or mine? I'd choose to not do it right now and I could explain that to the parents, tell them why it's better to wait, but I can't talk to them because that baby isn't my patient. Yet if Ellis persuades someone else to do it and the baby dies, will I, in part, be responsible?'

Maggie put her arm around his waist and hugged him close to her side. Bother the physical consequences. If ever a man needed a hug it was this man, and he needed it now.

'You and Alex make life-and-death decisions all the time,' she reminded him. 'You've held the lives of so many babies in your hands, but you know you can't save them all. Can you pretend this baby is in Melbourne, or somewhere else where it's physically impossible for you to be involved? Would that help?'

He smiled down at her and touched his finger to her cheek.

'Not much, but you do, though I have a feeling this could get nasty and you should distance yourself from the whole affair so you don't get hit by any of the fall-out.'

'Nasty?' Maggie queried, battling the urge to press her hand against the place where his finger had touched her cheek. 'Fall-out?'

'Annie's away as well, remember—which means we don't have a unit manager to fight our in-hospital battles. Ellis is powerful in this hospital and we're the relative new chums.'

'The hospital could make you do the op? But it

can't—not if you feel it's not in the best interests of the baby!'

Phil smiled again, but it was a weak effort.

'They can't make me operate, but they can make things uncomfortable for the unit—and for Annie and Alex when they return.'

'Damn hospital politics!' Maggie muttered. 'I can't believe it can intrude into decisions like this. I'd like to walk out right now, but I guess you don't want to.'

She'd put a little space between them but could still feel the shape of Phil's body against hers.

She needed a diversion.

She needed a coffee!

'Seeing as we're here, let's have another cup of coffee. I barely drank half of the last one.'

She led the way towards their suite of rooms where Annie had installed a state-of-the-art coffee-maker.

'Dr Park!'

Maggie recognised the voice of the hospital CEO, Col Bennett, though how Dr Ellis had got him to the hospital so quickly on a Sunday she couldn't guess. She turned with Phil and stood beside him as Col, with Dr Ellis yapping at his heels, approached.

'Dr Ellis tells me you don't feel confident about performing this operation.'

Maggie glared at the doctor mentioned, unable to believe his effrontery and misrepresentation of the facts. But if she was annoyed, it was nothing to the anger sparking from Phil's body.

'I am not confident of a successful outcome in so young a baby. It is my considered opinion that the operation should be delayed until the infant is older. I can produce a whole body of evidence that the operations to correct valvular aortic stenosis are more successful on babies over thirty days. The figures on operating on a neonate are abysmal to say the least. And as we can, and have in the past, successfully kept neonates with this condition alive for thirty days, I see no reason why Dr Ellis can't accept this case management.'

'Oh!' Col said, but before he could say more, Dr Ellis broke in with a long dissertation on the damage prostaglandin could do and why supportive measures, in this case, wouldn't work.

He was positively bristling with anger.

'You haven't yet seen the infant,' he fired at Phil.

'Because he is not, as yet, my patient,' Phil fired right back. 'Come on, Maggie, let's get that coffee.'

He took her by the arm and hustled her away, muttering when they were far enough for his words not to be heard, 'I'd have hit that man if I'd stayed there a second longer!'

Maggie pressed her hand against his, which was still on her upper arm, steering her along the passageway.

'Far better to walk away than to come to blows in the unit, but I can't blame you for wanting to wipe the smug smirk off that fellow's face. I wanted to slap it myself.'

They walked into the suite and she turned on the coffee-machine then found ground coffee and filter papers and set everything in motion.

'What I don't understand,' she said to Phil, who'd walked to the desk he used and was booting up his computer, 'is why Ellis is so adamant about the operation. Don't cardiologists usually prefer to go the medication or closed catheterisation route in most cases?'

'They do,' Phil said, his voice vague as if most of his attention was on his computer screen. 'But apparently the catheterisation didn't work, so it's my guess there's so much wrong with that poor baby, Ellis is afraid he'll die, and, having been called in as the specialist, he doesn't want the death on his hands. He'd far rather the baby died on the operating table, or from post-op complications. That way it's not his fault.'

He paused then added, 'And there's a more than fifty per cent chance—up to sixty-eight per cent chance, in fact—of that happening if he's operated on this young. I just don't believe the risks are worth that kind of result when by waiting, even a short time, the odds are considerably reduced.'

Maggie carried his coffee across to him and perched on the other side of his desk. He looked up at her and grinned.

'Thanks for sticking by me,' he said, and her heart turned over in her chest. The grin, the words—the man's dogged determination to do the right thing—all combined to remind her that what she'd felt for Phil had grown from the initial attraction at that first meeting to something very close to love.

Oh, dear!

Better to think about work.

'Is Dr Ellis right about prolonged use of prostaglandin? Are there concerns?'

'Yes. Various studies have shown problems with prolonged use of it, but it's been done often enough for intensivists to know how to handle the side-effects. It's politics again. Ellis has voiced these concerns to Col because the baby could well die anyway, and once again he will have someone to blame—me, for suggesting the prostaglandin option!'

'You keep talking about blame but surely this is one very sick baby who, without any supportive measures, would probably be already dead. In fact, the parents have probably already been offered the option of compassionate care—keeping the baby comfortable but not intervening in his condition. There shouldn't be any talk of blame. If the baby dies, it's no one's fault.'

Phil turned his attention from the computer screen to smile at her and she had to remind herself it was nothing but a colleague-to-colleague smile.

'Of course there shouldn't be blame laid at individual doors, but it happens every day. Everyone likes to palm off responsibility—you see it everywhere. Surely you've been in an op that's gone wrong—who's the first person the surgeon blames?'

Maggie smiled back at him—colleague-to-colleague!—although every smile from Phil caused an achy feeling in her heart.

'The anaesthetist—or sometimes the theatre sister. Sometimes even the assisting surgeon. You're right, it's a fairly normal, if unattractive, human trait to look around for somewhere to lay blame. But surely not in the death of a baby born with so many complications he might not survive anyway.'

'Wishful thinking, Mags!' Phil said, his attention now back on the screen as his fingers clicked keys to scroll through the information he'd brought up.

Mags again! No one had ever called her that. The thought warmed little corners of her body.

Sweet heaven! Was she going soupy over a nickname?

She sipped her coffee, watching Phil scanning the information on the screen, knowing he was so intent on what he was doing she could study him for a while.

Brown hair, slightly lightened, maybe by his weekend in the sun, longish and very straight, dropping forward over his forehead, touching his ears. Darker eyebrows—she could only see one, but knew the pair matched well—above the mid-blue eyes that caused flip-flops in her heart region when they smiled at her.

No smiling eyes recently, which, she told herself firmly, was a good thing. If her stomach was about to launch an early morning rebellion, she could do without heart flip-flops at the same time.

She continued her study, taking in the neat nose with a slight dip at the end—a Roman nose, she rather thought, although she'd never done much nose-typing. Clean-shaven pale skin, but she guessed from the shadow his beard was darker than his hair. Nice chin, not too obvious, with an indentation too slight to be a dimple but tempting her fingers to touch it every time she noticed it there.

You missed the lips, a snide voice in her head reminded her, and she turned away because just looking at those lips reminded her of kisses, and made her ache for more of them. But life was complicated enough already, without adding Phil's kisses to the mix.

'There it is—I knew I'd read it recently. Latest studies confirm that patients over thirty days fare far better short-term and have a higher long-term chance of survival than those operated on as neonates. I'll print this out and wave it in the face of the next person who mentions it.'

His fingers, long and thin, danced across the keyboard, and as the printer on the far side of the room began to chatter, the phone on Annie's desk rang and Maggie crossed to answer it.

'It's Alex, for you,' she said quietly, waving the receiver in his direction.

Phil cursed under his breath, but picked up the extension on his desk.

'Alex, I assume you're phoning about Dr Ellis's patient. Believe me, man, I'd as soon have operated as dragged you into this mess.'

'Don't give it a thought,' Alex responded. 'Col Bennett got me on my mobile and I told him exactly what you'd already told him. I just thought you might need some moral support.'

'Thanks, I appreciate it, and now you're on the phone, how do I actually stand within the hospital? I know they can't force me to perform an operation I truly believe will do more harm than good, but am I going to jeopardise your position or put pressure on the continuation of the unit? I know we're on fairly precarious ground as it is, with other services and units jealous of the money we've been allocated. Is this going to make things more difficult for you?'

'Too bad if it does, and as for your position, you're my fellow, employed and paid by me, so hang tough.'

They talked some more, Phil explaining what he knew about the patient, Alex confirming his own belief that the operation should be delayed as long as possible, running through the figures Phil had already considered, then repeating his opinion that Phil had done the right thing.

Phil knew he shouldn't feel relieved—he'd already had high cardiac surgical standing before joining Alex to learn more about the paediatric side of things—but he was.

'Thanks again,' he said. 'Now, you get back to looking after Annie and enjoying your honeymoon, while we hold the fort here.'

He hung up and picked up the now lukewarm cup of coffee. He sipped at it and grimaced, then smiled at Maggie who was perched on Annie's desk.

'Seems we're doomed as far as coffee is concerned today. Shall we give it up as a bad job, get the car and go shopping?'

She looked surprised but slipped off the desk and picked up her handbag.

'Sure. Why not?'

He knew she was humouring him, but couldn't explain his need to get out of the hospital. Maybe if he put his mind to something else he could forget about the ill baby. Forget that just maybe, by refusing to operate, he was denying the little fellow a slim chance of life.

'You're worrying about him, aren't you?' Maggie said a little later, removing the second, third and fourth bottles of coffee he'd absent-mindedly loaded into the trolley.

'Yes!'

'What did Alex say?'

'That I'd done the right thing—that he wouldn't operate either. We do some unavoidable procedures in neonates—do them all the time—but the heart muscle is so slushy in a newborn, doing anything is a risk. But that's not the issue, Mags. It's the voice in my head that's bothering me.'

'A voice suggesting an op at this stage might just save him?'

Phil smiled at his companion. She was wearing a red sweater and he wondered if maybe red was her favourite out-of-hospital colour. It was a cheery colour and he felt inexplicably cheered. By her presence and understanding more than the red sweater, but still...

'Damn voices!' he admitted and she laughed.

'We all have them. *Why didn't you try such and*

*such?* mine will ask when a protocol goes wrong, although I know full well it should have worked.'

And standing in the beverages aisle of the local supermarket, Phil was struck by how good it was to have Maggie around. As a colleague and a friend. He doubted he could remove lust from the equation altogether, but he could hide it, and enjoy her company both as a workmate and a housemate.

'You two taking up residence in front of the coffee?'

An impatient shopper reminded him of where they were, and he grabbed the trolley and began to steer it out of that aisle and into the next, pausing when Maggie stopped to select an item, pushing again as she moved on, telling himself this was the same as the occasional times he and Alex had shopped together and he shouldn't be feeling any more pleasure because it was Maggie sharing the task.

'OK, all done. We'll go to the greengrocer then home,' she said cheerfully, some half an hour later.

'There's that word again,' Phil said, because he *had* been feeling more pleasure shopping with Maggie.

She turned towards him, her brow crinkling with confusion so for a moment she looked like a puzzled child.

'Greengrocer?' she asked, and Phil had to laugh.

'Home,' he corrected, reaching out and ruffling her short dark hair.

Her dark eyes mirrored her concern as she said, 'Oh, Phil!' very softly, then turned her attention back to unloading the trolley onto the checkout counter.

'I'll pay for this—we're using your car and your fuel,' he said, feeling a need to take control after her murmuring of his name had loosened something inside him.

Anatomically, this was unlikely. He was a cardiac surgeon, he knew people didn't have heart-strings so it couldn't be those.

'You won't pay. We'll split it and later set up a housekeeping system so we both pay the same,' she told him, the practical anaesthetist Maggie back in place, although he could have sworn it was the other Maggie who had whispered his name.

But as she drove efficiently out of the shopping-centre car park, he realised they weren't done with the conversation.

'Do you have some mental image of the home you'd have liked to have?' she asked. 'Does the word conjure up mental pictures for you?'

He turned to look at her, wondering if she was just making conversation or really wanted to know. He couldn't think why she would, but from what he knew of Maggie, she didn't talk for the sake of it.

Anyway, she was his housemate and he liked her and so...

'If I tell you, you'll probably laugh!' he said.

She glanced his way, brow wrinkled again.

'Why would I laugh? I really want to know. I'm trying to put myself in your shoes—growing up as you did. I know when I was growing up, one of five kids, I longed to be an only child, with a bedroom of my own, and to live on a farm where I could keep a horse and ducks and geese. I never went much on chickens, but I had a thing for fluffy yellow ducklings.'

'Well, we had the horse and ducks and geese, though I remember ducks as creatures with no discretion at all when it came to where they did their business. Duck poo everywhere down by the lake.'

'I suppose there's a downside to everything,' Maggie

said, pulling into the lane that ran behind the row of houses and provided access to the garages. 'But I'm not going to be diverted by duck poo. Tell me about your dream.'

Phil sighed. He'd been right about her persistence.

'It's stupid,' he began, feeling narky at being forced to talk about something so trivial. Then suddenly, from wherever it had lain hidden for close to thirty years, a vivid image of the picture on which his dream was based flashed back into the forefront of his mind.

'Our old nanny—she'd been with my father so she really was quite old, not just old to small children—had a picture in a frame. It showed a little thatched cottage, with roses over the door, and hollyhocks standing straight and tall beside the wall. Flowers everywhere, probably a bird or two. But somehow I always felt, if I could open that front door—it was blue—inside I'd find a family. Mother in the kitchen, father and dog by the fire, small children at the table while a rosy-cheeked baby crawled across the floor. The image of what was behind that door was so clear to me, I finally realised it must have been another picture I'd once seen—maybe on a calendar in Nanny's room as well. It was the kind of sentimental tripe she adored.'

'Tripe? When it made such an impression on you?'

Maggie had stopped the car and she turned to look at him.

'Even a novice in psychoanalysis, knowing how you grew up, would be able to explain all that to you.'

She reached over and touched his shoulder.

'I think it's sweet. Like me and the farm and a bedroom of my own! I guess all kids have dreams. But *now*, Phil Park—what does the word home mean to you now?'

She hoped she sounded casual enough, asking this question, but this 'home and hearth' Phil didn't square with the playboy who flirted shamelessly and dated women as casually as she changed her clothes. And given her current state, it would be good to know which was the real Phil. So, although she'd brought up the subject of home to divert him from thinking of the situation with the sick baby, now they were talking it had turned into a good idea.

'I suppose it's wherever I'm living at the time—though none of the places I've been lately have felt like home because I've always known they were temporary arrangements. First in the US, where I started with Alex at one hospital then moved to another, then Melbourne, now here. I can feel at home just about anywhere, I suppose, but...'

He turned to look directly at her, and she knew he was about to share another bit of himself with her. This, she knew, was special, because in the nearly eight months she'd worked with Phil, she'd learned little of him, apart from an apparent attraction to blondes.

'A little bit of that corny thatched cottage is embedded deep in my subconscious. If I think at all of marriage—hypothetically, of course—I find myself reverting to a modern-day version of that particular picture. Myself in a chair by the fire—children chattering around the place—pets to pat—a wife in the kitchen. Totally unacceptable view in this enlightened day and age of equal rights and careers for women, I know, but the idea persists. I suppose because my parents' marriage *wasn't* like that—my mother lived her own life based mainly on good works, my father was always away—and it was such a disaster, I have this conviction that only something drastically different would work.'

He gave a huff of laughter—at himself, Maggie knew—but she also knew this was very real to him, and given his upbringing she could understand why he saw this dream as an ideal.

Diametrically opposite from her ideal but, then, it would be, she thought gloomily. That was the way life worked!

'I suppose the wife slaving in the kitchen is a blonde?' she heard herself ask, and hoped she didn't sound as bitchy as she must be feeling to have said it in the first place.

Fortunately Phil took it well, laughing as he opened the car door and began unloading the shopping bags.

'At least you stereotyped yourself, offering to do the cooking,' he reminded her. 'You can't blame me for that.'

'I will cook because I enjoy it,' Maggie told him haughtily, 'not because I'm a woman.'

Phil laughed again, then unlocked the back door, freeing a delighted Minnie who leapt about his legs with yaps of excitement before heading for Maggie to welcome her home.

'There's that damn word again,' she muttered to herself, half wishing she hadn't been so persistent in her questioning.

Phil dumped his load of groceries on the kitchen table, and began to unpack them, stacking things into the pantry or fridge. The woman in his childhood dream kitchen *had* been a blonde, but watching Maggie bustling about in this real kitchen was far more seductive than any dream.

'I think I'll go up to the hospital and see if I can see

the baby,' he said, as she stacked things on the bench beneath the window, apparently in readiness for some dish she was about to prepare.

She spun towards him.

'See Dr Ellis? Ask to see the baby?'

Phil shook his head.

'I doubt Ellis is still there. My bet is he's passed it back to the paediatrician. The baby will be in the SBCU—no, that's English, and PICU is American— special care unit you call it here, don't you?'

'We all understand PICU to be Paediatric Intensive Care Unit so stick with that. Yes, the baby will be there. So what?'

'So most of the intensivists we have working in our PICU also work in that one, and I know them all, so I'd like to take a peek at the notes and look at the scans. I imagine they did two-dimensional and Doppler echocardiography. A lot of these cases are associated with hypoblastic left heart syndrome—meaning the child has virtually no left ventricle. We can operate to help his heart function without one, but there again the mortality rate is high unless it's done as a carefully staged procedure—three stages to it—when the child is older.'

He pushed his hair back off his forehead—he had to get a haircut some time soon—and shook his head and sighed.

'I don't really know why I want to go up there, Maggie, just that I do. I can't get that baby out of my mind.'

Maggie shifted some of the things she'd put on the bench into the fridge.

'I'll come with you.'

He had to smile.

'To see the baby or be my support person?' he teased, then realised she wasn't smiling.

'I'll come because you're likely to decide that maybe there *is* something you can do for him, and if you operate, or opt to assist someone else to operate, then you'll need the best paediatric anaesthetist available in this hospital, and that's me.'

'Modest little thing, aren't you?' he said, as she ducked past him towards the front door.

'Not falsely so,' she said, turning to smile. 'But that's my goal—to be the best, not only in this hospital but in Australia, and after Australia the world. And I'll get there, too. I don't think it's boasting when we say things like that. We all know our limitations but surely we should also know our abilities as well, and be confident of them?'

And though he'd been seduced earlier by Maggie's domesticity in the kitchen, he now remembered other things he knew of her. Maggie was a career-woman through and through. In fact, her determination to learn all she could from working with Alex, and the expertise she had already developed anaesthetising neonates and very small infants, was what had persuaded Alex to bring her to Sydney as a member of the team.

'Would you give up work and be a stay-at-home mum if you had a baby?' he asked, as they set off to walk the short distance to the hospital.

She stopped dead, so suddenly he thought at first she must have turned an ankle or injured herself in some other way.

'Are you OK?'

'Of course I am,' she muttered at him, striding along again. 'But we're talking operations, and suddenly you're asking if I'd stop work to have a baby. Not that it's any of your business, but the answer's no. I've done as many years of training as you have—well, not quite as many because you're older. I'm a specialist with skills that go beyond those of general anaesthetics, skills I intend to keep improving and honing. Turn that question around. Would you stop work if you had a baby?'

'Good point,' he said easily, trying to regain some lost ground, but he knew the companionable ease they'd shared earlier was gone. Her voice could have scythed through bamboo! And he'd guessed that was how Maggie would feel, even though he couldn't remember motherhood and families coming up in previous discussions, so why had he been stupid enough to ask the question?

Surely not because of one night in bed with a colleague and a vague memory of a stupid childhood dream!

'If they have decided to go ahead with the operation, will you offer to assist?'

He glanced her way, wondering if she really wanted to know or if it was just her way of getting the conversation back on medical matters. The full lips that had figured in his dreams of late were set in a tight line, so he guessed it was a deliberate conversational shift.

He accepted it, thinking through his reply.

'I don't know,' he told her honestly. 'It's a matter of what's been decided. And it will depend on the surgeon. He—or she—may not want me there. Scott Douglas is the senior cardiac surgical registrar, and he's assisted at a lot of our ops. He's a terrific surgeon, lacking some experience of infants and neonates but getting there.'

Then something else struck him.

'Will you offer?'

She turned and smiled at him.

'It's a baby so, yes, of course I will. I'm lucky in that the decision to operate isn't mine, but my special skill is in giving the little one the best possible chance during and immediately after the op.'

She was silent for a moment, then she added, 'The best possible chance!' in a voice so soft he barely heard it, and shook her head as if to chase some persistent thought away.

# CHAPTER FOUR

THE first person they saw in the PICU was Rachel, the theatre sister who was part of their team.

'My guess is they're going to operate,' Maggie whispered to Phil, who nodded, his face set in an unreadable mask.

'Glad you guys are here,' Rachel greeted them. 'Someone from the hospital phoned Kurt and, thinking it meant Phil had a surgical patient, I tagged along. Now it seems someone else is operating. Kurt went through to Theatre—our theatre—to check his machine, but I don't know if they'll need me.'

She shrugged her shoulders and nodded towards one of the glass-walled rooms where a group of men and women was clustered around a crib.

'You doing the anaesthetic?' she asked Maggie, who looked from the group to Phil, her mind racing.

Although he'd said little, she knew he was still fretting over his decision. Would her going into Theatre with the other group seem like a betrayal?

Worse, how would he feel, definitely on the outside, while all his colleagues on the team were involved?

Purely for the sake of solidarity, should she refuse to help if asked?

'If they ask me to assist, I will,' she said, knowing her own ethical standards would dictate that choice, although her heart would have preferred to stand by Phil.

He nodded as if he understood, but his lips were tight in his grim white face.

She was asked to assist only minutes later, by Scott Douglas, who looked as haunted by what was going on as she felt.

'Phil,' he said, but spoke too hesitantly, for Phil had turned away and was walking not towards their rooms but to the lifts. Leaving the hospital—cutting himself off from them.

From her…

Routine took over, and she moved to the theatre complex, changing into theatre pyjamas then checking all the equipment and assembling the drugs and fluids she'd need.

A tall lanky man came in and introduced himself as Evan Knowles.

'I do this stuff over at the Kids, normally, but when one of the surgeons was called over here he asked me to come along.'

'Is he good?' Maggie asked, stepping back so Evan could familiarise himself with things in the near-new theatre.

'I try not to think about what the surgeons are doing and focus solely on what's happening with the patient.'

He smiled at Maggie, and added, 'To tell the truth, I'm not one hundred per cent certain about how much interference we should run on neonates and infants— how much gross surgical trauma they should have to endure. I've read a lot of studies on measuring pain in them and that's really where I'd like to go—long-term effects of pain in babies and children. Maybe there's none, but we tend to think about all the other things, like the possibility of brain damage and stroke—yet you and I both know, having managed pain in patients in Intensive Care, just how little we know about it in babies.'

Maggie warmed to the man who spoke so openly about his doubt, and, watching him check what she had ready, she felt confident he was a good anaesthetist.

Maybe she could slip away, join Phil at—at Alex's house.

'You will stay?' Evan asked, apparently picking up the thought in the air.

'Yes, I'll stay.'

It was a long and traumatic afternoon. The baby boy arrested on the operating table, and the shock cart was brought close to shock his heart back to action. Then the small heart was so badly deformed it seemed any kind of surgical intervention would be impossible, yet the surgeon did what he could, Scott and Rachel both helping. Rachel, who for years had worked with Alex, and in the US was known as a physician's assistant, seemed to know as much as either of the surgeons.

The first stage was to insert the cannulae, which would run his blood through the bypass machine, but the arteries and veins were so tiny it was a Herculean effort to get the plastic tubes into place.

The baby arrested again, Rachel reacting first, taking the base of the little heart in her fingers and gently squeezing it, keeping blood flowing to the baby's brain until he could be hooked up to the machine. Then Kurt had a problem getting the blood flow pressure low enough for the baby's vessels to handle it and yet sufficiently high to keep the little body perfused.

'This is not going to work,' Evan whispered to Maggie, who was reading out the temperature figures as the machine cooled the blood.

'I thought you didn't watch,' she whispered back.

'I don't,' Evan told her, 'but look at the monitor. Look at the blood acidity reading. If he arrests again— and he will—we won't be able to do anything.'

Maggie looked towards the tiny mortal on the table, so little of him in view, and her own pulse rate accelerated as fear clutched at her heart. What if it had been her child?

What choice would she make?

Operate on the slim chance he or she might survive?

'We'll get him through,' she said fiercely to Evan. 'We can fix acidity—we can fix anything!'

She was aware of his eyes, a nice grey colour, studying her, as if trying to make out what had brought on this sudden determination, then he said, 'Whatever!' and turned back towards the monitor.

Maybe she'd have to get out of this field, she thought, once again pressing her hand to her stomach. But even thinking such a thing worried her. She'd always been able to separate her work and personal selves—always been able to focus solely on work when she was working, even to the extent that she barely gave Phil a glance when he was in Theatre with her.

Well, maybe she did give him the odd glance, but she didn't, when in Theatre, think the lascivious thoughts about him that were likely to pop into her head outside the hospital world!

So all she had to do was to divorce the baby-carrying Maggie from the hospital one, and she'd be fine.

The operation dragged on. The tiny heart was stopped with cardioplegia, so the surgeons could open it up to fix the valves, but because its effect was only temporary, more had to be given after twenty minutes—the timing critical. Everyone was aware of the time, everyone knowing that the longer it stretched, the less chance this baby had of surviving.

Finally, he was taken off the bypass machine and his heart was stimulated, but the little organ refused to beat. Evan bagged the baby, forcing air into his lungs, while the surgeon's hands tried to stimulate the heart into beating.

Collective breaths were held, the air still with a dread anticipation.

'Shock again,' the surgeon ordered, but once again it was Rachel who saw the action.

'No, it's beating,' she said, and Maggie turned to the images on the wall-screens and saw the tiny, stitched heart valiantly pumping.

She had to blink away a tear, and swallow a lump that had risen in her throat.

Good thing the more observant team members weren't around—they'd have caught her out for sure, and her 'ice-cool Maggie' image would have been shattered for ever.

'Do you always get emotional?' Evan asked, and she realised she'd been sprung anyway.

'Hardly ever,' she told him, bringing the hospital Maggie back into place. 'Almost never.'

'I think it's OK to feel something,' Evan said. 'After all, these are babies you're dealing with, and being a woman you must feel some tie.'

Maggie contemplated kicking him hard on his ankle, but decided against it. He was probably only voicing a thought that ninety-nine per cent of men would voice— or at least think—in similar circumstances.

'Six hours—not too bad,' the surgeon said, finally stepping back from the table and letting Scott close the wound.

Maggie heard Kurt mutter something about the time on bypass, and knew he was worried about possible brain or kidney damage to the child. Anyone who had ever worked with Alex knew his feelings about not doing more harm than good, and he was adamant that too long on the bypass machine fell into the 'harm' category.

Rachel was assisting Scott now, explaining to him why Alex was fussy about the way the tubes and drains and wires were taped.

'It makes it more comfortable for the baby,' she said, 'and a comfortable baby recovers faster.'

'Does Dr Attwood do that with all his infants?' Evan asked, as he watched the procedure. 'Has he ever done any studies on measuring their post-operative comfort—things like pain levels?'

'I don't know about the post-op studies, but he swears post-operative care is just as important as the surgery.'

'Well, that must include post-op pain relief. I need to talk to this man. Where is he?'

'On his honeymoon,' Rachel told him, and gave a little laugh that sounded forced.

Had Rachel had a soft spot for the man with whom she worked so closely? Maggie had never considered it before, assuming, since Rachel and Kurt lived together, that they were a couple.

But she and Phil were now living together, and they certainly weren't a couple.

She shut her mind to these stray thoughts, upset to find her other self intruding yet again at the hospital.

'He's all yours now,' Scott said, and Maggie turned to Evan.

'I guess he's all yours really. You're the person called in.'

'But you're the local,' he said. 'You'll be seeing him in hospital. I guess we should share him.'

'He's arrested again,' Rachel said quietly, and the other theatre sister wheeled the crash cart back close to the baby, while the circulating nurse pressed the alarm button for the surgeon to return.

Surgeons pulled on gloves, the wound was reopened, the baby shocked again. Maggie injected drugs into his veins as the surgeon ordered them, her fingers trembling as she measured out the doses, her heart clinging to hope.

Muttered curses, demands, frantic, dramatic measures to save an infant who'd been born with the odds against him from the start—every member of the team rigid with tension as they willed him to survive.

Babies born with such huge problems die, Maggie reminded herself, but she desperately wanted this one to live.

For Phil's sake so he wouldn't feel badly later.

For her own, because she knew it could have been her baby...

But no amount of stimulation would bring him back and as they left the theatre, for reasons more to do with the stresses of the morning and the long hours in Theatre than her own condition, Maggie found tears sliding down her cheeks.

So she did cry for these babies, she realised, wiping them angrily away before Evan, or anyone else, saw them. But it was too late. The tall man had hooked his arm around her shoulder and drawn her close, and she put her head against his chest and cried for all the babies they couldn't save.

And cried for Phil, who would be devastated but, she guessed, would never cry…

'Very touching,' a cool voice said, and Maggie jerked away from the comfort of Evan's arms to see the man she cried for standing only feet away from them.

'The baby died,' Maggie said bleakly, then realised from the set expression on Phil's face she'd get no sympathy from him.

She got her confirmation in the shrug he gave as he walked towards their rooms.

'Boyfriend?' Evan asked, and Maggie shook her head.

'Colleague,' she explained, but didn't elaborate. Evan would go back to his hospital and get on with his life, while she and Phil would continue to work and live together.

The problem was, she'd get over the death of this baby far more easily than Phil would, for the demons that drove him would always be questioning whether he could have done better—could have saved the tiny boy's life.

She said goodbye to Evan, and was heading for the suite herself, needing a coffee and sugar jolt and a chance to unwind, when he called her back.

'Hey, don't rush off without telling me where I can get a decent cup of coffee around this place. Don't you guys have somewhere you unwind?'

They did, of course, but she had a feeling the atmosphere in the suite of rooms, with Phil there, wouldn't be very conducive to unwinding. More likely they'd get wound even tighter.

'There's the canteen,' she began dubiously, then heard Phil's voice again.

'For heaven's sake, Maggie, take the man into the suite and give him a real cup of coffee. I'm leaving, so you needn't worry about me getting in the way.'

He stalked past them and Maggie watched him go, seeing anger and something else in the stiff set of his shoulders and the swift strides he took.

'They asked him to do the op,' she explained to Evan as she led him into their rooms. 'He believed the baby was too young—that the operation had more chance of success in a month. Statistically, it's true, apparently.'

'Well, the baby died so maybe he feels justified.'

Maggie swung towards her companion, unable to believe he could have meant what he'd just said.

'I hope I'd never feel a baby's death was justification for one of my decisions,' she snapped, and Evan held up his hands.

'Hey, I phrased that badly. Don't jump all over me.' He peered down at her. 'Sure he's not your boyfriend?'

She didn't answer, fussing with the coffee-machine, and he continued, 'All I meant was that he's now been proved right. You're correct in saying it's a terrible way to be proved right, but he was, wasn't he?'

Maggie knew where he was coming from and nodded.

'But I don't for a moment think Phil will see it that way. His torment will be whether he could have done it better, and whether, by refusing to do it, he signed the baby's death warrant.'

'But that's like playing God,' Evan protested, accepting the cup of coffee and adding three sugars to it. 'Assuming you'd do better!'

'This is a stupid conversation,' Maggie said crossly. 'Phil's the last person who'd do a ''playing God'' routine, but he wouldn't be human if he didn't have some what-if questions rattling in his head.'

She stirred her coffee and shifted the conversation to Evan's work at the Children's hospital, asking about staffing and working conditions, general questions that couldn't possibly lead to an argument.

'Do you realise how late it is?' Evan said some time later. 'As neither of us have eaten, how about we grab a bite somewhere?'

Maggie felt and heard her stomach gurgle obligingly at the mention of food and looked at her watch. It was after nine, far too late to prepare the meal she'd planned for herself and Phil. And by now he was sure to have eaten. Hadn't he said he and Alex, when alone in the house, did their own thing?

'Good idea,' she told Evan, thinking of the added benefit of putting off going home so she wouldn't have to discuss what had happened in Theatre. 'You have a choice of Thai or Italian restaurants within walking distance. I like both so you choose.'

Evan chose the Italian but insisted on driving, although it was only a short distance. Over the meal, they talked shop, Evan expanding on some studies he'd done and what he'd like to do.

'You're probably aware that not so long ago, people believed neonates and infants didn't feel pain, and as recently as 1995 a study showed not all anaesthetists used pain relief during an operation.'

'It depends on the relief and the age of the child,' Maggie said. 'I'm wary of using opioids on premmie babies, but on most infants I use a cocktail of morphine, codeine and fentanyl for pain. I wonder if it's because babies seem to recover so well from really major surgery that we believe they either don't feel pain as much as adults or don't know what it is so it isn't a negative in their recovery.'

She finished her glass of wine and sat back in her chair, suddenly exhausted.

'I really should get going. Tomorrow's a workday and I only shifted house this morning and haven't settled properly in.'

'I could help you settle in,' Evan said, and Maggie caught the suggestiveness beneath the words.

She smiled at him.

'I think I can manage on my own.'

'Fair enough,' he said easily, 'but I'd like it put on record I'm single, uncommitted to anyone at the moment, disease-free and attracted to you. Any chance we might see each other again?'

Maggie hesitated. She'd had a pleasant evening, and had relaxed enough to enjoy Evan's company, but...

'You're seeing someone?'

She looked into his clear grey eyes and couldn't tell a lie.

'No,' she said, 'but I'm a bit up in the air at the moment. I haven't been in Sydney long, and I've just moved house for the third time in two months...'

'It doesn't have to be anything hot or heavy,' Evan said, picking up on her uncertainty. 'A few casual dates to see where things might go—you said you liked dancing, I do too—and I could take you to some great dance places in Sydney. You like the salsa?'

Maggie did and couldn't deny it, so she smiled at him.

'Maybe when I've settled in,' she said, as Evan signalled for a waiter then insisted on paying for their meal.

'I asked you to eat with me,' he reminded her, when she argued.

He drove her the short distance back to Alex's house, where lights downstairs told her nothing. Phil could be down there reading or watching TV—she realised she had no idea what Phil did in his spare time—or he could be out and have left the lights on for her.

'I'll see you to the door,' Evan said, opening his car door.

'Really, there's no need,' Maggie told him, realising she'd never got the key Alex had said he was going to leave for her at the house, and if the front door was locked she'd have to ring the doorbell.

And hope Phil *wasn't* out.

But having Phil open the door to find her and Evan standing there wasn't an appealing prospect either.

She hesitated, but Evan showed no sign of leaving, and by now Minnie had realised someone was outside and was doing a fierce watchdog imitation, yapping furiously from inside.

The door opened before Maggie could make a decision, and Phil stood there, the light behind him throwing his face into shadow.

'Forget your key?'

'Forgot to pick one up. Did you meet Evan properly? Evan Knowles, anaesthetist from the Children's. Evan, this is Phil Park.'

She managed the introduction, watched the two men shake hands—an awkward move for Phil who had quietened Minnie by lifting her into the crook of his left arm—then turned to Evan and offered her own.

'Nice to have met you and thanks for dinner. I'd be

pleased to hear more about your pain studies some time.'

She shook his hand formally, and hoped he get the message this was not the time to say something personal. Not that there was anything between her and Phil—apart from that one night and a pregnancy—but the tension in the air suggested something different.

Something possessive?

Surely not. For all Phil's talk of rose-bowered cottages and domestically devoted families, his dating behaviour suggested he was more a 'why buy a book when you can join a library' man, too scared of commitment to go out with any woman more than once or twice.

'Knowles,' he had growled in acknowledgement of the introduction, then he remained standing in the doorway, glowering like a cloud looking for a parade on which to rain.

'I'll give you a call,' Evan said, then to Maggie's surprise, he leant forward and kissed her on the cheek.

'Quick worker!' Phil muttered, while Maggie watched Evan walk down the path and through the gate—shutting it carefully behind him—then to his car.

Maggie contemplated pointing out to Phil that it was none of his business, then decided she had no desire to continue the conversation. She stepped forward, intending to move past him and up the stairs to her room, but he was too quick, shutting the door and setting Minnie down on the floor, then grasping Maggie's arm.

'But he hasn't a clue how to kiss a woman goodnight, has he?'

He swung her around and, before she had any idea of what he intended, his head descended then his lips claimed hers, so fiercely demanding she had to grasp his shoulder to remain upright.

*Don't kiss him back!*

The warning sounded somewhere in her head but it obviously didn't penetrate to her lips which were clinging to his, not only responding but making demands of their own.

For a few minutes Maggie managed to remain detached so she felt like an onlooker watching this passionate embrace from afar, then the heat the kiss was generating took control and her mind ceased to function.

Minnie saved the day—or night!—her hysterical noise finally penetrating Maggie's consciousness enough for her to pull away from Phil.

'Does she want to go outside?' she asked, too breathless to do anything more than mumble the words.

'She can get outside through the hatch in the back door,' Phil said, and Maggie was pleased to hear his usually precise voice was also a little strangled.

'I'll take her through,' Maggie said, bending to lift the little dog into her arms.

'Thank you,' she whispered when they were out of earshot. She pressed a kiss on the dog's soft downy head.

By the time she returned, Phil was gone, so she turned out the downstairs lights and went up to bed.

Alone.

Though she had doubts that would have been the case had the hot kiss continued any longer…

Agreeing to Alex's request that Maggie move in was obviously the worst thing he'd ever done, Phil decided as he tossed and turned in his bed that night. As if he hadn't had a bad enough day, with the decision not to operate and then the baby's death, then seeing Maggie with that lanky anaesthetist—first crying in his arms, then coming home so late they *had* to have been out to dinner together.

But you didn't need to kiss her, his picky conscience said.

No? libido replied. When that long skinny streak of misery had just pecked her on the cheek? Someone had to show her what a real kiss felt like!

Did you a lot of good! a new voice muttered, and Phil, tired of listening to voices in his head, listened instead for noises in the house. Noises that suggested Maggie might be on her way up to bed.

Alone!

It was better this way—that wasn't a voice, it was common sense, of which he had apparently retained a few shreds.

But his body didn't believe what common sense had suggested. His body longed to once again have Maggie's body tucked against it.

And not just for sex, though he'd be a liar if he said that didn't come into it.

Sure he wouldn't sleep, he counted sutures, spacing them just the right distance apart, and woke to daylight and someone tapping on his door.

'Come!'

The door opened a crack and Maggie peered dubiously inside.

'It's OK, I'm decent,' he assured her, pulling up the sheet to hide his bare chest, although on that one memorable night she'd seen more of his skin than that of his upper torso.

She edged into the room but only far enough for him to see the whole person rather than just the head.

'I'm on my way to work and I wasn't sure if you wanted to be woken. If you were called out during the night and trying to catch up on some sleep, I'm sorry, but I slept in myself and wondered if you might have done the same.'

Maggie sounded so flustered Phil checked to see he was decently covered. His sheet had become untucked, so his feet were poking out the bottom, but unless Maggie had a thing for feet, he couldn't see anything to embarrass her.

Damn! It must be the kiss. How could he have been so stupid? Only yesterday he'd decided how nice it would be to have Maggie as a housemate, then he'd blown the platonic colleague scenario to bits with his behaviour.

'Well, as long as you're awake, I'll be going,' Maggie was saying, still flustered he could tell, but apparently it was by his feet as that was where her gaze had been directed.

Hmm! Turned on by toes? libido wondered, but the real Phil slapped him down.

'Thanks for waking me,' he said. 'I doubt if anyone will be looking for me, but if they are, tell them I'll be there in half an hour.'

As he spoke, memories of the events—the medical events—of the previous day came rushing back, and the depression he'd managed to keep at bay with thoughts of kissing Maggie returned in full force.

'OK, I'll see you later,' Maggie said, and she fled down the stairs, one hand against her stomach as she made silent apologies to her baby.

It was Phil's fault—firstly because he'd slept in and

she'd had to go into his bedroom. Then for leaving his feet on show. Pale, slim, really elegant feet, with straight, well-manicured toes. Except that the second toe was longer than the big toe and Maggie had a sudden image of her baby, not nearly up to growing toes as yet, being born with the same distinctive feet—slim and elegant, with the second toe longer than the first.

As if it mattered what her baby's feet were like, she scolded herself as she hurried up the road to work—hurrying not because she was late but to put physical distance between herself and Phil.

Had she had strange thoughts flipping in and out of her head during her previous pregnancies?

Pregnancy, singular. She hadn't known about the first until she'd had her second miscarriage and had realised she'd been through it before.

And as for toes, in planned pregnancies, most women would have done some genetic comparisons with the baby's father, and toes were almost sure to have come up in conversation.

# CHAPTER FIVE

'AND what are you so deep in thought about?'

Maggie came back to earth to find Rachel standing just inside the gate that led into the hospital grounds.

'Toes!' Maggie told her, smiling when she saw Rachel's surprise.

Her colleague shrugged and said, 'As good a subject for contemplation as any other on a Monday morning,' then linked her arm through Maggie's and continued towards the hospital.

The gesture put all thoughts of toes out of Maggie's head. Rachel had never sought her out before, yet today it seemed as if she'd been waiting for her.

The events of the previous day—the loss of the baby—came flooding back. If the usually super-confident Rachel had felt in need of a little moral support to walk back into the hospital this morning, how much worse must Phil be feeling? Maggie wondered.

Not that Phil would appreciate someone pandering to him, but the questions that had bedevilled him the previous day must still be racing around in his head.

Which would explain his strange behaviour with the kiss. It had been a release of physical tension, nothing more.

'Maggie, you're wanted in the cath lab,' Becky Myles, their unit secretary, said when she walked in. 'Neonate with pulmonary stenosis.'

Maggie dropped her handbag into a desk drawer and grabbed her coat. The catheterisation lab was just off

63

the adult ICU, a room with a big glass window behind which the technician sat, talking through a microphone to the medical staff and controlling the huge X-ray machine that hung above the operating table. Pictures from the machine were visible on screens on the wall, so the person performing the procedure, which entailed passing a wire from the groin of the patient up into the heart, could see where the wire was going.

Babies were sedated before the procedure to keep them still, and with newborns the amount of sedation was critical, which was why the cardiologist had called Maggie in.

'The echo shows a problem with the pulmonary artery valve so blood's building up in the right ventricle instead of heading for the lungs,' the woman cardiologist told Maggie. 'I can usually open it with a balloon—it's a temporary measure but saves operating on a neonate.'

Maggie intubated the baby carefully, mentally apologising to the tiny scrap of humanity for the things she was doing to her. She wondered whether the cardiologist's words had a hidden meaning, whether the woman had heard of Phil's refusal to operate, though this was a different problem—or the same problem, but with the valves in a different artery.

Maggie watched the baby, worried about the rising blood gas levels, then glanced at a screen to see the wire inching up the blood vessel towards the heart. Once the wire reached its destination, a hollow tube would be slipped over it and the wire withdrawn, then a tiny balloon on the end of the tube would be inflated with water forced down the tube, and the inflating balloon should force the valves open.

It was delicate, precise work, with risks all along the way.

Maggie knew crossing her fingers wasn't going to make a scrap of difference, but she did it anyway.

Phil was walking up the street, considering whether there was any feasible way he could move from Alex's house and so escape life with Maggie, when his pager vibrated in his pocket.

'Hospital! Well, I'm nearly there,' he said, only realising he'd spoken aloud when two boys on their way to school walked carefully around him.

He picked up his speed, striding now, wondering what lay ahead of him this morning. At least thinking about escaping life with Maggie had stopped him thinking about yesterday's disaster.

Jenny Payne, the staff paediatric cardiologist, met him near the ICU.

'Newborn with a huge heart murmur—the echo shows a faulty valve on the pulmonary artery. I catheterised her to try to open it with a balloon, but it won't open,' she explained, handing him the case notes—a thickish file already, although the baby was only hours old.

*Déjà vu*! Phil thought. Another balloon valvuplasty that didn't work.

'Let me check these and talk to Becky. We have a four-year-old booked in for a first-stage repair of a tetralogy of Fallot, but there's no reason we can't delay that slightly and do the baby first.'

'You'll do the baby?'

Phil closed his eyes for a moment and told himself to remain calm.

'Jenny, the baby needs a shunt put in to get blood

from her heart to her lungs. Of course I'll do it. We've done three or four in the time we've been here. Why wouldn't I do it?'

She looked embarrassed, as well she might, and Phil took pity on her.

'A shunt is a minor op to keep the baby going until we can do a more complete repair. What Dr Ellis—I assume you've heard about the argument I had with him yesterday that you're looking so jittery?—wanted was a different matter altogether. He wanted me to do major surgery of a kind that has been proved to be more successful when the infant's older.'

'I know that,' Jenny said, 'and I should have known better than to listen to the stories Ellis has been circulating, but he's a dangerous enemy to have, Phil, so watch your step.'

Something else to keep his mind off Maggie, Phil told himself as he took the notes to the ICU desk, spread them out and looked at what they knew so far about Baby Creagh.

The team would already be preparing for the tet but if Maggie hadn't done the pre-med on their patient, a stalwart little boy called Pete, they could do the baby first.

He bundled up the notes and headed for their rooms, finding Becky there and alerting her to the change in schedule. She paged Maggie first, then Rachel, who would tell the others.

'We won't need Kurt for this first one,' Phil told her, as the phone rang on her desk.

Becky nodded and spoke into the phone.

'Maggie's on her way,' she said to Phil as she put down the receiver then lifted it again as the second page was answered.

Phil nodded and, notes in hand, left the rooms. He was at the sink in the theatre suite, scrubbing furiously at his arms, when Maggie came in. The hospital Maggie, all dedication and efficiency! He could handle this.

'I did the anaesthetic on Baby Creagh when Jenny did the cath. We had to use bicarb to neutralise acidosis even in such a short procedure. I'll have it on hand but be prepared for fibrillation if she's still unstable.'

Phil turned towards her, holding his dripping hands high in the air.

'Thanks, Mags,' he said. 'We'll watch it.'

And though this was the hospital Maggie he was talking to, he couldn't help but notice anxiety in her soft dark eyes and a tightness in her usually full and luscious lips.

Hospital Maggie with full and luscious lips? He was definitely losing his grip.

But the tightness bothered him more than his reaction.

'Are you all right? Are you still thinking about yesterday?'

The lips flashed into a smile.

'Depends what bit of yesterday you mean!' she said cheekily, then she darted off, leaving him wondering if she could possibly have meant the kiss.

And if so, did that mean she might consider resuming a relationship with him?

'Gore-tex shunt?'

He turned, arms still dripping water, to find Rachel hovering behind him.

'I'm sorry, what did you ask?'

'Nothing complicated,' she said with a smile. 'Just wondering if you'll use a Gore-tex shunt or do you want to try one of the new ones that rep brought in the other day? The information he had on them and rec-ommendations from surgeons back home all sounded good.'

Pleased to be able to focus on work, Phil considered the question. The new shunts had also been demon-strated at a conference he'd attended recently and looked good.

'Put a range of both out and we'll see. It would be good if we can find one of either make that is the exact size.'

From the beginning of his time with Alex, he had learned the importance of doing the little things right. He explained this to Scott a little later, when Scott had made an incision, not midline, but a small cut between two ribs on the side of the baby's chest.

'We're already invading this infant's body and put-ting in something that doesn't belong there, so the least we can do is make it the right size, put it in the right place and cause minimum disruption to the proper pat-tern of her blood vessels.'

With the light angled so he could see into the small hole they'd made, he inserted probes into an artery and a vein to keep an eye on the pressure in each, then carefully clamped the baby's subclavian artery, cut a small nick, and with swift but careful stitches sewed the shunt into place. Then did the same thing with the pulmonary artery, attaching the little tube with preci-sion. Blood would now bypass the blocked valves and be shunted into the lungs of the baby, picking up ox-ygen there and bringing it back to the heart to be cir-culated through the body.

Maggie's report showed all was well, and Phil felt a huge sense of relief, although this was little more than a minor procedure compared with what he would be doing later.

'There, that should hold her for a while,' he said. 'When she's a bit older—eighteen months, if she can make it that far—we'll give her a new valve and remove the shunt. There's a lot of work being done now on replacing aortic valves with working pulmonary valves and putting a new man-made valve in the pulmonary artery, which takes less pressure so the valve doesn't need to be as strong. They do it a lot on adults but it's still experimental with children, although lab tests suggest the transferred valve will grow with the child and save more surgery later on.'

Scott shook his head.

'I can't believe the stuff I'm learning from you and Alex.'

'Make the most of it,' Phil told him. 'I'm still learning but Alex is one of the best there is. And learn from Rachel, too—you won't find a better theatre assistant than her anywhere. It's my belief she could do my job as well as I can, if not better.'

The atmosphere was suddenly light-hearted, Rachel giving a huff of laughter and tension Phil hadn't known he'd been feeling draining from his body.

'OK, crew, take a break and be back in…'

He turned to Maggie, knowing she'd need to see young Pete before he came to Theatre.

'When?'

'Better give me an hour—I want to keep an eye on this baby for a while, then make sure there's a nurse available to sit with her. After that, there's pre-med for Pete. Yes, an hour. We'll still only be about forty-five minutes later than we'd originally scheduled.'

Maggie hoped she sounded more together than she

felt. The tension in Theatre when the operation had begun had suggested everyone had heard the stories Dr Ellis had spread. The worst of these was that Phil had choked—refused to do the operation because he'd been afraid he'd fail. No mention of the age of the baby or the statistics that backed up his decision not to operate.

So all the unit members had been on edge and the theatre had seemed to vibrate with tense expectations.

But Baby Creagh was fine, the operation to insert the shunt successful—although once again Maggie found herself surreptitiously crossing her fingers.

She uncrossed them and patted her stomach, telling the multiplying cells in there it must be their fault she was doing such foolish things. At least, she hoped it was the hormone havoc they were creating within her, not a symptom of something more permanent.

She walked with the baby back to the ICU, although she didn't expect her to be in there long. She hooked her up to the in-room ventilator and monitor, checked her blood saturation levels then stood and watched the infant until her anxious parents came in.

'Is she feeling any pain?' the mother asked, and Maggie shook her head, though since Evan had spoken of his desire to study pain in infants, she'd begun to wonder just how they could tell.

Stress leading to acidosis in the blood, she supposed. Or maybe brain activity if they had the infant's head wired to a monitor.

But wires might cause their own anxiety in the infant, so how could they tell what they were measuring?

'Are you worried about her?'

The question made her turn from where she'd stopped outside Baby Creagh's room, pondering these things, to face the questioner.

Phil!

'No, she's good. I was thinking about Evan—'

She stopped because unless she wanted to yell her thoughts at Phil's departing back, there was no point in saying anything more. He'd swept away as if summoned to a dire emergency.

Because she'd mentioned Evan's name?

Why should that upset him?

He'd made no attempt to pursue their relationship beyond that one night, so it was obvious it had meant nothing to him—beyond, possibly, a little embarrassment.

So he couldn't be jealous…

Puzzlement turned to anger. Here *she'd* been, feeling sympathetic and supportive towards him, and he'd walked away from her in a huff.

'Well, he can stay huffy,' she muttered to herself, making her way back to the rooms for a coffee before seeing little Pete to prepare him for the lengthy operation that lay ahead of him.

She walked into the rooms to find Phil there, with a surgeon from the Children's who'd assisted Alex in an operation some weeks ago, and, of all people, Evan Knowles.

Maggie greeted them politely, made herself coffee, then excused herself, explaining she had work to do. She supposed it was inevitable Evan would follow her out.

'When Phil asked Dave to assist, he—Dave, that is—asked me if I'd like to come along. I haven't seen a tet repair and he knew I'd be interested.'

'It's a complex procedure,' Maggie told him, 'and long, because there's so much that has to be repaired—the pulmonary valves, shifting the aorta, fixing whatever holes there are between the atria or ventricles. This is just the first stage. Pete will have two more operations after this before his heart can function as normally as possible.'

Evan loped along beside her while she explained this, then she introduced him to the little boy who needed their help to lead a normal life.

'Pete, this is Dr Evan. He's going to help me watch over you while you're asleep.'

Pete extended his hand and gravely shook Evan's, his short, slightly clubbed fingers lost in Evan's big palm.

'How do you do?' Evan said politely, and Maggie gave him full marks for treating this special patient with respect.

She explained to Pete what she was going to give him—'to make you feel a bit sleepy'—and how he would feel when he woke up.

'Dr Evan might visit you again after the operation,' she said, thinking the four-year-old might be able to articulate some of what he was feeling.

'I'd like to do that if it's OK with you,' Evan said, and Pete nodded.

'But Dr Phil will visit me, too?' he asked, anxiety screwing up his little face.

'Of course he will, and so will I. We'll all visit you,' she assured him.

She gave him the syrup that would be quickly absorbed into his bloodstream then unhitched the shunt in his hand from the drip line and got him ready to be moved to Theatre.

His mother had left the hospital earlier, having to see to her other four children, but Pete's father arrived before they took him away.

'How are you going, soldier?' he asked, his voice gruff with concern for his boy.

'Fine, Dad,' Pete managed to say, then Maggie explained she'd already sedated him.

'It's a long procedure, Mr Barron,' she said. 'You could go home and someone can phone you when he's nearly ready to come out.'

The big man shook his head.

'No, I need to be here, near him,' he said. 'I know that sounds stupid because he won't know if I'm here or not, but I've got to stay. My wife, too—she'll be back, just as soon as she's fed the baby and her mother comes to mind the other kids. We're all kinda upset, although we've always known he'd have to have these operations.'

His voice broke as he said the words, and Maggie reached out and touched his shoulder.

'Of course you are,' she said gently, 'but Pete's in the best of hands. No one could do this operation better than the two experts he'll have in there.'

Mr Barron rubbed his hands across his face.

'I know that,' he said, his voice hoarse with emotion. 'I can only thank God for them.'

A nurse arrived to move Pete to Theatre, and Maggie excused herself to go with them. Evan followed her, although she was hardly aware of his presence, her entire being concentrated on what lay ahead of them.

This operation *had* to be successful. For Pete's sake, and for his family's—they were all counting on it. And once again she thought about the burden of responsibility and the pressure family expectations placed on the shoulders of specialists like Alex and Phil.

How did they do it? Day after day, working to save

the lives of children? Knowing full well that one slip and the baby died?

Sometimes they died anyway, and that was another matter. How did they cope with the deaths?

Where in their inner selves were all those dead babies locked away?

'They're in my head, every one of them, and sometimes at night I think I can hear them all crying.'

It was six hours later and Maggie had asked Phil the question. They were sitting on the bed in the on-duty doctors' room of the PICU. Phil would stay the night, getting up at regular intervals to check on Pete, while Maggie was about to leave the hospital but reluctant to go home to an empty house when she was so full of emotion after the operation.

'But what you did today was textbook perfect. Dave said he'd seen Alex do the same op in the US but yours was even more beautiful.'

'Beautiful!' Phil snorted the word. 'We mess around in a small heart and leave it stitched and scarred, and someone calls it beautiful!'

Maggie shifted closer to him, sensing something very like despair in the way he spoke, while his words about the crying babies still echoed in her head and ached heavily in her chest.

'It *is* beautiful when you can take a mistake of nature and fix it so completely it looks as if that's how it always was. Yes, there are sutures and there'll be scar tissue, but when that little boy sits up in bed and smiles at you, and his lips are pink, not blue, won't that still some of the crying in your head? Won't his laughter— and we all know Pete can laugh—give you enough pleasure to cancel out at least one unavoidable death?'

Phil turned towards her.

'You'd think it would, wouldn't you?' he said, sounding so harsh and un-Phil-like she put her arms around him and drew his head down onto her shoulder, holding him tightly to her in an effort to banish his ghosts.

Not a good thing to do from her point of view as her body seemed to think this was a romantic embrace, not a comforting one, but she massaged his shoulders—so tense still—and kneaded her fingers into his scalp.

'Come on,' she teased, 'where's the post-op euphoria we shared after the transplant on Amy? You're usually on a high after an operation. Alex is the one who suffers letdown.'

'If I cheer up you'll stop massaging, and it feels like bliss, Mags,' he said.

'I won't stop,' she promised.

He lifted his head and she saw his eyes were smiling again—for the first time in what seemed like ages.

'You could massage lower down,' he said cheekily, and Maggie felt herself blush for the first time since she'd been fourteen and had walked in on a boy cousin in the shower.

'I only do shoulders on Mondays,' she told him, shifting so there was a space between them, though the air seemed so hot she might as well still have been touching him. 'Turn a bit so I can get at you.'

Phil chuckled and Maggie felt her cheeks heat again, but she ignored the connotation he'd put on her words and dug her fingers into the tight trapezius muscles stretching from his neck and sweeping down across his shoulders.

She remembered how her mother had massaged her neck and shoulders when they'd been tight from studying or working on an assignment on the computer, and wondered if Phil heard the babies crying because there was so much emptiness inside him. Did the crying echo through the spaces that in Maggie's life were filled with the love of her family and the memories of the joy and laughter they'd shared?

He was right about his image of home, whether he'd considered it consciously or not, she thought with a certain degree of bleakness. He needed the security of a stay-at-home wife and a family clustered around his feet, to fill him with the love he'd missed out on in his childhood. Surely then he would no longer hear the babies crying.

'Ouch! Getting a bit rough there.'

Maggie patted the place she'd probably bruised, digging in deeper when she'd realised where her thoughts had led.

'Sorry. Well, you're just about done. I want to check on Pete before I go.'

Phil turned to her again.

'We could both do that then have dinner in the canteen,' he suggested, and though a faint replica of the twinkle remained in his eyes she sensed he needed company and agreed.

And by the end of the meal, when they'd relived the tricky moments of the operation and laughed about the translation difficulties between English English and Australian English, Maggie felt peace had been restored between them and, providing she kept her innermost thoughts and feelings about Phil hidden from view—and her body stopped reacting to every casual touch—they could coexist as housemates in an enjoyable and companionable manner.

'It's dark, I'll walk you home,' Phil said as they were leaving the canteen.

'Don't be silly. It's not far and I've often walked back to Annie's in the dark.'

'I need some fresh clothes anyway,' Phil told her, 'so don't argue.'

He put his arm around her waist and steered her towards the hospital exit.

His touch sent pent-up tremors of excitement flooding through Maggie's body—so much for not reacting. She'd managed to hold lascivious thoughts at bay while she'd massaged him, thinking about the inner man, not his body, but just one touch had let them loose and she wondered if she'd have to revise her opinion about their coexistence!

She moved away from him as soon as they were outside, then shivered in the cold night air.

'You forget it's winter outside when you're shut in the hospital all day,' she complained, pulling a jacket out of her bag and shaking it free of creases.

'Winter!' Phil scoffed, lifting his arms and sniffing the night air. 'You call this winter? Four degrees of frost, a sudden storm that deposits fourteen inches of snow overnight, sleet that cuts into your bones—that's winter. This, Dr Walsh, is nothing more than a bracing summer evening.'

He took her jacket from her and held it while she put it on, then he wrapped it around her and gave her a tight hug.

'That's nothing more than a thanks-for-having-dinner-with-me hug,' he explained, when she stiffened in his arms. 'I had a few demons that needed exorcising and your company helped me do it.'

Ho! Back to coexisting in harmony, Maggie thought.

She might be having licentious thoughts about the man, but he saw her as a colleague, nothing more. Oh, he'd be willing enough to hop into bed with her again—she had no doubt on that score—but for Phil it would mean nothing while for her it would be torment of the worst kind—a tempting taste of what she couldn't have…

Minnie's almost hysterical delight when they opened the front door made Phil feel terrible.

'I should have come down earlier and fed her,' he said, lifting the little dog into his arms and cuddling her. 'Instead of all that navel-gazing you were kind enough to put up with.'

'She's been fed,' Maggie told him. 'I phoned Rod and asked him to come up. He has a key he keeps for the dog-walker so she can get in to collect Minnie each day.'

Phil knew he should have been relieved, but instead felt a contrary dissatisfaction. He could pinpoint it, too. Maggie talking to Rod.

He put Minnie down and took the stairs two at a time, wanting to get clean clothes and get out of the place—if only so his thoughts could fester in peace.

OK, so she'd rung him about the dog—fair enough—but for some weeks he'd harboured the idea that Maggie might be keen on Annie's father, and this chance remark niggled him.

The same way that lanky Evan Knowles irritated him!

Maybe he needed a psychiatrist or psychoanalyst. Someone to sort out his head which, though relatively uncomplicated in the past, had been getting some very strange ideas lately.

He chose clean clothes, packed them in a small overnight bag, put toiletries in with them then headed back downstairs.

Minnie and Maggie were in the kitchen, Minnie cavorting in circles around Maggie's feet while Maggie picked up what looked like the entire contents of the kitchen tidy from the floor.

'Problem?' he asked, and Maggie looked up and grimaced at him.

'She may have been fed but Minnie obviously felt food wasn't enough and showed her disapproval of our late arrival home by strewing the contents of the kitchen tidy across the floor.'

She dumped the last piece of rubbish into a plastic garbage bag, tied the top of it and washed her hands.

'Let's hope it's not a new habit she's developed,' Phil said, then added, 'What a bad dog!' to Minnie who was now leaping around his feet.

'I'll put the bin on the table tomorrow morning just in case,' Maggie told him, and smiled as he continued to tell off the dog.

'I don't think she understands the concept of "bad dog",' she said. 'I tried to point out the error of her ways and she seemed to think she'd been extraordinarily clever to have spread it all so far.'

'Do you want me to run a mop over the floor before I go?' Phil asked, and Maggie laughed.

'To prove how domesticated you are? No way—you get back up to the hospital to Pete, I'll mop.'

She smiled at him, and Phil saw the teasing laughter in her face and read it in her night-dark eyes.

'OK?' she said. Just one word. But again Phil felt that little hitch in the region of his heart and wondered what was happening to him.

Could he be falling in love with Maggie? he wondered as he walked back to the hospital.

Now, that *would* be a disaster! He didn't need a psychiatrist or psychoanalyst to tell him that. He wasn't in the first flush of youth and knew all about genetics, so he was reasonably sure he'd inherited enough of his father's genes to make him a poor prospect in the love stakes. It wasn't that he deliberately set out to hurt the women he fell in love with, it was just that, for him, love didn't seem to last and, having lived with pretence in his parents' marriage, he knew he couldn't live a lie himself.

So he'd always been honest. He'd told the women— there had only been three, not three dozen—that he no longer loved them, and had seen their hurt first-hand. Since the third of them he no longer dated seriously— just going out a few times with women who knew that was all a relationship with him would be. Something pleasurable, he hoped, but casual.

But Maggie was different. There was nothing casual about either the hospital Maggie or the dancing Maggie. Both lived their lives with intensity and passion, though the hospital Maggie kept these emotions under tighter control.

'So, Minnie Min, what do I do about that man?' Maggie asked when she'd finished mopping the kitchen floor and had decided to forgive the mischievous dog.

'It's the baby,' Maggie explained because the dog was the most receptive audience she knew and wouldn't pass on any secrets. 'I know I should tell him, and I will—if I manage to hang on to it—but when I do that, is he likely to go all Sir Galahad about it and insist on marriage?'

The thought of marrying Phil sent a shiver of delicious delight through her body, but a loveless marriage would be infinitely worse than no marriage at all, and she would hate to see Phil tied up that way because it would mean he'd be living out his worst nightmare—a replica of his parents' marriage.

'I'll just wait and see,' she finally decided, sharing this with Minnie in case the dog was worrying. 'If I do go past three months, it will still be wintry and I can bundle up in warm clothes and no one will notice for a while—though I guess even without warm clothes no one will notice for a while.'

But that thought depressed her immeasurably. Being pregnant was a great and joyous thing—exciting and exhilarating. She should be shouting her news from the rooftops, not moping in the kitchen, sharing the news with a dog, even if the dog in question did have understanding eyes.

She pressed her hand to her stomach and offered a silent apology to the small cluster of cells busy multiplying inside her.

'I'll tell my mother when I get to three months,' she promised them. 'She'll be excited with me.'

*For a moment or two*, Maggie amended in her head, *until she asks me who the father is and when we're getting married.*

But if all went well and she had the baby, her family would stand by her, so Baby Walsh would have heaps of cuddles and grow up wrapped in family love.

'But we're getting way too far ahead of ourselves,' she said, ruffling the curls on the top of Minnie's head. She lifted the little dog and put her in her basket, then turned out the kitchen light and made her way upstairs.

Passing Phil's room, even knowing he wasn't in it,

she couldn't help but feel a twinge of regret. Here they were, two adults, who'd already enjoyed a night of explosive and satisfying love-making and could, as they were living in the same house, continue to enjoy such nights, yet they were sleeping in their own rooms—alone in their big beds.

But in her heart she knew that spending even one more night in Phil's arms, in either of their beds, would only deepen what she felt for him, which would undoubtedly lead to her being tempted if the time came that he asked her to marry him. And there they'd be, she head over heels in love with a husband to whom the concept of love was foreign.

*Although if I did the stay-at-home-wife thing and provided him with all the love he needs, surely that might work*, a sneaky inner voice said temptingly, but Maggie knew it wouldn't. She'd feel cheated and become frustrated, and what kind of mother would she then be for her baby?

'You're a problem,' she said, patting her stomach, but she said it with love because she couldn't help the excitement building inside her, even if she wasn't shouting it from the rooftops.

Yet!

# CHAPTER SIX

THE solution to one of her problems, when to tell Phil she was pregnant, came much sooner than Maggie had anticipated. Not because morning sickness struck with such intensity she couldn't hide the fact but because of one small dog who had suddenly decided she didn't like being left alone in the house.

True, Mayarma, the dog walker, called for Minnie every day and took her for a long walk and play in the park, but Minnie still felt obliged to show her dissatisfaction with her lack of company by strewing rubbish across the floor. Remembering to put the kitchen tidy on the bench became as high a priority as locking the front door, but as Minnie rarely ventured upstairs, Maggie hadn't given a thought to the small waste-paper basket in her *en suite* bathroom.

'Not again,' Phil groaned as they came home together one evening and opened the door to see a trail of rubbish leading down the stairs. 'My turn to do the clean-up,' he said. He lifted the milk they'd bought on the way home out of the plastic bag, passed the bottle to Maggie and kept the bag for the rubbish.

Maggie, admonishing the little dog all the way, went on through to the kitchen to put the milk in the fridge.

With the door still open she pulled out some chicken breasts and an assortment of vegetables. She'd make a stir-fry and rice—easy meal to prepare yet filling enough to satisfy Phil's appetite. Her own appetite was on the wane at the moment, and though she wasn't feeling nauseous at any stage of the day she also wasn't hungry.

She was slicing celery into long julienne strips and pushing them across to sit beside the similarly sliced capsicum on the cutting board, idly admiring the contrasting colours, when she heard Phil come down the stairs, across the polished wooden floor of the living room and into the kitchen.

Would she always be as conscious of his footsteps?

Would her heartbeat continue to accelerate as he got closer, so whenever she was in his presence there was turmoil in her chest?

Should she leave work now—return to Melbourne—before this whole 'love for Phil' condition got totally out of hand?

He didn't say anything and she kept chopping, assuming he was getting a light beer out of the fridge, but she didn't hear the fridge door. In fact, she heard a chair scrape across the tiles and guessed he'd just sat down.

Determined not to give in to the urge to turn and look at him—looking at him at home was so different to looking at him at work—she pulled a head of broccoli towards her and began to separate it into small flowerets.

'Stir-fry and rice OK with you?' she asked, when the silence became too much to bear.

'Fine,' he said.

Hard to read much into a single word.

Was he reading something that he hadn't said more? Hadn't started some general conversation about work or housekeeping, the two subjects they both seemed to feel were safe?

Maggie began to slice the beans.

'Alex and Annie are due back Saturday.' Great—tell the man something he already knows, why don't you? 'I wondered if we should have them down for dinner Saturday night. And Rod, of course. And Henry if he's well enough to have Minnie clambering all over him. I thought I could do a Japanese meal. Is Alex into raw fish and seaweed and things like that?'

When silence greeted this offering Maggie realised there was something going on behind her back she didn't know about. Something she guessed she didn't want to know about!

She stopped cutting, terrified her suddenly trembling hands would send the knife slicing through her fingers if she continued.

Then she turned around to see Phil sitting exactly where she'd envisaged him at the table. On the table, on a tissue, directly in front of him, was the test strip from the second pregnancy kit, with its telltale stripe across it.

'I realise it's none of my business, and a gentleman should simply have dropped it into the bag with the rest of the rubbish. But then I thought about repercussions, your work as part of Alex's team, and also how you might be feeling yourself—up here without your family and as far as I know no man in your life to support you—so I thought maybe it would be best to talk to you about it.'

His eyes, expressionless, were fixed on Maggie's face as he said these things, and as she could feel her blood pounding through her veins, she guessed her cheeks were, by now, a bright, rosy red.

She opened her mouth to say something—anything, yell at him perhaps for not minding his own business—but no words came out.

'I won't hassle you, Mags,' he said gently, 'but I do want you to know that I'm here for you. I'll help you any way I can, listen if you need to talk things through, make cups of tea for you in the morning if you're sick—be there for you.'

He paused to smile at her, but it was the saddest smile Maggie had ever seen and its sadness pierced her heart.

'After all, isn't that what being housemates is all about?'

It was at this stage Maggie realised there was something wrong with the conversation.

Oh, she was hearing it all right, it just wasn't coming through in her head as clearly as it might be. Like trying to see through thick fog and catching only blurry outlines, what she was hearing was distorted in some way.

'Have you told the guy?'

The fog lifted—though in her head, not his. He certainly hadn't the foggiest notion that the baby might be his.

And why should he? They'd used protection, but somehow something had happened and it hadn't been enough…

Phil thought he'd got through the conversation remarkably well. His first instinct on seeing the test strip had been disbelief. How could Maggie have made love to him when she was seeing someone else?

Pain—jealous pain—that she *was* seeing someone else intervened!

Then anger had begun to smoulder—not at Maggie but at the someone else. Where was the blighter? He certainly wasn't around at the moment because Phil knew Maggie, apart from an occasional night out at a club, was, at the moment, leading as non-existent a social life as he did.

Was the father someone she'd been seeing in Melbourne?

Dancing with?

Questions bombarded him, which was just as well as they stopped him thinking about the nauseous feeling creeping over him, as if Maggie's pregnancy was a personal disappointment.

Anyway, he'd got this far, made his stand—he'd look after her, that was what he was saying—but she obviously hadn't caught onto the gist of it for she was still staring at the strip on the table in front of him with a kind of mesmerised horror.

Pity for her pushed him to his feet, and he walked around the table, put his arm around her and led her to a chair.

'I'm sorry if you'd have preferred I didn't say anything, but I wanted you to know I'm on your side— that you're not alone in this.'

He pressed a kiss to the top of her head, and thought ugly thoughts about the man who'd abandoned her. And abandoned she must have been to be keeping the pregnancy a secret.

Although maybe she'd only just found out.

Or maybe she hadn't kept it a secret. Maybe she'd told a lot of people, just not him.

Now disappointment surged through the turmoil of emotions he was suffering.

She pushed away from him and sank down into the chair he'd pulled out for her, then rested her elbows on the table and pressed her head into her hands, so all he could see was the pale nape of her neck where her dark hair parted and fell to each side.

Inappropriate thoughts about kissing that pale sliver

of skin formed in his head, but he held them at bay with practicality.

'Is there something I can get you? A coffee—no, best you don't have coffee! How early in pregnancy do you have to give up coffee? Do you know? I'll look it up for you. That'll probably be the hardest part for a caffeine addict like you. I'll make a cup of tea.'

Pleased to have something to do, he crossed to the bench, filled the kettle and turned it on. Seeing beans half-sliced, he finished them while the kettle boiled then made two mugs of tea and carried them across to the table, tea bag strings still dangling over the sides.

'I've never made tea for you before so don't know how you take it,' he said to the still bent head. 'Black, two sugars, like you do coffee?'

He was being so helpful Maggie knew she had to respond. But how? By telling him she hated tea and would sooner drink poison?

Talk about biting the hand that fed you!

'What you could do is get rid of that test strip,' she managed to say, her voice croaking out from somewhere near her boots.

'Oh, dear,' she heard Phil say as he bundled the offending article back into its tissue and dropped it in the kitchen bin. 'Do I take it you're not happy about this pregnancy? Are you thinking about a termination?'

Maggie sighed and lifted her head.

'How could I possibly be happy about it?' she demanded, knowing her words and her tone were too sharp when concern registered in his eyes. 'The six months I worked with you and Alex in Melbourne were great, but to be offered the opportunity to do another twelve months with him was better, in my opinion, than winning Lotto! With his name on my CV my dream of getting a fellowship at a hospital in the US might just have come true! Now this!'

He sat down opposite her and jiggled his tea bag in his tea.

'So, you're thinking termination?'

His voice was so full of sympathetic understanding she wanted to slap him, but she didn't, making do with a good yell instead.

'No, I'm not thinking termination!' she roared, frightening Minnie out of the room. The sight of the little dog scuttling to safety calmed her down somewhat and she added in a more reasonable voice, 'I'm sorry. This is bad timing but nothing more than that. I've only known a week—that test was the second one—and I need time to get used to the idea myself. And it's early days yet—think of the statistics, I may not hold onto it—but termination?'

Her anger died away completely and she shuddered, then hid it with a weak smile.

'It fits with some people's lives and at another time, under other circumstances, I might have considered it. But I've seen too many babies die, Phil—babies I've not been able to save, so, no, this baby is mine and if I can carry it safely through to term, I'm keeping it.'

She realised as she finished the sentence just how fiercely protective she'd sounded, and found that one hand had yet again crept to curl above her stomach.

Ridiculous when the embryo was still not much more than a heart in a curl of developing cells.

Even more ridiculous to get attached when she'd twice miscarried...

\* \* \*

*She must love the father, to be so definite about it. Maybe he's married. Bet if he is she doesn't tell him, she's so damn independent.*

Phil realised he was still jiggling his tea bag and looked down to see the liquid had turned a tarry black. He didn't like tea much at the best of times, but this would be impossible to drink.

Maggie didn't seem too keen on hers either. She was turning the mug in circles the way his nanny had done with the teapot as she'd waited for the leaves to settle.

Had the old woman returned to earth to haunt him that he was thinking about her so often these days?

No, it was Maggie's fault—with all her poking and probing about his home life.

He looked up from the tarry tea to see her watching him—Maggie, not his nanny's ghost.

Consideringly…

'I've never seen you drink tea,' she said, just when he thought their conversation might become deep and meaningful.

'I hate it,' he admitted, and she laughed and pushed her mug across the table to him.

'Me, too,' she said, 'though maybe I'd better get used to it. Or start drinking decaffeinated coffee!' She shuddered. 'Doesn't bear thinking about, does it? And as for the headaches! Believe me, I've tried to give up coffee before and the caffeine-withdrawal headaches are sheer murder. Days and days of them. And I won't be able to take anything to relieve them, so be prepared for a very cranky colleague.'

She pushed the chair back as if the conversation was now finished, picked up both mugs of tea and carried them over to the sink, where she emptied them out.

Then she returned to her cutting and slicing, throwing only the most casual of remarks over her shoulder. 'You didn't say if chicken stir-fry is OK with you?'

So much for sharing with your housemate!

So much for his offer of support!

'Yes, thanks,' he said, glaring at Minnie who'd come back in from the garden and was looking for some attention. Then he left the room, going not upstairs but to the downstairs room Alex had set up as a library. He'd look up some medical books and find out just when things like the mother's caffeine intake became unsafe to a foetus.

Whether Maggie liked it or not, he was going to be with her every step of the way through this pregnancy.

In fact, he was quite looking forward to it. A kind of surrogate fatherhood.

As he pulled down a tome on obstetrics he found himself hoping she wouldn't give up her job too soon—wouldn't move back to Melbourne to have the baby.

Though it was strange to be feeling so proprietorial an interest in it!

Maggie finished chopping the vegetables, sliced two chicken breasts and turned on the heat under the wok. She was concentrating so fiercely on what she was doing—to prevent thinking about the repercussions of Phil's discovery—she didn't notice her pager buzzing on the kitchen table.

'Hospital. A two-week-old being transferred from up the coast—aortic stenosis, picked up late, already treated with a balloon catheterisation that has failed.'

Maggie turned off the gas, tipped her sliced vegetables onto one plate, the chicken onto another, covered both with clingwrap and washed her hands. Personal problems were forgotten as she translated Phil's words into a rehearsal of what lay ahead of them.

For a start, the baby would require the operation Phil had refused to do the previous week, but this time there was no alternative. It was too late for prostaglandin to keep the ductus arteriosis open because the little duct would already have closed and be disintegrating, as it was supposed to do once a baby started breathing air. But a tiny balloon, inserted through a catheter and inflated to force the aortic valves open, had failed to do its job, and Phil would now have to operate to open them or refashion them into working entities.

'Rachel and Kurt on their way?' she asked, pausing in the hall to get her jacket. Phil already had it, and held it out for her to put on. She thought of the hug he'd given her last time he'd helped her into it, and knew this time he was the one who needed the hug.

But he was all business, and she knew he wouldn't appreciate the hug—probably wouldn't even know what it was for!

They walked briskly up to the hospital, at first in silence, each thinking of the tasks that lay ahead, then Phil said, 'Alex is so much better at talking to parents than I am.'

Maggie turned to look at him and saw a deep frown scoring his forehead.

'I wouldn't have thought so. The times I've heard Alex talk, I've wondered why the parents have gone ahead with the op.'

Phil's frown cleared as he offered her a brief smile.

'That's exactly what I mean. He's able to tell them the downside of things so matter-of-factly they accept it, while I hate having to say, ''There's a thirty per cent chance your baby won't come out of this alive.'' I *hate* having to tell people that, Mags.'

Unable to think of any comfort she could offer, Maggie took his hand and squeezed it, and they walked the rest of the way hand in hand.

Within fifteen minutes of the page they were talking to the parents, Maggie anxious to find out about previous procedures the baby had had and what reaction, if any, little Cain had had to anaesthetic.

Maria Cardella, Cain's mother, was sitting by the bed where her little son lay, hooked up to a ventilator and monitor, while Al, the father, paced the room.

'All operations, particularly on infants this young, carry an element of risk. In this case, we will be opening up Cain's chest, cutting through tissue to get to his heart and putting him onto a bypass machine that will put oxygen into his blood and keep blood flowing around his body. The machine has refrigeration that will cool the blood and cool Cain, so eventually we can turn off the machine for a short time to work inside his heart and fix the valve. By cooling him we reduce the demand for blood from other organs in the body.'

Maggie watched the faces of the two parents. They looked as if they were desperately trying to understand what Phil was telling them, but a glazed look in their eyes suggested it was too much information.

Yet they had to know.

'The way valves work is they open up as the heart pumps blood into the arteries, then close so it can't rush back into the ventricles. Because the base of the artery we're concerned with, the aorta, is inside the heart, we have to go in there to fix the valves. Once in his heart, we'll see just how bad his valves are. Hopefully, we can open them up by trimming them a bit, and they'll keep working just fine.'

Or Cain might need new valves grafted in, which would mean more operations as he grew to replace them when they became too small and started to leak.

Maggie, reading carefully through Cain's case notes, thought this but didn't say it. It was hard enough for parents to comprehend that their beautiful new baby had life-threatening problems, then to have to take in what the surgeons were going to do to him and understand enough to give informed consent to the procedure, without complications way down the track being pointed out.

Phil was answering Al's questions now, while Maria sat beside her infant son, fat tears sliding down her cheeks.

'We want you to do whatever you can, and if it doesn't work for him, that's how it has to be,' Al said at last, and Maggie wondered how he would feel when asked to sign the consent form, something a nurse would ask of him as little Cain was being wheeled into Theatre.

'Have you got all you need?' Phil asked, and Maggie, realising he was talking to her, nodded, but stayed in the room and spoke quietly to Maria.

'We'll take real good care of him,' she said, and the woman looked up and nodded, accepting Maggie's word that everything that could possibly be done for her baby would be done.

'I hate it when it's their first baby,' Rachel said, coming into Theatre while Maggie was checking she had all she'd need. 'I mean, they're so excited, first baby and all, then, whammo, some person they don't know is telling them there are terrible things wrong with their new son. *Terrible* things.'

Maggie looked at the theatre sister and saw the despair she'd heard in Rachel's voice mirrored on her face. In the nearly eight months she'd worked with Rachel, Maggie had never heard her upset—or even slightly downbeat.

'Are you OK?' she asked.

'There is no OK!' Rachel said, echoing something surgeons often said in Theatre. In top surgeons' eyes OK was just not good enough. Perfect was their aim and that's how they wanted things to be.

'There is for ordinary humans like you and me,' Maggie reminded her. 'Sometimes OK is as good as you can expect, although there's always hope we'll better it.'

Rachel smiled at her.

'I'm grumpy, that's all. I've been doing this work for eight years and I love it. I'm good at it. I can see things Alex and Phil can't see because they're focussed on what they're doing, and I can react to things when I see them because I've seen enough of all the ops they do to know how it should go, and now I hear the fellow who operated last week—when Phil wouldn't—is telling people things went wrong because of inadequate theatre staff.'

'He what?' Maggie couldn't believe it. 'But he's at Children's—how come the stories are circulating here?'

'By kind favour of the great Dr Ellis, of course,' Rachel snapped.

'And no Annie here to put out the fire,' Maggie muttered, thinking of the damage this could do the fledgling unit. 'But don't take it all personally, Rachel. I'm theatre staff too, I'm sure he's blaming all of us equally. What about Scott?'

'What about Scott?' that man said, coming into Theatre, a bright scarf wrapped around his head and his gown on, but not yet gloved.

'Dr Ellis's rumours,' Rachel said succinctly.

'Oh, that!' Scott said, his usual good cheer dissipating immediately. 'It shouldn't worry you, you work for Alex. What about me? These last two months have been like a revelation. I mean, I liked hearts and had decided cardiac surgery was definitely for me, but this stuff? Watching Alex and Phil work? It's so beautiful. I know for certain now that it's what I want to do, but if I end up carrying the can for that operation, who knows where I'd get another position in paeds cardiac surgery?'

'Damn Ellis!' Maggie said, but inside she felt a growing concern. Paediatric heart surgery required one hundred per cent concentration from everyone in the team, yet here were two members, three counting her, four counting Phil, who were already uptight before the operation began.

'Forget it all,' Kurt said, and Maggie realised she hadn't known he was there. Well, she probably *had* known, but he said so little from behind his machine they tended to take him as another piece of furniture. 'We've got this baby coming in. That's all we need to think about now. Later we'll talk about these rumours and work out a strategy for dealing with them, but the little fellow we're operating on today needs and deserves all of our attention.'

It was the most Maggie had ever heard Kurt say, and

she was impressed. She told him so, then left Theatre, wanting to supervise the transfer of Cain from his room herself.

Scott opened Cain's chest, Rachel sliding the stainless-steel clamps into place and cranking open the rib cage so Scott could go further, cauterising small vessels as he went. He cut open the pericardium, the tough fibrous sac around the heart, and put in a stitch to hold it to the chest wall so Phil would have a clear field around the heart.

Maggie watched her monitors, tensely alert for any change in the baby's status.

She felt rather than heard Phil come into Theatre, then his quiet 'Good job' to Scott confirmed his presence. She glanced his way. With mask and loupe and light all strapped around his head, it was hard to see skin let alone read expression, but listening to his voice, seeing the sure way his hands moved, she doubted he'd heard the rumours.

She prayed he hadn't, because the slightest lapse in concentration could lead to disaster.

Not that there wasn't a little of that. Phil's soft comment 'I've never seen a malformation like this!' was the first indication something was wrong.

'That's the left coronary artery,' he said to Scott and the other registrar assisting, 'and instead of curving around the heart to feed the left atrium and ventricle, it's shunted a large part of itself off into the inferior vena cava. I've read about it but never seen it.'

Without wasting more than a fleeting second wishing Alex was around, Phil began the process of attaching Cain to the bypass machine, first inserting cannulae to take the plastic tube to and from the machine.

Maggie administered the drugs to keep the baby's

blood from clotting and clogging up the machine, and more drugs that prevented the fragile blood cells being damaged, then Cain was on bypass and Phil could tackle the problem of the displaced coronary artery first.

'You have to wonder if lack of blood to the left ventricle has been preventing it pumping effectively enough to push blood into the aorta. Is it possible the valves are OK? Why wasn't this picked up? I wonder if anyone did an oesophageal echo to get a better view. Maggie, did you see one?'

'Not in the notes I read,' Maggie told him, but they all knew notes that followed a baby from one hospital to another were sometimes not complete.

'I guess they put it down to a left ventricle insufficiency—maybe a hypoblast, which is common with aortic stenosis,' Phil continued, almost speaking to himself, so Maggie wondered if he was just thinking it through out loud.

'Whatever they put it down to, it's our problem now, isn't it?' Scott said, and Maggie turned in time to see Phil nod.

She could almost feel his concentration. The problem with moving coronary arteries was that they could kink easily, and once kinked would starve the heart muscles of the blood they needed to keep pumping.

'We can take a vein from his chest if we need to, and use it to repair the artery or replace it,' Phil said as he worked, and Maggie had to admire the fact that he kept explaining what he was doing to Scott and the other registrar even when things were tough.

'Done! Now for the little fellow's heart.'

The bypass machine was turned off to stop it sucking in air when the heart stopped beating, then an injection was given into the coronary arteries to stop the heart. Now Phil worked swiftly, making an incision high up on the left ventricle to reach the opening of the aorta.

Maggie watched her monitors, checked everything was in place for an emergency and did her own monitoring of the tension levels in the room.

Not too tight, she decided, and the quiet buzz of orders suggested nothing major was going wrong.

So far so good!

'Now, make sure you suction all the air out of his heart before we put him back on bypass. We get air into the machine, we put it back into his blood and the poor kid has a stroke.'

Phil the teacher telling Scott what to watch for! He did it well, Maggie realised, and more consistently than Alex did, though both of them, when concentrating on the intricacy of the surgery they performed, would sometimes forget to explain.

'Pump back on,' Phil said to Kurt, when they were satisfied the tiny heart was airtight.

The noise of the pump, this time pumping warmed blood into Cain's body, thumped through the room, a background noise to Phil's quiet voice, telling Scott where he wanted drains and wires and catheters placed.

'OK!' One word, but it signalled it was time to breathe easily again. Maggie saw Phil step back so Scott could close.

Now Maggie, monitoring the atmosphere, could sense a general relaxation in the room.

'He's all yours, Maggie,' Scott said at last, and the surgical staff drifted from the room, leaving the theatre orderly and a junior theatre nurse to clean up the mess they'd left behind.

Rather than shift infants from Theatre to a recovery

room then into the ICU, Maggie kept them in Theatre until she felt it was safe to move them. With little Cain she wanted to wait until she was sure even something as unthreatening as changing his ventilation from the theatre lines to bagging him on the short journey wouldn't compromise his condition.

Twenty minutes later, she was sure he could make the trip safely and called up an ICU nurse and orderly to move him with her. And though the nurse would usually handle the bagging, squeezing air into his ventilator tube using a rubber device they called a bag, Maggie did it herself.

For some reason—and she suspected it had more to do with Phil than being pregnant—she wanted everything to go just right for Cain.

Once in his room she hooked him up to the ventilator again, while the nurse made sure the monitor leads weren't tangled and connected the monitor to the central nursing station.

His parents came in, peering anxiously at the still unconscious baby, and while Maria took the chair beside his bed Al paced.

'The doctor said it went well. He said there could be complications but so far everything's looking good. Is that right?'

Maggie knew she needed confirmation of what Phil had already told her, so she repeated the reassurances, but explained they still had a way to go.

'We'll keep him in here while he's on the ventilator,' she explained, 'but once he comes off that and is breathing on his own, he'll go into the infants' ward where nursing staff especially trained to deal with postoperative cardiac patients will look after him.'

Maria smiled at her.

'Every stage is a little step towards his being better, isn't it?' she said, and Maggie had to agree with her.

Very small steps babies made at times, but each one significant in its own way. It was good for a parent to understand this and take joy in each stage of the recovery.

Maggie left the room, though she knew she'd be back before she left the hospital, checking on how the baby was doing on the ventilator and if there was any sign of distress showing up. But right now the parents needed to be alone with their child and she needed a coffee.

Back in their rooms, the coffee-machine was on but the place was deserted.

'Just how badly are you going to be affected by caffeine?' she asked the embryo developing inside her, then she sighed and drank some water, just in case the word she hadn't heard had been 'badly'!

'Look, decaffeinated coffee-grounds.'

Phil swept into the rooms, waving the packet in the air.

'I knew the canteen served it, so I went down and begged to be allowed to buy some.'

Maggie hid the start of joy his sudden appearance had caused. Hid it with cross words!

'You put that stuff into the machine and you'll be lynched,' she told him.

'No one will know!' he said, still beaming with his cleverness. 'We tip it into the other packet and how would anyone tell? We all drink far too much coffee and we know caffeine's no good for us, so we're really doing the whole team a favour.'

Maggie looked at him, propped herself against a desk and shook her head.

'Phil, you can't do this! Of course people will know. Have you ever drunk decaffeinated coffee? It tastes like—well, it tastes terrible. And people will say so and Becky will get the blame for buying cheap grounds and they'll throw out that lot and buy new, and you can't keep replacing it with decaff!'

He was still holding the packet, but now looked so downcast she had to laugh.

'It's OK—we'll take it home and I'll drink it there.'

'And say what when the others ask what's happened to your eight cups a day coffee habit?'

'I'll tell them I've given up for Lent—no, it's too late for Lent. I'll say I'm doing it for a bet. You bet me I couldn't. They know we're living together, so they'll think it's something that's arisen from that.'

'Living together!' Phil echoed, then he added in a very quiet voice, 'It has other connotations, doesn't it, Mags?'

# CHAPTER SEVEN

MAGGIE got up from the desk and poured herself another glass of cold water from the jug in the small fridge.

'Of course it does,' she said, hoping the word 'bracing' might describe her tone but doubting it. Phil's question had gone directly to her heart, piercing the feeble defences she'd been building up around it. 'That's happened with so many words these days. Take ''partner'', for example. My sister is married, and she's also a partner in a decorating firm, but when I talk about her partner, people assume I mean the man she's living with, who is, in fact, her husband—'

'We weren't talking about words,' Phil interrupted, crossing to where Maggie stood by the fridge, sipping at the cold water, which was having no effect whatsoever on either her nerves or her caffeine craving.

He took the water glass out of her hand and set it down on a table.

'We're talking about living together.'

He put his hands on her shoulders, resting them there, not holding her, but she knew if she moved the pressure might increase.

'Is the father of this baby someone who's important in your life, Maggie? Is he still around? Will he take on the responsibility of a child? Does he want to marry you? Do you want to marry him?'

Yes, yes, I don't know, I don't know and...

If he'd stopped after any of the earlier questions,

Maggie wouldn't have known what to answer, because she hadn't yet thought through all the consequences of telling Phil the baby was his. But the last question was easy to answer.

'No,' she said. 'I don't want to marry him.'

No need to explain she couldn't bear the thought of forcing him into marriage—all she had to do was answer the question.

'You could marry me,' Phil said, and Maggie felt her knees give way, and was sure she would have dropped to the floor if Phil hadn't grabbed her.

'Damn,' he said. 'You haven't eaten and I'm keeping you here, talking.'

He sat her down and rummaged in the cupboard, coming back with a packet of biscuits.

'Eat a few of these then I'll take you down to the canteen for dinner. You've got to start thinking about regular meals, Mags,' he said, opening the fridge and taking out the milk.

He sniffed at it and shook his head, then, still holding the milk carton, he fixed his blue eyes on her and added, 'And I meant what I said about marrying you. Think about it. We're already living together, so the logistics would be simple. We work together, so we understand the stresses of each other's job—none better. The baby will have a hands-on father, and we were great together in bed.'

Maggie felt the air around her grow suddenly colder, then heard Phil repeat the words in a slow, hoarse voice.

'We were great together in bed!'

He stared at Maggie, disbelief and anger vying for control of his features.

Anger won.

'Is it my baby, Maggie?' he asked, his voice soft but no less furious for its softness. 'It is, isn't it? And just when were you going to share this little gem of knowledge with me? Just how long did you intend letting me believe it was someone else's?'

Maggie felt the icy wind of his fury and though she wasn't nearly ready for him to have found out, she found some relief in his anger because it fired hers up as well.

'For heaven's sake, Phil, I've only just found out myself. I'm still trying to come to terms with the fact that a one-night stand with a colleague has ended in a pregnancy! How do you think *I* feel? And what would you suggest I do? Front up one day in the PICU and say, "Oh, by the way, I'm pregnant and it's yours!" Hell, Phil, I know the kind of childhood you had, I know you have your own dreams of the way a marriage should work, and I also know that with the stupid male chivalry you carry around, the first thing you'd do when I told you would be to ask me to marry you.'

Maggie gave a mirthless laugh then added, 'You did that anyway—even thinking it was someone else's baby—so I was spot on, wasn't I?'

'This isn't about my offer of marriage—it's about you not telling me the baby is mine. It's about being a biological cipher all over again—an accident of paternity. Well, that's not going to happen.'

Maggie could feel his anger vibrating around the room, but she couldn't find words to deflect or defuse it, so she sat and let it wash around her.

'My child is going to know his father and know his father's love.'

It's about the baby, Maggie thought sadly. Only about the baby!

Phil finished speaking then heard the silence echoing back to him and realised he'd been shouting.

He glanced at Maggie, saw the way her hand curved protectively across her stomach and felt a momentary pang of compunction.

But she *was* wrong, not telling him.

She was also awfully pale and he remembered how she'd come close to fainting earlier.

'Come on,' he said, taking her by the arm and hauling her out of the chair. 'You need to eat and this is hardly the time or place to be discussing the matter.'

He knew he'd spoken brusquely, but her pale face and the lines of strain at the corners of her mouth had made him feel angry again—and protective—and…

Husbandly?

He had no idea how that would feel, but as he hustled Maggie towards the lift, he decided he'd better find out—and soon. There was no way a child of his would be born out of wedlock.

Was that a hopelessly old-fashioned attitude?

A relic of his upbringing?

Best not to say it to Maggie!

But there was no reason why he and Maggie couldn't make a go of marriage.

He must have spoken this thought out loud, because Maggie's 'Oh, please, Phil!' had to be in response to it.

Though when she added, 'I need food but not so badly I have to run all the way to the canteen,' he wondered if he *had* said it. Maybe she'd been protesting the pace.

Which meant he'd have to say it again!

He slowed down but kept his grip on her arm, telling himself it was a supporting grip not a proprietorial one, though something very like a proprietorial feeling, where Maggie was concerned, was creeping over him.

Would it take over from the 'race her off to bed' feeling he usually had to deal with whenever he was around her?

They had just reached the canteen when both their pagers went off.

'You stay here and eat,' Phil ordered, directing Maggie towards the food counter in the nearly deserted canteen. 'I'll check out what's wrong.'

'Nonsense. It's the PICU so it's sure to be Cain. I'm going straight up there.'

Don't let him die! Maggie found herself praying as they both hurried back to the lift, then felt a moment of shame because she was wishing this for Phil's sake, not the baby's.

But it wasn't Cain who was the problem, but little Amy Carter, who'd received the new heart two months earlier.

'High temp, evidence of infection. I didn't know if you'd have to take her into Theatre so I called both of you,' the sister in charge of the PICU told them. 'I've paged the rest of the team and will ask them to be on standby just in case, but I knew you two would still be in the hospital.'

The little girl had been hooked up to the ventilator and monitors by the intensivist who'd admitted her to the unit. She was obviously very ill, and her mother was shaking with anxiety.

Phil spoke gently to the little girl as he examined her, while Maggie led Mrs Carter to a chair and sat her down.

'She's been through so much,' Mrs Carter cried. 'First, being so sick, she needed the operation and then after it—you remember how everything went wrong for her. Then just as she's getting better, this!'

'Has she been with any other children who might have been in contact with chickenpox?' Phil asked, and Maggie wondered if he'd gone mad. What did chickenpox have to do with anything? The little girl was a heart transplant patient!

'Her cousins have all got it, but I keep Amy away from other children—I mean, she's not long out of hospital and Dr Attwood warned me about infection. I keep her in her own room whenever anyone is visiting.'

But family members would want to see her, Maggie thought, especially inquisitive children.

'She's got chickenpox?' she asked aloud, and Phil nodded.

'I think so. Poor pet! With the scar on her chest still healing, it's hard to tell if the small marks there are the beginning of chickenpox lesions, but I'd say they are. The blood tests should be back soon.'

'Chickenpox! It's only chickenpox!' Mrs Carter said, her voice so full of relief and joy Maggie didn't want to tell her the bad news.

But Phil would have to!

'I'm afraid it's not all that much of a relief,' he said gently, coming to rest against the bed in front of the sitting woman. 'Because Amy is on so many anti-rejection drugs, and these drugs are designed to damp down the body's immune system, a virus like this can take a terrible hold. I'd be lying to you if I didn't tell you we're in for a bad few days. But I'll be here with her all the time, and the staff are trained to be vigilant and know how to keep her as comfortable as possible.'

He took Mrs Carter's hands and continued, 'We haven't got her all this way just to lose her now, so hang in there. It'll be a fight, but it's a fight we can win, so don't give up hope.'

Maggie heard the commitment and determination in his voice and knew what he was thinking—he didn't want Amy Carter crying in his head in the years to come. Her heart ached for him, knowing just how hard he'd take it if he couldn't save Amy, and suddenly she wondered if marrying Phil might not be a good idea. He was deserving of so much love, and she could give it to him. Even if he didn't love her, wouldn't her love help him in some way?

But would he let her love him?

Let her fill some of the empty places in his heart?

She watched him sitting there, talking with Mrs Carter, giving of himself without asking anything in return, then he stood up and left the room, turning back to say to Maggie, 'You should be masked. I'm going to instigate total barrier nursing here, so the infection can't be carried by staff from one room to the next.'

Maggie stayed a little longer then, rather than risk carrying infection into Cain's room, she checked him on the monitors, satisfied herself he was doing well. With exhaustion from the long, long day washing over her, she left the unit and headed home. Forget food, all she wanted was to fall into bed and sleep for ever.

'I don't think I've ever been so pleased to see anyone in my entire life,' she said to Annie and Alex when they, with Annie's dog Henry, appeared at the house late on Saturday afternoon.

Minnie, banned from visiting Henry while he recovered from a series of operations, had gone berserk on seeing her friend, so the two dogs had been banished to the back yard.

Maggie gave both her human visitors a hug and invited them to come through to the kitchen.

'Inviting you into your own house, Alex. That's a bit weird, isn't it?'

'It's your home now—of course you do the inviting. Phil not here?'

'He's at the hospital.'

'Amy Carter?'

Maggie felt instant relief.

'Then he *did* contact you about her,' she said. 'He's so stubborn, I wondered if he would. He kept saying there wasn't anything you could do and you both needed a break and shouldn't be bothered.'

Alex smiled at her while Annie chuckled, and Maggie sensed the love the pair shared and felt a sharp twinge of envy.

'He didn't contact me but I kept in touch with him, not all the time, because the last thing I wanted was for him to think I was checking on him, but just occasionally. Hard to just cut off, you know, and after making excuses to go for a short walk so I could use my mobile, I found Annie had been doing the same, phoning Becky at the unit the moment I went out, just to see how things were going.'

The pair smiled at each other again, their love fairly buzzing in the air around them.

'So you heard about Dr Ellis and his stories.'

As soon as she'd said it she realised they hadn't, for both of them looked puzzled.

'Ellis the cardiologist?' Annie said. 'He doesn't do much work at Jimmie's.'

'Is he the one who wanted Phil to operate on the neonate?' Alex asked, and Maggie nodded, then knew she had to explain. She didn't want either of them walking into what could prove to be a battle, unprepared.

'He's been spreading stories about Phil's refusal to do the op—making out it was incompetence on his part. I know Amy's been terribly sick, and it's been a struggle to get her through this setback, but in some ways it's been good because between her and the scheduled procedures, Phil's been too busy to be worrying about any extraneous matters.'

'Are they affecting the unit?' Annie asked, and Maggie smiled to herself. Just like that, Annie had slipped back into work mode.

'The unit staff are sticking together, confident it was the right decision—but the staff working on the baby ward are finding things tough. I think probably the other staff members were already a little jealous that some staff had been singled out to care for our babies and children, so they've been making snide remarks. But I think the main problem is going to come from the hospital hierarchy.'

'Where there's also been envy of our funding and grumblings about our special treatment all along,' Annie said. 'But it's nothing we can't cope with,' she added determinedly. 'I'd be more worried about how it's affecting Phil.'

Though it wasn't phrased as a question, Maggie knew it was one, and she sighed.

'I honestly don't know,' she admitted. 'He's been all but living at the hospital since Amy was readmitted, and when we do talk it's about work.'

She paused then said to Alex, 'You know him better than the rest of us, but my impression of Phil is that he keeps things bottled up inside him. He's all the bright playboy on the outside—though there's been

precious little of that lately—but what's going on inside is a deep, dark and probably very gloomy mystery.'

Annie, perhaps hearing a faint shadow of despair in
the words, put her arm around Maggie's shoulders and
gave her a hug.

'And I suppose you've just gone on being Maggie,
quietly doing your job and keeping everyone focussed
on work, no matter what's going on around you.'

'Oh, Phil's done that, too,' Maggie said, trying desperately to swallow the lump of misery Annie's sympathy had brought to her throat. Self-pity, that was all
it was. 'And Rachel! Even Kurt's been heard to speak
his mind on the subject. All the team have hung tough.'

Alex had moved to the kitchen bench and was filling
the kettle with water, and Annie took the opportunity
of his distraction to ask another, quieter, question.

'You and Phil?' she whispered, and Maggie shook
her head. Annie was the only person she'd told about
her night with Phil, and eventually Annie—well, all the
team but Annie first—would have to know about her
pregnancy.

If it continued past the first trimester…

But right now there was a crisis at the hospital—two
crises really, although Amy was certainly getting better
so she hardly counted—and that was where everyone's
attention should be focussed.

'Black, two sugars?' Alex said, turning from the
bench with the jar of coffee in his hand.

'No, tea for me, thanks, Alex,' Maggie told him,
then seeing the look of disbelief on both their faces,
she told them the story she'd rehearsed on Phil.

'I bet Phil I could give up coffee,' she said, her voice
quavering slightly as she remembered the context of

that conversation and the delicate stage their discussion had reached when it had all been halted by Amy's return to hospital.

'How do you like your tea, then?' Alex asked, and Maggie smiled at him.

'Black, two sugars, but weak, because to tell you the truth I hate tea. I'd just as soon drink hot water with two sugars, but people would think I was crazy so I wave the tea bag over the top of the cup.'

She was aware Annie was watching her closely and wondered if she could possibly suspect.

From giving up coffee and only drinking very weak tea?

Surely not!

'I was going to have you two and Rod and Henry to dinner tonight to welcome you back, but even if Phil gets away from the hospital he'll probably feel more like sleeping than being polite to guests,' Maggie said, hoping to divert Annie's attention—just in case she was harbouring suspicious thoughts!

'We're tired, too,' Annie said, 'but knowing Alex, he'll be taking Phil's place at the hospital before I've even unpacked our bags.'

She paused then smiled.

'In fact, I might pop up there myself before I unpack. Just so anyone still considering whatever rumours Dr Ellis spread knows I'm around and I intend to fight back.'

Maggie felt a genuine smile spread across her face for the first time, it seemed, in weeks.

'It's good to have you guys back,' she said, and knew they knew she meant it.

They sat down at the table and drank the tea and coffee Alex had made, talking now about the mountains to the west of Sydney and the wonderful time the honeymooners had had exploring them.

'You must go up there while you're in Sydney,' Annie told Maggie. 'It's a really beautiful area.'

'I will,' Maggie promised, thinking a weekend away, on her own, in the mountains, might be the ideal place to think through her future.

Alex and Annie finished their coffee and departed, leaving Henry in the back yard with Minnie because they were heading not back to Annie's house but towards the hospital. Having guessed Alex would stay up there, Maggie wasn't at all surprised to hear Phil's key in the front door only an hour later.

She was in the laundry, doing some hand-washing, and he came through the house to find her there.

'The cavalry arrived just in time,' he said, leaning against the doorjamb and watching her dunk her sweater in soapy water. 'I doubt I'd have lasted another night without a proper sleep.'

Maggie looked at the lines lack of sleep and anxiety had drawn on his face, and her heart ached with a need to hold and comfort him.

Failing that, she could offer practicality.

'Would you like something to eat? I shopped this morning and bought some mini ham and cheese croissants. It would only take a few minutes to heat you a couple, or would you prefer to just fall into bed?'

'Bed, I think,' he said, but he didn't move and the word 'bed' reverberated around the room, heightening Maggie's usual awareness of her colleague and suggesting things it shouldn't.

She squeezed the soapy water out of the sweater and rinsed it under the tap, then emptied the bucket she'd been using and filled it with clean water, conscious all the time of Phil standing there, watching her.

Silence stretched between them—though 'bed' still whispered in her head—and she tried to think just where they'd been in a very awkward conversation earlier in the week before work had driven all personal matters from both their heads.

They hadn't reached any conclusions, she knew that much, and given the sleep deprivation Phil had suffered this week, maybe he'd forgotten the conversation altogether.

Forgotten he'd guessed the one thing she hadn't told him about the baby.

'Sleep deprivation hasn't killed all my brain cells,' he said, as Maggie once again squeezed water—clean this time—from her sweater. 'So, once I've slept we need to talk, Mags.'

She glanced his way and saw he looked even more tired than he had earlier, although earlier she wouldn't have thought it possible. She set the wet sweater down on top of the washing machine and stepped towards him, then put her arms around him and gave him a hug.

'We'll sort it all out,' she promised, though she wasn't sure they could.

But right now this man needed some reassurance before he slept, and how could she deny it to him?

His arms closed around her back and he drew her closer, resting his chin on the top of her head.

'I don't suppose you'd like a snooze yourself,' he asked, his husky voice and awakening body suggesting he wasn't nearly as exhausted as she'd thought.

Before she could think of a casual way to laugh off

the suggestion, he eased her away and used his fore-finger to tilt her chin so he could look into her face.

'I wouldn't do you justice today, but our time will come,' he said, the words a promise she guessed he intended to keep, then he bent and kissed her on the lips and for a few minutes she forgot all the tangled threads that wove around their lives and gave in to the seduction of that embrace.

# CHAPTER EIGHT

MAGGIE woke early, and though she felt lethargic and was tempted to have a lazy morning in bed, she knew she needed exercise. She'd get Minnie and go for a walk in the park. No, Minnie had gone to live with Alex at Annie's house where she'd have Henry for canine company and Rod, who lived in the flat downstairs, to see she was fed when all the humans were held up at work.

Well, people could walk in the park without a dog— no rule against that.

Only it didn't appeal.

Maybe she *would* stay in bed.

Not good for the baby, all this lounging around.

*OK, I'll walk*, she told the nag in her head. *But I'll drive down to the beach and walk there.*

With this decided, she still lingered, reluctant to leave her comfy bed, reliving the magic of the kiss she'd shared with Phil last night. Then a memory of the conversation they'd had before the kiss returned, and she decided she'd be better off being out of the house when he awoke. It was putting off the inevitable, she knew, but she might think more clearly after a brisk walk in the salt air had cleared the cobwebs from her head.

She pulled on a tracksuit and grabbed a jacket, knowing the wind could whip coldly off the sea.

Breakfast first or later? The question was about as much as she could handle this early in the morning, and she'd just decided on later—walk, then breakfast at the beach—when she reached the kitchen and found Phil already there.

'Good morning!' he said, so cheerfully she had to hide a shudder.

'I think that's always a matter of individual opinion,' she muttered at him.

'Not a morning person?' Phil teased. 'Shows how chaotic things have been at work that we've been living together for a fortnight and I didn't know.'

'You didn't need to know,' Maggie told him, then realised she was pursuing the wrong argument. 'Anyway, I am—a morning person, I mean. I like mornings. I'm up and I'm going for a walk. Would someone who wasn't a morning person be doing that?'

Phil looked around and Maggie knew he'd been about to make a smart remark to Minnie, then realised the little dog was no longer there. And the expression of loss on his face made Maggie realise how much Minnie had meant to him—she'd been part of his image of 'home', however temporary that home might have been.

'I'm going down to the beach for a walk—do you want to come?'

It had to be the surge of pity she'd felt that had made her ask. The last person she needed on a head-clearing excursion was Phil.

'Yes, yes I would. Great place to talk about the wedding. I suppose your folks will want you to have a proper one—with you being their daughter and all. Well, your mother probably would want it. Funny how it is with mothers and brides.'

'Phil!'

The name came out louder than Maggie had intended, but at least it stopped him rabbiting on and gave her the opportunity to have her say.

'There is no wedding to discuss. We're not getting married.'

He stared at her in disbelief.

'Of course we're getting married. We're having a baby.'

The look on his face told Maggie he'd realised this wasn't exactly a winning argument, but he recovered, coming towards her and taking hold of her hands.

'I put that badly. The thing is, I've been thinking about it all week and I'd really like to marry you, Mags, baby or not. We'd be good together. We know and understand each other's work and the demands it puts on us. Alex is confident of your work so I'm sure he'd offer you a place on the team in the US. Then when I finish my fellowship with him, we'll still be a team, working together wherever we decide to go.'

It was so exactly the life Maggie had always envisaged—working in partnership with the man she loved, partnership in the ultimate sense, in marriage and in their careers—that she almost weakened and gave in.

But this was her dream, not Phil's, and she doubted it would fill the emptiness in his life.

And what about the emptiness in her own life if she agreed? What about love?

Had she said those three words aloud that Phil's hands tightened on hers?

She must have, because the blue eyes were serious as he said, 'I can't promise that, Mags.'

'So it *is* all about the baby, in spite of what you just said about us being good together.'

He frowned down at her.

'You can't know that and nor do I.'

'Of course I know. Would you have mentioned marriage if I wasn't pregnant?'

'No, but—'

'There are no buts!' Maggie said, and she walked away, knowing the dream on offer wasn't what she wanted after all.

If Phil wanted to walk with her he could follow, but right now, more than ever, she needed that walk. Needed to think.

He did follow, protesting every step of the way, so in the end, as she backed the car out of the garage, she turned to him and said, 'Phil, I'm going for a walk to clear my head and have a think about things. For a start, it's far too early to be thinking in terms of a living, breathing baby.'

Her heart squeezed now with a different pain, remembered pain, and she realised, though she'd intended telling him about her previous miscarriages, she couldn't, fearing it might be an omen of bad luck for this pregnancy.

'Supposing it happens, I understand you want to be involved in the baby's life, and I appreciate that. But it doesn't mean you have to take over *my* life. Anyway, pregnancies last forty weeks—don't you think we've plenty of time to sort out minor details?'

She glanced his way, and saw again the lines of strain on his face, some of them, she knew, caused by her unexpected pregnancy. Then she remembered the stress he'd been under the last few weeks, and regret that she should be providing additional stress made her reach across and touch him lightly on the hand.

'We'll sort it out, but let's think things through first—not rush into the first solution that occurs to us.'

'At least you're saying *us*!' he muttered at her, then

he sighed, rested his head back against the headrest, and closed his eyes.

The parking area at the beach was almost deserted, and Maggie, seeing the wind flapping the crossed red flags that indicated the surf was unsafe for swimmers, wondered if the park might not have been the better option for her walk.

'It's blowing a gale out there,' she said, but Phil was already opening the car door.

'A nice bracing breeze,' he said, grinning at her in a way that started the flip-flops again in her heart. 'Come on!'

He was still too tired to be trying to sort things out between himself and Maggie, Phil had realised as they'd driven towards the beach. Instead of planning a strategy that might work with a fiercely independent woman like Maggie, he'd gone rushing in with his own assumptions and upset her. Now he'd have to go back to square one and start again.

The thought made him feel even more tired, but when they reached the beach and he saw the wind thrashing the tops of the swell to white froth, he felt invigorated, as if this cold, blustery weather would blow all his cares away.

Well, it wouldn't do that, but it would give him an excuse to put his arm around Maggie and maybe give her a warming kind of cuddle. That idea had taken precedence in his mind and all the rest of the stuff there could go hang for a while.

'Come on, you'll be blown away if I don't anchor you to the ground,' he told her, as she tried to escape the first part of his plan.

She turned and smiled at him and, with the wind whipping her dark hair across her face and bringing pinkness to her cheeks, she looked so delectable it was all he could do not to kiss her right there and then.

Caution prevailed, however, and he led her down the concrete steps to the beach, then across the dry sand towards the surf, rolling and crashing onto the shore. It was easier walking on the wet sand and though salt spray caught them occasionally, Maggie didn't seem to mind the dampness that misted in her hair and sparkled like diamonds in the bright morning sunlight.

Diamonds! Would she wear a diamond ring? No, she was a red girl. A ruby? Maybe a square-cut ruby with small diamonds around it. Or a baguette-cut ruby, with baguette diamonds each side. Would she think that too much?

He had no idea, though he did realise that in spite of Maggie's protestation that there'd be no wedding his mind was steadfastly following that track. Of course it would, it was the only sensible solution. In fact, it was such a great solution he felt his body responding every time he thought about it.

He glanced towards her, wondering if the walk was working for her, as far as thinking was concerned. For himself, well, he was thinking, but with her warm, soft body tucked up against his, his thoughts were getting raunchier and raunchier.

'This isn't working,' Maggie said, tugging away from him. 'I can't think with you so close.'

'No?'

Given where his mind had been, it wasn't surprising that hope began to hammer in his heart. Maybe it was hammering harder in other parts of his body, but he was sure it was in his heart as well.

She looked up at him, brown eyes serious, and

though he guessed she'd been feeling some of what he'd been feeling he was sure she was going to lie.

'No!' she snapped crossly. 'All I can think about was how good we were in bed together, and how much I'd like to do it again. I know it's probably just a hormonal thing from the pregnancy, but it's driving me nuts.'

Phil held in his whoop of joy, neither did he scoop her into his arms and run with her all the way back to the car, though both options were distinctly appealing. But he was a mature man of thirty-four, not a randy adolescent, so he made do with pulling her towards him and then kissing her so thoroughly he realised that carrying her off the beach might have been a better way to go. Because now, with the kiss broken off so they could breathe, they still had to get home, and if her legs were anywhere near as shaky as his were, just getting back to the car was going to be an effort.

'You want to do this?' he asked her, as they tumbled into the house, shut the back door and were about to resume kissing.

'So much!' she whispered, her eyes sparkling with desire, her lips so red and ripe his body ached to devour them.

They kissed their way through the kitchen, risked serious injury continuing it up the stairs, then finally he guided her onto his bed, still kissing, but now his hands were exploring her body, and hers his, further inflaming the passionate desire that flared between them.

Maggie could feel heat, but couldn't tell if it was his or hers. The inner heat was hers, but skin heat—that was different. Skin heat brought her nerve endings to life in a way she'd never before experienced, so they zapped and tingled at the slightest touch, the merest brush. She nuzzled her lips against the hot satiny skin of his shoulder and nibbled at his ear-lobe, while his hands explored her belly, fingers tickling at her belly button, sliding lower, her escalating desire causing little whimpering noises of delight and demand to flutter from her lips.

'So sweet,' he whispered, as his lips found hers once again, while his fingers worked a magic of their own. 'Sweet tempestuous delight, Mags, that's what you are.'

Maggie was beyond speech, which was probably just as well, for her words might just have been words of love, confessions of feelings too deep to be spoken of in other situations.

Then Phil slid over her, his body hard and soft and hot and made, it seemed, to fit hers, for he filled all the aching emptiness within her as they joined in the wild joy-ride of love.

Love-making, some remaining shred of common sense amended, but Maggie didn't care. This was Phil, taking her on a voyage of discovery of her own body and the sensual delights it could yield. And all the time he talked to her, sweet murmurs of allure, approval, passion and incitement, but never love, and although the final climax was momentous, leaving Maggie weak and trembling in his arms, that one small shred of common sense picked up that omission and clung to it, warning Maggie of just where she stood—or lay—in this relationship.

Phil was gone when Maggie woke on Monday morning. In her bed, not his. They'd shifted beds some time during the day, after foraging in the kitchen for food, and deciding Alex, as the landlord, had probably had the best bed in the house, and as it was now Maggie's bed, they were duty bound to try it.

Maggie felt a blush rising up from her toes as she thought of some of the other things they'd done, but it had all been fun, and the sex had been great, and they'd laughed in each other's arms and held onto each other as they'd slept.

'Like lovers!' Maggie whispered into the cold morning air. 'Which we are, of course,' she added, patting her stomach so the baby would know she was talking to it, and not think its mother was some nut who talked to herself.

And would continue to be, her head reminded her. After all, it would be stupid—not to mention hypocritical—to go on living in the same house and not continue to enjoy the physical delight they could offer each other. As Phil had pointed out some time yesterday, they'd already wasted two weeks.

She smiled at that and other memories, refused to think about the 'L' word that was absent from the equation and eased out of her nice warm bed. If she didn't get moving soon, she'd be late for work. Work! Had Phil been paged that he was already up?

She listened for noises in the house but heard none, and frowned, wondering why he hadn't woken her— let her know he was going.

No answer came to mind so she showered, blushing again at memories, dressed and went downstairs.

A note and a strange bouquet of leaves and berries from the garden were waiting for her on the kitchen table, the note explaining he had woken early and gone up to the hospital to get a start on the day, and apologising for the paucity of this floral offering, but it was all he'd been able to find so early in the morning.

Maggie smoothed the note with shaking fingers.

'Oh, Phil!' she whispered quietly. 'Don't be nice to me and make things harder than they already are.'

Then she wrapped her arms around her body and slumped down at the table.

He was so very much what she'd always wanted in a man, yet she was so wrong for him.

And because she loved him, she knew she couldn't marry him, condemning him to the loveless marriage his parents had endured.

Reminding herself there'd be no need to make any decisions if she lost this baby too, Maggie turned her thoughts to work. No paeds cardiac operations today, but she was scheduled to spend some time in another operating theatre, working in a supervisory capacity with some students doing their first paediatric anaesthetic.

She made toast and ate it with a glass of milk. She found milk nearly as revolting as tea, but she dutifully tried to drink some every day. Then she walked up the road to work, going straight to the paediatric ward where the children who would be her patients were waiting for her.

'We depend so much on patient weight in deciding the amount of drugs we give that if ever you have the slightest doubt about the weight of a child, weigh him or her again,' she told the three students. 'Ruby here is five and looks as if she might be light for her age, so the seventeen kilograms is probably right. Carry a weight-age chart so you can check if you need to, and when in doubt weigh.'

The students all nodded dutifully, then listened while Maggie explained to Ruby what she was going to do.

'I need to put a needle in the back of your hand so

the doctors can put medicine in there,' she told the little girl, already drowsy from the pre-med. 'Just a prick and we're done. You look at Mummy's face and see her scrunch it up when I put the needle in you. You watch and you'll think it's hurting her more than it's hurting you.'

While Ruby watched her mother who obligingly screwed up her face and said a loud 'Ouch!' Maggie sited a cannula in Ruby's hand and taped it into place.

'Ruby will be wheeled to Theatre by an orderly with a nurse accompanying her,' Maggie told the students. 'Because she's not on a ventilator, there's no need to bag her on the way, but with children who need oxygen, we bag them manually as they're moved. Although nurses usually do this, I like to go along with them.'

The orderly arrived to move the bed and Maggie, with the students trailing behind her, followed the little girl towards Theatre. Outside the door, Ruby's mother was asked to sign the consent form and agreed that, yes, it was her daughter going into Theatre and, yes, she was to have an appendicectomy.

Maggie was leading her crew into the changing rooms when a theatre sister who'd worked with the team a few times came out.

'Congratulations,' she said, beaming good-naturedly, then, as Maggie moved on, thinking the woman was talking to someone else, she thought she heard the sister add, 'He seems a great bloke, if something of a flirt.'

Puzzled, Maggie turned towards the two women students with her, but neither of them seemed to be responding to the conversation, and as the sister had, by now, disappeared from view, Maggie couldn't call her back to ask who she'd been talking to.

She found out later when, with Ruby and two other children safely out of the recovery room and back in their ward, she made her way to the rooms, hoping Annie might have been too tied up to eat lunch at the normal time and be willing to join her for a quick bite.

Annie wasn't in. In fact, apart from Becky, the rooms were empty. The secretary, who was usually full of good cheer, was obviously too busy for a chat, casting a glance towards Maggie then turning resolutely back towards the computer screen. So Maggie made her way down to the canteen alone.

'Oh, Maggie, I'm so glad for you.'

Annie was waiting for the lift on the ground floor and as Maggie stepped out, her colleague enveloped her in her arms and gave her a huge hug.

'It's so wonderful, being married, and I know you love Phil. I can't believe he's finally realised what a great woman you are. To think you've been there under his nose all this time while he played around with his blondes. Though I shouldn't be saying this, I know, but I really began to wonder about Phil—that he couldn't see just how good for him you'd be.'

Maggie, squashed in Annie's arms, took all this in, but her brain refused to process it.

Then the enormity of what Phil must have done struck her, and she was surprised she didn't self-combust so fiery was the anger that consumed her.

She broke away from Annie's embrace and opened her mouth to deny whatever lie Phil had spread, then saw the joy in her friend's face—joy that Maggie was sharing the happiness she and Alex had found—and knew she couldn't wipe that joy away.

Not now—not yet.

'Where is Phil?' she asked, hoping his name didn't come out as if she'd chewed broken glass before saying it.

'Just finishing lunch with Alex. He said you were busy today or we'd have waited.'

'I was busy,' Maggie said, stalled in the foyer outside the lift. She could hardly go into the canteen and rip Phil's head off—which was what she felt like doing—in front of Alex, and with this new news churning inside her, she doubted she could eat.

'And now I'm going home,' she said. 'Forgot to pick up the shopping list before I left this morning, and as I'm off this afternoon I may as well shop.'

*Home indeed!* she thought as she strode down the road. *It's a house, nothing more. The hide of the man, telling people we're engaged when I told him I wouldn't marry him.*

*I did tell him, didn't I?*

*Yes, I'm sure I did.*

Berating Phil, mentally at least, kept her moving quickly towards the house, but once there she had no idea why she'd come. She'd shopped on Saturday so certainly didn't need to shop again, but maybe she could pack her things and shift back to her sister's place.

But living there again, with her sister's four children, including two-year-old twins, might put her off children for life—right when she was hoping desperately to bring one into the world.

In thirty-something weeks…

Maybe…

Forget maybe, be positive!

'But with all that time ahead of us, why's Phil told people anything now?'

Even asked aloud, the question offered no answer, so Maggie went up to her bedroom, shut the door and collapsed onto the bed, staring at the ceiling and hoping some solution to her dilemma might just come to her.

Ripping off Phil's head still seemed the best solution, but some of her anger had dissipated by the time he came home later that afternoon, so all she did was yell.

'How dare you tell our colleagues we were engaged! I said no, Phil, remember, when you talked about marriage? No! No! No! Don't you understand the word?'

He looked dazed, as well he might, having breezed into the house with, this time, florist flowers in his hand, and an 'isn't life great' smile on his face, to be greeted by a small but furious woman.

'But I thought we'd established that yesterday,' Phil said lamely, offering the flowers then, realising they'd probably be flung at his head, dropping his hand back down so the bright blooms hung by his side.

'All we established yesterday,' an icy voice informed him, 'was that we were compatible in bed. Extremely compatible. Extraordinarily compatible if you like, but we probably suspected that from the first time. Marriage is more than compatibility in bed, Phil Park, and I would have thought even you were mature enough to have realised that!'

She wheeled away from him and stalked to the kitchen, her backside swaying so seductively it was all he could do not to scoop her up in his arms and take her back up to one or other of their bedrooms, where he could, he felt sure, sort the whole problem out in no time flat.

*No, she thinks I should have* some *maturity*, he reminded himself, but as no other solution offered itself, he followed her into the kitchen, allowing the fantasy to play in his mind.

'You'll have to tell everyone it's not true,' she told him as he entered, again proffering the flowers as if the second time around they might be more acceptable.

They weren't.

He set them down on the table and absorbed what she was saying.

'But why? Isn't marriage the best solution? Don't you think, as two mature adults, we can make a marriage between us work? Do you really want your baby to grow up with an absentee father?'

The last question snagged in his gut, and he had to protest it before she had time to answer.

'No, even if you do, that just wouldn't be acceptable to me, and as I'm half of the decision-makers here, I'm entitled to state that it won't happen. This baby will have two parents, both of whom live in the same house as he or she does, so there's absolutely no doubt in his or her mind who he or she belongs to.'

He got to the end of this appalling statement and realised why it had been so difficult, and why it probably didn't make sense.

'Should we give the baby a name now—some kind of unisex name like Mop or Gonk that we can refer to him or her by—so we don't have to keep saying he or she all the time?'

Maggie was staring at him as if he'd gone mad, but she didn't seem quite so angry. He considered trying the flowers again, then decided he was better off stopping while he was ahead so he crossed to the sink, searched under it until he found a jug, filled it with water and took it back to the table, where he picked up the flowers and stuck them into it.

'You should take them out of the paper, undo the string around them and cut off the bottom of the stems so they can take up fresh water,' the woman for whom they'd been intended said coolly, then she went to the fridge, took out the milk and some cheese, looked at both, put them back in, shut the door and sat down in a chair.

Suddenly.

So suddenly Phil looked more closely at her, and this time he didn't think of racing her off to bed.

'Have you eaten?' he demanded. 'Is that why you were at the fridge? Do you feel sick? If not, you have to eat. Even if you do feel sick, you have to eat. What? A cheese sandwich?'

He was so anxious and uncertain that Maggie had to laugh, and for a moment she thought how nice it would be to have Phil around all the time—bringing her flowers, fussing over her appetite…

Insidiously nice.

'I'll have a cheese sandwich. I'll get it in a minute. Just felt a bit woozy and thought it best to sit down.'

He fussed some more, insisting she stay sitting, scolding her for missing lunch, cutting the sandwich into little triangles and even finding a little bit of celery leaf to put on top so they looked appetising.

'And I'll make a pot of that decaff coffee,' he told her when he'd given her the sandwich. 'I know it's not like the real thing, but you probably need it, though you should drink it with milk to get some calcium.'

'Cheese has calcium,' she managed to say, although she had to swallow down a stupid lump of misery that had lodged in her throat—hormonal activity again, only this time it made her feel weepy for no other reason than that Phil was being nice to her.

But he was always nice to her, she reminded herself, chewing on the sandwich.

Not this kind of nice, herself said, although she knew this was a dangerous form of weakness, to be thinking of Phil's varying degrees of niceness and weeping over a cheese sandwich.

Especially when he didn't love her!

When it was all for the baby!

'None of this is making what you did right,' she told him when her body had been fortified and her will-power bolstered by the sandwich and a ghastly cup of milky coffee.

Phil was over at the sink, snipping the ends of the stems from the flowers. He turned his head towards her, his face serious—no twinkle in his eyes.

'No, if it's not what you want, then it isn't. I'm sorry.' He shrugged. 'I guess I can just tell Alex and Annie that we're not engaged—they'll spread the word.'

Maggie closed her eyes at the magnitude of *that* idea. Engaged one day, unengaged the next—the hospital gossips would have a ball and the grapevine would be buzzing with speculation.

She wasn't at all sure she could cope with the consequences. Not right now.

'Maybe not saying anything would be better. People might forget.'

'Of course,' Phil said politely, not meaning one word of it.

Neither did she, but a sudden wave of tiredness had swept over her and her brain had stopped working.

Maybe tomorrow she'd think of something…

# CHAPTER NINE

BUT before tomorrow could come there was tonight.

Where would she be spending the night?

Where would Phil be?

She sighed, and he came and stood behind her and kneaded her shoulders, as she'd kneaded his about a hundred years ago.

'You should have something more substantial than a cheese sandwich for dinner,' he said, kneading in such a firm, unsexual way Maggie felt her whole body relaxing.

'I'm not hungry,' she said, and he didn't persist, shifting his attention to her neck, working magic on her knotted ligaments with his probing fingers.

'Then when I finish you should go to bed. Have a good night's sleep. Things always look better in the morning.'

'By morning the entire hospital will have heard we're engaged,' Maggie said bitterly. 'I can't see how that's going to make things look better.'

Phil kept kneading.

'Not necessarily. We're isolated from most of the hospital staff, being in the unit. And it's not as if, like Annie, you were on the staff at Jimmie's before the unit was set up. It's only our lot that have taken any notice of the news.'

Maggie had to agree, but she wasn't letting him off the hook that easily.

'And it's our lot that have to be told it isn't true. That it was a fabrication. We're not engaged, Phil.'

'But we *are* expecting a baby. And some time that's going to become obvious. What then? There's no way I'll have whispers about the little scrap's paternity. I'll make sure they know it's my baby you're expecting, Mags. And people will realise just how pig-headed you are at the same time.'

'Pig-headed?'

Maggie twisted away from his hands, and turned so she could glare up at him.

'You spread an untrue story through the hospital and *I'm* pig-headed because I want to tell the truth?'

He smiled, which was his first mistake.

The second was uttering the words that followed the smile.

'Too pig-headed to marry me. You know we'd be good together. Just because it wasn't your idea, you've got all uppity about it.'

Maggie stood up, still glaring at him, wishing she was a man so she could punch him and release just a little of the fury bubbling in her body.

'I wouldn't marry you if you were the last man on earth, Phil Park!' she yelled. Then she stormed out of the kitchen, across the living room, up the stairs and into her bedroom, where she flung herself on the bed and burst into tears.

Phil told himself he was having trouble getting through to Maggie because her hormones were out of kilter but, although he believed her hormones could well be causing havoc in her body, he couldn't help but feel there were other issues at stake here.

Things happening in Maggie's head that he had no inkling of.

He looked around the kitchen, wishing Minnie was there so he could talk things out with her, but she wasn't, so he checked the fridge instead, grabbed a light beer, then pulled out a piece of steak and the makings for a salad.

If they had a potato—and they had—he was set for dinner.

But grilling a steak, sticking a potato in the microwave and tossing salad ingredients with some oil and vinegar wasn't a difficult enough task to keep his mind from wandering. Salads were so healthy, but how did you get infants to eat lettuce? Or shouldn't you bother? Go with the tried and true mashed vegetables for a while, and introduce salad things when they could chew.

Obviously that would be best—you could hardly give a toothless baby a carrot stick.

So much to learn.

Was it too early to buy a baby book?

And what baby book to buy?

From what he'd seen in his sorties into book stores, bringing-up-baby books accounted for about half the store's turnover.

Maybe a quarter.

He couldn't ask his mother. He doubted she'd ever read one in her life, any more than his nanny had. Who did he know with offspring? Someone must know the best book to buy!

As he ate his meal his mind switched from the baby—plenty of time to find out about the best book—to the woman carrying it. Here he was eating the ultimate in healthy dinners and she'd gone to bed with only a cheese sandwich inside her. She'd wake up some time in the night absolutely starving.

Would she come downstairs if she was hungry, or should he leave a sandwich—there must be something other than cheese in the fridge—beside her bed?

Maggie was asleep when Phil crept in to her room, lying face down across the bed, still in her hospital clothes, the bedside lamp casting enough light for him to see the tear stains on her cheek.

His heart squeezed in his chest, but he ignored this physical manifestation of weakness. She was going through so much, he had to be the practical one.

He set the sandwich he'd made and covered with clingwrap on the table by the bed, but took the glass of milk back downstairs. He'd make her a hot chocolate, and bring it up, wake her and help her into her nightwear—professionally detached no matter if it killed him!—and encourage her to have the food and hot drink before she went back to sleep.

But by the time he returned, she'd gone, and he could hear the shower running in the bathroom. He left the drink beside the sandwich and departed. He'd made her cry once already this evening, he wasn't going to risk it again.

Maggie came out of the bathroom to find a cup of hot chocolate beside the sandwich, which had appeared while she'd been asleep.

She wasn't hungry and a skin was forming on the chocolate so that just looking at it made her feel ill, but he'd meant well.

He probably meant well about the baby, too, but there was no way she was going to mess up both their lives by marrying him.

She took the chocolate into the bathroom and tipped it down the sink, then eyed the sandwich. Maybe she should eat some of it. She mightn't want to marry him but there was no need to insult him further by not eating the food he'd so thoughtfully prepared. She forced it down, then slid into bed, turning her mind resolutely to work. What did they have on tomorrow? An ASD closure first up. Phil was doing it. The patient was a little girl who'd only recently been diagnosed, when she'd taken up horse-riding and had become so breathless after cantering gently around a paddock that the riding instructor had suggested her mother take her to a doctor.

Phil would go into the chest through a median incision—Scott would do that part—then Phil…

Always Phil, in her mind, in her dreams, in her heart…

The atmosphere in the theatre was relaxed and Maggie tried to work out why. Usually as the surgeons prepared a patient to go on bypass, the tension rose, not to an uncomfortable level but enough for everyone to feel it.

Was it because Rachel and Scott were teasing Phil about the end of his freedom? She opened her mouth to say that there was no end to his freedom, that they weren't engaged, then closed it again. This was not the time to be creating problems for Phil.

'Atrial septal defects—holes between the atria— aren't uncommon in congenital heart disease,' he was saying to the same students Maggie had instructed the previous day. 'The patient can be asymptomatic for years. Though blood is shunting from left to right across the atria, it isn't until they show signs of pulmonary obstruction, as little Gemma did, that the defect is discovered.'

'They'll close all by themselves quite often, won't they?' one of the students, a really beautiful young woman—blonde, of course—asked.

Maggie glared at her, but Phil didn't even turn in her direction, concentrating on attaching Gemma to the bypass machine and letting Scott answer for him.

'Yes, they do,' he said, then Kurt took over, explaining to the students how the bypass machine worked, acting as both heart and lungs for the patient while the operation was performed.

Maggie was listening to him and watching her monitors at the same time.

'She's fibrillating,' she said, knowing the panicky beat of the heart could lead to a heart attack if it wasn't stopped.

'The cannula's not seating properly, so she can't go on the pump yet,' Phil said, ordering the drugs Gemma needed to settle her heart back to an acceptable rhythm.

Maggie added them to the fluid flowing into the little girl, watching the monitor, not the child, willing the frantic beating of the heart to subside but not to stop.

'OK, go to pump, Kurt,' Phil said, and everyone breathed again.

'So much for a relaxed atmosphere in Theatre,' Maggie muttered, and Ned, the theatre sister who assisted in most of their operations, gave her a nudge with his elbow.

'You should know not to even think about such things in Theatre,' he said. 'It's tempting fate.'

Maggie wanted to agree with him but, though she nodded, her mind was back on the child. Had the problem been something she'd done? Had she added something to the cocktail of drugs immediately before the heart had gone haywire?

Later, when she read through the notes she made as she worked, she'd have to check if there was anything that could have triggered the reaction. She'd seen it happen before, but usually in very sick babies or neonates, not in otherwise healthy five-year-olds.

'That was unexpected,' Phil said, much later, when Gemma had been returned to the ward and they were gathered in the unit, discussing the operation.

'No change in your usual protocol?' Alex asked Maggie, who held up the notes she still had in her hand.

'Nothing!' she said. 'But it was scary and I'm wondering if there's something I don't know about in these cases where we're operating on an older and healthier child. I'll stay here tonight and trawl through whatever info I can find on the Web, and there's an anaesthetist over at Children's who's pretty savvy. He might have some ideas.'

She noticed Phil's scowl but thought nothing of it until he announced, late that afternoon when she settled in front of the computer, that he, too, would stay back and do some Web surfing.

'But your work was textbook,' Maggie reminded him. 'I've seen Alex do ASDs and he couldn't have done it better. And the fibrillation was so early in the procedure, I don't see how it could have been caused by anything you did.'

'I'd still like to know if there's any paper or report of something similar happening,' he said, sounding so grouchy she decided to leave him alone.

Maggie was reading through an article on possible reactions between some pre-medications and the use of pain relief during surgery when a cheery voice interrupted her concentration.

'Two of you hard at work,' Evan Knowles said.

'And I bet you haven't eaten, Maggie. I missed lunch and I'm starving, so how about you guide me to this canteen of yours and we'll eat and talk? Phil can mind the computers.'

'Phil hasn't eaten either,' Maggie said, darting a quick glance in Phil's direction and catching a scowl as a reward.

She ignored it and continued, 'Come on, Phil, we'll all go and eat. We can talk to Evan over dinner—he might have some experience of what happened.'

Evan looked put out, Phil looked thunderous, and Maggie wondered why women ever put up with men! But eventually he stood up and, still glowering, took Maggie's arm and all but frogmarched her out of the room.

Evan walked on her other side, chatting on, either unaware of the vibes around him or choosing speech as a way of ignoring them.

'Oh, Maggie, I was hoping to see you.'

One of the nurses who cared for their patients on the open ward was waiting by the lift. 'I saw Phil yesterday and congratulated him, but I didn't see you. All the best on your engagement.'

'We're not engaged.'

The words came out before Maggie had time to consider the company—or the impact they would have on the two men standing next to her.

'You're engaged?'

That from Evan, who'd spoken too early to hear her denial.

'What happened to not saying anything?'

This from Phil, frowning down at her from what suddenly seemed like a great height.

The nurse looked embarrassed, muttered something about forgetting to check a list and hurried off.

'It was a misunderstanding,' Maggie said, mainly to Evan although the answer could equally apply to Phil's protest.

'Oh, yes,' Evan said, looking from one to the other. 'Happens all the time, I imagine, one half of a couple thinking they're engaged while the other half thinks they're not. Ordinary kind of misunderstanding!'

Maggie laughed.

'It's complicated,' she said, and Evan sighed.

'More so than you realise,' he said quietly. 'Anyway, I wanted to see young Pete while I was here, so how about you two eat on your own? Maggie, I'll check out some likely sites for anything about your problem and email you.'

He walked off before Maggie had a chance to stop him.

'Now see what you've done,' she said to Phil.

'I've done?' he echoed with totally false astonishment. 'I had nothing to do with it—it was the nurse who mentioned engagements.'

'And she'd have known if you hadn't told the world?' Maggie stormed at him, wanting to yell but knowing this wasn't the place for a really good argument.

Then Phil smiled at her, and all her anger melted.

'I know it's a terrible cliché, but you look beautiful when you're angry. Your cheeks go pink and your eyes spark fire, and all I want to do is kiss you.'

He spoke quietly, although they were now alone, the other people waiting with them having taken the lift.

'Phil, this is all wrong,' Maggie said. 'There's so much more to it—things I haven't told you.' Her stomach scrunched but she forced herself to add, 'Things that will probably make the engagement unnecessary.'

She knew it wasn't the ideal place to tell Phil about her previous marriage and two miscarriages, but it was time things were said, and she was ready to say them, so—

'Phil, Maggie, I think you should see Pete.'

Evan's voice betrayed his urgency and Phil and Maggie responded immediately, turning and striding towards the unit's PICU.

'He was fine, breathing well on his own with the machine assisting him, but he wasn't reliant on it, so we decided to try him off it,' the intensivist on duty explained. 'We intended keeping him on ventilatory assistance but getting him off the mechanical ventilator, so he's been fasting today in preparation for it and we cut his fluids right back, but there's obviously fluid collecting in his abdomen.'

The little boy, though awake, was far from alert, lying limply on the bed, his usual cheery smile nowhere to be seen.

'So, not feeling too good, soldier?' Phil said, while Maggie nodded to Mr Barron, on duty by his son's bedside today. Mr Barron called his youngster 'soldier' and most of the staff had adopted it, pleasing Pete enormously.

But today he didn't respond at all, just lying there while Phil poked and prodded at his body.

Let it not be kidney failure, Maggie prayed, then she reminded herself that Pete's kidneys weren't being overworked as he still had a drain in his abdomen and he was undergoing peritoneal dialysis.

Peritoneal dialysis! Her mind raced through what she knew of it. Usually done during the night while the patient slept, it was a way of cleansing the impurities from the blood and adding needed electrolytes, performing the tasks of the kidneys when they were too weak to function properly.

But one of the dangers of it was peritonitis, an infection getting into the abdomen through the catheters designed to keep the body healthy.

Phil was explaining some of this to Mr Barron, whose complexion had gone from a healthy, if somewhat ruddy olive to a dull, tired grey—a skin colour seen quite often in the exhausted family members of PICU patients.

Only, as well as grey skin, there was a blue tinge to Mr Barron's lips.

'Phil,' Maggie said, intending to nod towards the man in case Phil hadn't noticed, but it was too late. Mr Barron pitched forward off his chair, and little Pete's weak but frantic cry of 'Dad!' was one of the saddest things Maggie had ever heard.

She didn't hesitate, hitting the crash button in the room. Although the closest crash cart would be geared towards paediatric resuscitations, it would be better than nothing for Mr Barron.

Maggie moved around the bed, stepping over Phil who, with Evan, was giving CPR to the prone man, and stood so Pete could no longer see what was going on.

'Daddy's just fainted,' she lied to the sick little boy. 'Probably because Dr Phil was talking about such yucky things.'

But the monitors showed Pete's agitation and Maggie sent a nurse for a mild sedative. Just a little of the drug, added to what he was already on, would make him sleepy and unaware of what was happening, at least until they could move his father out of the room.

Better that way than having the already ill little boy deal with the chemicals his body would produce through anxiety.

He slipped peacefully into sleep, but Maggie stayed by his side. Someone else would contact Mrs Barron, who would then have to make arrangements for a friend or relative to mind the other children before she could get up to the hospital.

Mr Barron was defibrillated where he lay on the floor, and the collective sigh of relief told Maggie he'd responded. Within minutes of his collapse he was lifted onto a stretcher and wheeled out of the room, Phil and Evan following, the intensivist obviously wanting to go too, though he did turn back towards Maggie to check that Pete was OK.

'I knocked him out,' she explained. 'I'll stay with him because when he comes to again he'll want to know his dad's all right, and we still have to sort out his problem.'

She sat down and reached for Pete's hand, stroking it and talking to him as she waited for him to wake. No one really knew how much an anaesthetised person could take in, but Maggie believed some words filtered into the other world the patient temporarily inhabited, so she always talked to them as they came out of anaesthetic.

She told Pete he was going to get better, that they'd fight the infection, and before long he'd be going home to play with his sisters and brothers. She crossed her fingers again as she added, 'And your mother and father, too, of course.'

Phil walked back into the PICU and hesitated outside

Pete's room, looking through the glass at the woman who sat beside the child's bed, holding his hand and talking away, although Pete appeared to be comatose.

'You could have gone and had your dinner,' he told her, coming into the room and nodding towards the sleeping child.

'And leave him on his own—when his parents have been knocking themselves out to make sure someone's with him all the time?'

She smiled at Phil.

'And why did you come back? To sit with him, I bet!'

'To check on him, that's all. Though I might have known you'd be here—persistence personified, that's you.'

He knew she was still annoyed with him, but reached out to ruffle her hair anyway.

'It might be an irritating trait to your friends and family, but it pays off in your work, Mags. You worry away at things until you find not only a right solution but a perfect solution.'

As she hadn't objected to his touch, he dropped his hand onto her shoulder.

She didn't bite it off, which cheered him immensely, not because it was his operating hand but because she must be over the argument and they could be friends again.

Friends! More and more he was realising the importance of this friendship between them—valuing it, treasuring it…

Wanting it to continue.

He reined in his wandering thoughts, returning to the problem at hand.

'Though I doubt even you can find a perfect solution

to the Barron family's dilemma. Five children, one still desperately ill after major surgery, and the prospect of more surgery to come, and now the father in the coronary care unit.'

Maggie looked up at him and smiled.

'Have faith,' she said, 'but speaking of the Barrons' problems, how is Mr B.?'

'He should pull through. He's a bit overweight, but he's relatively young. The worry isn't the first heart attack, but the likelihood of a second.'

'And then a probably fatal third!' Maggie finished for him. 'Though surely, with drugs, and possibly a lifestyle change, the second and third can be averted.'

Phil nodded, his eyes now on Pete's monitors, which were showing a drop in the oxygen saturation in his blood. He touched the computer, then brought up the drug schedule. The intensivist had already given antibiotics for the peritonitis, but they'd take time to work.

'The fluid in his abdomen must be pressing his diaphragm upwards and compromising his lungs. I'm going to have to draw off some of the fluid. I'll need some for testing anyway,' he said. 'It might be easier on him to do it while he's still sleeping. How long have I got?'

Maggie looked at her watch, calculated the amount of drug she'd given Pete, his weight, other medications he was on and gave an estimate of fifteen minutes.

Phil asked the nurse who'd followed him into the room for the equipment he'd need, then with Maggie still holding Pete's hand and talking to him, and with the nurse assisting, he drew off two large syringes of fluid, putting some into smaller vials and sending them off to the pathology lab.

'Do you know if they have Dial an Angel or a similar organisation here in Sydney?' Maggie asked, but before he'd even made sense of the question, she answered it herself.

'No, of course you wouldn't. Probably don't even know what Dial an Angel is.'

'I do, so. It's an organisation that provides help for people who need it, mainly in the house, help with kids and housework and suchlike. But if you're thinking of it for the Barrons, and your organisation is like ours, it's probably not affordable for them.'

'No, but there are ways and means,' Maggie said, smoothing her hand up and down Pete's thin arm.

She looked up at Phil.

'If you're finished here, could you send Annie in— if she's still in the rooms, that is? She'll know how to go about things.'

Phil hadn't a clue what she was up to but he had finished, and as Maggie seemed to have no intention of leaving to have dinner with him, or for any other reason, he may as well go and talk to Annie.

He was at the door before she asked the question he'd expected earlier.

'Where's Evan?'

'He had to go,' Phil said, and hoped Maggie wouldn't pursue it. Hoped so much he nearly crossed his fingers as he had done when wishing for something as a child.

Not pursue it! This was Maggie!

'Go where? And why?'

'Back to the Children's, I guess, and why, because he's a worker like the rest of us. He probably had a child waiting to go under even while he was over here dallying with you.'

'It's eight o'clock at night, so an op's unlikely, and

he came so we could talk about the anaesthetic,' Maggie reminded him. 'Though when I phoned, he said he was coming anyway, wanting to see Pete and talk to him about pain.'

'Well, there you are,' Phil said, delighted Maggie had handed him an excuse. 'With Pete so ill, then his father collapsing, Evan probably felt he was in the way here at Jimmie's.'

Maggie nodded, and though it didn't seem to be a nod of total acceptance Phil took it as such and slipped away.

It wasn't as if he'd thumped the man, he comforted himself as he walked through to their rooms. All he'd done had been to let slip the information that he and Maggie *were* engaged, though he was in trouble for telling people before her family had thrown them a party and made an official announcement.

He'd felt slightly guilty, feeding Knowles this lie, though not about the lie, more about the fact he knew absolutely nothing about Maggie's family, and didn't even know if they'd want to give a party or make official announcements.

He had a feeling such arrangements, like the man asking the woman's father for her hand in marriage, were things of the past.

Annie had already heard the news of Mr Barron's collapse, and agreed that something needed to be done to help the family.

'I don't see what you can do,' Phil told her, but she bustled off to see Maggie anyway.

Maggie was excited. Annie knew just the right organisation to contact to arrange help for the Barrons, and though they'd agreed to wait until one of them had talked to Mrs Barron before making final arrangements Annie had gone off to find out exactly what was available.

'But you're his anaesthetist, you shouldn't have had to sit with him,' Mrs Barron said to her as she came anxiously into Pete's room.

'I wanted to,' Maggie told her, 'and I wanted to talk to you as well.'

She indicated the little boy, now sleeping naturally and less flushed as well, a sure sign the antibiotics were clearing the infection.

'I knew you'd come to see Pete once you were satisfied Mr Barron was in good hands, so I stayed on.'

She pulled the second chair close to the one she was using, then swapped places so Mrs Barron could hold her son's hand.

'We all know the trouble you've had juggling your family at home with the hospital visits and Mr Barron's work, and with this, you must be nearly frantic.'

Mrs Barron smiled at her.

'I don't think frantic comes anywhere close,' she said, blinking away a tear. 'I know I have to be strong because so many people are depending on me, but I've always depended on Joe. He's been my rock. I'd never have got through all the problems little Pete's had without Joe being there, telling me all the time we've got to see it through.'

Maggie put her arms around the other woman and let her cry for a while, then, as Mrs Barron straightened, Maggie told her about the charitable organisation that could arrange support for her.

'It has to be what *you* want,' she said. 'Help that will make things easy for *you*. It could be a live-in person to take care of the kids or someone to come in to clean and cook. Someone to drive you to and from the hospital, or money for taxis, someone to drive the kids to school if you like. Whatever you need, these people will give it to you until you've got Joe back home again. After that, too, if you need support for a little while.'

Mrs Barron looked at Maggie as if she'd gone mad.

'But there are loads of people in the world far, far worse off than us. I've got Mum, who will come and stay, and while I know doing everything will be too much for her, it gives me peace of mind to know she's there. Joe, too—he wouldn't like to think a stranger was with the kids.'

'Then maybe someone to clean and cook, do the washing and ironing and leave your mother free to see to the children. Would you accept that?'

Mrs Barron nodded, but she was frowning mightily.

'Why us?' she asked, and Maggie smiled at her.

'Because you need help and you need it now. Think about it, about what would help.'

Maggie watched her face and knew she was weakening.

'If someone could come in the morning at eight and take the kids to school, then give Mum a hand around the house, I could spend the nights at the hospital and stay with Joe and Pete in the mornings, then go home in time to collect the kids. That way I can give them time in the afternoons and see to their homework, and fix their lunches for the next day.'

She looked at Maggie.

'Are you sure these people exist? And they're free?'

'They exist, and while they charge for their services, the organisation will pay, not you. We'll make sure we get someone with a car big enough for all the children and your mother, because you'll both feel better if she goes in the car to the school the first week or so.'

'Week or so? They might come for more than a week?'

Mrs Barron began to cry again, and as Maggie comforted her, holding the weeping woman and patting her on the back, she raised her eyes to the ceiling beyond which she still believed heaven existed, and said a quiet thank you.

Big miracles, like getting Pete and Mr Barron better immediately, were beyond her but, thanks to what had been a tragic loss ten years ago, small miracles were within reach.

# CHAPTER TEN

'Come on, I'm taking you home.'

Maggie looked up from the computer and pushed her fingers through her hair. Her earlier high, when she and Annie had arranged for an 'angel' to help out at the Barrons', had disappeared, mainly because her search for something similar to what had happened today had proved fruitless. All she'd found out was that peering at the screen for an hour gave her a pain in the neck.

'I don't know!' she complained to Phil. 'Computers are good, but they can also lead you on endless wild-goose chases. I'd pick up something in search results that sounded similar and follow it through, only to find it was a different matter entirely—fibrillation in octogenarian patients or fibrillation as a result of metabolic disturbance.'

He'd come closer and rested his hand on her shoulder as he, too, peered at the screen. Any of their colleagues would have done the same thing, but only Phil's touch warmed her skin and eased the stiffness in her neck.

Until she realised why he was so interested in the information on the computer—not fibrillation at all. Frustrated at not finding anything similar to what had happened with Gemma, Maggie had run a quick search on personal medical matters, and although the search engine hadn't delivered any results when Phil had first walked in, they were all up on the screen now—page one of one hundred and eighty-four—all concerning spontaneous abortion in the first trimester of a pregnancy.

Phil's grip tightened on her shoulder and he crouched beside her.

'You haven't lost the baby, have you? Today? You shouldn't be here. Why didn't you say something?'

He was so pale and seemed so upset Maggie stopped any further speculation by putting her hand across his mouth.

'I haven't lost the baby,' she told him, then hesitated, took a deep breath and added, 'but I might. That's why I really didn't want to say anything, Phil. To you or to anyone else. Back when I was still a student, I was married. Jack was my first boyfriend—we'd been together at school, then at uni, we got married, I got pregnant...'

'You lost the baby?' Phil guessed, hoping he sounded OK when in reality his mind and body were coping with some strange reactions to the news Maggie had once been married.

Surely that hot, tight sensation in his gut couldn't be jealousy!

And coming on top of the shock discovery—however wrong—that she'd lost the baby, it was almost too much to cope with right now!

He decided to ignore all the internal commotion going on and concentrate on what she was telling him.

'That one and the next. But by the time I lost the second one I wasn't married any more, and I was also determined to get back on track with my career, so I didn't do anything about investigating why it had happened.'

She hesitated and Phil could read the fear lurking in her dark eyes, and again experienced a physical tightening of his gut—though this time for Maggie, for how she must be feeling.

'Now I wish I had,' she whispered. 'Wish I'd found out if there was some reason why I miscarried twice. Wish I knew if it was likely to happen again…'

Phil eased up from his crouched position and put his arms around her, drawing her to her feet so he could hold her properly and offering her the warmth and comfort of his body.

But while physically he was offering comfort, mentally he was nearly as upset as she was. They might lose this baby? That would be bad enough, but with no baby there'd be no reason for Maggie to marry him, and that thought bothered him more than the losing-the-baby possibility.

So, they'd better not lose the baby.

'Did you find anything? On the computer?'

Maggie obviously understood what he meant, for she pushed away from him.

'You saw the screen—the results have just come up. I hadn't looked at anything, let alone found anything.'

Phil heard the strain in her voice and pulled her close again, thinking now of practical matters.

'About a million hours ago, we were on our way to the canteen for dinner. Did you ever eat?'

She shook her head against his chest.

'I got over being hungry.'

'Me, too, but that's not good for either of us. Let's close this computer down, order something nutritious and delicious to be delivered, and go home. By the time we get there, the food will be on its way. We'll eat then go to bed. We can do a search tomorrow.'

He tilted her chin so he could look into her eyes.

'We could even consult an obstetrician—there's sure

to be a couple somewhere around the hospital. But for now let's go home.'

'Now *you're* saying the word,' she said, to hide the melting sensation in her bones his 'let's go home' had caused.

He smiled.

'Home? I guess I am—and do you know what, Mags? It feels like home. Or it does when we're not at odds with each other.'

He brushed his lips against her forehead and crossed to Annie's desk, where a list of all the local restaurants that delivered food was taped on the outside of the hospital phone directory.

'Italian?'

Maggie nodded. She was still absorbing what he'd said about their house feeling like a home and telling herself not to get too excited about it. He'd already told her he could feel 'at home' wherever he was working.

'Delivery in three-quarters of an hour. That will give us time to pop in on Pete before we leave—if you don't mind.'

They walked briskly through to the PICU, and Phil, rather than disturb the sleeping boy, or his mother who was dozing in the big chair by the bed, stopped at the desk and checked the monitor to see how his charge was doing.

'Temp's down, oxygen sats up, more fluid building in his abdomen, but we'll drain some more off during the night if it affects either his heart or his lungs,' the intensivist who'd joined Phil at the desk said.

They were turning away when Mrs Barron came out.

'Oh, Dr Walsh, I wanted to thank you again for the angel. I visited Joe and he was conscious but worrying, and as soon as I told him about the angel, the nurse said all his readings got better.'

She gave Maggie a hug, sniffed back a tear and beamed at Phil.

'This is some woman you've got yourself,' she said, then she returned to continue her vigil by her son's bed.

'Angel?' Phil queried as they went down in the lift.

'Annie and I arranged some home help for Mrs Barron, so she's not worrying herself to death about the family at home while she's visiting the hospital.'

'Most places I've worked, it could take weeks to organise home help. Unless, of course, you've got the wherewithal to pay for it, which I doubt is the case for the Barrons.'

'There are ways and means,' Maggie told him, not wanting to get into those particular ways and means.

'What ways and means?'

So much for not wanting to get into it.

'Annie and I are "locals"—well, she's a local and I'm from Melbourne, but it's the same country and a number of the same organisations exist in all the states.'

'You're waffling!'

They'd reached the hospital exit and Maggie stopped to pull on a jacket, Phil once again taking it from her hands and holding it for her to put on.

He couldn't resist the urge to hug her, once again wrapping his arms around her bulky, jacketed figure and drawing her close to his body. Then he freed her and in case she thought he'd lost the track of the conversation, he gave it a nudge.

'Ways and means?'

'I know this charitable trust that does small things like pay for home help in emergency situations. Annie found the helper and I'm arranging the finance for it. That's all.'

He was sure it wasn't all, but she wouldn't tell him more—not until she was ready. She was as stubborn as she was persistent, his Mags.

*His* Mags? Now, where had that come from?

The food arrived soon after they got home, and they sat together in the kitchen, eating what was now a very late dinner.

'I was hungrier than I realised,' Maggie said, tucking into a bowl of pasta with a chicken and pesto sauce, taking a break occasionally to help herself to some salad as well.

'Eating for two,' Phil teased, then regretted it when he saw the fear in her eyes. Fear for this baby, or remembered fear?

A different fear clutched at Phil's heart. Annie, they now knew, had lived in fear of an abusive husband, and with reason as the man had found and shot her, luckily only wounding her. Was this Maggie's fear as well?

'What happened, Maggie, that you weren't married any more when you had the second miscarriage?'

She looked surprised, then frowned and toyed with her fork, twirling it in the bowl.

'We'd known each other for ever, it seemed,' she said quietly. 'At school and then at uni—Jack doing engineering, me medicine. He wasn't well and we put it down to exhaustion. He was working part time as well—we both were—so he didn't see a doctor soon enough. He had leukaemia, acute, the prognosis terrible because it had been discovered too late. What he wanted most was to leave something behind. Something of himself—a child to go on living for him. We got married and I fell pregnant before he began radiation treatment, and just to be safe we also had some sperm frozen so if anything happened with the first pregnancy I could have another go.'

'And you miscarried twice!'

Phil took her hand and held it, his heart aching with pity for the young student she had been.

'He died?'

Maggie nodded.

'He died before he knew I'd lost the second baby. That was the only good thing—the timing of the loss. He died thinking the baby was OK and he'd live on in his son.'

She raised her head and offered a watery smile to Phil.

'Silly man—he was so sure it would be a son!'

'And you didn't try again. Didn't want to, later on?'

Maggie shook her head.

'I can't make myself believe that dead people know what's happening back on earth. I like the idea of a heaven, but I'm a doctor. I believe people live on in the memories of those who loved them, and in the people whose lives were touched by them, or are still touched in some way. Jack lives on that way.'

'Jack still touches people's lives?'

Maggie's face cleared of the grief he'd seen wash across it.

'He does,' she said simply, then she smiled at Phil. 'He's the charitable institution I talked about earlier. The one that will pay for the Barrons' angel. Jack's Way, it's called, because he always believed you should show people how you feel about them in a practical way.'

She hesitated but Phil wanted—needed?—to know more.

'Go on,' he encouraged, and won another smile, this one slightly embarrassed.

'It's funny to think how young we were!' Maggie said softly, still smiling.

Then she looked into Phil's eyes.

'When we were students, first and second year, we spent so much time sitting around talking, nearly always putting the world to rights. Were you the same? I imagine most young people are. Anyway, Jack maintained you should do what you can to help others who were trying to help themselves. Helping themselves was the important part. People who didn't try—who just took whatever they could get from government agencies or charities—infuriated Jack, but real battlers, well, he always had time for them.'

'So Jack's Way helps out battlers?' Phil prompted. He wasn't sure he wanted to know any more about this obviously saintly husband, but at the same time he was learning more about Maggie than he ever had before. 'Do you fundraise? How did you set it up?'

Maggie ate another piece of chicken then pushed her bowl away.

'He had a huge life insurance policy. Neither of us knew that, but his father had taken it out when Jack was young, thinking he could eventually cash it in when he wanted to buy a house. The last thing anyone expected was that a young healthy man would die.'

She paused and Phil waited.

'I didn't want the money,' she added in a small voice, 'so, with some friends, we founded Jack's Way and now every year the university students' union puts money into it as well, so we don't ever have to touch the principal but can use interest and donations to fund things like some help for the Barrons. We tend to do the small stuff that big agencies don't handle—things that don't cost much but, because we can put help in place immediately, can make a tremendous difference for families in times of crisis.'

Phil shook his head.

'What else have you done?'

Radiance shone through her smile this time.

'We've done the most amazing things, but they're simple things really. Flying a woman to South America after her daughter was injured in a car accident, bringing a grandmother out from England to take care of a suddenly orphaned family, paying for a young boy who'd lost his legs to go to the US for special prosthetics. We don't publicise the donations or help we give, but the larger agencies know about us, and hospitals in Melbourne are aware we exist, so somehow people in need seem to find us. It's confidential, the help we give—no, anonymous is probably a better word. I've only talked to you about it because of the Barrons.'

'And because you wanted to think about something other than miscarriages?' Phil said, reaching out to take her hand. 'Come on, it's very late. Let's go to bed. My bed, so I can hold and comfort you. It's way too late for anything but sleep. OK?'

Maggie looked at him, aware that the relationship between them had shifted into a different dimension.

Whether for better or worse, she wasn't sure, but she knew with the ghosts she'd raised this evening still floating around her head, her own bed would have been a very sad and lonely place.

But…

'Phil, I don't think that's a good idea. Going to bed with you—continuing a physical relationship…' She paused and even managed a smile. 'And don't tell me we wouldn't get physical no matter how late it is. It's just going to make things harder in the end.'

'In what end?' he asked, looking genuinely puzzled.

'In the end when we say that it's over.'

'But why need it be over? Why will this end come? We're good together, Mags, and be positive—we'll have the baby. And more babies to keep the little scrap company—that's if you want more babies—'

Maggie held up her hand to stop him talking before he dug himself into more trouble. She knew she'd reached the stage where only the truth would do, but she was so used to keeping all her feelings bottled up inside her she found it hard to put them into words.

'Being good together isn't enough for me, Phil. I married once for convenience. Oh, I loved Jack dearly and would have done anything for him—marrying him was no sacrifice. But if I marry again, it has to be for love. Not because I'm pregnant.'

She looked into the blue eyes of the man who'd sneaked in under her guard and stolen her heart, and saw confusion and more than a little pain. Standing up, she moved around the table and bent to kiss him on the cheek.

'I love you, Phil, but one-sided love's a desperate, lonely place to be. Let's wait and see about the baby, then make arrangements when and if we need to.'

It was as good an exit line as any, she thought as she walked out of the kitchen, her unfinished meal still on the table.

It was Phil's job to clear away and stack the dishwasher anyway, she told herself, as she dragged her weary body up the bed.

And you will not cry, she added silently. Not tonight and not any night. Your hormones aren't in that much of a mess.

But waking in the morning, she found her pillow strangely damp and realised her willpower hadn't worked while she'd slept.

The house was empty, a note from Phil saying he'd gone to work early tucked under the vase of flowers she'd never thanked him for.

Phil found her in the small lounge off the theatre, writing up notes on the operation they'd completed earlier. She hadn't heard him come in, and he watched her for a few seconds, the words she'd said last night echoing in his head.

He'd thought of Maggie as self-contained—right from when he'd first met her—but was that self-containment a cover for the lonely place she spoke of? Had she loved someone else who hadn't loved her? Someone after Jack?

Or was he, Phil, the one who'd sent her into exile there?

She'd said she loved him but there'd been despair in her words, and it had been that despair that had haunted him throughout the night.

Oh, she'd mentioned love earlier—even, if he remembered rightly, asked if he could offer it to her. But he'd brushed it aside, thinking love was connected with his dream—thinking about his version of what love might be, not what he might gain from giving it.

But if he said that now, told her he loved her as

Maggie and she was more important to him than any childhood dream, would she believe it?

Probably not! He was finding it hard to believe himself—this tumultuous shift in his emotions.

So rather than rush into action as he had already—engagement announcements and flowers, to name but two incidents—he had better make sure he explained what he was feeling in a very convincing manner.

And at an appropriate time...

Which wasn't right now.

He moved towards her, speaking quietly.

'I've made an appointment for us to see the obstetrician at four. He has rooms on the sixth floor—six-four-seven.'

She looked up and frowned, as if trying to place him, then she shook her head.

'You know once a woman's pregnant it's too late to do any tests to find out why she might have miscarried previously? All an obstetrician will say is wait and see.'

'But between eight and twelve weeks you can have a scan to date the baby's birth—I was reading up on it last night. They do a measurement called CRL—crown-rump length—and from a scale can tell exactly when it's due. Great, isn't it?'

He'd been fascinated by the things he'd learnt but Maggie didn't seem to be sharing his fascination. In fact, her frown seemed to have grown deeper.

'I'm not having a scan,' she said firmly.

'But—'

'No, Phil, I'm not! Neither am I seeing an obstetrician—not yet.'

She sighed, then closed the book she had beside the file on the coffee-table.

'Look, I may not have sought medical advice about

why I'd miscarried twice or had tests done, but I was a med student, for heaven's sake. I *did* look into it. If you want facts and figures, twenty per cent of pregnant women miscarry—that's one in five—most too early to recognise it as a miscarriage. Usually it's because of a foetal abnormality but occasionally it's a physical problem. The woman has an infection, there are environmental factors like smoking and drinking or even stress, which I was certainly suffering at the time. Then there are endocrine disorders.'

She sighed.

'The list goes on, Phil, but without knowing the exact cause, the best obstetrician in the world wouldn't be able to do anything right now.'

Maggie watched him, hoping this was sinking in—hoping mostly that he'd just walk away.

But hope didn't seem to be on her side right now. He came closer to sit on the couch beside her.

'I understand all of that, but why no obstetrician appointment? Why no scan?'

She turned to face him, then turned away again, her hand moving to protect her stomach. Then dipped her head so he wouldn't read the pain she felt in her face.

'Because having it confirmed—worse, seeing it on a scan—would make the baby so much more real. I'm sorry, but, knowing I might lose it, I can handle things—just—the way they are. But if I see its shape—at eight weeks it's got a face, Phil, the beginning of features, even a chin—no, I don't want to know this baby that intimately, thank you.'

The final words croaked out past all the emotional turmoil in her chest, but she got them said. Whether Phil understood or not, she didn't know and tried not to care.

But she did care, wanting his understanding nearly as much as she longed for his love.

Surely understanding wasn't too much to ask for…

'Ah, glad to find the two of you together. We're in strife—we as in the unit—and Alex wants to talk to the whole team in the rooms a.s.a.p.'

Had Annie, standing in the doorway, heard their conversation? She looked concerned but she would be, if the continuation of the unit was at risk.

'We'll be right with you.'

Phil answered for both of them, but though Maggie rose immediately to her feet he was slower, taking his time, waiting until Annie had departed then pulling Maggie into his arms and holding her close.

'It's your call, Mags,' he said softly. 'Whatever you want. Whatever it's in my power to give you. I mean that.'

She held him close for a moment, then pushed away, looking up into his face.

'Except love,' she reminded him.

And it was too late for him to tell her.

Love was forgotten as they joined the team, propped against desks in the suite of rooms, no one sitting down, which seemed strange. Until they learned of a medical negligence case being brought against the hospital following the death of Dr Ellis's patient.

Bad news apparently required you to be upright when you heard it!

'Are we mentioned specifically in the charge? Me? The unit?' Phil asked.

Alex shook his head.

'The charge is against the hospital but although it could take years to get to court, the hospital is taking it seriously and moving towards palliative—if that's the word in law as well as medicine—measures now.'

'Like blaming us and closing the unit?'

Rachel asked the question in all their minds.

'Something like that,' Annie explained. 'That way, when the case comes to court, or if they decide to go to mediation, the hospital can say, well, the problem was within this trial unit we'd set up, and we've now disbanded it so it won't happen again. A copout.'

'But the hospital would still have to pay if negligence is proved,' Maggie put in.

'The hospital has insurance, we all have insurance, it's only the insurance companies who pay,' Rachel said.

'Yes, they'll make the actual pay-out—part with the money—but they're also the ones who'll look for someone else to blame,' Kurt told her. 'The hospital's insurance company will come gunning for the unit, or for the insurance company that provides cover for the unit members.'

'But they have to prove negligence,' Annie said. 'Maybe we're getting all worked up over nothing.'

'They can't and won't prove negligence against us,' Alex said grimly. 'Phil made the absolutely correct decision, but don't tell me the administrators wouldn't prefer us as the scapegoat rather than Dr Ellis. After all, they'll figure most of the current unit staff will be gone before the case comes to court. Other hospital interests have already been clamouring to have both our funding and our theatre. They can offer a sop to the complainant's solicitors and placate their own departments all at once.'

'But if they use us as a scapegoat it will tarnish your and Phil's reputations. Phil's specifically,' Kurt pointed out. 'There's no way we can accept some kind of compromise or be shuffled quietly off into the sunset to give them something to offer to the other side's solicitors.'

'I could leave.'

Maggie knew she wasn't the only one who'd been struck dumb by Phil's pronouncement, but she was probably the only one whose heart stopped beating.

'Nonsense!'

Annie put everyone's feelings into one succinct word, but Phil held up his hand before anyone else could object.

'No, listen to me. It's the only sensible solution. If I get out, the team's reputation remains untarnished.'

'But yours...'

Rachel moved to stand beside him, unable to put her argument into words but wanting to show support.

'There's no way I'd allow that,' Alex said, also moving a little closer to his friend and colleague.

Maggie watched and wondered if any of them had noticed their physical reactions—if they were aware of moving closer to Phil.

She was by his side anyway, but had never felt further away. She had no idea what to say or do, but her heart, which had resumed beating, now ached with a weary kind of confusion. Was it because she was standing next to Phil that she sensed the pain his words had caused him? Or was it because she loved him and love had unconsciously discovered all the little nuances in his voice, and speech, and movements?

'You wouldn't have to allow it, Alex,' Phil said quietly. 'I'd resign.'

'You're not through your fellowship,' Alex said, angry now. 'And you'd be letting me down—and the whole team. We *are* a team, remember, and we stick together.'

'Scott can take my place. He's not had the experience, but he's going to be very good. Possibly better than me. For difficult cases, you can always get someone over from Children's. It's the way things were done here before—a paeds cardiac surgeon from over there, helping one of the adult surgeons from here.'

'But you can't leave with a cloud over your head,' Annie protested. 'It will ruin your whole future, and it's such a bright future, Phil.'

'Is it?' he said, then, after touching Maggie lightly on the hand, he turned and left the room.

Maggie knew the rest of the team was looking at her, waiting for her to follow him—talk some sense into him—but her legs wouldn't have carried her anywhere and, as she felt her knees give way, she sank down onto the nearest chair.

Talk broke out around her, but she barely heard it, wondering what had pushed Phil to take this stance. Then she heard Alex calling for quiet.

'Are we all agreed we'll fight this business as a team and not let Phil accept the role of scapegoat?'

Loud noises of agreement.

'And that we'll fight whatever the hospital administrators want to throw at us?'

More agreement.

'Good,' Alex said. 'That's decided. Now, if you'll excuse me, I'll go find my fellow and beat some sense into his stupid head.'

He glanced Maggie's way but she shrugged away the unasked question. She was too confused herself to be able to offer any advice whatsoever.

'OK, let's get out of this place. How about the Thai

restaurant down the road? We can get that big table in the alcove and have some privacy to talk this through.'

Maggie was surprised to hear Kurt organising things, but Rachel, Ned, Scott and the theatre and nursing staff present all seemed content to follow his lead.

'I've work to finish here,' Annie said, 'but you lot go ahead.'

'I'll stay and help you,' Maggie told her, knowing she couldn't sit through a meal where Phil's position was being discussed.

'Do you know why he offered to resign?' Annie asked, when the others had departed.

'Because he's Phil!' Maggie said. 'There's a lot of old-fashioned gallantry, and ''doing the right thing'' in our Phil. He felt by sacrificing himself he'd save the unit.'

She sighed.

'He's been upset about that baby since it happened. Upset about all the babies that die. Maybe he's just had enough.'

But she knew it wasn't true. Losing a baby—a child—would only make Phil work harder to save the next one, make him learn more, try something different, test out the widest parameters—anything to save a child.

To save having one more baby crying in his head...

'He needs a break,' Annie said. 'Alex was saying as much the other day. Phil carried on when Alex was distracted by me being in hospital, then we had our honeymoon, but Phil hasn't had a holiday in over a year. The work's too emotionally fraught for them to just keep going.'

She was talking sense, but Maggie knew she was also waiting for a contribution from the woman who was supposedly engaged to Phil—herself. But she had nothing to contribute. She loved him, and knew more about him now than she had when they'd moved in together—knew things about him she doubted many people knew. But most of what went on in his head was a complete mystery.

There were no lights on at Maggie's place when she and Annie walked home an hour later.

'They must both be down at my place,' Annie said. 'Come home and have a bite to eat, and find out what's happening.'

Not wanting to go into the dark, empty house, Maggie agreed, although she doubted Phil would be at Annie's, a doubt confirmed when they walked in.

'He's taken leave, packed a bag and left for the airport. Reckons if he's standing there, a seat will turn up on a flight to London sooner or later.'

Alex explained this while he poured them each a glass of white wine.

You'll just have to forgive me this lapse, Maggie told the baby, taking the glass and sipping gratefully at the wine.

'Why London?' someone said, only realising who the someone was when Annie and Alex answered together.

'Because his family's there,' they chorused, and Maggie knew she couldn't tell them he didn't have a concept of 'family' in the way most people did.

But, still, they *were* his family, and maybe in times of stress everyone turned to family, no matter how dysfunctional they were.

He certainly hadn't turned to her!

Although he'd left her a note.

'Take care of yourself, Mags. I'll be back. Love, Phil.'

Love, Phil! Her brothers signed their emails with 'Love, Jonah' and 'Love, Ryan', even Tom occasionally added a 'love' to his sign-off 'T'. That kind of 'love' meant nothing.

'Not quite the kind of note you clutch to your heart and treasure for ever!' Maggie muttered, but she did fold it into four and tuck it into her pocket, patting it from time to time as she walked up the stairs to prepare for bed.

# CHAPTER ELEVEN

SOMEHOW Maggie got through the next few days. Even before the court case drama blew up, Alex had asked Annie to juggle their operating load so he could give Phil some time off, so only simple operations were scheduled.

But having a less frenetic workload gave her more time to think, and she found herself missing Phil so badly she began to wonder if love had to be a two-way street for a marriage to work.

To make matters worse, the hospital's insurance company had appointed investigators, who were gathering information for a legal defence against the negligence claims. With Phil gone, they were targeting herself, Rachel and Kurt, making it obvious they were gunning for Alex's team and willing to throw the unit to the wolves in order to save the hospital's reputation.

'It's stupid,' Alex said, when he and Annie called in for a coffee after dinner. Knowing Maggie was lonely, they'd brought Minnie with them and suggested she stay with Maggie for a while. 'The hospital's defence team should be concentrating on the facts—on things like statistics showing the number of babies born with such defective hearts die anyway. On statistics showing the results of operations on neonates. They should be doing that, not badgering my staff about what happened during the op.'

'Their story is they have to know everything that happened because the other side could bring up something, and if they don't know about it, they can't argue against it.'

'Seems a strange way to be doing things,' Annie said, reaching out to pat Minnie who was snuggled up on Maggie's lap.

But Alex looked interested.

'Was there anything went on? Do you think there could have been a problem during the op?'

'The baby was on bypass for a long time. Kurt mentioned it at the time. And Rachel manually kept his heart beating just before he went on pump, but I've seen her do that when you and Phil were operating.'

Maggie paused and looked at Alex.

'I don't think we should be looking to blame our colleagues, even those from other hospitals,' she said quietly.

Alex nodded.

'You're right, but neither should we cover up mistakes. That's happened too often in the past in the world of medicine. The old joke that doctors can bury their mistakes has a lot of truth in it. Be fair, be honest in all you say, but try also to be detached. Tell it like it was without worrying about consequences. Think of the consequences of covering up a colleague's incompetence.'

Maggie nodded.

'I know what you're saying, and I've been totally honest about my recollections of the op. I've let them see my notes, but I can't and won't make judgements about the other staff's abilities or conduct. I know what I did and what Evan, who was the anaesthetist in charge, did, and I watched other stuff from time to time, and heard things like Kurt's comment, but I wouldn't have a clue if the surgeon tied the right kind of knot or not.'

Annie laughed, easing the tension that had grown in the room, but no amount of laughter could ease the tension that pervaded the unit over the next week.

'We can't go on like this for the rest of the year, or for however long it takes for the case to get to court,' Maggie said to Annie as they walked the two dogs in the park the following Saturday. 'Everyone's so uptight, something's got to give.'

'At least Pete and his father are both on the mend,' Maggie reminded her, although she too had wondered how long they could go on before something fired the tension into an explosion that would tear the whole unit apart.

'It would have been easier if the hospital administrators had stuck by us and tackled the case head on, rather than trying to weasel out of it by blaming us.'

'Why can't they blame Ellis?' Maggie asked. 'He's a consultant, not on staff.'

'Because he's the one that suggested the parents sue. I imagine they were so upset he used the suggestion to divert them. Probably didn't think they would, because he's not going to come out of this too well.'

'But it's Phil whose career will really suffer,' Maggie said, the sadness she carried within her pressing against her breastbone so she had to hold her hand against it for a moment.

'Yes,' Annie said, finishing the conversation, because there was nothing more to say.

Somewhere someone was making a terrible noise. At first Maggie thought it was in her dreams, but when she finally shook herself out of a deep sleep, she realised it was Minnie, barking furiously at the front door.

Clambering out of bed, Maggie grabbed her old chenille dressing-gown and wrapped it around her body. A quick glance at the clock told her it was well past midnight, and the fact that she could now hear knocking at the front door suggested it was unlikely to be a burglar asking to be let in.

Downstairs, she quietened Minnie by picking her up, then she turned on the porch light and peered through the spyhole. A bit of a blue and red striped tie, white shirt and suit lapels came into view, but try as she may she couldn't see a face.

'Who is it?' she called through the heavy door.

'Callan Park.'

She must be hearing things. Or the man wasn't very good at aliases. Even people from Melbourne knew the old mental asylum in Sydney had been called Callan Park. These days it housed a number of small organisations, but that didn't explain the man…

'Who?'

'Phil's brother, Callum. Callum Park.'

Oh!

'Phil's not here.'

That wasn't right, yelling such an unwelcoming statement through the door, but recent events had her dithering uncertainly.

'Phil's on his way,' the stranger said. 'We could only get one seat on the flight I came on, so he's following. He'll be here tomorrow morning but if you'd rather I went to a hotel, that's all right. But I've sent the cab away…'

*Phil's on his way*. The words rang like music in her ears and she opened the door.

'I'm sorry,' she said to Callum, who was frowning at her in exactly the way Phil so often did.

'No, I'm sorry,' he said, his beautiful voice making the words seem special. 'I should have phoned first, or asked Phil to phone. You really shouldn't be letting strangers into your house at any time, let alone at one in the morning.'

He looked so like Phil she smiled at him, and lifted Minnie higher for his inspection.

'Not even when I have my fierce watchdog to protect me?'

'Ah! This, I assume, is Minnie.'

He reached out to fondle the squirming dog.

'Why are you here? What's happening? Where's Phil been that he's flying in in the morning?'

'He's been home,' the man who looked like Phil said, then he leaned forward to kiss Maggie on the cheek. 'To see his family,' he added, then lifted his bag and looked expectantly at the steps. 'Spare bedroom upstairs?'

Totally bemused by now, Maggie nodded.

'Last door on the left,' she said. 'The bed's made up.'

'Great!' Callum announced, and he headed up the stairs. 'I can never sleep on planes, no matter how long they make the bed.'

Too awake—too excited—now to be able to consider sleeping, Maggie carried Minnie through to the kitchen, where she put the dog back in her basket, then opened the fridge, hoping to find something to munch on while she considered this latest development in her life.

Though it wasn't in *her* life, it was in Phil's.

His brother had come to visit—so what?

But no amount of plain talking to herself would banish the feeling of excitement simmering inside her.

Phil was coming back—that was part of it. But he was coming home as well, she felt sure of it.

Then the wetness came, and she knew exactly what was happening. She rested her head on the door of the fridge and cried.

Although her previous experiences of miscarriage had been so long ago, she still remembered how it would progress. She couldn't stay leaning on the fridge for much longer.

On leaden legs she made her way up to her bathroom, turned on the shower, stripped off her clothes and stood under the cascading water while her hopes and dreams, and an embryo barely three centimetres long, were washed away.

Her tears mingled with the cleansing water—tears for the baby, for Phil and what might, in time, have been. Then she began to shiver—the water was running cold. She left the refuge of the shower stall, dried herself, pulled on a comfortable old flannel nightdress and crawled into bed.

Later today—no, today was Sunday, tomorrow— she'd see a doctor, book in for a curette, do what had to be done and maybe even arrange for tests to find out why she couldn't carry a baby.

Though she doubted she'd worry about the tests…

She doubted it would ever be important.

Her heart felt as if the blood was seeping out of it— her life washing away with that of the tiny embryo.

She woke to find the day had begun without her, bright sunshine streaming through her window.

Too bright, too sunshiny! It should have been raining—gloomy as her mood. Dull as the ache in her chest.

She pulled on her dressing-gown and headed downstairs. At least she could drink real coffee now. Cups and cups of it.

And focus on her career again—on saving the lives of other babies.

She was at the bottom of the stairs before she heard the voices and remembered she had a visitor. But voices? Was he talking to himself?

Minnie! He'd be talking to Minnie.

But such common-sense explanations didn't cut it with her body, which was showing all the signs it usually did when Phil was in the vicinity.

Phil—what would Phil think?

He'd be relieved.

He'd have to be.

The thought made her even sadder and she swallowed hard.

No self-pity!

Neither would she dash back upstairs—to hide or even to change into something more attractive.

Maggie continued doggedly on her way.

Phil was sitting in his usual chair, Minnie on his lap, his brother opposite him, and, most surprising of all, Annie and Alex were also at the table.

But it was Phil who saw her first, his face breaking into a smile that faded as she watched. Then he was on his feet, depositing Minnie on the floor, walking towards Maggie and taking her arm, guiding her out of the kitchen, out of earshot and away from watching eyes, then taking her in his arms and holding her close for a long, long minute.

He cuddled her close, murmured her name then kissed her on the top of her head, before easing away so he could look at her.

'Mags! What is it? Are you OK? Is it the baby?'

Maggie couldn't answer. Oh, there were heaps of things she'd have liked to say. *Why should anything be wrong?* would be a starter, and *Why should you care about the baby?* should follow straight after it. But her voice wouldn't work and Phil must have realised it for he folded her once again into his arms and whispered, 'Oh, love,' in such a broken voice it was all she could do not to burst into tears all over again.

'When did it happen?' he asked, still holding her tightly.

'Last night.'

'Damn that Ellis. I should have been here. Mags, I'm sorrier than I can ever say! Sorry I wasn't here, but sorry too about the baby.' His voice cracked as he added, 'Our baby!'

Maggie let him hold her, drawing strength from his arms and warmth from the genuine sense of loss she could hear in his voice. Then his arms tightened and he was talking again, saying things she'd never thought to hear—saying things she hardly dared believe.

'But there'll be other babies, Mags. For both of us—and if there aren't then we'll still have each other.'

He tilted up her chin and kissed her on the lips.

'We will have each other, won't we?' he whispered, his usually confident voice shaky with emotion. 'Because I love you, Maggie Walsh, with all my heart and mind and soul. You asked me for my love once and I backed away, offered no guarantee, but that was before I realised how important you are to me—far more important than a fantasy cottage with fantasy roses climbing over the door. More important, Mags, than life it-self.'

He held her for a long time, rocking her back and forth, then he lifted her into his arms, carried her up the stairs and tucked her back into bed, taking control both of his emotions and the situation—being practical—talking all the time.

'Stay there. You're sheet-white. You don't look after yourself properly. I'll get you something. Coffee and toast? I'll send the lot in the kitchen down to Annie's house to talk and we'll have this place to ourselves. Stay right there. Don't move. I'll be right back.'

Maggie stared at him, still trying to make sense of what was happening.

All of what was happening…

'You love me?' she whispered, and won a funny, twisted kind of smile from Phil.

'So much you wouldn't believe,' he told her, the half-smile still hovering around his lips. 'But food first. I'm famished, too. I don't know how that can be because I did nothing but eat on the plane.'

He bent and kissed her—hard—then left the room.

Maggie stared up at the ceiling, wondering how one person could be so sad yet so happy at the same time. And she was really perfectly OK—physically—so why had she submitted to Phil's fussing?

Especially when a meeting of some importance was obviously going on downstairs.

But Phil was here—he'd said he loved her and now he was bringing coffee and toast, so she snuggled down deeper into the bed and waited for him to come back.

'Callum's a barrister who did medicine first then switched to law so he's become an expert in medico-legal work,' Phil explained, much later, when he was lying back against the pillows on the other side of her bed.

They'd talked about her miscarriage, established she'd do all the right things as far as seeing doctors went and held each other close again to ease the ache of loss. Then practicality had exerted itself and they'd demolished a large plate of toast and strawberry jam. Now Maggie was savouring her first real coffee in ages and watching the man she loved as he sought for the words he wanted to say to her.

'You made me think of Cal,' Phil added, turning so he could kiss Maggie's cheek. 'You and your talk of home and family. He'd been in my mind for a while—he and Laura, my sister. So when this blew up, I thought I'd go and see him, to talk about the case but also to talk about other things. About our upbringing and family and what it meant to him and Laura. The problem was, we hadn't ever talked about it. We'd been close as children—united against the world when we were small—but then we all went off to boarding school and saw so little of each other that the sibling closeness seemed to fade away.'

Maggie put her coffee cup on the bedside table and moved so she could hold his hand, her body pressed closer to his, although she was in the bed and he was on it.

Phil kissed her cheek again, as if in thanks, then lifted her hand to his lips and kissed the back of it.

'I let it fade away, Mags,' he said. 'I told myself it didn't matter. Oh, I always saw Cal and Laura when I was in the UK—we'd have a drink, a meal, but that was it. We never talked.'

Maggie turned to look at him and saw the tiredness of travel in his face, but below that there was warmth, as if he'd found something special that had been missing from his life for a long time.

'You talked this time?' she prompted quietly.

Phil beamed at her.

'Talked and talked, all three of us. We even dragged Mother in at the end and talked with her as well.'

He hesitated and then added, 'I found I had a family after all.'

Maggie swallowed the lump in her throat—couldn't blame hormones this time—and tried to concentrate on where this conversation had begun.

'And Callum?' she asked, but Phil was sound asleep, a small smile of contentment lingering on his face.

Maggie rolled over so she was curled against his body, though a sheet, two blankets and an eiderdown separated them, and went quietly off to sleep herself.

Callum stayed a fortnight, spending most of his time locked in conference with hospital officials and insurance officers, making it exceedingly clear the unit staff would not accept anything less than complete exoneration in the tragic death of the baby.

'You've got to see something of Australia while you're here,' Phil told him, late in his visit, on one of the rare occasions he, Maggie and Cal were eating dinner together at home. 'You can't go back to England without seeing anything of the country.'

'Not this time,' Cal said. 'But I'll take a month's leave when I come out for your and Maggie's wedding, and do some travelling then.'

'Wedding?' Maggie said.

Cal smiled at her.

'Don't tell me he hasn't asked you yet! He was like that as a small boy—always putting things off because he felt there had to be a perfect moment to do or ask whatever it was. Of course, there's never a perfect moment.'

'I think there are,' Maggie said stoutly, thinking of the whispered 'Oh, love' she still carried in her heart.

'Don't tell him that,' Cal groaned. 'You'll never get him up to the mark.'

'Have you ever thought Maggie might not want me?' Phil said.

'Drivel! Of course she wants you. Even Minnie knows she's head over heels in love with you.'

The little dog, hearing her name, came to sit at Callum's feet.

'Don't you, Min?' he added, and Maggie was grateful his attention had been diverted as she knew her cheeks would be scarlet with embarrassment.

Phil did know she loved him—she'd told him so— but she wasn't going to let his brother bully him into doing something he didn't want to do.

'Love's just a word that has different meanings in different contexts,' she told Callum. 'Some love is transient, ephemeral—not strong enough to build a relationship on, let alone a marriage. Marriage is about for ever and the love you need for that is gut-deep.'

Then, embarrassed by the conversation, she stood up.

'I've got to go back up to the hospital for a while,' she said, knowing Phil would insist on walking up with her. 'When you boys finish arguing you can stack the dishwasher.'

Phil was on his feet before she reached the door.

'You can't walk up there in the dark on your own. Callum can stack. I'll come with you.'

Maggie smiled to herself, partly because she'd been

right in her prediction but also because there'd been so much going on, and with Callum in the house she and Phil had spent very little time together.

'I'm OK,' she said to him, when they were walking out the gate. 'I understand where things stand between us. Even if you do love me, we want such different things from marriage it would never work, so don't let your brother bully you into doing something you don't want to do.'

She was holding his hand because it seemed a natural thing to do, and she felt his response in the pressure of his fingers.

'It's hard, Mags,' he said, drawing her closer, their hands still clasped together. 'Hard because what Callum said is true—I do put off important things, thinking there should be an optimum moment. And what you said is true about knowing where things stand—or it was true, up until the time I went away. That's when I realised how much you meant to me. Far more than any dream of a picture-perfect home, or some image of a stay-at-home wife. I went to see Callum as a barrister who would help us with the court case and ended up seeing him as a brother, because suddenly it was important to me that I had a family—that I understood family as you understand it.'

He stopped and turned towards her.

'It was important for me to learn what family meant, because I knew I didn't have a hope of persuading you to marry me if I was still vague about the concept. And if I didn't understand it, then I'd lose my wise, passionate and, oh, so compassionate Maggie.'

He paused and brushed a kiss across her lips.

'I had to learn that home and family are about people, not places—that it's the people and the love they share that makes a family complete, that makes any place they dwell in home. For some reason I'd let my fantasy tarnish the love I feel for my own family, and let it blind me to the love the members of it have for me.'

He paused again, to kiss her once more, but also to draw breath because he hadn't finished all he had to say.

'But I know the difference now, Mags, between fantasy and reality. You're reality—you and me. That's reality. But I needed to leave you—to be away from you—to realise just how much I love you. Love you gut-deep—I couldn't have put it any better.'

She looked up into his face, and saw the plea in the way he stood, and read anxiety in his eyes.

They were near the main road now, the footpath too brightly lit for them to see the stars. The air was redolent with petrol and diesel fumes, and the only music was the roar of traffic, the occasional squeal of brakes and the occasional blare of a car horn.

'Is this the perfect moment you've been looking for?' Maggie teased, and Phil let out a huge sigh of relief, gathered her in his arms and kissed her soundly.

'Woohoo!' a young voice cried, and two teenagers skirted around them.

'I love you, Mags. Will you marry me?' Phil asked, and Maggie snuggled close to him again and nodded.

'No, I need to hear the words,' he said, so Maggie looked up at him and said just one word.

'Yes.'

# THE ITALIAN SURGEON

### BY
### MEREDITH WEBBER

# CHAPTER ONE

RACHEL dropped her mask and gown into the bin as she walked out of the operating theatre. Too tired to be bothered showering and changing immediately, she headed straight for the small theatre lounge, where she slumped down into an armchair and pulled off her cap.

'I think it is close to criminal that such beautiful hair should be hidden under such an ugly cap,' a deep, accented voice remarked, and Rachel, her fingers threaded through the hair in question, turned in alarm.

The voice certainly didn't belong to any of the members of the paediatric cardiac surgical team here at Jimmie's—she'd all but lived with them for the past year, at first in Melbourne, where the team had spent six months, and since then in Sydney!

The body didn't belong to anyone on the team either—here was a serious hunk, not overly tall, but solid in a way that would make any woman want to experience being held in his arms.

This was a dispassionate observation—made on behalf of all womankind—not personal at all. She no longer did personal observations of men.

Now an ultra-white smile flashed from the kind of face Rachel had only ever seen in ads for men's fashion—expensive men's fashion. But this was no photographic image—this was drop-dead handsome in real life.

5

She suspected her observation was becoming a tad less dispassionate, and was puzzled by it.

Dark eyes, set beneath ebony brows, met hers.

'You don't know me. I was late arriving—too late for introductions. I am Luca Cavaletti, here to observe and learn from Alex and all his team.'

He smiled again, then added, 'Including you.'

Bemused by some very unaccustomed physical re-actions to a man, she could only stare at him, though she did clench her fingers, which desperately wanted to move to her head again and fluff up the hat-hair she knew was on show. Hat-hair tousled into knots by her fingers' initial foray through it.

'You were in Theatre?' she asked, her eyes, fasci-nated by his strongly boned face, strayed to clearly delineated lips then moved back to study the dark, piercing eyes.

Crikey, it was as if she'd never seen a man before!

Thanks to a show she'd watched on TV back home in the States, 'Crikey' was about the only 'Australianism' she'd known before she'd come down under with Alex and the team, and she used it in her thoughts all the time.

'I thought it seemed a little more crowded than usual, though Alex and Phil always draw a number of onlookers.'

'Ah, but I'm more a student than an onlooker. I'm a qualified paediatric cardiac surgeon, but Alex has techniques we don't use in Italy, and the whole team has a cohesiveness that is known throughout the world. I'm fortunate enough to be here for four weeks,' the man said, taking the chair across from Rachel so she was no longer looking up at him.

Maybe from this new angle her hair didn't look quite as bad!

Maybe she should have a brain transplant to stop this reaction thing happening.

She let her fingers escape for one quick ruffle at the front, and tried to remember what Alex had said about someone coming to observe for a few weeks.

Someone fabulously wealthy! She stole another glance at the man, though she doubted she could tell a rich man from a poor one just by looking, especially if both were in that great leveller—theatre pyjamas!

'There's coffee in the pot over there and sandwiches in the refrigerator,' she said, not because she felt obliged to play hostess but because she was back to cataloguing the stranger's physical attributes and couldn't think of anything else to say.

And she'd found a flaw—a slight scar running across his left eyebrow, marring the perfect symmetry of that feature but adding to, rather than detracting from, his beauty. No, beauty was far too feminine a word when this man was masculinity personified.

She touched her own scar, a far more jagged and less appealing mark, running down her hairline from left temple to left ear, the result not of anything dramatic but of falling off her bicycle onto broken glass when she'd been five. Then, thinking again of the man's good looks, she smiled to herself, wondering what Kurt would make of him.

'Can I pour you a coffee?' he asked.

And sit here in theatre scrubs, no make-up and impossible hair while the archetypical Latin lover was sitting opposite her?

She might not be interested in men, but as a woman she had some pride!

'No, thanks, I need to grab a shower and change. I just came in to sit down for a little while to gather up the energy to make the next move.'

'Of course, of all the team, you have the longest time in Theatre—seeing everything is ready first, then assisting the surgeon who makes the primary incision and prepares the heart for Alex, as well as assisting him. With the added tension of operating on such tiny infants, you must be exhausted by the finish.'

Seduced more by the understanding in his words than by the soft accent that curled around them, Rachel smiled.

'I don't think the tension I feel is nearly as bad as the stress the surgeons are under,' she said. 'Yes, I have more theatre time, but my job is the easy one.'

He shook his head and smiled, as if he knew better, but then he turned away, apparently taking up her offer of a coffee. She struggled to her feet, told them to walk, not run, and left the room, escaping to the washrooms where, if necessary, she could resort to the time-honoured convention of a cold shower.

Though wasn't it men who usually needed cold showers?

And, physiologically, why would they work?

Did blood really heat in a sexual reaction to another person?

It certainly wasn't a topic she remembered covering in nursing school.

And she couldn't possibly be having a sexual re-action to the man, anyway. No way! He was another colleague, nothing more. And his charm was probably as natural to him as breathing.

What had he said his name was? Luca—she remembered that part, because the way he'd said it had lilted off his tongue.

What would he make of Rachel?

How would her name sound, whispered in that husky accent?

She banged her head against the wall of the shower stall. Kurt was right. She really should get out more.

'You OK in there?'

Maggie's voice.

'I'm fine, just bumped against the wall,' Rachel lied, but hearing Maggie reminded her she *was* going to get out more—starting tonight! Maggie and Phil's engagement party at the Italian restaurant not far from the hospital—a restaurant the whole team now frequented.

But going out to eat with other members of the team—even attending an engagement party—did not constitute 'getting out more', Rachel reminded herself. Getting out more, in Kurt's view, meant dating—going out with a man, perhaps having a relationship.

She shuddered at the thought, and felt a suggestion of old pain, like a hidden bruise, somewhere deep within her, but then an image of the Italian's face flashed up in her mind's eye, and the shudder became a shiver…

She showered—under hot water, damn the cold—dried herself and dressed, hoping she wouldn't run into tall, dark and deadly again because she'd woken late this morning and dragged on the first clothes she'd put her hands on—a pair of comfy but far from young sweat pants, and a bulky, misshapen sweater her mother, during a knitting phase of her exploration of various handicrafts, had knitted for her.

Knitted with more love than skill—the love ingredient ensuring Rachel had worn it to death.

She poked her head out of the shower stall. The changing room was used by both male and female members of the team, and she usually checked she wasn't going to embarrass anyone before emerging.

The unspoken but commonly agreed standard of embarrassment was total nudity. Underwear was OK, though the thought of seeing Luca whoever-he-was in tight black briefs made Rachel's mouth go dry.

The reality of him in that identical garb had her reaching for the door of the shower stall for support.

Kurt was definitely right about her getting out more, though the thought made her heart quail and again the remembered pain pressed against her ribs.

Perhaps she could just date. Go out with a guy a couple of times—really casual—enough to get used to being around a man again.

Though she worked with men all the time, so it wasn't lack of male companionship that had her reacting the way she was to the temporary team member.

'You are finished in the shower?'

She opened her mouth and formed her lips to say the word, but whether a 'yes' came out she wasn't sure. None of the other team members had olive skin stretched tight across their chests—skin that clung lovingly to flat slabs of muscle.

Well, not that she'd noticed, anyway…

'Talk about buffed!' Kurt whispered in her ear, appearing from nowhere, taking her arm and guiding her across the room to the washbasins and mirrors. 'The man is gorgeous, but I'm pretty sure he's all yours.

No signals at all in my direction, and I'm not wearing my very worst clothes.'

'You know I don't care!' she snapped at Kurt. 'I couldn't be less interested.'

But in spite of her defiant words, Rachel glanced down at her unglamorous attire and winced, then looked up at herself in the mirror and groaned.

'In any case, there's no way a man like him— Didn't Alex say something about him being rich and famous? Famous in his own country?'

She didn't wait for Kurt's nod, but continued, 'Well, a man like that wouldn't be interested in a woman like me, even at the best of times. But today?' She smiled at Kurt. 'I think we both miss out. Anyway he was probably snapped up years ago. Married with two point five children would be my guess.'

'He's not.'

Rachel stared at her friend's reflection.

'Not what?'

'Not married. No ring. Continental men were into wearing wedding rings long before we Americans adopted the custom.'

'But no one wears a ring in Theatre, so you can't tell.'

Kurt sighed, as he often did when he was shown what he called the depth of her ignorance of the male sex.

'The guy's got naturally olive skin, but he's tanned as well—babies aren't born that delectable bronze colour. And there's no pale mark around his finger where a ring has been.'

Rachel poked her tongue at him.

'Smart-ass!' she said, but her silly heart was skipping with excitement as she dragged a comb through her wet hair. A whole string of 'crikeys' echoed in her head, the only possible means of expressing the disbelief she felt about this situation.

Here she was reacting to a man as if she were a teenager—she, who hadn't been interested in a man for years. True, from time to time she tried to pretend, mainly when well-meaning friends threw men at her, but none of them had ever sparked the slightest physical response or filled her with an urge to get involved again.

In fact, the thought of getting involved again made her stomach clench.

'Damn this hair. It's impossible to manage. I shouldn't have let you talk me into growing it.'

Kurt took the comb from her hand and carefully drew it through the tangled curls.

'It's beautiful hair,' he reminded her. 'So beautiful it was a sin to keep it cropped short purely for convenience. Besides, as I pointed out to you when we first came to Australia, how would you have known a good hairdresser from a bad one? And for short hair you need the best. Far better to have grown it.'

Finished, he handed back the comb, while, behind them, Luca emerged from the shower, this time with a snowy white towel draped around his hips. It didn't do anything to diminish his good looks!

He came towards the mirror, nodding to Kurt who had hurried to grab the shower before someone else went in. With only two stalls, the competition among the team was usually fierce.

'You and Kurt are a couple?'

Still conversing in the mirror rather than face to face, Rachel saw herself as well as the dark-featured man. So she also saw the frown that drew her eyebrows together, and the look of puzzlement in her own eyes.

'Me and Kurt? No.'

Not knowing why he was asking—he couldn't possibly be interested in her as they'd barely met—she wasn't prepared to offer any more information. She tucked her comb into her toiletry bag and carried it over to her locker, pleased to have a reason to move away from the double whammy of the man and his mirror image.

'Good,' he said, following her and holding open her locker door. Far too much bronzed skin, now Kurt had drawn her attention to it, far too close to her body.

'So perhaps there is someone else in your life?'

'Are you coming on to me?' Rachel demanded, more angered by her reaction to his presence than by the pace of his approach. 'Why? Because I'm convenient? Save you looking elsewhere for someone to while away the off-duty hours for the time you're here?'

She grabbed the door of her locker away from him and slammed it shut, then remembered she needed to get her shoulder-bag out and had to open it again.

Luca whoever was staring at her with a puzzled expression in his so-dark eyes.

'I'm sorry. I've offended you.' His accent was more marked now, and he did sound genuinely regretful. 'But I know Maggie and Phil are a couple, and Annie and Alex also. I thought perhaps you and Kurt...'

He held out his hands in a typical Mediterranean gesture.

'Not in this world, or the next, though I love the

woman dearly.' Kurt, who must have heard the conversation, smirked as he sashayed past them.

What was it with these men that they were in and out of the shower so quickly?

And what had got into Kurt that he was talking and joking this way? Kurt the silent was how most people thought of him, though Rachel knew him better and understood why he usually listened more than he talked.

Loud conversation signalled the arrival of more members of the team: Alex Attwood, team leader and top paediatric cardiac surgeon; Phil Park who was all but through a five-year fellowship with Alex; and Scott Douglas, the surgical registrar here at St James's Hospital, who was currently on roster with their team.

'Ah, Luca, you've met these two indispensable members of my crew,' Alex said, coming towards them. 'Rachel, as you no doubt saw, is the best physician's assistant any surgeon could ever have, while Kurt's refinements to the heart-lung bypass machine have made operating on neonates far safer for the patient and far easier for me.'

Luca put out his hand to acknowledge Alex's introduction to Kurt, then turned, hand still extended, to Rachel.

'We've not been formally introduced,' he said to Alex, but his eyes were on Rachel, and though she was reasonably sure eyes couldn't send subliminal messages, she was certainly receiving something that made her feel tingly all over, even before his hand engulfed hers, and strong, warm fingers applied gentle pressure.

'Luca Cavaletti.'

He released her hand but his eyes still held hers.

By this time Rachel was so thoroughly confused by her physical reactions to him, her mind had stopped working.

Or almost stopped working…

'Rachel Lerini,' she managed to respond, and wasn't surprised when the man to whom she'd spoken let fly in a stream of Italian.

'Whoa there!' she said, recovering enough composure to hold up her hand. 'My great-grandfather brought the name to America and while it's been passed on, his language certainly wasn't. *Ciao*, *prego* and pasta—that's the limit of my Italian.'

'Perhaps I will have time to teach you new words,' he said softly.

Rachel frowned at him. She hadn't totally forgotten how things worked between men and women in the dating game and from what she remembered, this man was moving far too fast for her to feel comfortable.

Actually, her physical reactions—silly things like tingles and shivers—were making her more wary, rather than more attracted. It was so weird.

So unlike anything she'd experienced before…

So new…

She was so busy trying to work out what was happening, she didn't realise the man was still there—and talking to her!

'Are you already going with someone or would you like to be my date tonight at the party?'

'No.'

The word positively erupted from her lips, so blunt it sounded rude. Politeness forced her to explain, 'It's not that kind of party. It's a celebration for Phil and Maggie, and a double celebration in a way because some bad stuff that's been happening for the team has

been resolved. But it's a team party—everyone
goes—so you don't need a date.'

'Besides, if she did need a date, she's got me,' Kurt
said, turning from the washbasin a little distance away
where he'd been pretending to wash out a small bottle
while listening avidly to the conversation.

'She's the cat's mother!' Rachel spat the words at
her well-meaning friend. She definitely wanted to
fend Luca off—to slow him down—but she wasn't
altogether, one hundred per cent, absolutely and utterly certain that she wanted to lose his attention altogether.

And *that* thought was even scarier than her physical
reactions. Crikey—it was hard to know what she
wanted.

Though given that it had been months since she'd
had even a casual date, and four years since her marriage had ended in the most disastrous way possible,
maybe a four-week flirtation with Luca Cavaletti
might be just what the doctor ordered.

The person inside her head groaned at the weak
pun.

'I'm going to the office to do some paperwork,'
Rachel said, hoping the Italian would take the hint
and move away to torment someone else. 'I'll see you
at home, Kurt.'

She walked away, but escape was never going to
be that easy. Stopping outside the changing room to
talk to Annie, who was checking the lists for the following day, meant Luca caught up with her and then
accompanied her to the suite of rooms the team used
for an office.

'You live with Kurt?' he said, following her into

the room, his voice alerting Becky, the secretary, who was manning the front desk.

'Yes.'

'But he flirts with me! He's gay, isn't he?'

Rachel wasn't sure if he was being sexist or not, but years of defending Kurt, her best friend, had her hackles rising.

'So?' she demanded, and Luca's smile lit up his face as he stretched his arms wide to each side and shrugged his broad shoulders.

'So he's not your boyfriend, just your friend,' he said, then he turned and winked at Becky who was staring at the two of them as if this was a show put on solely for her amusement.

'Mr Cavaletti—or Dr Cavaletti—whichever you prefer,' Rachel said, trying hard to sound icily in control while in reality the smile and shrug had turned her bones to jelly and she was considering returning to the shower to try the cold-water treatment. 'Just because Kurt isn't my boyfriend, it doesn't mean I don't have one. I don't know how you do things back in Italy, but for an American woman, you're moving far too fast. If you're anxious about the limited time you have here in Australia, then go sweep someone else off her feet. Mine are staying firmly on the ground.'

'I'm sorry, but I felt an attraction—the hair maybe—I don't know...' He offered an apologetic smile. 'I'm not normally impulsive.'

Shoot—it was with difficulty she stifled the 'cri-key'—but the man's remorse was nearly as good as his smile! The feet, which she'd said were firmly planted, now seemed to be floating several inches above the floor.

Luca touched her lightly on the shoulder.

'You *do* have a boyfriend?'

Rachel stared at him. Big opportunity here! The lie—a simple yes—hovered on the tip of her tongue. An easy word to say—a single syllable—but she'd left it too late, because he was smiling again.

'I will slow down!' he said softly.

Then he leaned forward and kissed her, first on one cheek, then on the other. And while Rachel pressed her hands to the burning patches of skin, he walked away.

'If you don't want him, give him to me,' Becky said, her awed tone conveying loads more than the words themselves.

'Feel free,' Rachel told her, but Becky shook her head.

'It seems he's only got eyes for you.'

Embarrassed, both by Becky's words and the little pantomime that had been played out in front of the secretary, Rachel shook her head in denial.

'It's the hair,' she told Becky. 'Apparently it's not a common colour in Italy.'

'It is beautiful, your hair,' Becky told her. 'A true red-gold. Makes us blondes look ordinary.' She eyed Rachel consideringly before adding, 'Although I'd always been given to understand Italian men went for blondes. What are you wearing tonight?'

The question was so transparent Rachel laughed.

'My old flannel pyjamas with Snoopy all over them?' she teased.

'That might work,' Becky said, 'though if he's hooked on your hair he probably wouldn't notice anything else. Pity, because Alex was saying he's rich as well as gorgeous—well, Alex didn't say he was gorgeous, that was me.'

Rachel chuckled and headed for the desk she shared with Kurt. So Luca *was* the wealthy man Alex had mentioned.

And with looks and money, he was probably used to women falling at his feet, when he went into flirt mode.

Well, if he was expecting her to fall anywhere near his feet tonight, whatever she was wearing, he was in for a disappointment!

Ignoring a twinge of regret she didn't want to analyse, Rachel turned her attention back to work. She wanted to check on the paperwork from today's operation—make sure all the team members present had signed it—then look at the programme for the following week. Alex had suggested she take some time off, but she didn't want to leave him with a new assistant for any complex cases.

Tonight could wait...

# CHAPTER TWO

SHE wore black. A slinky silk jersey dress Kurt had
talked her into spending an entire pay cheque on
when the team had been working in Melbourne. She'd
worn it to Alex's wedding to Annie, the team's manager, and would probably have to wear it again when
Phil and Maggie, the team anaesthetist, were married,
as she certainly didn't want to splash out on another
expensive outfit.

'No one will recognise it as the same dress,' Kurt
assured her as they walked the short distance to the
restaurant. 'The wedding was in the afternoon, and
you wore it with a white jacket and those divine white
and black sandals. Tonight it's pure sex appeal.'

Then, without giving Rachel time to protest, he
added, 'Though my guess is you could be wearing
your Snoopy pyjamas for all the attention the Italian
will give to your clothes.'

'Ho!' Rachel scoffed, but just thinking about Luca
brought butterflies to her stomach, and she wondered
how she was going to get through the evening.

And why, after all this time, she was feeling such
strong physical reactions to a man...

'That is a beautiful dress, but no more beautiful
than the woman wearing it,' Luca, standing outside
the restaurant as if expecting her arrival, greeted her.

'That kind of over-the-top compliment might be
flattering to an Italian woman,' Rachel told him, cross
because now her heart was racing and, with the but-

20

terflies fluttering wildly, internally she was a mess. 'But American women are more embarrassed than flattered by people saying things like that.'

'Is that so?' Luca responded, quite matter-of-factly, as if she hadn't been deliberately rude to him. 'Then, as well as slowing down, I must tone down my compliments, although they're no less genuine for being—what did you call it?—over the top?'

He took her arm and led her up the stairs. Kurt, who'd walked ahead when they'd reached Luca, was watching from the top with a grin of teasing delight. Rachel glared at her best friend, though she knew he wasn't the cause of her consternation, because in spite of her denial she was, in some peculiar way, both flattered by Luca's compliments and excited by his company.

And his touch…

No way! She was definitely not going there!

Dating was one thing, but a relationship?

Though if he was only here for four weeks…

She drew away from him, unable to believe the way her mind was working. How could she even consider such a thing? Especially with a man like this— so far out of her league they were practically different species.

Maggie and Phil were waiting just inside, Maggie reaching out to take Rachel's hand and draw her close for a kiss.

'If I wasn't so besotted by Phil, I'd be throwing myself at that man,' she whispered to Rachel. 'Isn't he gorgeous?'

'I guess so.' The reluctant admission was forced from Rachel's lips, making Maggie laugh. Rachel moved on, kissed Phil and offered her congratulations once again, then Kurt was by her side, leading her to a table on the far side of the room.

'Thought you might have needed a breather from that walking sex god,' he said, and Rachel nodded, thinking if she stayed away from Luca, the butterflies might settle enough to make room for food in her stomach.

It might also give her mind time to sort out what was happening, and remember all the reasons she no longer did relationships.

With *any* man!

But avoiding Luca was like avoiding Aussie flies in summer. Impossible. The meal was no sooner finished than he appeared by her chair.

'You will dance with me?'

Maggie and Phil were already on the dance floor, and a number of the nursing staff and their partners had joined them. Rachel glanced at Kurt who offered no help at all, announcing he and Becky were going to show the team how real dancers danced.

Rachel stood up, then realised immediately how big a mistake she'd made when Luca put his arm around her waist to guide her towards the floor. The clasp was as light as thistledown, but even so it alerted every nerve-ending in her body.

Finally, Luca had the woman in his arms. Why it had been so important, he didn't know, but he'd seen her first in the theatre and had been fascinated by her total competence and composure, then, meeting her afterwards in the lounge, he'd felt attraction stir.

That, in itself, had been enough to confuse him. Lately he'd been so busy with his work, and plans for the new clinic, he'd had no time at all for a social life—a fact his long-term fiancée had pointed out with some bitterness, just before she'd flung the engagement ring at him and gone off to marry the industrialist who'd been after her for so long.

But that had been six months ago and half a world away. Now here he was, with another woman in his arms—a very different woman—one with something special about her—something that had drawn him to make a fool of himself with his compliments and behaviour earlier. Now he held her loosely, fearing she would break away if he tried to hold her close. Her tension was so palpable he could feel it vibrating between them.

But why?

She was beautiful. She must be used to men falling at her feet. She should carry the assurance that came with the combination of beauty and experience. Yet her tension suggested there was more behind her reaction to him than a wish for him to proceed more slowly.

He would find out.

'You like theatre work?'

Rachel nodded, and he suspected, as he watched her slide her tongue surreptitiously across her lips, that it had been safer to answer that way than to try to form words.

'You're good at it, I saw that. You chose it because it suits your skills?'

She didn't answer immediately, and he felt a hitch in the smooth movement of her feet, then she lifted her shoulders in a little shrug as if either his question or her reply was unimportant.

'It's detached,' she said, a slight smile curving up the left side of her lips. 'Working in Theatre, I don't need to get involved with either the patients or their families.'

A slight pause then her head tilted upward and warm golden brown eyes met his.

'I don't get involved with men either, Luca,' she said quietly.

And she meant it. He knew that immediately, but refused to be daunted.

'You've been hurt! I can see that in your—your defensiveness. Will you tell me what happened?'

He felt a tremor run through her body and regretted his curiosity, but that curiosity was part and parcel of who he was, and he could no more have not asked than he could have stopped his heartbeats.

'No!'

She whispered the word, almost under her breath, but he caught it anyway, and drew her just a fraction closer.

'That's all right,' he assured her. 'You don't know me, so why should you tell me personal things? My family all talk too much. We talk about everything—our hopes and dreams and fears and worries. We dramatise, cry, yell, fight, hold and hug each other over the talk we share, so I ask questions an American or Australian man might not ask.'

She looked up at him, a smile in the eyes that were widely spaced and slightly elongated, like the eyes of a very beautiful cat.

'And do you mind if you don't get answers?'

He couldn't help but respond to that smile.

'Ah, but I did get an answer. You don't get involved with men. You told me that much. So I remind you now I am not men in general.' He held her lightly so she wouldn't feel trapped. 'I am a man, singular, and we will be working together a lot of the time. If I promise to take it slowly, will you consider seeing something of me when we are both off duty?'

He heard the words and knew he'd said them, but in his head he was wondering why.

How much easier to find someone else to flirt with—the little secretary, Becky, for one? She would go out with him, show him the city that was her home and, he was reasonably certain, they would have a good time together.

But, glancing across to where Becky danced with Kurt, Luca knew it wouldn't work.

No, for some reason that defied rational argument, he knew if he was to enjoy a relationship with anyone during his short stay in Australia, it would have to be with the woman who danced so reluctantly in his arms.

Was it fate that Luca's temporary abode was in a high tower of serviced apartments right next to the very unserviced building—there wasn't even an elevator—where she and Kurt shared what their landlord called a two-bed flat? Kurt had made rude remarks—not to the landlord—about liking his beds flat, but they'd both known, after six months in Melbourne—learning the language, as Kurt said—that 'flat' down under didn't mean an even surface, but an apartment.

Not that the standard of accommodation had anything to do with Rachel's discomfort as she'd walked home from the party with the two men. Mostly it was due to Luca's presence, though anger had seethed as well because Kurt, in an excess of good spirits—no doubt brought on by an excess of the wine that had flowed—had asked the man to dinner the next evening.

Saturday night!

Which was fine, except her presence at the dinner table made it obvious she had no man in her life. Why else would she have been dateless on a Saturday night?

But Kurt had done the asking so she hoped she didn't appear desperate as well as dateless!

Kurt cooked a delicious meal, and was at his most charming best, but Rachel found the evening uncomfortable, and Luca's company unsettling. Physically unsettling in a way she couldn't remember ever feeling before.

Tension meant she had more than her usual two glasses of wine so when Luca asked, as he was taking his leave, if they would join him for dinner the following evening she thought it a wonderful idea and said, yes, her assent no sooner out than she heard Kurt pleading another engagement.

So here she was late on Sunday afternoon, surveying a wardrobe that consisted mostly of jeans and sweat pants with a variety of tops she wore according to the weather—short-sleeved if it was hot, long-sleeved if it was cold.

She did have one green T-shirt she particularly liked, but she'd worn it to death so it was faded and out of shape and she knew, if Kurt had been here, he'd have forbidden her to wear it.

So she'd wear the black one she'd picked up at a market in Melbourne and had never had occasion to wear, because it was definitely a 'going out' type top—V-necked, long-sleeved, slinky kind of fabric, with a feathery bird printed on it in some kind of gold paint.

Jeans would stop it looking too formal…

Why the hell was she doing this?

She didn't date—or if she did it was with men in whom she had not the slightest interest. Not that she was interested in Luca, not really. It was just some glitch in her body chemistry—some cellular attraction in her body to the pheromones he shed so effortlessly.

Working this out didn't make her feel any better.

Neither did Luca's behaviour, which was exemplary from the moment he collected her from her flat, walking her down the stairs with only an occasional touch on her elbow for support, holding an umbrella over her as he ushered her into the waiting taxi, talking casually about the weather, which had turned bleak and wet, and what he'd seen of Sydney through the rain when Alex and Annie had taken him for a drive earlier in the day.

The restaurant was above a row of shops and looked out over the promenade, the beach and further out to a turbulent dark ocean. White spray from the crashing waves lit its blackness, but it seemed to have a brooding power—not unlike the man with whom she shared a table.

'You like the ocean?' Luca, playing the perfect host.

'Love it! Though usually when I've been down here to Bondi I've seen it in happier moods.'

'I have raced on yachts across the Atlantic,' Luca said, 'but I prefer the Mediterranean where the weather is more predictable.'

'Of course,' Rachel said, again realising what worlds apart they were, that he could speak so casually of racing yachts and a sea she'd only heard and read of.

'You like boats?'

The question had been inevitable.

'The ones I've been on,' she said, then grinned at him. 'Ferries on Sydney Harbour! I live a long way from water back at home.'

'So tell me about your home.'

He was still being the good host, but 'home' wasn't a subject Rachel wanted to discuss. Once she was thinking of home, it would be too easy to think of other things. Fortunately, a waiter arrived, and began to list the specials available that night, and listening to his recital then discussing what they would eat diverted the conversation to food.

'You will have some wine?'

Rachel shook her head.

'Work day tomorrow, and a big work day. I know Alex has a TAPVR listed first up, and they can be tricky. And if the first op overruns its time, we'll be late all day, which is when people get frazzled.'

Luca smiled at her, and just about every cell in her body responded, so she had to remind them it was just a chemical reaction and nothing was going to happen, so to cool it.

They talked about the operation—far safer, especially as Rachel had assisted in so many total anomalous pulmonary venous return ops with Alex that she knew it inside out. And because talking work helped keep her mind off her physical problems, she asked Luca about his work—about the operations he liked doing—knowing most surgeons had their favourites.

'Transplants.' His answer was unequivocal. 'I haven't done many, but there is something about removing a terribly damaged heart and replacing it with a healthy one that fills me with wonder. I know the operation is only the first part of the battle, but I find that battle—to keep the patient stable, fight infection and rejection—a great challenge. It's a fight, so far, I've been fortunate enough to win, so perhaps that is why the operation is my favourite.'

The passion in his voice affected Rachel nearly as badly as the attraction. She understood it, because she loved her work in the same way. Every operation was a new challenge, and her total focus, whether she was handing instruments to the surgeon, suctioning, or massaging a tiny heart, was on providing the best possible outcome for the baby or child on the table in front of her.

She felt the bond between them but at the same time was aware this was a very different kind of attraction and an infinitely more worrying one.

Talking about work was still the best option so she asked about places he'd trained and surgeons with whom he'd studied.

It should have been safe, innocuous conversation, but beneath it the attraction still simmered, and when he passed her a bowl of freshly grated Parmesan cheese to sprinkle on her pasta and their fingers brushed together, she felt heat flash through her body.

Crikey, she was in trouble…

'Phil as a surgeon.'

And she was missing the conversation.

She looked at Luca—at the dark eyes, and bronzed skin, and strong-boned face—and tried desperately to guess what he'd been saying.

'He's terrific,' she managed to get out, hoping he'd asked her about Phil's ability.

He hadn't! That much was obvious from the delighted grin that spread across his face.

'You were thinking of other things?' he teased.
'Too much to hope it might have been of me.'

'Far too much!' she snapped—perhaps too snap-
pishly! 'I was thinking about the TAPVR.'

'Ah!' Luca murmured, dark eyes smiling at her so
she knew he didn't for a moment believe her. 'Of
course!'

But those smiling dark eyes not only seemed to see
right into her soul, they made her feel warm and excited and, damn it all, sexy!

And *that* feeling was so unfamiliar she had to mentally question it before deciding, yes, that's what it
was.

Somehow she got through the rest of the meal, refusing dessert or coffee, anxious to get home now her
hormones seemed to be totally out of control.

Again they took a cab, Luca paying the driver off
outside Rachel's building before offering to walk her
up the stairs.

She thought of the dim lighting on the landings and
the temptation the gloom would provide and insisted
she could walk up unattended.

'That is not right,' he protested. 'I should at least
see you to the door.'

Rachel smiled at him.

'Not right but probably safer. I'm not at all sure
about this situation, Luca. I meant it when I said I
don't get involved with men.'

But her heart was thudding so loudly he could
probably hear it, and her body was leaning towards
his even before he put his hands on her shoulders and
drew her close.

'It is up to you,' he said softly, the little puffs of air from the words brushing her cheek as he bent his head and kissed her on the lips.

By this time she was so wired—so jumpy—her brain forgot to tell her lips not to respond. And the heat she'd felt earlier with an accidental touch of fingers was nothing to what she now experienced.

Hard, hot and horrifyingly exciting—her lips clung to his as her body awoke from a long, long sleep and desire spiralled deeper and deeper into her body.

An impulse to drag him inside, rip off his clothes and give in to the urges she was feeling came from nowhere and her startled brain was actually considering it when two young lads walked by.

'Get a room!' one of them yelled.

Mortified by her thoughts *and* her behaviour, Rachel pushed away from the man who was causing havoc in her body, muttered her thanks for the meal and hurried into her building.

Luca watched her disappear—watched the door shut firmly behind her—and wondered just where things now stood between them.

He could no longer doubt that Rachel felt the attraction between them as strongly as he did.

So why was she resisting it?

Because they barely knew each other?

But giving in to it would help them know each other better…

He walked slowly along the pavement to his apartment building, thinking about attraction and a woman with red-gold hair and amber eyes who had, so unexpectedly, appeared in his life.

\*     \*     \*

'I've called you all together because it's the first TAPVR operation we've done at Jimmie's and I wanted to run through the whole procedure.'

Alex stood on the dais at the front of the very small lecture room the unit used for staff meetings. Rachel, whose job today was to explain to the theatre staff exactly what they'd need, sat at a nearby table, uncomfortably aware of Luca in a seat directly behind her.

Not that she needed his presence to remind her of his…eruption—that was about the only word that fitted—into her life. He'd dominated her thoughts all weekend, both when she'd been with him, fighting the physical attraction, and when she hadn't been with him, when she'd wondered about it!

Now here she was, having to sit in front of the man and pretend nothing had happened—which it hadn't, apart from a mind-blowing, bone-melting, common-sense-numbing kiss.

Pretend nothing had happened, when her toes were curling every time she looked at him?

Could it be because of one kiss?

Was this what lust felt like?

And, if so, what did one do about it?

The problem was, she'd been out of circulation for too long for any of this to make sense. Remembered pain had been an effective barrier to involvement for the last four years, but she sensed the barrier was crumbling beneath the onslaught of her attraction to Luca.

But involvement led to vulnerability and she'd vowed never to be vulnerable again…

*Never* again!

Especially not when all that could possibly occur between herself and Luca was a brief affair.

She tried to focus on what Alex was saying. No doubt he'd begun by explaining that TAPVR stood for total anomalous pulmonary venous return. Put simply, Rachel knew, the blood vessels bringing oxygen-rich blood back from the lungs to the heart had hooked themselves up to the wrong place. Instead of coming into the left atrium to be pumped into the left ventricle and then out the aorta to be distributed throughout the body, some mistake had occurred during the heart's development and the blood returned to the right ventricle and was recirculated through the lungs, causing problems there while starving the rest of the body of oxygen.

'When does it happen?' someone asked, and Rachel realised she'd heard Alex's explanation so often before she was at the right place in her head.

'Usually during the first eight weeks of pregnancy, which is when the heart is developing from a double tube into a complex muscled organ.' Phil explained this to the nurse who'd asked the question and, looking at the young woman in the back row, Rachel realised the questioner was pregnant.

And worrying.

Been there, done that, have the T-shirt, Rachel thought, but, though she might act tough, remembered pain had her feeling sympathy for the pregnant woman.

Luca had also turned towards the speaker, and now he said, 'You shouldn't worry. You'll have had scans by now, and it would have shown up if your baby had a problem.'

It's nice he feels for people—even those he doesn't really know.

The thought sneaked up on Rachel and she had to

remind herself that Luca's niceness wasn't her concern.

The operation was her concern, and explaining what the theatre staff would be doing during it was her immediate concern.

Right now, apparently, because Alex was waving his hand in her direction and asking her to take over.

'You would make an excellent teacher,' Luca said an hour later when, the briefing over, he had managed to walk out of the room beside her. 'Have you thought of doing more academic work?'

'Not often,' Rachel told him honestly. 'I really love the theatre work I do, and Alex is good in that he encourages me to be part of the explanations as I was today, so I get to do a bit of teaching that way.'

Luca nodded.

'Yes, I like the way he includes everyone, theatre and PICU staff, in his briefings. I think I'll learn more than I even imagined I would from him—in administrative matters as well as surgical skills and techniques.'

Rachel felt a glow of pride for the man his team called Alexander the Great, then Luca was talking again.

'Have you worked with other surgeons back in the US? Are they all as meticulous in their planning? As thorough in their briefings?'

'I've occasionally assisted other surgeons. I suppose assisted sounds strange to you, but back at home I'm what's known as a PA—a physician's assistant. Anyway, since Alex joined the staff at the hospital where I trained, I've worked exclusively on his team, assisting whoever on the team is operating. Alex usually has a fellow working with him, Phil being the current one, and a registrar or surgeon in training, and then there are other surgeons, like yourself, on short-term visits.'

'So you would assist me if Alex asks me to be the lead surgeon in an operation while I am here?'

They'd talked as they walked towards the theatre the team used, Rachel fending off the strange sensations being close to Luca caused and answering his questions automatically. It was only after they'd parted, Luca to join Alex, who would have a final talk with the baby's parents, and she into the theatre to check all was ready, that she wondered if he'd been talking to her because he wanted to know more of the details of her job or to give him an excuse to walk with her.

Nice thought, that, but did she really want to break her commitment to non-involvement? Or want to have an affair with Luca just because her body was behaving badly?

The answer to both questions was no, but that was her brain talking at eight thirty-two in the morning, when the man was no longer in the vicinity so his body wasn't zapping hers with seductive messages.

Kurt was in the theatre, explaining the finer points of the heart-lung bypass machine to Ned, an Australian theatre sister who'd been seconded to their team and was being trained in the work Rachel did as a PA.

'Fantastic party Friday night,' Ned said cheerfully.

'Huh!' Rachel replied, but didn't elaborate. There was no need for the entire team to know she was in a tizz over Luca. She turned her attention to work, and addressed Ned and the other theatre staff.

'Although the echocardiograms suggest the pulmonary veins are connected to the right atrium instead of the left, the films are never as accurate as we'd like so we have to be prepared for surprises. I always make sure I've got extra patches and shunts in case they're needed, and the runner...' she nodded to the pregnant nurse '...knows where to put her hand on more if we need them.'

'I've got a full range ready,' the woman answered. 'I've put out the ones you usually use on the trolley, and have back-ups.'

She smiled at Rachel.

'I worked on an op with Phil a couple of weeks ago and he went through five shunts, snipping and shaving them, before he got one exactly the size he wanted. Since then I've made sure I've got plenty on hand.'

'Great,' Rachel said, and she meant it. The longer a baby was on bypass, the more chance there was of doing damage to its fragile circulatory system and organs. It was unacceptable to have hold-ups because the theatre personnel weren't properly prepared.

'The problem with TAPVR is that you can use so many patches and shunts. The surgeons have to detach the veins from wherever they are and patch the holes they left, then rejoin them up to the back of the left atrium and patch the hole between the two atria, which has usually been made bigger by the cardiologist during a catheterisation procedure. Then sometimes the veins are too small, and we either use a stent to hold them open or a patch to make them bigger, so, like the Scouts, we have to be prepared.'

She checked the trolley, automatically noting that

the instruments Alex would need were in the right places, then went to change.

'Teaching again,' a now familiar voice murmured.

Luca was standing in the doorway, and had obviously heard her little lecture to the nurses.

'That's not teaching,' she protested, while her body suggested her head had been wrong about the two decisions it had made earlier.

'Ah, but it is, and you are very effective.'

He touched her lightly on the shoulder, then went on his way, while she took her muddled thoughts into the changing room and wondered if physical attraction would get stronger or weaker if one gave in to it and enjoyed an affair purely for the satisfaction and undoubted delight it would bring.

# CHAPTER THREE

THE operation took longer they any of them had expected, the baby's left atrium being small and underdeveloped, so in the end Alex had to splice the four pulmonary veins so he ended up with only two, then use another shunt to join them, attaching it to the tiny heart.

'It's a damn shame,' he said much later when he'd seen the baby's parents and had returned to where most of the team were gathered, holding a general debriefing. 'It means she'll need more operations as she grows, because the shunts won't grow with her.'

'I know you can use tissue from the baby to make patches,' Maggie said, her hands cupped around a mug of coffee. 'Could you also use a vessel from the baby instead of a shunt?'

'I've used veins taken from another part of the body for a small repair but for a vein as large as the pulmonary vein, I've never tried it,' Luca said, looking enquiringly at Alex.

'I have,' Alex said, 'and found it didn't work as effectively as the shunt. Because it was small, and possibly because it didn't like the insult of being transplanted from one site to another, it closed off almost immediately. Until we work out some way of successfully growing spare vessels inside the baby—which might not be that far away considering how science is advancing—then I believe we're better using shunts. At least the subsequent operations to replace them shouldn't require putting the patient on bypass.'

It was a fairly normal post-op conversation but there was nothing normal about Rachel's feelings, sitting as she was next to Luca who'd pulled a chair up close to her desk.

This distraction had to stop. So far she'd been able to keep one hundred per cent focussed in Theatre, all but forgetting Luca was in the room, but if, as he'd suggested, she was one day called upon to assist him, even a tiny distraction could lead to trouble.

She was due time off. She'd take it. Get right away. Maybe even, if she could get a cheap flight, go home to the States.

She was planning this little holiday in her head when she realised Alex was talking again. Something about a trip to Melbourne.

'I'm sorry, did you say you're going away? Does that mean we're all off duty for a few days?' She couldn't go home to the States for a few days but she could go north to somewhere warm—perhaps North Queensland.

Alex grinned at her.

'No, it doesn't mean you're all off duty for a few days. I know you're due time off, Rachel, but if you can just hang in for this week, I'm sure we can work something out after that.'

He paused and Rachel sensed something bad was coming—it was unlike Alex not to come right out with things.

'Problem is, Phil, Maggie, Kurt and I are flying to Melbourne tomorrow to do this op. We're taking an early morning flight, and will overnight there to make sure the baby's stable before we leave, then be back about ten on Wednesday.'

'Not me?'

She didn't particularly want to go to Melbourne, but if the core of the team was going, why not her?

Alex smiled again.

'It's not that I wouldn't like to take you—but you know you trained that theatre sister down there well enough to do your job. Besides, I need you to be here.'

Another hesitation, so Rachel prompted him.

'You need me to be here?'

A nod this time—no smile.

'I do indeed. We've an op scheduled for midday on the day we get back—a first-stage op for a baby born with HLHS—hypoplastic left heart syndrome. The Flying Marvels, that organisation of private plane owners who volunteer their time and planes, are flying the baby and his parents to Sydney early tomorrow morning. I need someone to do the briefing. Luca can explain the operation to them—what we'll be doing—but I'd like you, Rach...' his eyes met hers in silent apology '...to explain the post-op situation to them. What to expect when the baby comes out of Theatre—the tubes and drains and special equipment that will be protruding from his body.'

The words hit against her skin like sharp stones, but with the entire team looking at her with varying degrees of interest or concern, depending on how long they'd known her, she could hardly throw a tantrum and refuse Alex's request. Especially as he wouldn't have asked if there'd been any alternative! She'd be here, she knew his work, she knew exactly what the

baby would be attached to when he left Theatre—so
who better to explain?

'No worries,' she said, using a phrase she'd heard
repeatedly during her time in Australia. And if her
voice was hoarse and the words sounded less convincing than when an Aussie said them, that was too
bad. It was the best she could do under the circumstances.

With duties handed out, the meeting broke up,
though Alex signalled for Luca and Rachel to stay.

'Luca, if you wouldn't mind having dinner with
Annie and me tonight, I'll give you a run-through of
how we do the procedure. Actually, Rachel, you
should come too if you can. I'll give Annie a quick
call to let her know she has extra mouths to feed,
then, Rachel, can I see you privately for a moment?'

Rachel nodded glumly, and watched him walk behind the partition that provided the only bit of privacy
in the big room.

Luca turned to her.

'Did I imagine something going on there, a tension
in the air? Is Alex perhaps aware you don't like to
get involved with patients? If so, why is he asking
you to do this?'

Luca's dark eyes scanned her face and the sympathetic anxiety in them, and in his voice, weakened
the small resolve Rachel had built up during a kiss-
less day.

'He's asked because there's no one else, and he
wants to see me privately to give me a hug and say
he's sorry he had to ask.'

'You know him so well?'

Rachel smiled at Luca's incredulity.

'On Alex's team we're a bit like family—a grown-up family that doesn't live in each other's pockets—but we've shared good times and bad times and we stick together through them all.'

Alex appeared as she finished this explanation and Luca politely left the room, though the scene panned out exactly as Rachel had foretold.

'I'm sorry to ask you to do this,' Alex said, giving her a big, warm hug.

'That's OK,' Rachel told him, and though, deep in her heart she wasn't at all sure it *was* OK, she was also beginning to think it was time!

'You'll be all right with it?'

She stepped back and looked at the man with whom she'd worked for a long time.

'And if I'm not?' she teased, then was sorry when she saw him frown.

'Of course I'll be all right,' she hurried to assure him. 'Quit worrying.'

He hugged her once again, but she doubted he'd obey her last command. Alex worried over the well-being of all his team.

She'd just have to prove herself tomorrow.

Or maybe she shouldn't, because she certainly didn't want this patient-contact stuff to become a habit…

Luca was waiting for them outside, and, though she could practically hear the questions he wanted to ask hammering away in his head, he said nothing, simply falling in beside her as they walked to the elevator, and staying close in a protective way that should have aggravated Rachel, but didn't.

He held her jacket for her before they walked out into the cool spring air, and brushed his fingers against her neck. His touch sent desire spiralling through her, although she knew it was a touch of comfort not seduction.

This was madness. It was unbelievable that physical attraction could be so strong. And as surely as it fired her body, it numbed her mind so she had difficulty thinking clearly—or thinking at all a lot of the time!

So she didn't. She walked between the two men, and let their conversation wash across her, enjoying the sharp bite of the southerly wind and the smell of smoke from wood fires in the air.

Annie greeted them as if she hadn't seen them an hour or so earlier, and introduced Luca to her father, Rod, and Henry, her dog.

Henry, Rachel noticed, seem to approve of Luca, bumping his big head against Luca's knee and looking up for more pats.

There's no scientific proof that dogs are good judges of character, she told herself, but that didn't stop her feeling pleased by Henry's behaviour.

Which brought back thoughts of brain transplants…

Annie ordered them all to the table, already set with cutlery, plates and thick slices of crunchy bread piled high in a wicker basket in the middle. She then brought out a pot only slightly smaller than a cauldron, and set it on the table.

'Lamb shanks braised with onions and cranberries,' she announced. 'Help yourselves, and take plenty of bread to mop up the juice.'

Discussion was forgotten as they tucked into the appetising meal, and it was only when they were all on second helpings that Alex began to explain exactly what the upcoming operation entailed.

'It is the same procedure I use,' Luca told him, when Alex had finished speaking. 'I'm confident I can explain it well to the parents. I've seen you in action with explanations, remember, and I know you always tell the families of the problems that can arise during an operation, as well as the hoped-for outcomes.'

Alex nodded.

'We talk about ''informed decisions'',' he said, 'but I fail to see how parents can make informed decisions if they aren't aware their child could die, or suffer brain or liver damage, during open-heart surgery. And it is equally important they know they will still have a very sick child after surgery, and be prepared to care for that child for however long it takes.'

'In your experience, do most parents accept this?' Luca asked. 'Have you had parents who opted not to let you operate?'

Alex hesitated, his gaze flicking towards Rachel.

'Many of them over the years,' he admitted. 'And I have to respect their decision, though in some cases I was sure the outcome would have been good. But family circumstances come into play as well. Not all families can afford a child who will need a series of operations and constant medical attention for the rest of his life, yet this is all we can offer them in some cases.'

'It is a terrible choice, isn't it?' Luca said.

'It is, but I refuse to end a pleasant evening on such a gloomy note,' Annie declared. 'Dad, tell us some murder stories—that's far more fun.'

Rod, an ex-policeman who now wrote mysteries, obliged with some tales of bizarre and intriguing true-life cases from long ago.

\* \* \*

'Rod's stories might not have been ideal dinner party conversation,' Luca said, as Rachel guided him on a short cut home across a well-lit park, 'but they got us away from that depressing conversation.'

He spoke lightly, but he'd been sitting beside Rachel at the dinner table and had felt her tension—which had begun back when Alex had asked her to speak to the patient's parents—escalating during the meal. There was a story behind it and much as he wanted to know more, he was reluctant to ask, fearing it might break the fragile bond he believed was developing between them.

He glanced towards her. She was walking swiftly, her hands thrust deep in her jacket pockets, her head bent as if she had to concentrate on the path beneath her feet, but the unhappiness she was carrying was so strong it was like a dark aura around her body.

This was not the Rachel he knew, she of the glorious hair, and the sunny smile, and the smart remark. This was a person in torment, and her pain, unexpectedly, was reaching out and touching him. He could no more ignore it than he could refuse to help a child in trouble.

He put his arm around her and guided her to a seat in the shadow of a spreading tree. Her lack of resistance reassured him, and once they were seated he tucked her body close to his and smoothed his hand across her hair, holding her for a moment in the only way he knew to offer comfort.

'Will you tell me what it is that hurts you so much? Why Alex had to give you a hug?'

She turned and looked at him, studying his face as if he were a stranger, then she looked away, back down at the ground, her body so tight with tension he was sure he could hear it crackling in the air around them.

Then she nodded, and he held his breath, wondering if she'd tell the truth or make up some story to stop him asking more.

But when it came he knew it was not make-believe, because every word was riven with raw pain.

'Years ago, I was going out with this man. I found I was pregnant, we got married, the pregnancy was normal, the scans showed nothing, but the baby was early. I was staying with my parents at the time and had the baby in the local town hospital. He was diagnosed with HLHS, which was ironic considering I was working even then with Alex. Yet I hadn't given having a baby with a congenital heart defect more than a passing thought. I haemorrhaged badly during the birth, and had blood dripping into me, and drugs numbing my mind, so the paediatrician spoke to my husband, explained the situation, told him to talk to me and think about the options, which included transferring the baby to Alex's hospital. But that didn't happen. My husband made the decision not to operate.'

Rachel's voice had grown so faint Luca barely heard the final words, and he was repeating them to himself—and feeling something of the horror and loss Rachel must have experienced—when she spoke again.

'It didn't matter, as it turned out,' she said harshly. 'The baby died that night, before he could have been transferred.'

*Dio!* Luca thought, drawing the still-grieving woman closer to his side and pressing kisses of comfort, not desire, on the shining hair.

'Oh, Rachel, what can I say?' he said, and knew the emotion he was feeling had caused the gruffness in his voice. 'You are a very special person. I knew this from your work, but to know your sorrow and see you helping other people's babies, assisting them to live—that shows more courage than I would have. More than most people in the entire world would have.'

He felt the movement of her shoulders and knew she was shaking off his praise, and perhaps a little of her melancholy. Something she confirmed when she straightened up, moving away from him, and said, 'It was four years ago. I don't usually crack up like this. I guess Alex asking me to talk to the parents brought back memories I thought I'd put away for ever.'

'No matter how deeply you might bury it in your brain, I doubt you could ever put the loss of a child completely away,' Luca told her, hearing in his voice the echoes of his own buried memories.

She stood up and looked down at him, and even in the shadows he could see the sadness in the slow smile she offered him.

'Maybe not,' she said, 'but you do get past thinking of it every minute of every day, so maybe now it's time for me to get past seeing other babies who are ill, and thinking of my Reece.'

Luca stood up too, and took her hand, the clasp of a friend.

What happened to your husband? he wanted to ask. Her name was her own, he knew that, and she wore no ring. Had she divorced the man who'd made the decision not to try to save her baby? Because of that decision?

But surely, with his wife so ill as well, it could not

be held against him, especially as the baby died anyway!

'My husband visited me in hospital the next day,' she said suddenly, making Luca wonder if he'd asked his question out loud. 'He brought his girlfriend and explained that she, too, was pregnant, and he'd like a quickie divorce so he could marry her.'

She stopped again, and this time, in the light shed by a lamp beside the path, he saw mischief in the sadness of her smile.

'I threw a bedpan at him. Best of all, I'd just used it. The pan hit him on the nose—I'd always been good at softball—but she didn't escape the fallout. Petty revenge, I know, but it sure made me feel better.'

Luca put his arms around her and hugged her tight.

'Remind me never to upset you when you have a scalpel in your hand,' he teased.

Then they continued on their way, friends, he felt, not would-be lovers.

Not tonight!

# CHAPTER FOUR

IT WAS both better and worse than Rachel had thought it would be, walking into the room where two anxious parents sat beside their infant son. Better, she had to admit, because Luca was there, not holding her hand but standing shoulder to shoulder with her, as if he knew she needed some physical support.

Worse, because the baby was so beautiful. She tried so hard not to look at whole babies, preferring to concentrate on the little bit of them left visible by the shrouding green drapes of the theatre.

But this baby drew her eyes and she looked at him while Luca introduced them both.

She shook hands automatically, her attention still on the physical perfection of the tiny child. Smooth soft skin, downy fair hair, rosebud mouth and dusky eyelashes lying against his cheeks. A chubby baby so outwardly perfect her arms ached to hold him and hug him to her body.

The perfection, however, was spoilt by the tube in his nose, and the hum of the ventilator, and the drip taped to his fat little starfish hand.

'He's wonderfully healthy,' Luca said, examining the baby boy.

'Apart from his heart,' the father said.

'Yes, but some babies with the same problem have not done well *in utero*,' Luca told them, 'so they are very fragile even before we operate. Your…' He hesitated momentarily and Rachel filled in for him.

49

'Bobbie.'

Luca smiled at her, a special smile that started the faintest whisper of attraction happening again.

Damn, she'd thought she'd got rid of that last night!

'Your Bobbie,' Luca was saying, 'is so well, we will not hesitate to operate unless you decide otherwise.'

He went on to explain exactly what the team would do, how long it would take, and what would lie ahead for the family.

'You will have been told,' he said, 'that with hypoplastic left heart syndrome, this will be the first of three operations to rebuild Bobbie's heart into a properly functioning mechanism. This first, which we call the Norwood, is the most complex, and carries the most risk, and Bobbie will have the longest recovery time from it. Maybe three or four weeks in hospital. Then, when he's four to six months old, we do the second stage, a Glenn, and finally when he is two or three, we will do an operation called a Fontan. These operations are usually called after the surgeon who first performed them, which is why they have strange names.'

'And then? After three operations?' the mother asked.

'He will still need constant monitoring and regular visits to the cardiologist, but the outlook is quite good,' Rachel said, knowing it because she'd read up on all the outcomes for the operations they did—and practically knew the stuff on HLHS by heart. 'He won't have any significant developmental delays—apart from those caused by frequent hospitalisation during his first few years. He'll be able to play sport, though he shouldn't undertake really vigorous exercise.'

'So these operations won't make him totally better? They won't make him normal?'

It was the mother again, and Rachel, though she doubted anyone could define 'normal' satisfactorily, understood her concern.

'No. We can remake his heart so it works, but it will never be a so-called normal heart,' she said, then she glanced at Luca.

He must have read her thoughts for he nodded.

She turned back to the worried parents.

'Look, you two have a lot to think about. Why don't you talk about it? And when you want more answers, or want to know more about the operation or Bobbie's post-op state, ask the sister to page us and we'll come straight back. We'll just be in our office on the other side of the PICU.'

Bobbie's parents looked relieved, so Rachel ushered Luca through the door.

'We tell them too much at once,' she said to him, upset and frustrated because she could sense the parents' doubts. 'I know we have to explain it all to them, because otherwise they can't make an informed decision, but it's hard for people to assimilate all the medical terms and the possible outcomes when they're worried sick about their baby to begin with.'

Luca nodded. 'I sometimes think it is the worst part of my job—that, and telling parents I could not save their baby.'

His choice of words startled Rachel.

'Do you say ''I'' or ''we''?' she demanded, only realising how strident she must have sounded when Luca turned to her in surprise.

'I say "I",' he responded.

'But that's taking all the responsibility on yourself, and that puts more pressure on your shoulders. It's a team effort. You should say "we".'

Luca smiled at her.

'I'm serious,' Rachel told him, 'You're operating on tiny human beings. There's enormous pressure on you anyway, so why add more?'

He touched her lightly on the shoulder.

'I am not smiling because I think you are wrong, but because of your passion. It tells me much about you.'

His words slid like silk across her skin and she shivered in the warm hospital air. Last night she'd thought friendship was replacing the attraction she'd felt for Luca, yet one word, huskily spoken in his beguiling accent, and her nerve-endings were again atwitter while her body hungered for his touch.

Passion!

She wasn't entirely sure she understood exactly what it was. But unless she found something else to put the brakes on what was happening, she might soon be finding out.

Back at her desk, Rachel took a cautious sip of coffee, sure it would be too hot, then glanced at Luca as he fished in his pocket.

'I had my pager set to vibrate rather than buzz. It seems the parents have talked and we're needed again. Only this time it will be your turn.'

He looked anxiously at her, banishing her thoughts of passion, which, contrarily, made Rachel angry.

'I didn't tell you stuff last night to make you feel

sorry for me, but because I thought you should know. I'm a professional—I'll do my job in there.'

'I know you will,' he said, 'but do not tell me what to feel in my heart.'

He walked away, leaving her to follow, uncertainty dogging her footsteps, though this time it was to do with Luca, not with what lay immediately ahead.

Do not tell him what to feel in his heart?

He barely knew her, yet he was saying things that confused *her* heart.

Forget it!

Non-involvement, that's your go!

Think work!

She caught up with him so they walked into Bobbie's room together. Luca answered all the questions the parents had, then talked again about the procedure, before explaining that Rachel would tell them about the immediate post-operative period.

Rachel looked at the couple, wondering how much they could absorb, then looked again at the baby on the bed.

So beautiful her heart ached for him, knowing what lay ahead.

'He's already on the ventilator, so you probably understand that what it does is breathe for him—not all the time, but when and as he needs extra help. It saves him the energy he would use if he was breathing entirely on his own.'

'So he'll be on that again when he comes out?' the woman asked, and Rachel nodded.

'I was reading in the papers someone gave us where it's sometimes hard to wean a baby off a ventilator,' the father put in. 'Is that likely to happen?'

'It can happen,' Rachel said cautiously, then she

smiled. 'But we rarely send our kids off to their first day of school with a bottle of oxygen so you'd better believe we can get them off!'

Both parents smiled back at her and Rachel knew the tense atmosphere in the room had relaxed slightly.

Time to take advantage of it.

'He'll have a nasogastric tube—up his nose and down into his stomach—to keep his stomach clear of acid and gas that might have built up during the op. He can also be fed nutrients using this tube. Will you be expressing breast milk for him?'

The woman nodded.

'Good, because not having to change from formula to breast milk will be better for him later when he's able to feed for himself. If necessary, the hospital dietician might advise staff to give him supplemental calories, which will be added to the milk. These will help him grow while allowing him to take in less fluid. Speaking of which, he'll have a urinary catheter, and he will be given diuretics to make sure his body isn't retaining excess water. What happens is the surgery upsets all the body—especially in a body this small—so during the immediate post-op period other organs might not do their jobs as well as they should.'

She paused, knowing all the information must be mind-boggling to the parents, and wanting to give them time to assimilate at least a little of it. Then, thinking carefully so every word would count, she continued.

'Sometimes we leave a tube in the abdomen to help the liver flush out toxins and he'll definitely be on a heart monitor and maybe have a tiny pacemaker to keep his heartbeats regular while he recovers from the insult of the operation. It will look like a thin wire protruding from his body, and will be attached to a battery-operated device that will stimulate the heart if it falters.'

'So he'll come out with tubes and drains and wires poking out of him, and his chest all sewn up, and we have to stay calm?'

The baby's father had stood up and was by the bed as he spoke, smoothing his long forefinger across his son's head, looking, Rachel guessed, at the perfection of a body that would soon be marred.

'No, you don't have to stay calm,' Rachel told him. 'You can be as upset as you like. You should be. The little fellow is going to go through major surgery that would take an adult months to recover from, but your little boy will probably be out of here—the cardiac paediatric intensive care unit—in two or three days, a week at the most. Infants are amazingly resilient. Once he leaves here he'll have another couple of weeks in the babies' ward, then you can take him home.'

'You will be given plenty of instructions and information and support when you take him home,' Luca said, sitting in the husband's chair beside the woman and taking her hand. He must have noticed how distressed she was getting, Rachel realised, while she herself had been yammering on and probably making things worse, not better.

'I'm sorry,' she said, coming to kneel beside the distressed mother. 'It's hard to take in but it's best that you know what's going to happen.'

'It's not that, it's the decision,' the woman cried. 'Why do we have to decide? Why can't the doctors decide?'

'You have to decide because he is your baby,' Luca said gently.

'Then tell me what to do for him—tell me what is best,' the woman demanded. 'What would you do if it was your baby?'

The air in the warm room grew very cold—or at least the bit of it surrounding Rachel's body developed an icy chill. She looked at the baby on the bed—twice the size her Reece had been—outwardly perfect, apart from a blue tinge to his lips. Jake had known he would be leaving her—that decision had been made—so had he listened to the doctors explaining what they had to do, then decided Rachel wouldn't be able to cope with a very sick baby on her own?

Was that why he'd decided to say no to an operation?

'Is your marriage strong?' she asked, and realised she must have spoken harshly because all three adults in the room spun to look at her. 'That's probably a rude question, but it's important, because you'll need each other's strength to get you through this. There'll be bad times, and worse times, and you'll need each other more than you ever realised. So it has to be a united decision. You must both agree to it, and not hold grudges or lay blame later on. But, that said, then, yes. I'm not a doctor, but if Bobbie were my baby, I'd opt for the operation. I'd give him a chance, and if it doesn't work—if the worst happens—at least you'll know you tried.'

Realising she'd become too emotionally involved with the entire situation, she tried a casual shrug and smiled at the bemused parents.

'But, then, as I said, I'm not a doctor,' she said. 'It's Luca you should be asking.'

She hurried out of the room, sure if she stayed another moment she'd burst into tears.

Crikey! What was this about? She hadn't cried in years! It couldn't have been seeing the baby, could it?

Or was it because she'd broken her vow not to get involved?

She blinked and sniffed back tears, fumbling in her pocket for a handkerchief, glad she'd made for the less-used service foyer and no one was around to see or hear her unprofessional behaviour.

'Are you all right? *Dio*, it was wrong of Alex to ask you to do that.'

Luca was there, his arm around her, drawing her close. And for a moment she gave in to the need to be held and comforted, then she pushed away, knowing he was comforting her for all the wrong reasons.

'No, it wasn't wrong,' she said, smiling weakly at the man who looked so concerned for her. 'Alex probably knew me better than I knew myself. I had to get past what happened—I should have got past it long ago—and as long as I was avoiding situations like that, I wasn't going to.'

She turned away, and leant against the wall—not as comforting as Luca's body but infinitely safer.

'I didn't get upset over losing Reece—not when I was talking to the parents. I got upset because for the first time I looked at Jake's—my husband's—decision from his point of view. He'd been unfaithful, sure, but we hadn't been that committed to each other when we married. We'd been going out together, having fun, and vaguely thinking our relationship might lead somewhere. When I realised I was pregnant, he thought I should have an abortion but, as a nurse, the idea of doing such a thing horrified me, so we made the absolutely wrong decision right there and then, and got married. Don't get me wrong, I loved Jake but I knew he didn't love me in the same way. By the time Reece arrived, although I dearly wanted that baby—already loved him, if you know what I mean—we both knew the marriage wasn't working.'

An aide walked past and looked curiously at them.

'This is not a conversation I should be having here,' Rachel said, straightening off the wall. 'Or with you,' she added, as embarrassment at how frank she'd been began to surface.

'It is often easier to talk to strangers, though I hope I am more than that to you,' Luca said. 'And here and now is as good a place and time as any. Will you finish telling me?'

Rachel thought about it, then decided she might feel a whole lot better if she did finish, if she explained to someone—anyone—the revelation she'd had in that room.

'I've always blamed Jake. I thought the decision not to operate stemmed from selfishness, from him not wanting to be saddled with a sick child for the foreseeable future, but in there, talking to those parents, I realised he'd already made his big decision. He was moving on, child or no child, and he was thinking of me, and how I'd cope. I'd have had to give up work, and he knew how much I loved my job and how much it meant to me.'

She looked bleakly at Luca.

'I've blamed him all these years for that decision yet I realise now he made it for my sake.'

Luca thought he knew a fair bit about women. After all, he'd grown up with four sisters. But this woman's pain was new to him—new because he couldn't grasp where it was coming from.

But his lack of understanding didn't make her condition any less real. He took her in his arms and though she stiffened momentarily she then relaxed enough to return the embrace, holding him close against her for a moment, then lifting her head to look into his eyes.

'Thank you for listening,' she said softly. 'For being there.'

Amber eyes repeated the message, and her lips parted softly, so it seemed only natural to kiss her.

Very gently! Feeling her emotional fragility, and not wanting to take advantage of it.

Not wanting to take advantage?

Weird thought, that, when the idea foremost in his mind most of the time was getting her into his bed!

Equally gently, he disengaged.

'Come,' he said. 'The parents are talking again with other family members, and a man I think is a priest has also come to talk to them. We didn't have time to drink our coffee last time. Let's go to the rooms and try again. The parents know to page us if they need us.'

He wanted to put his arm around her shoulders again, but knew from the way she held herself that it would be wrong. She was gathering her strength, renewing her reserves of courage—he could see it in the proud tilt of her head, and the stiffening of her spine—and he guessed she would not welcome sympathy right now.

'Shoot, but I'd hate to be Alex—or you, for that

matter—doing this stuff before every single operation.'

She was striding towards their suite, and threw the remark over her shoulder at him, confirming his reading of her change in attitude.

'Not all of our conversations with parents concern life-or-death decisions,' he reminded her.

'No, I guess not,' she said soberly, then she turned and smiled at him. 'You were right—talking to a stranger definitely helped. Kurt's been telling me for years I should see an analyst. Maybe that's how psychologists and psychiatrists achieve their success— simply by being strangers mixed-up people can talk to.'

Luca would have liked to protest the stranger tag, but he sensed there was a brittle quality to Rachel's change of mood so he said nothing, merely offering to fix the coffee. When Becky, who was at her desk, said she'd do it, Luca took himself across to the desk he used and made notes about the talk they'd had with the little patient's parents.

He would then have to check on the baby they'd operated on yesterday, while no doubt Rachel would be busy preparing the theatre for the operation.

'Coffee for the sexy Italian!' Becky said, depositing a mug of strong black coffee on his desk, then put a small tray with two chocolate-coated biscuits beside it. 'And sweets for the sweet,' she added cheekily, pointing at the biscuits.

Luca had to smile. She flirted as naturally as she breathed, the pretty blonde Becky. What puzzled him was his lack of inclination to flirt back. Certainly his pursuit of Rachel wasn't getting far, and now that he understood her reluctance to get involved he doubted it would progress at all.

Yet something apart from her glorious hair attracted him, and beyond that he was coming more and more to think what an asset she'd be at his clinic. If he stole her heart, could he steal her away from Alex?

Not an honourable thought at all, but beneath their emotional exteriors most Italians were innately practical.

He nodded to himself, pleased to have this sorted out in his mind, though he doubted Americans could think as practically when love came into it. In his experience, love to them came with roses and chocolates and heart-shaped balloons—practicality was nowhere to be found.

He wrote his notes and drank his coffee, then began to worry why he hadn't been paged. Alex would be back soon and would want to know if the operation was to go ahead. In fact, Alex fully expected it would go ahead, having already spoken to the parents via a phone conference hook-up at the hospital where the baby had been born.

So if he, Luca, with Rachel, had ruined this plan with their explanations, how would Alex react?

'I think we should see if they've reached a decision before Alex gets back.'

As if summoned by his thoughts, Rachel stood at his desk. Luca nodded his agreement, and pushed his chair back, straightening up while Rachel waited.

'You don't have to come,' he told her, not wanting to subject her to more distress.

'They might have questions about post-op care,' she replied, in a voice that told him not to argue. So, together, yet in separate worlds, they walked towards the baby's room, where the man in the clerical collar was the only person waiting for them.

'The Archers have asked me to speak to you on their behalf,' he said. 'They have decided not to go ahead with the operation on baby Bobbie.'

Luca heard Rachel's gasp and moved closer to her. They might be inhabiting different worlds, but her world right now needed support.

'But he's so healthy,' she protested, and Luca took her hand, squeezing it to show his sympathy but also to warn her to think before she spoke.

'It is the parents' decision,' he reminded her, then he turned to the priest. 'Can you tell them we understand, but that Dr Attwood, who is head of the team, will need to hear it from them when he gets in from his trip to Melbourne.'

The man nodded. 'I'll tell them. It'll be hard for them, but I'll be with them.'

He looked from Luca to Rachel, then back to Luca before he spoke again.

'They didn't reach this decision easily, and they are deeply upset about having to make it. But they have other children—four—and in giving so much to this one, with regular trips to the city for his check-ups with specialists after the three operations, they would be denying the others. That is part of it. The other part is the uncertainty of the outcome. Even with the operations there are no guarantees that Bobbie will be healthy. Today it is hard for them to say they will let him go, but to lose him when they have loved and nurtured him for maybe four or five years—how much harder would that be? These are their thoughts.'

Luca felt the cold tenseness of Rachel's fingers and squeezed them, silently begging her not to argue—

not to fight for this baby's one chance at life. They had given the parents all the facts they needed to make a decision—to not respect that decision now would be deplorable.

The priest offered his hand to Luca, hesitated in front of Rachel, then made do with a farewell nod and left the room. Rachel sank into a chair, and though Luca guessed her legs would no longer hold her up he still urged her to her feet.

'Come. The parents will want to sit with Bobbie, and there are alternative arrangements that must be made,' he said. 'We'll find somewhere else.'

He guided her out of the room and, because it was closest, chose the little bedroom just off the PICU used by on-duty doctors at night.

'Here, sit!' he said, gently easing her onto the bed. Then he squatted in front of her and took her cold hands in his.

'Alex will talk to them. Maybe that will change their minds,' he said, hoping to wipe the dazed, blank look from her eyes.

She shook her head so violently her hair flew out in a wide arc the colour of molten gold.

'No, you were right. We told them what they needed to know, and they put that information with the other circumstances of their lives and decided. I have no doubt it is the right decision for them, but that baby, Luca?'

Desperate gold-amber eyes met his.

'He is so beautiful. To just let him die! It seems so unfair. So many people have healthy babies they don't really want or need, yet that one…'

She began to cry, not noisily but with deep, gulping sobs, then shook her head as if to shake the misery away and straightened once again. He wondered if she practised yoga, for she breathed deeply now, and he could see the inner strength he had seen before shoring up her defences. She even found a smile of sorts, though it was so pathetic it made Luca's chest hurt.

'Alex *will* be pleased! Not! He spoke as if the op was definitely on. The team members were coming back from Melbourne expressly to do it.' She glanced at her watch. 'Is there time to let them know it's off? They might prefer to stay on down there.'

She looked at Luca, who'd shifted to a chair, and continued, 'My brain's not working properly. Of course there's no time. It's a short flight—they must be almost back in Sydney by now.' A pause, then she added, 'I'm so sorry I fell apart all over you. This isn't the normal me, you know. I'm Rachel-who-can-cope-with-anything!'

Her courage was like a hand gripping and squeezing at Luca's heart, but he found a smile to give back to her.

'I think it is normal to feel emotional about a situation such as this. If we, as medical people, divorced ourselves from all our emotional reactions, we would become automatons instead of human beings. Medicine is about humanity, and we should all remember it—and be grateful, not negative, when we are reminded of it.'

'Spoken like a true Italian,' Rachel teased, and Luca knew she was feeling better, although her words reminded him of the thoughts he'd had earlier—emotion versus practicality!

'Contrary to what the world at large might think,

we are not entirely ruled by our emotions,' he told her.

'No?' She was still teasing, but this time she sounded more relaxed and he knew she was recovering. He was considering his reply—he would tell her about the practical side of the Italian psyche— when she spoke again.

'So if I kissed you here and now, just a thank-you-for-being-there-for-me kind of kiss, would you respond, or tell me to get back to work?'

His heart upped its beat, and his body tightened, but the kiss she brushed across his lips was definitely a thank-you-for-being-there-for-me kind of kiss.

He could, of course, take hold of her shoulders and draw her close to respond but, though Rachel might read it as a think-nothing-of-it kiss, his body might be misled into thinking it was serious, and walking around the hospital with an obvious erection wasn't something he could contemplate.

'You are tempting fate, my beautiful Rachel,' he said softly, then he stood up, touched her lightly on the head, and left the room.

# CHAPTER FIVE

RACHEL followed, but more slowly, knowing she would have to walk past the baby's room, and not sure how her muddled emotions would react.

If she hadn't been so stubborn about not getting involved with their tiny patients, would she have recovered from Reece's death more swiftly?

Would she feel less bad now about the decision Bobbie's parents had taken?

Had she been holding back her recovery through cowardice?

And if non-contact with babies had been crippling her, then what was her non-involvement with men doing?

'You're only thinking that because you're attracted to Luca,' she muttered to herself as she made her way back to the rooms. 'Involvement with men is entirely different to involvement with babies. Involvement with men leads to pain.'

You are such a wimp!

Fortunately she'd stopped thinking aloud and this last admonition was in her head, so Becky, who'd looked up as Rachel walked through the door, didn't hear it.

'The boss is back. He phoned from the airport. ETA at the hospital in twenty minutes.'

'Great!' Rachel found she was muttering again. Where was Luca? If he didn't turn up, would she have to tell Alex of the decision?

Determined not to think any more about the baby, or the past, or even Luca, she went to her desk and grabbed all the untended mail sitting in her in-tray. It had been weeks since she'd seen the bottom of it, dealing with urgent matters and shuffling the rest back into the tray for some day when she had plenty of time.

Like today, because there was no op this afternoon...

She turned the pile over and started at the bottom, staring at an invitation to attend a theatre nurses' seminar two weeks ago.

Binned it and lifted the next item. A circular advertising a range of clothing for theatre nurses. Why on earth had she kept that? The hospital supplied their scrubs and who cared what they wore beneath them?

She flipped the paper over, saw a phone number printed on the back and smiled.

Scott Douglas, the registrar who was working with the team, had written down his home phone number. It had been after he'd asked her out for the fifth or possibly the sixth time, and he'd finally said, 'OK, when you feel like company, you call me!'

Right now a night out with Scott might be what she needed. She could ease back into male-female involvement without the high risk attached to doing it with Luca.

But Scott had had a pretty brunette with him at Maggie and Phil's party, and they'd seemed to be quite attached to each other.

She binned the leaflet with the number on it. Too late to use it now!

Her theatre nurses' association magazine, forwarded on from her US address, came next, and she shoved it in her handbag. She'd read it at home to-night.

An invitation to her cousin's wedding. She'd already sent a gift, so why had she kept the invite?

She turned it over, wondering if it too might have another pencilled message, but apart from two golden, entwined hearts, the other side was bare.

'Ah, golden hearts—you are a little sentimental after all?'

Luca's voice startled her so much she glowered at him, though her pulse had accelerated at the sound of his voice—badly enough for her to consider pulling the circular out of the bin and phoning Scott tonight, brunette or no brunette.

'This is how sentimental I am,' she said, and dropped the invitation into the bin.

Luca nodded, as if acknowledging her rebuttal, then settled into the other chair at the desk and said, 'Alex is back. He is talking to the Archers.'

Seconds later, Kurt joined them, propping himself against the desk and lifting one eyebrow as he looked her way.

'Good trip?' she asked, hoping her reaction to Luca's closeness wasn't noticeable to her friend.

'Successful,' he said, but he sounded tired.

Rachel raised her eyebrows, and Kurt hesitated, then said, 'I don't know, Rach. We do such terrible things to those fragile babies, then expect them to get over it. What about the ones who don't? Or the ones who suffer brain damage while on pump? Or have a stroke later because an air bubble has escaped someone's attention and filtered through their bloodstream to the brain?'

'Statistically, that rarely happens in Alex's ops,'

Rachel reminded him, wondering if he'd already heard this afternoon's operation wasn't going ahead.

'I know, but there was a little boy in the PICU down there in Melbourne. Surgeons had fixed his heart, but he'd had a stroke two days after the op. The parents were blaming the surgery, and they were probably right. It just makes me wonder about where and when to draw a line, that's all.'

He stood up again, and moved restlessly around the desk, then shook off his negative mood and smiled at Luca.

'Well,' he demanded, 'did you take advantage of my absence to get this woman into bed?'

'Kurt!'

Rachel's protest was lost in Luca's angry protestations.

'You should not talk of your friend that way,' he said. 'You should know she is not a woman who bed-hops indiscriminately. To suggest such a thing is...'

He broke off, apparently unable to find the English for what he needed, and finished with a stream of Italian.

Kurt's startled face made Rachel laugh, and she grasped Luca's arm as it seemed he could any minute explode into a physical fury against Kurt.

'It's OK,' she explained. 'I know he's teasing.' Then she looked at Kurt. 'We haven't had a lot to joke about this morning.'

'Ah!'

'And Rachel has already been unduly upset!' Luca added, bringing not an 'ah' this time in response from Kurt but a quick frown.

'Rach?'

'I'm fine,' she said, catching his eye and silently

begging him not to pursue the subject, because she wasn't entirely sure just how fine she was.

Surely she wouldn't cry again…

Fortunately, Alex and Phil walked in at that stage, and Rachel could tell from their faces they'd heard the news.

'The baby is being transferred back to his regional hospital. He'll be cared for there for whatever time he has left,' Alex said, but his eyes were asking questions Rachel didn't want to answer.

'It was a family decision,' Luca told him, standing up and walking across to the two men, shaking hands with both of them, then remaining close by to explain. 'We spoke only to the parents, and we left them to talk to each other, then they called us back and eventually asked the inevitable question.'

'Whether we would operate if the child was ours?' Phil said, sympathy in his voice.

Luca nodded, but before he could reply, Rachel stood up.

'I answered that one,' she said, looking directly at Alex. 'I said if he was mine I would operate, but my answer wasn't an emotional one, Alex. It was nothing to do with what happened with Reece. I just pointed out how healthy little Bobbie is and said we'd operated on children who were far smaller and less well developed. I said his size and general health would make a difference in the overall result—make the risks much less—then the family arrived…'

She couldn't go on—telling Alex she'd given an unemotional reply to the question yet choking up now as she talked about it.

Though for Bobbie, she was sure, not because of the past.

'It is their decision to make and we have to respect it,' Alex said wearily, 'but, like you, Rachel, I felt he was so healthy, that little boy, he stood an excellent chance of getting through not just this op but the next two.'

'But we can't promise normal life even after all the operations, can we?' Luca said. 'And it was my impression that's the promise those parents wanted.'

The gloom in the room was palpable, but then Annie whirled in.

'OK, you lot, no operating this afternoon, so let's have a unit meeting over lunch. I've booked a table for us at the Seasalt Café down by the shore and have liberated one of the hospital minibuses to take us there.'

It was the last thing Rachel felt like doing—socialising with the others—but she knew they all needed to be jolted out of the depression that was already settling in, and put on a brave face as she congratulated Annie on her brilliant idea.

'Let's go!' she said, slinging her handbag over her shoulder and heading for the door. 'Before our usually budget-conscious unit manager changes her mind!'

The others followed her out, Kurt introducing a safe topic of conversation—food. More specifically the virtues of various brands of sea salt he'd tried while in Australia.

'He's a clever man, Kurt,' Luca said, moving smoothly through the others to walk beside her. 'He not only senses the mood of people, but can find a way to change it. Did he know Maggie is as interested in cooking as she appears to be?'

'I suppose we all know that—we've eaten at her

and Phil's place often enough. But Kurt's clever in that he thinks to change the subject. Me, I'd just have plodded gloomily along.'

'Never gloomily,' Luca contradicted. 'There is too much sunshine in your nature for you to be gloomy for long. Sad, yes, but that is different. Sad is natural. Gloomy—pah! Not you!'

He waved his hands, dismissing her gloom as ridiculous, then leant closer and whispered in her ear.

'If we sit together, may I hold your hand on the bus?'

'Like two kids at school?'

Luca smiled.

'I suppose a bit like that, but I was not thinking childish thoughts.'

'I know you weren't,' Rachel told him, but what she didn't know was how to deal with her own thoughts, let alone how to handle Luca's.

The Seasalt, to Rachel's delight, was situated on a cliff near the head of a narrow inlet, so the waves washed in beneath it, broke over the rocks in a sparkle of spray and a flurry of foam, then rolled out again, providing nature's music as an accompaniment to the meal.

'This city is so beautiful, with the beaches and the ocean close enough for us to lunch above them,' Luca said, breathing deeply to inhale the 'sea-salted' air.

The meal, too, was special, Rachel choosing a dish of squid barbecued with a chilli marinade, while Luca pronounced his grilled swordfish the best meal he'd had in Australia.

But when the plates were cleared, Annie called them to attention.

'I warned you it was a working lunch,' she said. 'As you all know, this unit was set up as a prototype of a small paediatric cardiac surgical unit, but it was always in the nature of a trial. So I thought you might like to know that the higher-ups at Jimmie's and in the Health Department are all very pleased with the way things are going, and the board of Jimmie's has just committed to keeping the unit running.'

Someone cheered and there was a general raising of glasses in a toast. Then Annie silenced them again with an upraised hand.

'But now the unit will be permanent we need to start getting things together, so the people who will be appointed when the US members of this team go back home have everything already set up for them. We're already training theatre and nursing staff, and specialist paediatric cardiac surgeons are being approached to head up the new unit. But there are little things that need doing. Up to now, we've been using information sheets Alex brought with him from the US, updated and changed to fit with Australian hospital procedures but still copies of other hospitals' info. I think we need our own, and I want help from all of you to make sure the information we give out to parents is easily understood and covers all they need to know. Not an easy task, but we'll do it.'

'I'll be revamping the surgical procedure ones,' Alex said, taking over from his wife. 'And Phil is doing general information on congenital heart disease. Maggie, I'd like you and Kurt to work on a glossary of terms, explaining in simple English the words, phrases and acronyms parents will hear all the time.'

He paused, then turned to Rachel.

'We'll also need to revamp the information we

send home with parents—post-op care info. I'll get Susie from the PICU to do wound care and dressings and the pharmacy to do medication. Would you like to tackle feeding babies with congenital heart defects? I'll give you what I have from other hospitals, but you'll have to check with the pharmacy about supplements available here.'

He paused, then added, 'Luca, you're not obliged to do any of this, but maybe you have some suggestions for Rachel of what, in your experience, is offered to parents.'

'I'll be happy to work with Rachel on this project,' Luca said. 'And as we apparently have the bonus of a free afternoon, maybe we can start when we return to the hospital.'

He turned to smile at Rachel, who knew this wasn't nearly as good an idea as he and Alex seemed to think. She needed to be avoiding Luca, not having more opportunities for them to be together thrust upon her.

The general conversation turned to what parents needed to know. Keep it practical, Scott suggested. Keep to simple notes but with web sites and contact phone numbers of support groups so families could find out more when and if they so desired. This suggestion came from Kurt, who had designed an information pamphlet on the bypass machine that was now used in many hospitals throughout the US.

Rachel began to think about what she knew about feeding. Babies with congenital heart disease grew more slowly than healthy babies, and those with congestive heart failure, as a result of their defect, might grow in length but put on weight very slowly.

'They need a greater caloric intake, because their

hearts have to work so hard, yet they usually take in less food because they breathe rapidly and are more easily fatigued.'

As Luca spoke, Rachel knew they were on the same wavelength. Papers on feeding infants with congenital heart disease would be available in every large hospital in the world, but she understood Annie's desire to have one specifically designed for the unit here at Jimmie's. But to work with Luca on it?

Not ideal!

'It was a good idea of Annie's, taking everyone to lunch,' Luca said, when he'd followed Rachel off the bus and they were re-entering the hospital. 'And to have a job to do—that, too, will take people's minds off the baby.'

Rachel nodded but he sensed she was distracted, and he wondered if mentioning the baby had been a mistake.

But when she turned to him and asked, 'Do you think Annie asked us to work together because she thinks there's something going on between us?' he realised how far off the track his assumption had been.

'Would that bother you? For people to think this?'

She looked at him, amber eyes serious, scanning his face as if to commit his features to memory.

'I don't know,' she finally replied, and he knew from the little frown creasing her forehead that she spoke the truth.

He smiled at her.

'Maybe we shall have to test it out. Get something going on between us so you can see if people knowing worries you.'

For a moment he thought he'd lost her, then she

smiled, not only with her lips but with her eyes as well.

'Maybe we shall,' she said softly, and Luca felt his body respond, not to the smile but to the implication in her words.

This was not the time, however, so he set it aside, sitting at her desk with the folder of information pamphlets Annie had collected on feeding infants with heart problems.

'Let's read them all, mark the pieces we think are excellent, and take notes about what we don't like.'

Rachel handed him a small pile of maybe ten information sheets and folded pamphlets.

'Half each!'

They read, but Luca found his attention wandering, and he wondered if Rachel was as aware of his body beside her as he was of hers.

'Pooh! Too much information in most of these,' she said some time later, setting the last of her pile aside. 'I wonder if we're trying to generalise too much. Maybe we should have a computer program with a variety of options, and printout sheets according to specific needs. Say, infants awaiting surgery who need to be built up to a certain weight. Their needs are different to a neonate post-operatively and different again to a two-year-old who's had a minor adjustment to a shunt. Then we've got babies who've come off the ventilator and don't take kindly to oral feeding—there's such a wide range of patients.'

'Special printouts are an excellent idea,' Luca said, 'and so is dinner. Do you realise everyone else has gone home? We are the last two here.'

She looked around in disbelief, and Luca laughed.

'Did you really not hear people say goodbye to you? People leaving?'

Rachel shook her head.

'I'm very good at focussing,' she said, and he knew she must be. To have continued working in Theatre with babies with heart defects when her own baby had died of a similar condition, it would have required a tremendous effort of divorcing her work from her emotions—tremendous focus.

'Then could you now focus on food,' he suggested. 'I know I had a good lunch, but my stomach is thinking seriously of dinner.'

Keep it light, Luca's head warned, and he smiled at her.

'If we're to check out if it worries you that people think there is something going on, what better way to get started than to eat together? We can talk about the papers or computer program we will prepare. Besides, when Kurt left he said he was going to visit some friends, so he'll not be waiting for you at home.'

He paused, then, sensing hesitation, pressed on.

'Think of it as colleagues sharing a work-related meal.'

She looked startled and he realised he'd kept it too light.

'Is that all you want us to be? Colleagues?'

His heart seized with something that felt very like panic, then he saw the little smile playing on her lips and was able to breathe again. But he still took a few seconds to slow his pulse before answering.

'No, it is not,' he said, and he leaned towards her and kissed her on the lips. 'And you know that very well, my lovely Rachel. But I have promised not to rush you.'

Was one more very gentle kiss rushing things?

Perhaps not for she kissed him back, tentatively at first, but soon her lips firmed as if they wanted to take equal responsibility for the pleasure they were sharing.

Then she drew away.

'It's about trust,' she said, and he'd learned enough about her to know what she meant.

'I can understand trust is hard for you when your first husband left you the way he did,' Luca said. 'But it's also about attraction, surely. The attraction is there for both of us—a strong attraction, Rachel. Can we not just follow our instincts with it and see where they lead us?'

'Straight to bed,' she teased, smiling at him, though her eyes were still wary. 'But then what happens? In four weeks' time you fly back to Italy and that's it?'

She smoothed her fingers across his jaw-line, a tentative exploration, then tried to explain.

'I know I can't expect commitment—who could in such a short time?—but...'

'But you are afraid you will be hurt again.'

Luca put his arms around her and drew her close, kissing her cheek, her temple, pressing his lips against her forehead.

'Believe me when I say I wouldn't hurt you for the world. Trust me on that, Rachel. If, in four weeks' time, our relationship has developed to the stage where we believe it has a future, that will be a cause for happiness, not pain. And if it hasn't developed that way, then there'd be no pain.'

She drew away, studied him for a moment, then this time she initiated the kiss, whispering, 'I guess not,' as her lips closed on his.

'Uncomfortable,' she said at last, drawing away from him again. 'Not an ideal kissing position, sitting side by side on office chairs.'

'I can think of an ideal position back at my place,' Luca said, pushing her hair back from her face and tucking stray bits of it behind her ears so he could better see her clear skin and fine features.

'I can guess where,' she said, smiling as she touched a finger to his lips. 'But I think you mentioned being hungry. Perhaps we should eat first and discuss positions afterwards.'

Excitement pulsed through Luca's blood, certain of the promise in Rachel's words.

'Let me take you somewhere special,' he said. 'You have been in Sydney for, what, five months? You must know the best places where we can have a sumptuous meal.'

Her smile slipped a little, and she shook her head.

'I don't need fancy courting, Luca,' she said. 'And I'm not much good in "the best" restaurants.' She used her fingers to make inverted commas. 'I like the local places, where I feel at home.'

He understood what she was saying, but not why it made her look sad. He wanted to ask, but one thing he'd learned about Rachel was that if he asked, she'd probably tell him, and he wasn't entirely sure he wanted to know the answer.

'We shall go to the Italian place again?'

She shook her head.

'Half the team will be there, and the other half will probably be at the Thai place on the other side of the park. But there's a Spanish restaurant not far down the road from where we live. It's further from the hospital so the others haven't discovered it—or maybe they don't like Spanish food. Kurt and I go there sometimes—or I go on my own if he's busy. It's run by a lovely family—they make you feel as if you're a guest in their house, rather than someone visiting a restaurant.'

An anxious look, then she added, 'Do you like Spanish food?'

'I love it,' Luca assured her. 'We shall go there, then after eating we can walk back to our temporary homes.'

He stood up, and held her chair while she, too, stood, then, because she was so close he touched her, and they kissed again. But this time, their bodies touching, the kiss grew more impassioned. Luca drew her even closer, fitting her soft, slim litheness hard against his body, knowing she'd feel his arousal—wondering how she might react.

With encouraging fervour, he realised, and, as lust banished hunger from his mind, the practical Italian he claimed he was wondered what there was to eat in his refrigerator.

Nothing Spanish, that's for sure.

'You're buzzing.'

The words, whispered against his lips, were, coming from Rachel, totally unexpected, but he met the challenge.

'In every cell,' he told her, smiling as he kissed her once again.

Rachel chuckled but drew away from him.

'Not your body, your pager. It's in your pocket. I could feel it vibrating.'

'*Dio!* I should have turned it off.'

His fingers fumbled as he dragged the demanding little machine from his pocket.

'Could you do that?' Rachel asked. 'Turn it off?'

He looked at her and hesitated, then went for the truth, though he'd lost one woman from his life by his commitment to his job and his refusal to be out of touch with his workplace.

'No. I never have been able to,' he admitted, and was relieved to see her smile.

'I can't either,' she said, 'and I can hear mine buzzing in my handbag.'

Luca was already dialling the number when Rachel looked at her own pager and confirmed it was Alex wanting them.

'Hospital, a.s.a.p.,' he said when he answered. 'The Archers have changed their minds but they want the op done now. Mr Archer spoke to me. He says his wife can't stand the strain of waiting any longer, and if we leave it until tomorrow, Bobbie would have to go into the queue after the other operations.'

'I understand,' Luca told him. 'Rachel and I are still at the hospital. I'll get her something to eat while she prepares the theatre and we'll both be ready when you wish to start.'

'Good. Maggie's on her way to do the pre-op stuff so she'll be there before too long. I have to round up Kurt and some theatre staff. See you shortly.'

'You'll get me some food?' Rachel said.

'You are surprised I would do that? Because I'm practical, or that I care enough to make sure you have something to eat before you have to stand in Theatre for many hours?'

Her soft chuckle rippled in the air between them.

'Both, I guess. I'm not used to someone looking after me. Apart from Kurt, and though he cooks because he loves it, he'd go without food for days if he was thinking of other things.'

Luca looked pleased with her answer, and as Rachel followed him out of the room, she sensed their relationship had shifted more in that small interchange than it had in the heated kisses they'd exchanged.

Relationship? Where had that word come from? OK, she was coming to terms with the attraction, but relationships were a whole other ball game…

And the conversation they'd had earlier—when he'd asked her where they should eat—had reminded her of the huge gap between their lives.

No, for all Luca's talk of trust there was no way whatever happened between them could be anything but a brief affair.

She walked into the theatre, turning on lights, her mind switching from personal matters to work, but, in spite of her common-sense reading of the situation, there was a warm fuzzy feeling inside her that she hadn't felt for a long time. As if the ice around her heart might finally be melting.

Now, *that* was a dangerous thought.

'Work!' she told herself, and set about checking the preparations that had been done earlier, and not disturbed because much the same things would have been needed for their morning list.

Blood. Maggie would see to that. Fluids, drugs, spare drapes, spare swabs…

# CHAPTER SIX

'I JUST love working with you guys.' Ned had arrived. 'Halfway through a delicate negotiation with a chick from A and E, and the pager buzzes. It's enough to give a man a heart attack, and I think, well, all's lost now with this woman, but, no, she thinks I'm just the greatest—having a pager and being on call for paediatric heart surgery. I tell you, Rachel, I've gone up so far in her estimation, it'll be straight to bed next date.'

'Men!' Rachel said. 'You shouldn't talk like that—not about any woman.'

'Hey, I was joking. I've been taking Katie out for ages now, and we were cooking dinner, not really having sex.'

'Who was not having sex?'

Luca came in at the exact moment Rachel was wondering if she'd scolded Ned because her own passionate kiss-fest had been interrupted.

'None of us tonight,' Ned said gloomily. 'I don't know about you, Rachel, but I come out of these operations seriously whacked.'

'It's the emotional strain on top of physical tiredness,' Rachel told him, in softer tones. 'Much as we try to pretend it isn't a tiny infant on the operating table, we can't entirely divorce ourselves from the facts. And it's human nature that babies and children grab our hearts in ways older people don't.'

'Because they are so helpless,' Luca said, then he

changed the subject. 'I brought a meal for you. It is in the lounge. Will you have coffee?'

Rachel glanced around the theatre, checking again that all was in readiness.

'Yes, please,' she said, then crossed to check the trolley that held spares of everything the surgeons could possibly need.

'That's pretty nice, a doctor getting food for a theatre nurse,' Ned said. 'The guy sweet on you?'

Sweet on me, or looking for a pleasant sexual liaison for the four weeks he's in Sydney? For all Luca's talk of trust, Rachel still didn't know, but the big problem was that she wasn't sure she cared...

In fact, an affair without emotional entanglements might be just what she needed to finally get over Jake and his defection.

With an affair, there'd be no need to worry about the future—no question of having children...

'I don't think so,' she said to Ned, but he'd obviously decided she wasn't going to answer and had left the theatre.

She followed him out, but to the lounge not the changing rooms. Luca was right—she needed something to eat before the operation started. During lengthy daytime ops, they always had extra staff on hand to take over so the main staff could take a coffee-break, but not tonight. Tonight the team was on its own.

'It's not Spanish food, but I hope it will be good,' Luca said, putting a steaming cup of coffee beside the plate of food. He looked anxiously at Rachel then added, 'I can't stay and talk while you eat. Alex has asked me to do the opening with Scott so I'd better change.'

'You're excused, then,' Rachel joked, but she wasn't sure she should be joking, for his face, as he walked away, was very serious. It had been an odd thing for Luca to do. Mind you, it had been odd for a man to even think of getting a meal for her, but to apologise for not sitting with her while she ate?

Maybe it was Italian politeness—not letting someone eat alone.

Once again she felt the gulf that stretched between them—not only the difference in their financial status she'd felt earlier when he'd talked of fancy restaurants, but the cultural differences between them.

Though that shouldn't matter. Not if all that happened between them was a pleasurable affair.

Now *she* felt unaccountably serious…

Bobbie Archer came through the op like a little champ. So often, when Alex switched a baby from the pump to fending for itself, there was a time when the heart had to be operated manually, either the surgeon's or Rachel's fingers squeezing it gently to simulate its normal action and remind the little organ what it was supposed to do. But this time, while the team held their collective breath, the heart began to pump immediately and a cheer went up from the tired men and women who were present in the quiet theatre.

'He'll do well,' Luca said, as he, Kurt and Rachel walked home together a little later. Phil and Maggie would remain at the hospital overnight, but all the signs were good, and there was a feeling of contentment among the medical staff who had worked to save Bobbie's life.

'He will,' Kurt agreed, 'but in such a short time

he'll need another op then, in a couple of years, the third. It must put a tremendous strain on the family, to be getting him better, then having to see him go downhill again with each op.'

'I would like to help those parents,' Luca said. 'Do they get help from the government? From church organisations? I know their worry was the cost to the other members of their family—do they have in Australia financial support for people like the Archers?'

'I don't know,' Rachel said. 'I know there are support groups similar to the ones we have in the States, but I've never enquired about financial support.'

'We should look into it,' Luca said, and again she felt the warmth she'd experienced earlier, as if Luca including her in this project was special in some way.

'But you can't help all the families who are financially strapped,' Kurt pointed out. 'No one person could.'

'No,' Luca agreed, 'but do you ever read the stock-market reports? Which companies are among those making the most profits? Pharmaceutical companies, that's who. We use their products, we help make them their huge profits, so why should they not give back more to the patients we serve?'

'I think most of them donate to research,' Rachel suggested, although she wasn't entirely sure.

Luca gave a snort of derision.

'And take the money back as contributions to their own research scientists in some cases. But you are right, they do give in some areas. What we need is to wheedle some money out of them to go into a fund to provide financial support where it is needed.'

He nodded decisively and Rachel realised he was no longer thinking of the Archers.

Something he confirmed when he said, 'I must see if I can set it up in conjunction with my own clinic.'

My own clinic? The guy owned a clinic? And as he was into hearts, then it would undoubtedly do cardiac surgery—the highest income-earner for hospitals in the US.

No wonder Alex knew the man was wealthy.

Again the difference in their status struck home and Rachel was glad Kurt was with them. In spite of the physical attraction between them—or perhaps because of it—she needed to think things through a bit more thoroughly before getting deeper into a relationship with Luca.

What if she fell in love with him?

Truly and deeply in love?

It was one more thing to worry about on top of her unwillingness to get involved because of the past…

She'd known from other things he'd said that he was from a different world to hers—different in more ways than language and culture—and while Cinderella had married her prince, Rachel doubted her foot would fit Luca's glass slipper.

They had reached the building where she and Kurt lived, and she echoed Kurt's goodnight, putting out her hand to shake Luca's. In the glow cast by the streetlight she saw his disappointment, but he took her hand, shook it politely and added his own goodnight.

'I thought you guys had advanced at least as far as goodnight kisses,' Kurt said as Luca walked away. 'I was going to do a "vanishing quickly into the building" act so you'd have some privacy.'

'Don't bother on my account,' Rachel snapped at him, though Kurt wasn't to blame for the situation.

He must have sensed her mood, for he put his arm around her as they climbed the stairs to the third floor.

'Love's a bitch, isn't it?' he said gently, and Rachel nodded.

'Not that I'm in love with him,' she hurried to point out.

'Yet!' Kurt said, echoing her own unhappy thoughts. 'Tell me at least you're attracted to him. How could you not be? He's a seriously attractive man.'

'And a seriously wealthy one. He owns a clinic! And from the way he spoke, that's the equivalent of a small, private, specialist hospital back home. You know how much money those places make. And to set it up would have cost a bomb!'

They reached their landing and Kurt unlocked the door of their flat.

'Can't see yourself in the role of Cinderella?' he teased, though his eyes were full of sympathetic understanding.

'With these feet?' Rachel said, lifting one of her normally sized feet for his inspection.

'Maybe glass slippers come in larger sizes,' Kurt suggested, heading for the kitchen to fill the kettle.

'Then the ugly stepsisters would have fitted their feet in,' Rachel reminded him, then she said no to his offer of a coffee, wished him goodnight and headed for bed. It had been a long and stressful day, made more stressful, not less, by what had been, until recently, a peaceful walk home.

\*   \*   \*

Bobbie Archie continued to do well. Rachel knew this from personal experience, as she'd been drawn, for the first time in years, to the PICU so she could see the baby for herself. Her visits there became so regular Mrs Archer now treated her as a friend, showing her photos of her other children and chatting on about them.

Children!

For the first time in four years Rachel considered— rationally—the possibility of having other children herself. After all, if she was done with non-involvement, might not children be somewhere in her future?

But to lose another baby?

Go through that pain?

She wasn't sure it would be possible...

Luca had been with the Archers the day after the op—the first time she'd peered through the glass windows into the small room to see how Bobbie was faring. Luca had brought in another chair and had been sitting in front of the couple, talking earnestly.

Offering them money?

The thought had made her feel slightly ill, though she'd known the Archers desperately needed help. But it was yet another reminder of Luca's wealth that had churned inside her.

He'd glanced up and seen her, immediately excusing himself to the couple and coming out.

'It is you who should be in there,' he said, studying her as if to gauge if she could take the emotional fallout. 'They were thanking me for explaining things—apologising for their back-flip and saying how your words kept coming back to them. It changed their minds—the things you said about giving Bobbie a chance.'

'I don't think I need to talk to them again,' Rachel told him, mainly because her heart, which she'd thought she'd brought under control with reminders about the difference in her and Luca's respective lives, was behaving very badly, and a return to her non-involvement policy—with babies and with men—suddenly seemed a very good idea.

'But they want to thank you,' Luca protested, warm brown eyes smiling persuasively down at her.

'I was only doing my job,' Rachel told him, and she walked away. But later in the day she returned, drawn to the beautiful little boy, and so the friendship began, and thoughts of having babies sneaked back into her heart.

Not Luca's babies, of course.

She was telling herself this as she walked to work a few days after Bobbie's operation. She was on her own, as she wanted to get there early and Kurt was still in bed. Today's list was long, and although some of the operations they'd perform were only minor, she still had to see all was in readiness, not just for the first procedure but for all the ensuing ones.

Luca, standing at his window and looking out at the sun rising over the ocean, saw her leave her apartment building. Something had come between them in the last few days. One day the woman had been kissing him with such passion it would surely have led to bed, then suddenly she had withdrawn, talking, joking with him, but with an invisible barrier erected between them.

Did she regret telling him of her child who died? Or had her involvement with Bobbie brought back thoughts of her ex-husband, who maybe, in spite of her protestations, she still loved?

Even from this height he could see the easy way she walked, and he could picture her face, lifted to the wind that blew pink petals from the flowers on the trees that lined the road. But who could understand women? He had enough problems with Italian women, in spite of growing up with four sisters, but American women—sometimes it seemed they were a different species altogether.

Yet he knew enough of Rachel to know he wanted her—physically, more than any woman he'd ever met.

Beyond that? He had no idea, apart from the fact that she'd be an asset to his clinic. Was that a better reason to be pursuing her than lust?

Surely it was. It had substance, and purpose and practicality all going for it, though a squirmy feeling in his guts suggested a woman might not see it in the same light.

Especially a woman like Rachel.

She disappeared around a bend in the road, and he walked away from the window. It was time to shower and dress and go to work himself.

'Will you do the PDA on Rohan Williams?'

Luca turned to find Alex behind him, about to enter the rooms they all shared.

'Of course. I have his notes. Will Scott assist?'

'Scott and Phil,' Alex told him, 'but I thought you might like to take the lead.'

'I would indeed,' Luca said, proud that he was considered enough of the team to take this position in a procedure—albeit a simple one.

He realised it might not be quite so simple when

he saw the theatre crammed with medical students and knew he'd have to explain every move he made.

'Not afraid of operating with an audience, are you?' Rachel whispered to him, her eyes alight with glee, the barrier he'd sensed apparently lowered for the duration of the operation.

'More afraid of operating so close to you,' he murmured back, so only she would hear him. 'Such proximity between us can be very dangerous.'

He knew she was smiling behind her mask, and he felt a surge of hope that everything would be all right between them once again.

Then his mind leapt ahead, taking a giant stride as it conjectured that maybe one day this could be their life—working together to save the lives of infants. He hauled back on this flight of fancy. It was enough that Rachel was teasing him again!

'I'm sure you all know,' he said, addressing the students while Phil made the initial incision, 'that the ductus arteriosis is a small duct between the aorta and the pulmonary artery that allows the maternal blood in a foetus to travel all around the body. This duct will normally close soon after a baby starts breathing.'

Someone, presumably a lecturer with the group, had flashed up a diagram of a heart on the wall, with arrows showing normal blood flow and the small hole of the duct between the arteries.

'Sometimes the duct doesn't close, and we have to do it. The echo will show you more of what we need to do.' Kurt was in charge of the echocardiogram machine and he manipulated the probe so a picture of Rohan's heart, as small as a green peach, was flashed on another screen in the state-of-the-art theatre.

'You will see it does not have clean lines like the

drawing, but ligaments and blood vessels attached to it, and the pericardiac sac around it—plenty of areas for a mistake. So, first, after opening the pericardium and using small stitches to hold it in place—temporarily, of course—against the ribs so we get a good view, we separate out the tissues until we can clearly see the two arteries.'

He was good, Rachel realised as she worked beside him as lead surgeon for the first time. His movements were neat and sure—no hesitation, no fumbling.

But it was a relatively simple operation and, explaining every move, Luca completed it, then as Phil sewed up the incision, Luca gave the students a talk on how important sutures were, and how, by placing them precisely, at an exact distance apart, the surgeon gave the wound a better chance of healing without infection and, as a result, minimised any scarring.

'You talk about me teaching!' Rachel said to him when she caught up with him in the changing room late in the morning. 'You handled those kids brilliantly. Do you deal with a lot of students in your clinic?'

Luca, who, fortunately for Rachel's peace of mind, was fully dressed, grinned at her.

'I don't have a clinic yet,' he said. 'Well, I have a clinic building, and some staff already appointed, and even a waiting list for procedures when I return and the clinic opens officially, but I have lectured students in hospitals were I worked and trained, and I enjoy imparting what I know to them. Especially the ones who are eager to learn—they are a delight to teach.'

Rachel smiled to herself at his enthusiasm. Only a good teacher would enjoy his students so much. She would have liked to know more about the clinic as well—would have liked to ask—but she held back. She'd managed to put a little distance between herself and Luca over the last few days—mainly by avoiding him as much as possible, using the excuse of visiting Bobbie to not walk home with him and Kurt.

Surely she wasn't going to be tempted back to a closer relationship just because the man was a good teacher and surgeon? Surely the less she knew about Luca the better.

She showered and changed, intending to walk back to her flat for lunch, knowing the exercise would get the kinks out of her body and relax her muscles before the afternoon session.

Had Luca guessed her intention that she saw him just ahead of her on the pathway leading out of the hospital?

Two choices. Walk behind him all the way back to their separate apartments and be acutely embarrassed if he turned for some reason and saw her stalking him.

Or call his name.

She called his name.

'You're going home?' he asked, slowing his pace so she could catch up with him.

'I often do when we have two sessions in Theatre in one day. I find the fresh air clears my head and the walk helps me unstiffen.'

'Unstiffen—I like that word.'

Relief helped the unstiffening process. They were going to have a nice, neutral, non-involvement conversation. The distance she'd cultivated so carefully would remain!

'I'm not sure it is a word,' Rachel admitted. 'But it does describe what I feel I need. It's not that I'm tense during operations—well, not during most of them—but my joints seem to seize up and I need a brisk walk to shake them loose.'

Luca laughed and put an arm around her shoulders.

Casual as it was, it still did away with the nice, neutral, non-involvement idea.

Maybe not from his side, but the heat skating along her nerves with silken insistence certainly had ruined it from her side.

Would a wild romp in bed with Luca unstiffen all her joints as effectively as walking?

Unstiffen something, she thought irreverently, then she chided herself for such an earthy thought.

What was happening to her, that sex was so often in the forefront of her mind?

Sex and babies, though of the two, the 'babies' part was infinitely more scary!

Could she put it down to the long period of time where there'd been none of either in her life—when she'd avoided babies like the plague and hadn't felt even mildly interested in a physical relationship?

And, forgetting babies, could that be nothing more than a build-up of frustration, though she was reasonably sure she hadn't felt frustrated?

'Is it such a puzzle you are contemplating?' Luca asked, when they reached the entrance to her building. She turned to him, eyebrows raised in query.

'You are frowning—almost fiercely. I'm hoping I'm not the cause.'

'Only in part,' Rachel told him, smiling because it was the truth. For whatever reason, she was attracted to Luca—in fact, there had to be a stronger word than attracted, though she couldn't think of it. And if the operation on Bobbie Archer hadn't been called for that evening when they'd kissed, she knew there was a ninety-nine point nine per cent chance they'd have ended up in bed.

And if that had happened, she'd no longer have been frustrated, and that would no longer have been a reason for how she was feeling.

Luca was watching her as if trying to read her thoughts, and she was glad he couldn't because if they didn't make sense to her, they certainly wouldn't make sense to him.

# CHAPTER SEVEN

THEY talked of the operation as they walked, and of Bobbie Archer's progress, but beneath the conversation something else was going on. Like sub-titles in a foreign film, Luca's body spoke to hers, and for all she tried to stop it, her body responded.

'Well, here we are. I'm off upstairs for a quick peanut butter and jelly sandwich.'

Luca's face showed such disgust she had to laugh.

'It's comfort food,' she said to him.

'And you need comfort?' His voice, deep and husky, and his eyes, suddenly hot with desire, told her just what manner of comfort he was offering.

'Not that kind of comfort,' she said, though her heart was beating erratically, and her breath coming fast and shallow. 'Peanut butter and jelly—they're reminders of home, and childhood—of simple things and simpler times when I didn't know beautiful children like Reece and Bobbie could be born with heart defects.'

'I, too, like simple things,' Luca said, and Rachel hesitated. Should she invite Luca into her house? The fairy-tale that still fluttered around in her thoughts switched from Cinderella to Red Riding Hood, and though Luca was no wolf, he nonetheless represented danger.

'Well, peanut butter, jelly and bread are the only things I know for sure we have in the pantry. Some days the refrigerator harbours cheese and ham and

97

fruit, but on other days its shelves are bare, apart from mystery objects sprouting hairy blue mould.'

'I need to collect some papers from my apartment,' Luca said, and Rachel laughed.

'Very subtle! In that case, I'll see you later.'

'You will indeed,' Luca promised, then he leaned forward and kissed her on the lips. Rachel felt a tremor of desire begin, not at the point of contact with Luca's lips, but deep inside her belly.

A barely heard whimper of need fluttered from her lips. Luca drew her close, hugged her tight, then stepped away.

'It's as well you only had peanut and jelly to offer. Had I come inside we might not have wasted time on food. I'll meet you back here in twenty minutes, and we will walk decorously back to the hospital together.'

He smiled and touched a finger to her lips. 'So proper, though proper is not how I wish to be with you.'

It was all too much for Rachel and she moved swiftly away, amazed she hadn't melted with desire right there on the footpath.

What would a puddle of desire look like? she wondered as she climbed the steps. And if a kiss could turn her boneless, what would making love with Luca do to her?

Oh, dear!

She unlocked her door and stepped into the flat. With her knick-knacks scattered around and Kurt's jazz musician posters on the walls, it should have felt like home, but it still had the soulless feeling of rented space—of a temporary abode too long inhabited by people passing through.

Was that what she was doing? Physically, she was making a sandwich—and, having found a fresh to-mato, using that instead of comfort food—but was she just passing through life? Had the death of Reece and Jake's defection turned her into an onlooker in life rather than a participant?

It was a sobering realisation, and though she argued she actively participated in work and work-related matters, she knew as far as her social life went, it was true.

'So?' she asked herself as she walked back down the stairs.

The word echoed in the stairwell but no one an-swered—the ghosts of those other people who'd passed through before her not offering any advice at all!

Luca watched her walk out the front door. Long-limbed and lithe, she moved with an unconscious grace that he knew was as much a part of her as breathing. He also knew if he complimented her on it, she would be embarrassed rather than pleased.

He had dated American women before, and had not found them so different, but this one? At times it seemed she was from another planet, not just another country.

She did not like compliments or fancy restaurants and though she had kissed him with such passion—or perhaps because of it?—she then changed and held him some way apart, so he had no idea whether his pursuit was gaining ground or losing it.

'You move beautifully, gracefully.'

'Crikey!' she said, then she laughed.

'I knew you would laugh if I told you,' Luca muttered at her. 'Why are you so afraid of compliments? I wouldn't offer false praise, but I see your grace and it feels right to speak of it.'

She turned towards him and he could see her embarrassment not only in a high wash of colour on her cheekbones but in her expressive eyes as well.

'I'm sorry, but I'm not used to people telling me things like that. I don't know how to react.'

He took her hand and brought it to her lips.

'You smile at me, and you say, ''Thank you, Luca.'' Is that so hard?'

'No, I guess not, but if I accept your compliment— that I walk gracefully—I know for sure the next thing I'm going to do is trip over something and make a complete fool of myself. I'm not good at this stuff, Luca.'

She had walked on and he kept pace with her.

'Then let me teach you,' he suggested.

Silence, though he felt her body tense, and he knew she was thinking of lessons of another kind—as he was all the time when he was with her. Though they would teach each other in the bedroom—he was not vain enough to think otherwise.

Then she smiled and he felt as if the sun had come out from behind clouds. Such a cliché, he thought, but what other way to describe a feeling that made the day brighter and his body warmer?

'OK,' she said, and he knew she understood the implications of both his suggestion and her own reply. Their relationship had moved in the right direction at last!

But the afternoon was tough, and the final operation on an eighteen-month-old boy with coarctation of the aorta—a significant narrowing of the body's main artery, preventing blood circulating properly through the body—became complicated when Phil, who was operating, discovered the little patient's body had produced subsidiary vessels in an attempt to fix the problem and, rather than just removing the narrow part of the aorta and rejoining the ends, he had to find out where the new vessels led before he could move them.

'Damn, that's a coronary artery we've cut, Scott, not a subsidiary,' Phil said, as blood spurted everywhere.

'I'll sew it up,' Luca said calmly, 'while you continue with what you are doing, Phil.'

But the coronary arteries supplied the heart muscle with the blood they need to keep pumping, and without that blood the heart grew sluggish. Rachel could see the little organ swelling as blood collected within it.

'Damn!' Phil said again, while Rachel gently squeezed the bloated heart to help it pump.

Luca, she knew, would be sewing swiftly, reconnecting the two ends of the severed artery neatly and efficiently. This was what being part of a team was all about.

But the stress level had risen and when they were finally done, they all suffered let-down.

'We need better information before we cut,' Alex said later, when the team was gathered in the lounge after the final operation. They were all still in various degrees of theatre garb, as a caffeine fix had seemed more important than a shower.

'Better echo pictures,' Rachel said. 'Surely subsidiary vessels that size would have shown up in echocardiograms.'

'They should have,' Phil said, 'but when you think of the maze of vessels running around, into and out of a baby's heart, it's a wonder we get as much information as we do.'

'You're right,' Alex said, 'but maybe in future we should try to build a model of the situation so we've a three-dimensional representation of what we'll find before we get in there.'

'We don't have time for model-building in most situations,' Phil reminded him.

'And with patients like that baby—Andrew, wasn't he?—most of the information we had to hand was from the transferring hospital.'

'I know, but we still have to do better.'

Alex turned to Luca.

'In your clinic will you have your own specialist radiologist—an echocardiologist—so you can ask for the pictures you want?'

'He's already appointed and, like me, is currently expanding his knowledge, but in a hospital in London.'

'That's good,' Alex told him. 'We have our own man back home, but I'm beginning to believe to make a small unit like this work properly we need an echocardiologist attached to the team. He'll soon learn exactly what we need, and can do the follow-up scans on the patients and also be used in the cath lab for catheterisations. There'd be enough work.'

Alex sounded tired, although he hadn't been in Theatre for the final operation.

Luca looked around the room and realised just how much of themselves this team put into their work. It was already after eight at night, and they all still had to shower and dress and make their way home.

Although he suspected Alex would remain at the hospital until he was sure all today's patients were stable.

It was what he, Luca, would have done in the circumstances.

But these were not his circumstances, and as Alex declared a day off for the whole team for the following day, Luca glanced across at Rachel, who met his eyes and smiled.

Just a smile, but his body responded with a burst of testosterone that had his heart thudding in his chest.

*Dio!* He was hardly so frustrated that a smile could do this to him! Even with the promise behind the smile, he should not have been affected quite so strongly.

Was it more than lust he felt for Rachel?

Not that it was just lust—he liked her a lot. She was already, he thought, a friend.

But beyond lust?

Unable to answer any of the questions in his head, he stood up and headed for the changing rooms. He'd have a shower, dress, then walk her home. Maybe tonight they'd get to the Spanish restaurant. It was sure to be open late.

And after that, with a free day ahead tomorrow— well, who knew?

More excitement stirred and he hurried to the showers.

Rachel sat in the lounge while the team filtered out, timing their moves for when they thought the showers would be free.

Kurt, who'd followed Luca out, returned, all shiny clean and with the air of a man with fun on his mind.

'Don't expect me home,' he said to Rachel, bending to drop a kiss on her head. 'And if you've got an ounce of sense, you won't be home tonight either.'

Rachel looked up at him, and saw concern as well as mischief in his eyes.

'I'm scared about this,' she told him, and he sat down on the couch beside her and put his arm around her shoulders.

'Of course you are. You're practically a virgin, for all you've been married and had a baby. And you've still got all the old hang-ups in your head. Will he still respect me in the morning, and all that rubbish. Forget it, Rach, and go into it to have fun. Think pleasure and enjoyment. You're not Cinderella. You've got a full and rewarding life, so you don't need rescuing from the kitchen, but you do need some relaxation.'

Rachel laughed.

'I guess that's one way of putting it, but aren't there deep-breathing techniques for relaxation? Or I could take up yoga.'

'You know what I mean,' Kurt growled at her. 'And if he asks you out somewhere swish to dinner, wear the black. Do not climb into your ancient jeans and that green T you're so fond of. And take that sexy black trench coat I bought you for your birthday if you need warmth, not your old, bulky knit cardigan.'

'Yes, master!' Rachel saluted him, but his words had given her confidence. OK, her jeans and the green T might give her more confidence, but the fact that Kurt cared and, knowing that whatever happened, he'd always be there for her filled her with gladness.

He kissed her cheek and departed, leaving Rachel alone in the lounge, knowing she had to shower and change back into civvies, then...

Then what? Maybe she was making mountains out of molehills—cliché central!—and Luca hadn't even waited for her.

Maybe she'd misread the sub-titles earlier and all he intended teaching her was how to accept compliments gracefully.

She stood up and walked through to the changing room, deserted now except for Maggie who, as the anaesthetist, always saw their young patients safely back to the PICU so was always last to shower and change.

'Going to do something exciting on your day off?' Rachel asked her, and Maggie nodded.

'Very exciting, as far as I'm concerned. I'm going to spend the entire day in bed. The problems we've had lately, I can't think when I last had a sleep-in, let alone a day in bed.'

Then she blushed and Rachel laughed.

'I pictured you sleeping, not doing anything else,' she hurried to assure her friend.

Maggie smiled at her.

'Well,' she admitted shyly, 'there might be a little of something else.' Then she changed the subject. 'And you? Any plans?'

Rachel felt the heat start in her abdomen and rise towards her face so she was certain her whole body was blushing.

'Nothing special,' she managed to gulp, then she dashed into the shower cubicle and turned on the taps.

*    *    *

Luca, no doubt guessing she'd eventually return to their rooms to sign off on the operation, was waiting for her there.

'You've been thinking new thoughts about the situation between us?' he said quietly. 'I said before I wouldn't rush you.'

'Second thoughts, we call them.' She was slightly put out by the ease with which he seemed to read her mind. 'I suppose I have, but you're not rushing me.'

He smiled and she felt the last resisting chips of ice around her heart melt, and her body go on full alert, her nerve-endings so attuned to him that her nipples tightened.

'I refuse to kiss you here, for if we start we may not get home. We'll eat first. You will show me your Spanish restaurant, then let the night unfold as it will.'

He waited while she tidied her desk then they left the rooms together, not touching at all, though Rachel was so sensitised to his presence that every movement he made sent tingling messages of desire through her body.

Let's forget dinner, she wanted to say, although common sense told her she needed food, but when they exited the hospital they were barely on their way to the front gate before Luca guided her into the shadow of a thick bush beside the path. He took her in his arms, and common sense was forgotten.

His kiss met and matched the urgency her body had been experiencing and she trembled in his grasp, her need so great she thought her knees might give way.

'Let's forget dinner,' she managed to whisper, though her lungs were strangling in the tightness of desire and her breath was coming in little desperate gasps.

'I have food at my apartment—beyond what we know is in your pantry. You will come there?'

Still held tightly to him in the shadows, she nodded against his shoulder. He turned her and, with his arm firmly around her waist, guided her back to the path and along the road towards his temporary home.

'I suppose we'd look silly if we ran,' Rachel said, hoping even a weak joke might break the tension.

'Extremely so,' Luca said, his arm tightening momentarily as if in appreciation of her comment. 'Especially as I'm not at all graceful in my movements.'

'But you've got great hands in Theatre,' Rachel told him, feeling one compliment deserved another then flushing when she realised the implication behind the words.

They didn't run, but it seemed no time before they were at his apartment, and Rachel, who'd imagined this might be the moment when doubts and second thoughts reared their heads, found her excitement, far from abating, had grown, and Kurt's admonition to have fun was ringing in her head.

'What a beautiful place,' she said, when Luca opened the door to the penthouse and she saw the view out across her much smaller building. To the north were the city lights and to the east the seaside suburbs, the foreshores brightly lit and the moon shining on the night-dark ocean.

'It is sufficient,' Luca said, so offhandedly she knew he was used to such luxury—to places as luxurious as this, and maybe even more so! But the difference in their lives was not going to bother her tonight. She was going into this affair with Luca with her eyes wide open. She was going to have fun!

'Champagne?'

'Why not?' she said, walking towards the kitchen where he had the fridge door open and a bottle held aloft in one hand.

'And some things to nibble on while we drink a toast.'

He handed her the bottle, and bent again to the fridge, bringing out a large plate with an array of tiny, tempting hors d'oeuvres.

The implication of this platter struck her like a blow to the head. He'd planned for her to be here. The talk of the Spanish restaurant had been just that! No doubt there was an apartment manager somewhere in this building, part of whose job was to provide whatever food a tenant wanted.

Seduction food!

Luca must have heard her thoughts, for he put the platter on the bench and took the champagne from her, placing it on the bench as well, then he pulled her to him and held her close while he explained.

'I asked the manager to organise some food for our supper—I was thinking supper, not a meal, but our hunger for each other—well, it brought us here, and it was mutual, wasn't it?'

He had tilted her head so he could look into her eyes as he asked that last question, and looking into *his* eyes—dark with sincerity—Rachel couldn't doubt him.

She smiled, and shrugged.

'I'm sorry,' she said. 'I seem to be thinking either in fairy-tales or clichés these days and the champagne and tiny nibbles—a seduction cliché if ever I saw one.'

Luca answered her smile with a warm one of his own.

'Then I shall proceed to seduce you, my beautiful Rachel. With champagne and nibbles and compliments that will make your skin glow with colour, and your eyes sparkle like bright jewels.'

He leaned forward and kissed her gently on the lips then drew away, opening the champagne, pouring out two glasses, peeling the plastic wrap from the platter and setting it in front of her.

He passed her a brimming glass, and lifted his own in salute.

'To seduction!' he teased, and Rachel felt the colour he'd spoken of heat her cheeks.

'To seduction,' she echoed, but the fun seemed to have gone out of things. She sipped the champagne— dry bubbles fizzing off her tongue—and thought back, realising that perhaps she'd harboured in her heart the thought this might be more than a seduction—realising she'd been more caught up in the Cinderella story than she'd thought she'd been!

No, it wasn't that, she decided as Luca pressed her to take from the plate a tiny biscuit with soft cheese and a strawberry topping it. She didn't want the castle, or a prince, but being with Luca, working with him, seeing him with her friends—somewhere along the line she'd fallen just a little bit in love with him, and her silly heart must have harboured thoughts of love returned.

So the seduction scenario had struck deeper than it should have, although her head knew damn well an affair was all there'd be between them.

It was also all she wanted between them, she reminded herself.

He had guided her, while her thoughts had run riot, to a couch that looked out through wide glass windows towards the view, and was over by a CD player, organising music.

He'd put the food on a coffee-table in front of her, and the champagne was in an ice bucket beside it. Soon he'd come and sit beside her and, she had no doubt, she'd be an equal partner in whatever seduction might take place. But deep inside she felt a thin layer of ice building up again around her heart, and her head chided her for her folly in letting it melt in the first place.

'You are sad now, thinking perhaps of your husband, and of the pain he caused you,' Luca murmured, settling beside her on the couch, the warmth from his body transferring to hers where their thighs touched.

'No way!' she told him, glad she could answer honestly. 'Jake's a closed book as far as I'm concerned. I realised later that I was never really in love with him.'

'I'm glad,' Luca said, taking her empty glass from her fingers and setting it on the table, 'for I don't want thoughts of him coming between us.'

He held her gently and his kiss was more an exploration than a seduction, though as his hands touched her body, feeling their way across her shoulders, neck and back, she knew it *was* seduction.

But such sweet seduction, especially now his hands had slid across her belly and circled breasts that ached for his touch. So she became a participant instead of an onlooker and through touch explored his shape—broad shoulders and the strong bones of his skull, neat ears flat against his head, soft hair as black as midnight.

She caught her breath as he brushed his thumbs

across her demanding nipples, and bit his lip—gently but with insistence—wanting more, wanting pain herself, feeling pain from frustration.

'Strong, soft and beautiful,' Luca whispered, his hands beneath her shirt now, warm on her skin. 'You are a very special woman, Rachel, and so enticing—so exciting.'

His lips, parted from hers for speech, moved to her neck, where a nibble against her pulse had her crying out in need. Then he was gone—but not gone far, simply standing up and taking her hand, helping her up off the couch and guiding her towards a bedroom.

'Where we will be more comfortable,' she heard him say, though her mind had gone AWOL and her body simply followed where he led.

The bed was the size of Texas, but she had little time to take much notice of it, for Luca was undressing her, undoing buttons, kissing and murmuring endearments against her lips as he did it—stripping away any faint strands of resistance she might have been able to muster as he stripped away her clothes.

'Beautiful—I knew you would be,' he said, when he had her naked and she stood before him, embarrassed yet somehow proud he found her beautiful. 'Now it is your turn,' he said, holding out his arms, so serious she almost laughed.

But stripping Luca, she soon discovered, was no laughing matter. His body called to hers, his skin, like satin beneath her fingertips, tempting her to press her lips against it. And if she had any doubts about his readiness for love-making, they vanished when she put her hands against the black silk of his briefs.

Desire rendered her light-headed, almost dizzy, but

then Luca was kissing her again, and together, naked and entwined, they found the bed.

'You will make the pace, remember,' he whispered, as he drew a line with his finger from her breast to the junction of her thighs. 'You'll tell me to go fast or go slow.'

'I can barely think, let alone talk,' Rachel replied, teasing him in turn. 'Let's just go with the flow.'

'Go with the flow,' Luca repeated, moving his mouth from her lips to one pebble-hard nipple and slowly teasing it to even greater excitement with the tip of his tongue.

Rachel felt herself drowning in sensation, her nerves singing with anticipatory delight, the world reduced to here and now—to this bed, and the man who was making magic in her body.

'Ah, so sweet, so giving,' he murmured, though even without the words she knew her response was delighting him.

Then touching and kissing was no longer enough, and as Luca's fingers teased her open and his exploring thumb found the tight nub of her desire, she cried out his name, and helped him slide inside, deeper and deeper until he filled her to overflowing, his movements matching hers, bringing more and more delight until she shattered into a million glittering pieces, clutching him tight, crying his name now, feeling him expand to help her explode again, only this time he cried her name, and clung to her as if he needed an anchor to keep him tethered to the earth.

'Crikey!' she managed to croak when she finally drew breath. She hoped her attempt at weak humour might hide the awe she felt at what had just occurred.

She'd just had an orgasm of truly seismic proportions—so what was she supposed to say?

Thank you?

She probably should, but right now it was all she could do to breathe and cling to the man who'd lifted her to such incredible heights.

He moved so his weight was no longer on her, but kept his arms around her, holding as tightly to her as she clung to him. His chest rose and fell as he drew in deep breaths, and for once the man who always seemed to have so many words at his command said nothing.

But the kisses he pressed on her hair and her skin were gentle—even loving—and she knew from the tremors she'd felt in his body that his satisfaction had been as great as hers.

He lifted himself on one elbow and looked down into her face, tracing her profile with his finger.

'If I get the champagne and food, will you be upset?'

She couldn't read his eyes as the only light in the room came from beyond the open door, but she could hear uncertainty in his voice.

She raised her head far enough to kiss him on the lips.

'I'll only be upset for as long as it takes you to get them,' she told him. 'Once you're back again, I'll have no reason to be upset.'

And she wouldn't, she told herself as she sat up and turned on the bedside light so she could untangle the sheet and pull it over her body to hide her nakedness.

Making love with Luca had been a revelation of just how wonderful an experience it should be, and she had every intention of enjoying it again. As often as possible over the next three weeks.

She was going to have fun and if, at the end, losing Luca meant the ice-pack would once again form around her heart, then too bad.

He returned, set the glasses on the bedside table and filled them, then sat beside her on the edge of the bed. He pressed one glass into her hands, drew the sheet down so he could see her breasts, and raised his glass to hers.

'To love between us,' he said, sipping the cold liquid then bending, his tongue still cold, to lick at first one nipple then the other.

'I'll choke to death if you do that while I'm drinking!' Rachel told him, taking a big gulp of her drink and telling herself they couldn't possibly make love again just yet.

Luca raised his head and smiled.

'I love the way you joke while we make love,' he said. 'That word you used—"crikey"—it said so much I should have echoed it.'

He sipped his drink again and this time fed her lips with the taste of champagne from his tongue, but his hands were on her breasts, and her heart was pounding.

In a couple of effortless minutes Luca had readied her for love again, and her body called to him to take it and make his magic within it once more.

'It should not be possible,' he said, taking her hand in his and guiding it to the irrefutable evidence of his readiness. 'You have potent powers, my beautiful Rachel. Too potent for resistance.'

But this time it was she who took the glass from his hand, and she who led the way along the path to their ultimate satisfaction, teasing him until he groaned with needing her, positioning herself so she took charge and brought them both to shuddering climaxes together.

# CHAPTER EIGHT

RACHEL woke to find sunlight flooding the big bedroom. Beside her, Luca still slept, his bronzed back turned towards her. Memories of the night they'd spent together brought heat to all parts of her body, while concern over what might happen next stirred uneasily in her stomach.

Shower! She'd find a shower. There were sure to be two in an apartment this size, so she wouldn't have to use Luca's *en suite* and wake him with the noise she was sure to make. Once clean she'd be able to think what to do next.

Would serviced apartments this luxurious come complete with bathrobes? Putting on the clothes she'd worn to work the previous day had no appeal at all. How could she have been so totally disorganised?

Muttering to herself, she left the room, tiptoeing quietly away down a short hall to a second bedroom which, to her delight, not only had an *en suite* but the requisite towelling robe.

She showered, washing her hair in shampoo far more expensive than the brand she normally used and lavishing the body creams she found in the bathroom all over her skin.

'You smell like spring.'

Luca was in the kitchen and it was obvious that while she had revelled in the luxuries of his second bathroom he'd woken and made use of the first, for his hair was still damp and his cheeks shone with a freshly shaven look.

He was beautiful—not a good word for a man, but Rachel could find no other, especially not when her heart was racing and her lungs felt as if they'd never breathe properly again!

He was also wearing a matching bathrobe, which gave Rachel the impression she might not need clothes after all. This thought did nothing to calm her rioting pulse.

'I've ordered breakfast to be delivered for us. The least I could do as I cheated you of dinner, but I can make coffee if you'd like it while you wait. Or juice? I have orange only, but can order whatever you would like.'

He sounded strangely formal, and the skittering sensation in Rachel's heart changed to one of dread.

That was it? He was going to give her breakfast then say goodbye?

Panic attacked her and lest he guess her feelings—there'd been times she'd been sure he could read her mind—she walked away, over to the windows of the living room, pretending to take in the view of the ocean while in truth her eyes saw nothing. Or maybe her eyes saw but her brain didn't register the view, too intent on trying to work out what to do next.

Then Luca was behind her, his hands on her shoulders—strong, warm and steadying.

'You're feeling sad? Uncomfortable perhaps? Please, don't be embarrassed with me, Rachel, for we are friends, are we not? And what we shared—that was wonderful.'

His touch fired her senses but his words, which should have comforted, cooled her heating blood because, try as she might to make something more of them, they sounded like goodbye.

'I won't have breakfast. I'll put some clothes on and go home.' She could hear her voice breaking, and tried for levity. 'I've bread for toast and plenty of peanut butter and jelly.'

'You want to go?'

Luca sounded so astounded Rachel turned to look at him.

'Don't you want me to? Weren't you saying goodbye just then?'

'Saying goodbye? To the most incredible woman with whom I've ever made love? I don't want to ever say goodbye! I want to keep you by me always— preferably in my bed. We are so well matched, Rachel, why would I say goodbye?'

Rachel's misbehaving heart, which had picked up its dancing beat again when Luca had said he didn't want to ever say goodbye and had then slipped back into morose mode when he'd talked of keeping her in bed, now settled to near normal, while her head began to work again.

There was no easy answer to his question, for how did you explain gut feelings? But ignoring that, what else was going on?

An affair—that's what was going on.

Luca had left her to answer the door. Now he let in first a young man pushing a trolley laden with food, then a middle-aged woman pushing a rack on which hung a number of long, black plastic bags, no doubt covering Lucas's shirts and suits—back from the laundry.

The two new arrivals were thanked, and no doubt tipped, though Rachel had turned back to the window.

Then she heard the door shut, and Luca called her name.

He was unloading silver dishes from the trolley to the table, having pushed the rack of clothes to one side.

'We'll eat then you can see if some of the clothes from the shop downstairs fit you. I think we should spend some of our day exploring the city and I know you wouldn't want to be wearing your yesterday's clothes.'

I could have ducked home in them and changed, Rachel thought, but didn't say because curiosity about what was in the plastic bags was vying with an uncomfortable feeling that she was in danger of becoming a kept woman. Breakfast was one thing—but dressing her? That was taking on a whole different dimension!

But how to tell him?

Bluntly!

'I'm not happy with the clothes thing,' she said, coming cautiously towards the table.

Luca looked puzzled.

'I'm not trying to buy you, Rachel, merely being practical. If you don't wish to, you don't need to even look at the clothes. They're from a shop in the foyer and can all be returned.'

He spoke stiffly and she knew she'd offended him, but she'd felt…not offended exactly but definitely uneasy, so she wasn't going to apologise.

She reached the table, saw the food spread out on it and, in spite of lingering discomfort, had to laugh.

'Well, you've certainly covered all the bases,' she said, still chuckling as she saw not only crisp bacon, scrambled eggs, hash browns and pancakes, but toast, muffins, pastries and even small jars of peanut butter and jelly. 'Can you return what we don't eat as well?'

Luca looked at the woman who smiled at him across the table. With her hair still damp from the shower, and the bathrobe revealing the slight swell of one breast, she was so enticing it was all he could do to keep his hands off her. Yet she didn't seem to know it. She was edgy, and ill at ease, and he didn't know how to make things right between them again.

At least the breakfast had made her laugh.

He walked around the table and held a chair for her while she sat down, the perfume of her body so potent he could feel his own body responding.

'We must eat,' he said, sliding one hand into the opening of her robe and cupping one full, heavy breast. 'Or we won't have the energy for more lovemaking.'

He was practically croaking, so great was his confusion and desire, but when she tipped her head up towards him and he saw her smile, he knew it would be all right.

For now!

For the future, he had no idea, for she was so different, this woman, to any other he had known. He dropped a kiss on her drying hair and murmured her name, then walked away before he could give in to the urge to scoop her into his arms and take her straight back to bed.

'You'll help yourself to what you like?' he said, sitting down across from her.

'Anything?' she teased, and he knew from the glint in her eyes that she, too, was aroused.

'Food!' he reminded her. 'Any of the food!'

'And later?'

'There will be time for other choices.'

He breathed more easily now, certain they were over whatever had caused her uneasiness earlier. But he must tread carefully because, more and more, he was realising that this woman was important to him.

'This is wonderful,' she announced, helping herself to pancakes and syrup and bacon and coffee, and eating with a gusto that made Luca smile. 'I hadn't realised how ravenous I was.'

She finished what was on her plate then she smiled at Luca.

'Will you think me a terrible pig if I have a pastry with my second cup of coffee?'

'I will think you honest, and delightful, as I usually do,' he said, but when he saw colour sweep into her cheeks he wondered if he'd gone too far and hurried to cover his mistake.

'I know you don't like compliments, but I can't help what I feel.'

Her eyes met his, then her gaze moved across his face, studying it as he often found her doing.

'I could get used to the compliments,' she said, her voice softened, he thought, by emotion. Then she smiled a cheeky smile that made his heart race, and added, 'As long as they don't get too over the top.'

'Ah, over the top—you warned me of that the first day we met.' He smiled back at her. 'I hope I'm learning.'

She nodded, and bit into her pastry, watching him all the time. Luca thought it the most erotic action he'd ever seen.

'If you don't behave, we shall have to leave exploring Sydney for another day, and do some more exploring of each other instead,' he warned, and she laughed, a natural, whole-hearted sound that made him feel less uncertain about the situation.

As it turned out, they did both, spending the morning back in bed then, after Rachel slipped home to change, getting a cab to a part of the city called The Rocks, where old warehouses had been turned into shops and galleries. They found a restaurant that looked out over the beautiful harbour and ate while ferries carried their passengers back and forth across the water and sleek yachts cruised beneath the famous bridge.

They returned, first to Rachel's flat where, in a burst of practicality mixed with a welter of embarrassment, she shoved her toiletries and clothes for work the next day into a backpack, then left a note for Kurt.

'I'm not too good at this affair stuff,' she explained to Luca, as, her colour still high, they walked back down the stairs.

'Will it be over the top if I say it shouldn't please me but it does?'

He stopped her on the second landing and placed his hand on her shoulders, then kissed her lightly on the lips.

'To me it means I must be a bit special to you.'

So special, Rachel's heart murmured, though her lips were still. All day her love for Luca, revealed so unexpectedly the previous evening, had grown until she knew it had become a huge force in her life.

Common sense, when she could summon it, predicted hurt at the end of the 'affair', and cautioned her to hold back, but that was impossible. She was already committed and for now it was enough to enjoy the bliss of being with Luca, and the excitement and satisfaction his body could offer hers.

Back in his apartment, the rack of clothes mocked her from beside the door, and though curiosity prompted her to take a peek—to see what he'd ordered be sent up—she ignored it, refusing to let them worry her as they had earlier in the day.

'We'll go to the Spanish restaurant,' Luca announced. 'It's a favourite with you so there will be no more putting it off.'

But first they had to shower and change, which took a while—the showering part far longer than the dressing, for they showered together and discovered how erotic it could be.

'We won't be showering together in the morning,' Rachel warned Luca as he towelled her body dry. 'If we did, we'd never get to work.'

'We could wake earlier,' he suggested, nibbling at the skin on her shoulder and sending new ripples of desire through her body.

'Enough!' she said, moving away from him. 'We'll never get to the Spanish place at this rate.'

But they did, and the proprietors greeted Rachel with their usual delight. She introduced Luca and the wife clucked over him, embarrassing Rachel by praising her to Luca.

'She's as bad as my mother,' Rachel said, when the woman had bustled off to bring them drinks and menus.

'Your mother would like you to be married?' Luca asked.

'My mother wants grandchildren,' Rachel explained. 'So badly it's a wonder she hasn't adopted some married couple purely so she could be a granny to their kids.'

'But she must understand your reluctance, given what happened in the past. Is the sole responsibility for grandchildren on your shoulders? You have no siblings?'

'Two,' Rachel told him, holding up two fingers. 'Two brothers, both adventurers who are far too busy tasting all life has to offer to tie themselves to wives and children.'

'Do you feel being married and having children must necessarily be a tie?'

Their drinks arrived, giving Rachel time to study the man who'd asked the question.

And to think about the question!

Had it just been idle conversation, or was he asking something more?

Get real! she told herself. As if a man like Luca would be thinking marriage after one admittedly wonderful night in bed.

As if a man like Luca would be thinking of marriage with someone like her at all…

She answered the question anyway.

'No, I don't, though I must admit I haven't given the subject much thought. Back when I was married and pregnant I knew I'd have to keep on working because we'd have needed two incomes to start saving for a house. There were good child-care facilities at the hospital so it wouldn't have been a major problem.'

She paused, sipped her drink, then raised her shoulders and spread her arms in an I-don't-know gesture.

'Since then…'

Luca took her hand and held it on the table.

'You've not wished to think about it. But it was what? Four years ago, I think you said. You've not a met a man since who made you think about it?'

Until now! Rachel thought, but she answered no, because she *hadn't* thought about it.

And wouldn't now.

'But you would like children with a man you loved, or would being pregnant worry you? Would you worry about the same defect occurring?'

Crikey, he was persistent!

'I don't know, Luca, because I haven't thought about that either.'

She spoke too bluntly, but images of dark-eyed babies with silky black hair had suddenly popped into her head and filled her heart with longing. She reached out and touched his hand.

'That's not entirely true,' she admitted. 'Since Bobbie's operation—my involvement with him—and, to be honest, since my involvement with you, Luca, I have started to think about it—but that's all I've done. I haven't come to any conclusion, I guess because the thought of loss persists long after the pain diminishes.'

She paused then raised his hand to her lips and kissed his knuckles.

'But I owe you thanks, Luca, for at least *making* me think about it and, to that extent, releasing me from the past so I could become more than an onlooker on life,' she said softly, hoping he wouldn't notice the emotional cracks in her voice.

Maybe he had, for he squeezed her fingers then changed the subject, talking about an opal shop they'd visited at The Rocks—and where she'd refused to allow him to buy her an expensive piece of jewellery.

'I couldn't believe the colour in the stones,' he said. 'I'll go back there to buy gifts for my mother and my sisters—they, too, will love the colours.'

A pause, then he added, 'You'll come with me and help me choose?'

'Only if you don't insist on buying me a gift as well,' Rachel warned him, pleased to find the atmosphere between them had relaxed again.

Though perhaps Luca had been relaxed all the time and it had only been her who'd grown tense with the conversation about marriage and children.

Their meal arrived, the Spanish woman having decided what they'd eat.

'She always does that,' Rachel explained. 'I know she gives the guests a menu, but whether they have the other dishes on it I don't know, because she seems to take one look at me and decide what it is I need to eat.'

'It's delicious, and I'm glad she decided, for I'd have been far less adventurous,' Luca said, spooning the soup-like stew into his mouth.

Rachel watched him, thinking of the magic that mouth had wrought on her body, feeling desire rise like a tide within her.

'I do hope I settle down when I get back to work,' she muttered, and Luca smiled, no doubt knowing exactly what she was thinking.

'You will,' he promised her. 'You're too much of a professional to be distracted from your work.'

His prediction proved true for, although Rachel's body hummed with love whenever Luca was around, she found her concentration was, if anything, sharper.

It was as if her new sensitivity made her extra-aware of everything happening around her.

The days flew by, as if the time she spent not with Luca went especially fast, while the time with him, like the following weekend, which they spent exploring Sydney and learning more about each other, went on for ever.

Monday's operating list was always short, and she finished in Theatre well before lunchtime, so she walked through to the PICU to check on Bobbie, as she did most days.

Mrs Archer greeted her with relief.

'Oh, Rachel, would you mind sitting with him for a few minutes? I promised the other kids I'd take some photos of him then realised I didn't have a camera. I know the kiosk downstairs has those little disposable ones. I'll just duck down and get one.'

Rachel was quite happy to sit with the baby she thought of as her special charge, and smoothed her finger across his soft, warm skin.

He raised his eyelids at her touch and she could swear the big, smoky blue eyes were smiling at her.

Dark-eyed babies would start off with blue eyes, too, she thought, then shook the thought away as the eyes she was looking at filled with fright. A siren was wailing through the building.

Not loud, but strident and urgent-sounding, its cry, rising and falling insistently, made the hairs on Rachel's arms stand on end.

She looked at Bobbie, thought of Luca—where was he?—then quelled the panic rising in her chest.

It's a practice drill. All you have to do is listen to the instructions. ICUs will be excluded.

Her head told her these things but her heart still

beat erratically, a jumble of emotions skittering through her body.

'Attention, please. There is no fire so do not panic, but we are experiencing a bomb scare and would like all visitors to leave the building immediately. Staff have been trained in clearing the wards, so patients should remain where they are until instructed to move by a staff member. Staff should follow evacuation procedures as practised.'

Rachel heard the words but couldn't believe them, a disbelief she saw reflected on the faces of the two sisters monitoring the patients at the desk. Then, as the message was repeated, one of them was galvanised into action, leaving the desk and poking her head into the room where Rachel hovered protectively—though no doubt ineffectively—over Bobbie.

'Have you done a fire drill? Do you know how to bag a baby on the way to the secure rooms in the basement?'

Rachel nodded. The entire team had done a fire drill soon after their arrival at the hospital, and she'd been amazed at the extensive facilities deep below the hospital grounds where all intensive-care patients could be kept on the machines that were vital to their lives.

'Then you take Bobbie,' the sister said. 'The service elevators work on generators so even in a fire they'll take you down there. They will be set automatically to stop first at the ICU floors.'

As calmly as she could, Rachel detached the bag of fluid from the drip stand and set it on Bobbie's small bed. Then she detached the heart monitor. There were monitors where they were going, and the less gear they had to carry, the better.

Then finally she unhooked him from the ventilator and attached a bag to his breathing tube so she could squeeze air into his lungs while they made the journey to safety.

'We'll be OK, kid,' she told him, though her heart was thudding and she wondered just how safe anyone could be in a world that had gone mad. To plant a bomb in a hospital? Who would do such a thing?

She stared in dismay at the innocent face of the baby in her charge, and shook her head in disbelief.

Beyond his room a couple of aides were ushering reluctant family members out of the unit, assuring them the children would be well cared for. One near hysterical woman had to be physically moved away from her baby, a large orderly treating her as gently as he could, but with a firmness that brooked no resistance.

'OK, let's go,' the sister called, when the unit was cleared of visitors. With one nurse to each small patient, they pushed the small beds out of the rooms and formed a queue out to the service elevator foyer, pressed the button and waited their turn to go down into safety.

Waited in outward calm, but were they all hiding the inner turmoil Rachel felt?

She wished she knew these staff members better. Wished she'd spent more time in the PICU!

'So many of these things are false alarms,' one of the women said, while an aide who was with them began to sob.

'If you haven't got a baby, you should get out of the building,' the sister in charge told the crying woman. 'Use the stairs and go down to ground level and then to the muster point. Our floor is muster point five—the colour's blue—out to the right of the main gate.'

The woman looked at her as if she didn't understand, then she sobbed again and turned and fled, not towards the stairs but back into the ward.

'I'd go after her, but I can't stop bagging and patients come first,' the sister said, but Rachel guessed they all felt as tense as she did, and apprehensive for the woman who hadn't gone down the stairs—worrying what might happen to her.

To them all!

But once in the deep basement, she discovered the practice sessions had proved worthwhile for though there was an air of urgency as they pushed the small beds along a wide corridor, there was no panic. Arriving at the designated safe area, they fitted the patients back to equipment with a minimum of fuss and maximum of efficiency. A doctor circulated between the groups from the different ICUs and the CCU, making sure medication was administered on time, and that all patients were closely monitored.

'Poor Mrs Archer, she'll be going nuts,' Rachel said to the nurse who was beside her.

'Someone will explain to her—and we couldn't bring the parents down here as well—look how crammed we are as it is. Far better to have people here who can be useful.'

'Yeah,' a male nurse said. 'And far better to bury a few staff under all the rubble if the hospital does blow up than families who might sue if their loved ones are caught up in the chaos!'

'Gee, thanks for reminding us of the buried-alive scenario,' Rachel told him. 'Just the kind of thought we need in order to keep calm!'

'You're a theatre sister—you're always calm,' the fellow told her. 'Throwing tantrums in Theatre is the surgeon's prerogative, not the nurses'.'

'Such cynicism,' Rachel murmured, but the conversation was helping everyone relax, though the mention of surgeons brought Luca back to the forefront of her mind.

Worried as she was for him, she still smiled to herself, thinking of the pleasure they'd shared, glad they'd had their time of loving. If the worst did happen then she'd have no regrets.

As long as he got out.

Survived…

'They'll have to search the hospital, floor by floor, I guess,' one of the other nurses said. 'I wouldn't like that job.'

'I don't think staff have to do it. Aren't there bomb-disposal people for things like that?'

'Whoever does it, it will take time,' Rachel said. She'd decided Luca had probably left the hospital before the alarm, and this decision filled her with an inner peace. Although every time she looked at Bobbie, dozing peacefully on the small bed, she thought what a waste it would be for the baby to have gone through such a big operation and then to lose his life because someone had a grudge against the hospital.

The minutes ticked slowly by, with announcements every now and then so they could follow the progress of the clearing of the building, and the search of each floor by members of an anti-terrorist squad.

Six hours after the original alarm had sounded, the siren wailed again, and the announcement that followed told them they were cleared to return to the wards, though the intensive care units were to wait where they were until further advice.

It was after eight that night when Rachel finally pushed Bobbie's bed out of the service elevator and back into his room, where his anxious parents were already waiting.

'I'll take over,' the nurse who was standing by told Rachel, and she walked gratefully away. An overwhelming relief was washing through her but she guessed exhaustion would be close behind.

Her feet led her automatically towards the team's rooms, knowing there'd be coffee and, with a bit of luck, some food in the refrigerator. The lights were on, and as she passed Becky's desk she realised the whole team was gathered—on chairs or perched on tables—and the expressions of their faces didn't reflect any of the relief Rachel felt.

'It's over, you guys!' she said. 'They've sounded the all clear. You should be looking happy.'

'Rachel! You're all right! I've been trying to find you.'

Luca came straight to her, put his arm around her and drew her close. She could feel his tension in the touch, and knew he'd been worried. It was nice to have someone caring about her—which thought in itself was scary.

Having someone care wasn't something she should get used to.

'I was in the ICU basement—I was with Bobbie when the alarm went off so I took him down,' she explained, feeling more tired by the minute.

But not so tired she couldn't see that her explanation had done nothing to relieve the tense atmosphere in the room.

'Something's wrong! There *was* a bomb? What don't I know?'

'The women shouldn't be part of this,' Luca declared. 'We've men enough to do the operation without them.'

Phil smiled at him.

'I feel the same way, Luca, but I'm glad I didn't say it out loud,' he said. 'Maggie would rend me limb from limb.'

'Let the women speak for themselves,' Maggie put in. 'But, first, someone should explain to Rachel what's going on.'

Alex nodded and came to stand in front of Rachel, while Luca moved just a little away.

To dissociate himself from Alex's news, or from her? By now Rachel was too stressed out to care.

'We've had a request to operate on a baby with HLHS—the same first-stage operation we performed on Bobbie Archer. But this baby is the son of a man who has political connections in a country where his politics aren't one hundred per cent popular. The people who know about these things—I'm talking anti-terrorism specialists—believe today's bomb threat was connected to the hospital's agreement to treat the baby. Somehow the parents' political enemies got wind of the arrangement, and thought a threat to the hospital might make the high-ups at Jimmie's change their minds.'

He paused and looked around as if gauging the reaction to his statement so far, then, with his eyes on Annie, he continued.

'The baby has to have the operation or, as we all know, he dies, so mind-changing isn't an option as far as I'm concerned. Annie has been in conference with the terrorism specialists and they suggested we perform the operation tonight. They feel that as soon as the night staff members are on duty, and all but ICU visitors have been cleared from the hospital, the entrances and exits to the hospital can be guarded more effectively.'

'We hope!' This from Kurt, who was looking anxiously at Rachel, no doubt seeing how tired she was, as he knew her better than the others.

'Once the operation is over, and the baby stable, he can be moved to another location. Hopefully, the people who are now in charge of that aspect of things will be more successful in keeping the location secret.'

'What gets me,' Kurt said, heading straight for the crux of the matter, 'is that if the new location's kept secret, and whoever is threatening him thinks he's still here, then the secrecy isn't much use to us. Jimmie's could still be targeted.'

Alex waved away his concerns.

'We can make it public that he's been moved. In fact, it's already been noised about that Jimmie's won't have him here at all because of the bomb scare.'

'I don't think the bomb scare is the issue,' Maggie protested. 'The baby is. You can't move him immediately post-op.'

'With life-support measures in place, we should be able to,' Alex said. 'It's a baby, Maggie. We fly them huge distances on life support in the US to bring them to specialist centres for treatment.'

'Well, I don't like it,' she said, and Rachel understood her concern. As anaesthetist, Maggie was the one who worked most closely with the baby post-operative—she and Kurt, who would be responsible for the ECMO device which could be used to provide oxygen to the baby's tissues after the operation until the surgeons were certain the repairs they had done were providing good circulation.

'Moving him is not our concern,' Alex said. 'We do the operation, and other people have to make decisions about the baby's safety.'

'I can't believe this,' Rachel said, speaking so quietly that the others who'd been arguing amiably among themselves had to stop talking to listen to her. 'We're going to operate to keep this baby alive just so some terrorist somewhere can kill him?'

The depth of emotion in her voice reminded Luca of the little he knew of this woman who had fascinated him since he'd first seen her.

She'd spent nine hours in a basement with a seriously ill baby, and now this. Was she regretting her renewed involvement with a patient?

And would that lead to regrets over her renewed involvement with men?

With him?

Alex was explaining that other babies they operated on could die in car accidents—that there were no guarantees in this world—but Luca could tell his words were falling on deaf ears where Rachel was concerned. She was pale, and he could see her knuckles gleaming whitely on her clenched fists.

Alex had moved on, throwing the meeting open to discussion, assuring everyone it was a voluntary job and if they didn't want to be part of it, no one would blame them. The team members began to talk among themselves, but no one left the room.

They would stick together and all perform their usual roles in the operation, Luca realised.

He steered Rachel towards a chair, then settled into the seat beside her, sorry he could do little more than be near her.

He took the tightly gripped hands in his and rubbed warmth into them.

'The baby might *not* be killed by terrorists. Have you thought of that? He might grow up into a fine leader, and bring peace to his country.'

She turned towards him and smiled, and what started off as a polite expression of gratitude warmed into a sheepish grin.

'Thank you!' she said, and he knew she meant it. 'My mind had got so out of kilter I'd all but lost the plot. I think I was ready to take up arms and fight for the little babe when all we have to do is get the first-stage op right so he can live to have the next one.'

She leaned forward and kissed him on the cheek, and he felt a surge of pride that she would make even that small emotional gesture in front of the others!

'Come, we will go and get you a meal in the canteen,' he said, helping her to her feet. 'We have all already eaten.'

She allowed him to help her up then smiled at him again as they left the rooms.

'You know, for an emotional Italian you're also a very practical man, Luca,' she teased. 'Always seeing to it that I'm fed!'

'It's because I love you,' he said, in much the same way he might have said because cows eat grass. 'But I said I wouldn't rush you—that I'd let you set the pace—so I don't talk of love to you, except when we're in bed.'

Rachel heard the words echo in the tired, empty cavern inside her head and tried to make sense of them.

'You love me?' Her voice was as tentative as her heartbeats, as faint as the breath fluttering in her throat.

'I do,' Luca said, pressing the button to summon the elevator.

Being practical.

Matter-of-fact!

Detached?

He didn't look at her, intent on watching the numbers light up above the door.

Rachel watched them for a while as well, but they didn't offer any help.

Luca loved her?

How could he know so soon?

*She* knew!

But he didn't know she loved him, so he wasn't saying it in a 'me, too' kind of way.

The elevator arrived and he guided her inside, though it felt more as if she'd stepped onto a cloud.

With every possibility she'd fall right through it and land back on earth with a bump!

'You love me?'

She heard her own voice repeat the question, saw the other occupants of the metal conveyance turn to stare at her, and registered both Luca's deep chuckle and the warmth of his hands as he pressed one of hers between them.

'I do, though I probably wouldn't have shared it with the whole world just yet.'

'It's not the whole world,' Rachel told him, 'only...' she stopped to count '...five people.'

The elevator reached the ground floor and the five grinning passengers disembarked, all offering their good wishes, and luck, one woman adding, 'I'd stop arguing if I were you, and snaffle him up.'

She would if she could just get her head around it.

'It's a funny time to tell me.'

Luca made a grab for the closing door and it slid open again. He guided her out, then turned so he was looking at her, still holding one of her hands in both of his.

'When the siren went off, I didn't know where you were. There was a bomb scare. I thought of something happening to you. Of you dying! It was as if I'd died. Then the agony of you dying without knowing how I felt about you—I had to tell you.'

'Agony for you?'

'Agony for me,' he said softly, then he leaned forward and kissed her on the lips before reverting to the practical Italian once again and leading her towards the canteen.

# CHAPTER NINE

'I WILL not have men with guns in my theatre!'

'We are the baby's bodyguards—we go everywhere with him.'

'Not into my theatre!' Alex sounded adamant—and not a little angry.

It was two hours later. Rachel had eaten. Well, she remembered putting food into her mouth, though for a million dollars couldn't have said what it was.

Mostly, she'd tried to think. Looking at Luca and trying to think and then, when that didn't help clear the confusion in her head, not looking at Luca and trying to think.

'Do not fret about it,' he had said at one stage. 'I would not have spoken if I'd known you'd be so surprised. I thought you must have known, but now you're worrying and that won't do. I do not ask that you love me back, only that you accept how I feel. So, relax and let your mind focus now on the operation.'

They'd parted in the lounge, she to change and check the theatre, he to go into conference with Phil and Alex. So now she was waiting in the theatre for the patient to be wheeled in, listening to a conversation nearly as bizarre as the one she'd had with Luca earlier.

She'd turned at the sound of Alex's voice and now realised the baby was here, though whether he'd come further than the door depended on whether Alex won the argument he was currently having with two burly men.

Through the open doorway she could hear a woman crying softly, and men's voices conversing in a language she didn't understand. Annie's voice as well, explaining, placating, trying desperately to sort out the situation.

Then Alex's voice again.

'I don't care if they wait on Mars, but they're not coming into my theatre.'

Luca came in from the changing rooms, crossing the theatre towards Rachel, the anxiety and concern in his eyes warming her.

'You are all right?'

As ever, when he was stressed, his English became more formal.

'I'm fine,' she assured him. Utter lie! 'Don't worry about me, worry about that baby.'

She nodded towards the double doors that led from the passage to the theatre.

'There's more trouble?' Luca's voice expressed his disbelief.

'Only men with guns,' Kurt told him. 'Strange as it might sound, Alex doesn't want them in Theatre.'

'I should think not,' Luca said, moving closer to Rachel. 'This is a ridiculous situation, particularly with women involved.'

'Hey, Luca, enough of this protectiveness where Rachel and I are concerned,' Maggie, who'd followed him into theatre, told him. 'Women fought long and hard for equal rights—and now we've got them, we have to take equal responsibility.'

'I still don't like it,' Luca said stubbornly, and

Rachel smiled at his insistence. It was old-fashioned but nice, that kind of chivalry.

And he loved her?

Now movement at the door suggested Alex had prevailed, as he and Phil walked beside the trolley bearing the baby boy.

Rachel studied the face of the man with whom she'd worked for so long. It was set and hard, his eyes grim, and she wondered if he was having second thoughts about operating.

'Luca, would you and Scott open while Phil and I scrub? Maggie, you set to go? Kurt, Rachel, you two ready?'

He barely stayed for their nods before crossing to the scrub room, where a nurse waited with gowns and gloves for both surgeons. Maggie hooked the baby to her monitors, Ned set up a metal frame over the baby's head so it was protected during the operation, and Rachel spread drapes across his little body.

'I wonder why the incidence of congenital heart defects is higher in boys than girls—with nearly all the different defects, we seem to see more boys than girls,' Kurt said, making conversation while checking that the plastic tubes that would run from the baby to his machine and back again to the infant were all out of the way of the operating staff.

Rachel knew one kinked tube could mean death for an infant and, though nobody was saying anything, she was pretty sure they all felt the threat of the men with guns outside the theatre doors.

'The men with guns, who apparently are the baby's personal bodyguards, have been replaced by hospital security men—also with guns,' Alex explained when he returned, ready to take over the lead role from

Luca. 'They will wait in the corridor outside Theatre while the other bodyguards—and there are four in all, two for the father as well—will wait with the family somewhere up on the admin floor.'

'Does that mean that if the baby happens to not live through this operation, we won't be gunned down in Theatre?' Kurt's plaintive question made everyone smile and released some of the tension the men-with-guns scenario had built up.

'No, they'll wait and gun us down in the street,' Ned said, but Rachel had spent more than enough emotion for one day and didn't find it a joking matter.

'This baby will not die,' she said fiercely. 'Not if you all concentrate on your jobs, instead of thinking about what's happening outside.'

'Hear, hear,' Alex said, carefully cutting a small patch from the baby's pericardium and setting it in a liquid solution in case he needed it later. 'This baby is no different to all the others we have operated on. We will do our best for him—no one can ask more than that.'

But it seemed fate could, for the baby fibrillated badly when he went onto the bypass machine, and had to be resuscitated on the table.

Alex gave sharp orders and Maggie fed different drugs into the drip line—drugs to prevent fibrillation and to restore the balance of chemicals in the baby's blood. Anxious moments passed, Rachel's gaze going from the baby to the monitors and back again.

'Should we shock?' This from Phil, while behind him Ned stood by with the generator and paddles ready should they be needed.

'No, he's stable again,' Maggie said, but the tension in the room had tightened considerably, so it seemed to Rachel the air had become solid and now vibrated with the slightest move.

Alex worked swiftly and, though his fingers seemed too big and clumsy to fit within the baby's small chest cavity, he cut and stitched with delicate efficiency.

'His blood's thickening,' Kurt warned, and Alex ordered more drugs from Maggie to thin the blood so it would pass more easily through the machine. Too thick and it could clot, too thin and the slightest mistake could lead to a bad haemorrhage—it was a razor-sharp line they walked as the surgeons worked, re-aligning blood vessels and opening valves in an attempt to give the little one a chance of life.

'OK, three minutes and we'll be off bypass,' Alex announced. 'I'll give the word, Kurt.'

But no one breathed easy until the pump stopped and they saw the little ill-formed heart beat valiantly.

Alex stayed and closed, as if this baby were more important than others, but Rachel guessed he couldn't walk away from his team and chose to close rather than make it obvious he was hanging around in case of trouble.

He closed each layer with fastidious care, first the pericardium, then the chest, looping one curved needle into the bone on one side, then the needle on the other end of the thin wire into the other side, positioning four wires before he and Phil, using plier-like needle-holders, crossed them over and knotted them tight, then clipped off the ends and pressed them flat so they wouldn't cause problems to the baby later.

Finally the skin was closed, and the wound dressed. They were done!

'Maggie's right,' Alex said, when he finally

stepped back from the table and unplugged his headlight, rubbing wearily at the indentations it had left on his forehead. 'We can't transfer him immediately. We've all we need to keep him stable right here in Theatre. What say we keep him here until morning, see how he's doing, then make a decision?'

That way, Rachel realised, the men with guns wouldn't scare the living daylights out of all the parents sitting by their children in the PICU, and they were not endangering anyone else's life.

'I am happy to stay,' Luca said, 'but surely most of the staff should leave.'

'He's my responsibility post-op so I'd be staying anyway,' Maggie said. 'I might as well watch over him here in Theatre as anywhere else.'

'Well, if you lot are in, so am I,' Rachel told them, 'though I might do a bit of my waiting in the lounge. Shall we take turns to have a break in there?'

'Good idea,' Phil replied. 'Alex, you and I will go first. We'll take a break, grab some coffee and a bite to eat and be back in about an hour.'

Alex didn't argue, and Rachel, who knew how fiercely he concentrated during an operation, thought tiredness had probably prompted him to accompany Phil so meekly out of the door. But Maggie had a different idea.

'They're plotting something, those two,' she said, looking questioningly at Luca. 'Are you in on it?'

Luca spread his hands wide.

'Me? We've all been here, gathered around the table, concentrating on the baby—what chance has anyone had to plot?'

'Well, I know Phil, and he's plotting,' Maggie announced.

'Alex will want to see the family,' Scott suggested. 'He always does straight after an op.'

'Maybe he'll call Annie from the lounge and have her do it,' Ned suggested, and Rachel realised they were all feeling residual tension, for the whys and wherefores of the two men's departure to be so closely analysed.

The theatre phone rang an hour later, and Ned answered it, spoke for a while, then hung up.

'That was Alex, apologising for keeping us in the dark, but apparently Phil had a brilliant idea and they had to run it past the parents—using Annie as a go-between.'

'So tell us!' Maggie demanded, but at that moment the inner door opened and Alex ushered in two people, a man and a woman, both so obviously distressed Rachel knew they were the parents.

Phil, like Alex, still in theatre scrubs, followed behind them.

'Let them be with the little boy for a few moments,' Alex said, and the team members, with the exception of Maggie at the monitor, all fell back. The pair spoke quietly, their eyes feasting on their child, then the man put his arm around the woman's shoulders and she lifted a handkerchief to her eyes. Alex joined them and all three walked out into the corridor. Phil waited until the doors closed behind them, before explaining.

'They had to agree to our idea, and then to see the baby, but we are giving out that he died during the operation. I thought of it when he fibrillated—thought it might be an answer to how to keep him safe post-op. As far as the world—and that includes everyone in the hospital who is not in this room—is concerned, what you saw was the parents' last farewell to their son. The baby died in Theatre. Annie is organising all the things that have to be done, including a memory box, and while some of you might feel this is tempting fate, it's the only way we could see of keeping the baby here, yet removing any risk to the hospital and staff.'

He paused, then looked at each of them in turn.

'To ask you to swear you won't betray this child would be melodramatic, but you must all know in your hearts how important it is to maintain the charade. We've had a devil of a job convincing the baby's bodyguards that they must also leave with the coffin that will be arranged, or the plan won't work, but having got them out of the way, then it would be really bad if someone on the team gave the game away.'

Luca watched the team members all nod, and wondered at the unity Alex had achieved among his staff—though some of them had not been with him for long. Would he be able to bring such a team together when his clinic opened?

And would that team include Rachel?

Dared he ask her?

What of her loyalty to Alex?

Luca found that he, who usually planned his life so carefully, finding answers to all his problems through thought and application, had no idea of the answers to these questions. Things had seemed to be going well until his fear for her earlier today had prompted him to mention his love.

Since then it was as if she'd departed to some other place, where words alone were not enough to reach her. Tonight, or tomorrow—whenever they could be alone—he would show her as well as tell her of his love.

He would also tell her of his plan for them to be a team in every way, building up the clinic together, sharing the future.

'Well, I for one am desperate for coffee,' Kurt announced. 'Seeing a dead baby breathe does it to me all the time.'

And that was something else, Luca thought, watching Kurt hook his arm around Rachel and guide her out of the room. Would his team joke and fool around to relieve tension in the theatre? This was something he hadn't come across before. Leaving the circulating nurse, Ned, Maggie and Phil in Theatre with the baby, Luca followed Kurt and Rachel to the lounge where Kurt was already pouring coffee.

'One for you, Luca?' Kurt asked, waving the coffee-pot in the air.

'Please,' Luca said, then he sat down beside Rachel and took her hand.

'You're all right?'

She turned towards him with a tired smile and he noticed the lines of weariness on her face and the dark shadows beneath her eyes. Guilt that he might be responsible for some of her tiredness struck him, but he didn't think an apology would work. Not here and now, anyway.

'It shouldn't be long before the baby can be moved somewhere else,' he said, hoping to contribute to the lightening of tension, 'and we can all go home.'

'It's not the staying here that bothers me,' Rachel told him, accepting the cup of coffee from Kurt with such a sweet smile Luca wished it had been for him.

'It's the state of our world when a tiny baby needs two bodyguards.'

'But kids all over the world, from wealthy, or famous or in some way important families, have bodyguards, Rach,' Kurt reminded her. 'Having fame or money isn't all it's cracked up to be—it makes people very vulnerable.'

'Well, I wouldn't like my kids—if I had them—to have to spend their lives shadowed by men with guns, so maybe it's a good thing I'm not wealthy or famous or even a little bit important.'

Rachel turned to Luca.

'You grew up with money. Did it bother you?'

She saw his face close as she asked the question and immediately regretted it, but it was too late to take it back.

'How can you be so innocent, so trusting?' he demanded. 'Lots of terrible things happen all over the world, they always have done and will continue to do so, yet you still believe the world is a safe and wonderful place.'

'But it is, by and large,' Rachel argued. 'I know bad things happen to good people but on the whole there's a lot more positives than negatives happening. Look at the development in cancer cures, particularly the results for childhood cancer.'

'And take our own field,' Kurt put in. 'Not so long ago, babies with HLHS were cared for until they died, but now we can fix them to the extent they can lead near-normal lives.'

Luca smiled at him.

'Yes, here is plenty to be optimistic about. Maybe the pessimism I sometimes feel is to do with my own personal experience.'

'Well, I brought up the gloomy subject,' Rachel admitted, 'talking about bodyguards, and guns. Maybe we can agree to disagree.'

But although she spoke lightly, she was aware that she'd lost the closeness she'd felt with Luca earlier. Her personal question had struck some kind of nerve, and erected a barrier between them.

Perhaps that was just as well. In spite of the wondrous nature of the time they'd spent together, and the joy they'd shared in their love-making, she was still uncertain about their affair and afraid, for all Luca's words of love, that it was doomed to be just that—an affair.

Rachel stayed on in the lounge, but Luca had departed soon after the strained conversation with her and Kurt about the state of the world.

Kurt, too, had wandered off, so she was on her own. And although she was physically tired, her mind buzzed with speculation about what lay ahead—for the baby, and his parents, for herself and Luca…

No, better not to think about herself and Luca! He'd talked of love, but had he meant it?

And even if he had, what did it mean?

Her tired mind couldn't decide, but neither could she stop it going around in circles, getting nowhere.

Remembering she'd shoved her theatre nurses' newsletter into her handbag some days ago but still hadn't read it, she went to her locker and found her bag, pulling the magazine from its depths.

Back in the lounge, she flicked through it, wondering if there were any articles to hold her interest in her current state of near-exhaustion.

Nothing caught her eye, though on her second pass through it she saw the ad.

Or the photo of the man in the centre of the ad.

Luca!

Exhaustion forgotten, she spread the flimsy newsletter out and stared at the double-page spread. A photo of a sparkling new building took up a quarter of the page opposite the photo, and below it were lists of staff positions that needed to be filled. The ad had been placed by an agency in the US that Rachel knew by name, mainly because it was so big it recruited staff to work in jobs all over the world.

Some positions had been filled, but the largest and seemingly most urgent advertisement sprang out of the page at her.

Physician's assistant—twelve-month renegotiable contracts—the pay range enough to make her eyes widen in disbelief. Luca was offering serious money for someone to assist him in Theatre.

Language would be no barrier, the ad assured would-be candidates. Lessons in Italian would be provided for all foreign staff.

Reading through the qualifications and experience required, Rachel knew the job description could have been structured just for her, but with this knowledge came suspicion.

She tried to banish it with common sense. The magazine was a month old or even older, and the position had probably been filled.

But what if it hadn't?

One way to find out! Newsletter in hand, she headed for the phone, trying to work out the time difference in her head. It would be morning in

California where the agency had its head office. A quick phone call—that's all it would take.

'I'm sorry,' a female voice told her, after she'd been switched from one person to another for what seemed an interminable time, 'but the advertiser has recently advised us he has someone in mind for a PA. But we're involved with another surgeon putting a paediatric cardiac team together for a hospital down in Australia. St James's Children's Hospital in a city called Sydney. Starting date in about three months' time. Would you like to work there?'

Without bothering to explain she was already working in that exact location but in the trial unit, Rachel hung up.

So the advertiser for the clinic in Italy had someone in mind, did he?

Someone called Rachel Lerini?

Had Luca been wooing her, not because he loved her, as he'd so recently professed, but because he needed a PA for his new clinic?

Was that why he'd once asked her about working after marriage?

Although maybe marriage wouldn't come into it!

Maybe he thought good times in bed and the mention of love would be enough to entice her away from Alex.

Could this really be happening? How could she have given in to attraction against all her better judgement, then—worst of all—fallen in love with the man, and not realised he was using her?

What was she? Stupid?

Damn it all—the signs were all there. He'd *told* her Italians were practical! But when he'd questioned her on her feelings about having more children, and combining a family and work, she'd thought he was being understanding and empathetic, concerned only for *her*!

What a fool she'd been.

Pain she'd sworn she'd never feel again seared through her. The pain of loss, grief, betrayal…

She folded the newsletter and shoved it back into the depths of her handbag.

'You mustn't frown like that. You are right. The world, on the whole, is a good place. And if we do not keep believing that, and accepting adjustments to our way of life so we can continue to live in freedom, then the bad guys win!'

Luca had returned, unnoticed by her while she was fuming—angry at herself for being conned by a handsome man with a smooth tongue and enticing accent.

Angry at the pain!

So angry she barely heard the words he'd said—barely remembered the conversation that had prompted them.

He sat beside her, but when he put his arm around her shoulders she moved away, her body rigid with distress. Unable to find the words she needed to accuse him of betrayal, she reached down and pulled the newsletter out of her bag, smoothing out the page before shoving it in front of him.

'Your ad?'

He looked at the ad, then at her, studying her intently, as if trying to read her thoughts.

'My picture is there—you must know it is an advertisement for my clinic,' he said quietly, but quietness did nothing to soothe her increasing agitation.

'And is the PA's position filled?' The ice forming

again inside her made the words cold, and as clear and sharp as scalpels.

Not that she'd draw blood. He was heartless. Bloodless! He *had* to be!

'I do not know,' he said slowly. 'I had hoped...' he added, then stopped, confirming Rachel's worst fears.

Ice gave way to molten rage.

'Hoped I might fit the bill? Is that why you made such a play for me? To get a PA for your precious clinic? Is that why you paid me ridiculous compliments, chased after me, even went so far as to say you loved me? Is that what it's all been about?'

He looked at her, sorrow in his dark eyes, and the love she felt for him pierced her anger, weakening her to the extent she was silently begging him to deny it.

Just one word—that's all she needed.

One small, gently spoken, slightly accented 'No'.

She held her breath then let it out in a great whoosh of despair when he said, not no, or even words that meant it.

'I cannot honestly say it never crossed my mind,' he told her. 'But my feelings for you—they're for you the person, not you the PA. That's the truth.'

She stared at him, unable to believe he wasn't protesting more. He should be trying to convince her of his love. Assuring her of it—kissing her even!

'Truth! It's just a word to you,' she snapped. 'Like trust! I *did* trust you, Luca, and look what happened. It's like the clothes you had sent to your apartment without consulting me. You think money buys everything—that whatever you want you can have, and whatever is best for you must be right for anyone else involved. You could have told me about the job, asked me if I'd be interested, but, no, you have the hide to phone the agency—when? The day after we spent the night in bed? That soon?—and you tell them the position is filled. So sure of yourself—of your charm and looks and money—it never occurred to you I might not want your stupid job, or that I might just be having an affair with you for the sake of it.'

She paused, drew a deep breath, then added one huge lie, 'And I was! It was therapeutic—nothing more. To get over my non-involvement with men. So there!'

The 'so there' was definitely childish but she was so upset it had just popped out.

Luca stared at her.

'Rachel—' he began, then Alex walked in.

'Luca?'

'One moment, Alex, and I will be with you.'

Rachel looked from Luca to Alex, then back to Luca, feeling tension that had nothing to do with her own distress vibrating through the air between the three of them.

She waited for Luca to finish what he'd been about to say, but all he did was look at her with sorrow in his eyes, then he took her hand, lifted it to his lips, and pressed a kiss on it.

'I must go now,' he said, and she had the strangest feeling he was saying goodbye, not just for now but for ever.

And in spite of betrayal and pain and rage, she felt her heart break as surely as it had broken when Reece had died.

Numb with despair, she watched him stand up, cross the room to where Alex waited then, with a final glance in her direction, he followed Alex out of the door.

Out of her life?

Why would she think that?

But, given what had happened, why should she care?

# CHAPTER TEN

AT FOUR-THIRTY that morning, two long black cars with tinted windows drew up outside the hospital's staff entrance and a sombre procession led by two burly bodyguards, one carrying a small coffin, trailed from the building to the cars. Two more men assisted a woman who was obviously near collapse, while Alex walked with his arm around a man's shoulders, talking quietly.

He saw them into the cars, watched them drive away, then went back inside the building, past security men who nodded respectfully at him.

At eight a.m. an ambulance, which had come through the city traffic with its siren shrieking, screamed into the emergency bay at A and E and unloaded a blood-spattered patient. Doctors and nurses ran beside the gurney as it was pushed into A and E and the ambulance drew away, waiting in a parking bay until the attendant who'd accompanied the patient completed his paperwork and returned.

The ambulance driver hated waiting in this particular parking area as it was close to the service exit and laundry trucks were always pulling up there. Service staff milled around, bringing great bundles of laundry out to load into the truck, while other trucks brought fresh linen back, delivering it to the same door, causing traffic chaos because there were never enough parking spaces.

But the chaos helped disguise the fact that a very

small baby had been loaded, wrapped like laundry, into the ambulance, and the specialist staff waiting in the back of the vehicle had already hooked him up to monitors and machines that had been put in place earlier at another hospital.

The driver and his partner knew nothing more than that the baby had been the victim of an attempted kidnapping and was being moved in secrecy to another hospital.

Interstate, presumably, as the ambo driver had orders to take his passengers directly to the airport.

At seven-thirty, as weary staff left the hospital at the end of their night shift, the members of Alex's surgical team who were still in the hospital mingled with those departing and headed for home. Rachel was grateful for the support of Kurt's arm around her waist. She was so tense with tiredness she felt a loud noise might split her open, but the tiredness was a boon, for it stopped her thinking about Luca—and about love and betrayal and pain and loss.

*Almost* stopped her thinking!

She heard a groan escape from her lips and felt Kurt's arm tighten around her waist.

'He'll be quite safe, you know,' Kurt said, and it took a few minutes for the words to sink in.

'What do you mean, he'll be quite safe? Who do you mean?'

She'd stopped walking and Kurt turned to look at her.

'Luca, of course.'

She watched horror dawn on Kurt's face.

'You don't know?'

He sounded upset, and hesitated, as if uncertain what to tell her.

'Well?' she demanded.

'Luca went with the baby. I thought you knew. I was sure he'd have told you.'

'He went where with the baby? I fell asleep, remember, and next thing I know the baby had gone.'

'Back to his own country—the baby's country, not Luca's. He went as medical support. Maggie, Phil, Alex, they all wanted to go, but Luca pointed out it would be suspicious if any of the team suddenly disappeared for a few days, while he was not a team member and would not be missed by anyone, even hospital staff, who would assume he had completed his time with Alex and returned home.'

'And will he return home when he can leave the baby?'

Anguish that she might never see him again—and guilt that they'd parted as they had—bit into her.

Kurt held his arms wide.

'I don't know, Rach. I assumed he'd be back but no one actually said anything. I mean, he left with the baby—he didn't go home and pack or anything.'

'He has a manager at his apartments who can rustle up food and clothing at the drop of a hat—no doubt he'll do it for him anyway,' Rachel said, adding bitterness to all the other hurt inside her. Even in her exhausted state, she could feel her heart icing over.

Luca *had* been saying goodbye.

'Did you see the news this morning?'

Maggie asked the question as Kurt and Rachel walked into the rooms the following morning.

'What news?'

'Early morning news on TV—they had film of fighting in the streets. Apparently the government in the baby's country—you know what baby—has been overthrown, and the army is now in control.'

Fear that was colder than the ice around her heart gripped Rachel and though she opened her mouth to ask questions, it was Kurt who spoke.

'Was the baby's family with the old government? Do we know that for sure? Maybe the father was connected to the army who are now in control.'

Maggie shrugged.

'Phil understood they were part of the old governing body,' she said, 'but you'd think if they were, they'd have had advance warning of a coup and not returned there.'

'They would need a hospital for the baby,' Rachel said. 'Where else could they have gone?'

'With Luca on board the plane, maybe they went to Italy. He could have arranged for the baby to be admitted somewhere there.'

But within a day the team learned the plane had landed as scheduled, the family apparently unaware of the new turmoil in their country.

'They landed and walked right into the hands of the people they'd been trying to avoid,' Kurt said, as he and Rachel watched the news bulletin that evening. 'What a waste all our deception was if the rebels got the baby anyway!'

'There's no mention of Luca or the baby—just that the family have been imprisoned along with the rest of the previous government,' Rachel told him, furiously flicking through channels on the television in the hope another news broadcast might tell her more.

'He's a foreigner on a humanitarian mission—they won't hurt him,' Kurt said, but Rachel found no comfort in the lie. Kurt knew as well as she did that members of humanitarian missions were considered fair game in war-torn countries. 'And surely they wouldn't have hurt the baby.'

'Ho!' she said. 'As if! We're talking about the people who threatened to bomb our entire hospital in order to kill the baby.'

'Maybe not,' Kurt argued. 'As far as we know, all they really wanted was to stop us treating him. I would say that the worst scenario is that Luca's at the hospital with the baby, and under a kind of house arrest—hospital arrest.'

Kurt was trying to cheer her up, but memories of the way she'd parted from Luca haunted Rachel, and regret for the way she'd spoken—the accusations she'd made—made her heart hurt.

Needing something of him near her, she found the newsletter that had prompted her anger, searching through it for the ad—for his photo.

She ran her fingers across the beloved face, trying to will him safe. She felt helpless, and frustrated by her helplessness.

'Have you read the article?' Kurt asked, coming to sit beside her and looking across at the magazine.

Rachel shook her head.

'I read the ad and that was it,' she said, looking at the words beneath the photo but unable to focus because of the fear she felt for him.

'Then give it here. I'll read it.'

'Reading a stupid article won't help rescue him,' she snapped, not because she was angry with Kurt but because she didn't want to pass over the photo.

Which was dead-set pathetic!

Kurt refused to be put off, easing it from her fingers

and bending his head to read the article that accompanied the photo.

'Forty-bed clinic specialising in cardiac surgery. Apparently his sister is also a cardiac surgeon, but treats adult patients. They'll both work there.'

'He's got four sisters,' Rachel said, pulling the stray memory from some recess in her mind.

But Kurt was no longer listening and something in the way he sat drew her attention.

His eyes raced across the page, and every now and then he muttered, 'Oh, no!' but it wasn't until Rachel tried to snatch the newsletter away that he shared what he'd learned.

'Luca was kidnapped as a child! Remember that funny conversation we had in the lounge—about living with bodyguards? Well, apparently, when he was five he was kidnapped and held for two weeks.'

'And now he's being held prisoner again,' Rachel whispered, horror weakening her bones. 'Think of the memories it will bring back. Poor Luca!'

Her hands twisted in her lap, desperate for occupation, and in the end she knew she couldn't sit around doing nothing.

'I'm going to Italy,' she announced. 'I'll find his family—find out what they're doing, whether they've had contact with him.'

She looked beseechingly at Kurt.

'Would that be OK, do you think?'

'I think it would be a great idea,' he said gently, 'but you don't speak the language, Rach. For all you know, Cavaletti might be like Smith or Brown in Italy. How will you find the family?'

'I'll take the magazine and point. There's a photo of the new clinic. I'll show it to people until someone tells me how to get there—and once I've got that far, surely I can find the sister who's a doctor.'

Kurt shook his head, but whether in disbelief or disapproval she couldn't tell, neither did she care. She got up and crossed to the phone, dialling Alex's number, reminding him, when he answered, that she was due holidays.

'You're not going to do anything stupid?' Alex asked, and she realised everyone in the team must know about her and Luca. Remembering a conversation they'd had on this subject, she found she didn't mind one bit.

'I'm going to Italy,' she said. 'I can't sit here not knowing what's happening. Ned's good enough at his work to take my place.'

'You go with my blessing—our blessing, because Annie's here by my side. You phone the airlines and I'll see if I can get in touch with someone at Luca's practice—it will be morning over there. Call me back when you have a flight number and arrival time.'

Rachel let the phone drop back into its cradle, tears she couldn't control sliding down her cheeks.

'Damn it all! Alex gave you bad news over the phone!'

Kurt was beside her, hugging her, patting her back and smoothing her hair in comfort.

Rachel couldn't speak but shook her head and let the tears dampen his shirt. Then the storm passed and she raised her head.

'It wasn't bad news,' she said, smiling weakly at her comforter. 'But Alex was so kind and understanding and helpful, it was too much for me, and suddenly I was crying.'

She sniffed back the last remnants of tears and offered him another watery smile.

'I'm better now. I have to phone the airlines.'

'I'll do that,' Kurt offered. 'You get yourself a cup of coffee and sit down.'

Two hours later she was booked on a flight that left Sydney early the following morning for Rome with a connecting flight to Milan.

'Someone will meet you in Milan,' Alex, who'd insisted on driving her to the airport, told her as he followed her as far as the security check. Then he took her hand and said, 'Good luck, Rachel. You know all our love and best wishes are with you. If ever a woman deserved a happy ending, it's you.'

He kissed her on the cheek, and with tears again coursing down her cheeks she walked through the metal detector and waited for her hand-luggage to be scanned.

Security checks!

Luca had been right—if they didn't accept the adjustments they had to make, and get on with their lives, then the 'bad guys', as he'd called them, would win. In the world of medicine, there was no differentiating between the good guys and the bad guys— if people needed care they should get it. And in so many instances there were no good or bad guys, just people with different beliefs.

Thinking philosophy was better than thinking of Luca in danger, so she pondered the problems of the world as she boarded the plane, then ate her meal and settled herself to sleep her way across half the world.

At Rome airport, she went through customs and more security checks before boarding a local plane for Milan. Somehow, in the ten hours between making her booking and leaving the flat, Kurt had managed to get hold of an Italian phrase book for her though, looking at it now, she doubted it would be much use to her.

She didn't think she'd need a phrase for 'Where can I buy shoes?'

But she flicked through the phrase book anyway, remembering words Luca had whispered to her, and learning they were, as she'd suspected, words of love.

His voice, husky with desire, echoed in her head and she felt a little of her hard-won control slipping. But falling apart wasn't going to help Luca. She had to find his family and plan what *would* help him.

Milan airport was even more crowded than Rome, although she'd only been in transit in Rome so probably hadn't seen all of it. But walking off the plane into a sea of excited Italians, all calling and gesticulating to friends and relations, made her realise just how alone she was.

Until someone grabbed her arm and a small woman with grey streaks in her severely pulled-back dark hair said, 'You are Rachel?'

Rachel looked at the stranger and nodded.

'Ha, I knew!' the woman said, turning away to beckon to someone in the crowd. 'Beautiful hair, Luca said, so I knew at once, though Sylvana and Paola did not believe.'

Two more women, younger, joined them, both smiling and both looking so like Luca Rachel had to bite her lip to stop from crying yet again.

'I am Paola,' the taller of the two said, then she introduced her sister and her mother. 'Our two other sisters and their husbands are all talking to the diplomatic people. My husband is trying to find out things from a newspaper magnate he knows.'

Rachel tried to absorb this information but all she could think of was the kindness of these people, and how they seemed to consider her as family, wrapping her in the security that came with belonging.

Had Luca told them more than the colour of her hair?

'We will go to my place, which is near the clinic,' Paola said. 'I'm the other surgeon in the family. We have good friends at home by the telephone, and at Luca's office at the hospital, so if any news comes, we will hear it as soon as possible.'

Rachel allowed herself to be led away, first to the baggage retrieval area, then out of the airport to where a long black limousine waited at the kerb. A chauffeur leapt from the driving seat to take her case and open doors, and they all clambered in, Mrs Cavaletti sitting next to Rachel and holding tightly to her hand.

And suddenly Rachel felt what the older woman must be going through—the risk of losing a beloved only son, and not for the first time.

'How do you stand it?' she asked, and Luca's mother smiled at her.

'With a whole lot of faith,' Mrs Cavaletti said. 'Faith in Luca for a start—he is strong and he has so much work left to do in his life he will not give up easily. And faith that things will come out right in the end.'

She gave a little nod, and squeezed Rachel's hand. 'That is the strongest belief. We must never for a moment think it won't come out right.'

'Mamma is big on positive thoughts,' Sylvana, who was on the jump-seat opposite the other three, said, and Rachel was struck by the strong American accent in the English words.

'Have you lived in America?' she asked the younger sister, and Sylvana rushed to explain how a year as an exchange student had led to her continuing to do a university degree over there.

'Sylvana is engaged to a young doctor in New York,' Paola explained, then she smiled at Rachel. 'We have been saying we shall lose one sister to America, but that country, from what Luca has told us, will be giving one back to us.'

Rachel's heartbeat speeded up. She remembered Luca saying his family talked about everything—and laughed, cried, hugged and generally shared. But for him to have spoken so much of her? Maybe his love was genuine.

Or maybe he'd just been assuring Paola he had a good PA for the clinic…

'No negative thoughts,' Sylvana murmured, and Rachel realised she must be frowning. But Sylvana was right—the first priority was to get Luca home safe, and after that…surely they'd have a chance to talk, to sort out things like love and trust…

Paola's apartment was in a tall, glass-fronted building, the inside decorated in white and black and grey, sleekly modern and quite stunning though, having driven past some really beautiful old stone buildings, Rachel was a little disappointed not to be seeing the inside of one of them.

'Luca's apartment is in an older building,' Mrs Cavaletti said, and Rachel turned to the woman in surprise.

'I sometimes thought Luca could read my mind,

but I didn't know it was a family trait,' she said, and Mrs Cavaletti smiled.

'Your face tells all—it is so expressive it is no wonder my son could read it.'

'That can't be true,' Rachel protested, thinking how she'd never told Luca of her love, but wondering just how often it might have been written on her face.

'It is,' Sylvana told her. 'I'm not as good as Mamma and Luca at reading faces, but even I could see it.'

Paola, who had disappeared when they entered the apartment, returned with a tray holding a coffee-pot and cups.

'No news, but I'll call my husband shortly and see if he has made any progress.'

By late afternoon Rachel knew one more cup of coffee would have her hanging from the ceiling, and if she didn't get out in the fresh air, she'd fall asleep in the chair.

'I think jet-lag is catching up with me,' she said. 'Would you mind if I went out for a walk?'

'I'll come with you,' Sylvana offered, then she laughed. 'I can see you want to be alone, so I won't talk to you, just make sure you don't get lost.'

Rachel thanked her, but found she didn't mind Sylvana talking, especially as the younger woman prattled on almost ceaselessly about her fiancé in New York and the wedding that was planned for January.

They returned an hour later, Rachel feeling revived, though she didn't remember many of the details of dress, flowers or wedding cake. Three men had joined the waiting women, and Paola introduced Rachel to her husband, a colleague of his and another man who was from some government department.

'The government has word of Luca,' Mrs Cavaletti said quietly, her dark eyes sombre as she looked at Rachel. 'It appears he was offered safe passage out of the country, because the people now in command have no bad feelings against our country, but the hospital is largely unstaffed and what staff remains is over-worked, treating wounded from the fighting, so Luca has elected to remain, in part to care for the baby but also to help out in other ways.'

Rachel felt her knees give way, then someone grabbed her shoulders and led her to a chair, where she sank down and rested her head in her hands.

'Stupid, stupid man!' she muttered, oblivious to the stupid man's family gathered around her. 'Why would he do that? Why not leave and come home? The baby is going to need another operation in a few months, and if there's no one there who can perform it he'll die anyway. But, no, Luca has to stay and care for him.'

She shook her head, the last of the anger leaching out of her, then she looked up at the people watching her in various degrees of amazement and distress.

'I'm sorry—of course he'd have chosen to stay. Being Luca, he couldn't have done anything else, but it's all so senseless, isn't it? First the baby's parents risk their lives to get him to Australia for the operation, and probably put their government at risk because the coup happened while they were gone, and now this—a situation that's lose-lose whichever way you look at it.'

'But it may not be,' Sylvana said. 'When things settle down, the hospital in that place will find new doctors and maybe one will be a surgeon who can do the next operation on the baby.'

Rachel had to smile.

'I remember Luca saying something like that to me on a day when I was thinking negative thoughts. Thanks for that, Sylvana!' Rachel turned to Mrs Cavaletti. 'And that's the last negative thought from me,' she promised.

She looked up at the government official.

'If you have learned this from someone in the country, is there two-way communication? Can you speak to people over there?'

The man looked dubious, but perhaps because he didn't understand her, for one of the other men translated.

'We are talking to them, yes,' he said to Rachel.

'Then maybe you can offer them help. Tell them you have heard the hospital is understaffed and you know a nurse who is willing to go over there.'

'You can't do that!' Sylvana shrieked, while Paola added her own protest, but Mrs Cavaletti seemed to understand, for she took Rachel's hand again and held it very tightly.

'I can and will go if it's at all possible,' Rachel said to Luca's sisters, then had to explain. 'You see, for a long time I've been…well, uninvolved is the only way I can explain it. Detached from life—living but not living. Luca reminded me just how rich life can be, but it is he who has made it that way. Without him, well, I think it would lose all its flavour again, so I might just as well be with him over there as dying slowly inside without him here in Italy—or anywhere else for that matter.'

She looked directly at his mother.

'You understand?'

The woman nodded, then she took Rachel's face in

her hands and kissed her first on one cheek, then on the other.

'You will go with my blessing.'

At ten that night, when Rachel had been dozing in a chair while Luca's family members and friends had come and gone around her, the man from the government returned.

'We have found a doctor who is joining a Red Cross mission due to leave from Switzerland in the morning. He will collect you in an hour. You will drive to Zurich, then fly part of the way and finish the journey by truck. The Red Cross people have cleared you to go with the mission.'

Rachel couldn't believe it had all been so easy—or seemingly easy. She shook herself awake and stood up, looking around for her luggage. She'd take only necessities—change of panties and toiletries, a spare pair of jeans and a couple of T-shirts, water—in her small backpack.

Paola was ushering her towards the bathroom.

'It might be the last running water you see for a while,' she joked, and Rachel realised the whole family was thinking of her.

But excitement soon gave way to tiredness and she slept as they drove through the night, missing the views of the wondrous mountains she knew must be outside the window of the car, too tired to even register a trip through a foreign country.

'I'm sorry I wasn't much company,' she told the man who'd driven her as they left his car in a long-term car park—talk about positive thinking!—and walked towards the airport building.

'You have travelled far,' he said, understanding in his voice.

Inside the terminal, they found the rest of the party easily, for all were wearing, over their shirts, white singlets with the distinctive red cross of the organisation across the chest and back.

'Here's one for each of you,' the team leader said, introducing himself as Martin Yorke, an English doctor who had worked for many years in the country and was now returning in the hope of helping people he thought of as his friends.

The rest of the team, when Rachel had been introduced and had woken up enough to sort out who was who, were technical people, drafted to help get essential services working again. Phone technicians, pumping experts, mechanics and structural engineers—all would have a role to play in helping the country back to stability.

What surprised Rachel most was the enthusiasm they all showed, as if they were off on an exciting adventure.

But twenty-four hours later the enthusiasm had waned considerably. They had been bumping along in the back of an old van for what seemed like for ever. Dust seeped through the canvas sides and every jolt on the road hurt the bruises they were all carrying.

'Not as bad as East Africa,' one of the men said, and talk turned to other places these volunteers had served. And as she listened, Rachel felt her own enthusiasm returning, her doubts about what lay ahead—what would Luca think of her arriving?—set aside as she contemplated how, if things didn't work out with him, she could make a new life for herself on missions such as this.

They crawled into the capital at dawn, the vehicle stopping first at the hospital as most of the supplies were medical.

Now the doubts returned, and with them fear that Luca might not still be there. Might not even be alive…

'He will be all right,' the doctor who'd driven her to Switzerland assured her, and Rachel frowned at him. Now virtual strangers were reading her face!

The hospital, though the corridors were crammed with patients, smelt and felt like hospitals did all over the world, the familiarity helping soothe Rachel's agitation. Martin spoke the language and it was he who asked for news of Luca.

A long, involved conversation followed, accompanied by much waving of arms.

'He's here, in a ward at the end of this corridor,' Martin said at last, then he hesitated, shrugged his shoulders and added, 'But if you could see him really quickly, this man was telling me they're about to operate on a child who's had the bottom part of both legs blown off and they have no theatre staff. We'll need you there.'

Luca was at the end of the corridor, but a child who'd been very badly injured was in Theatre?

'Let's go straight to Theatre,' she said to Martin. 'Some of those boxes have theatre instruments in them. Shall we carry them through with us? These people are busy enough handling their patients without having to lug boxes.'

Martin beamed at her, then spoke to the man again.

'I have told him to let Luca know you are here,' he said, following her back towards the old truck.

'You wouldn't believe where the shrapnel's got to,'

Martin said, an hour later. He had tied off blood vessels and neatened the stumps of the child's legs, but during the operation the patient's blood pressure had dropped so low, the makeshift team of Martin, Rachel and a local nurse, doing the anaesthetic, had realised there was something else seriously wrong.

The child had stood on a land-mine, but as well as the immediate damage to his legs, shrapnel from the blast had pierced his bowel and all but severed his inferior mesenteric artery. Now, with the artery fixed and the damage to the bowel removed, Martin was searching for missing pieces of metal, afraid that if he missed one, all the work they'd already done to save the boy's life would go to waste.

'There!' Rachel said, spotting a piece close to one kidney.

'It wouldn't be so bad if we could be sure they'd stay where they are,' Martin grumbled, 'but if they start moving around the abdominal cavity and one pierces the bowel again or, heaven forbid, the kid's heart, he'll be in trouble.'

Rachel used saline to flush out the abdomen again and again but, conscious of limited supplies, she didn't flood the cavity but drew the fluid into a syringe and squirted it around.

The operating table was low, and her back ached, while tiredness from too much travel and not enough sleep tightened all the muscles in her shoulders and neck so even the slightest movement was agony.

Then the tension eased, as if someone had wiped a magic cloth across her shoulders. Wonderingly, she raised her head and looked around.

Luca stood just inside the room, a mask held across his mouth and nose, his eyes feasting on her—his face, for once, as easy for her to read as he found hers. For amazement, disbelief and, most of all, love were all reflected in his eyes. She knew he smiled behind the mask before he shook his head and left again.

The young local who was doing the anaesthetic spoke to Martin, his voice excited and emphatic.

'Seems your boyfriend has been all but running the hospital, operating day and night, never sleeping, teaching people to take care of their sick and injured relatives, performing minor miracles right, left and centre,' Martin explained.

And although she couldn't see his mouth, Rachel knew he, too, was smiling, and the warmth of the love she felt for Luca spread through her body, banishing pain and stiffness—even banishing her doubts...

# CHAPTER ELEVEN

THEY caught snatched moments together over the next few days, but time only to hold each other, not to talk. Well, not to talk much, though Luca had scolded her for coming, and called her a fool and idiot, but in a voice so filled with love Rachel knew he didn't mean it.

He was exhausted, and Martin, who was now nominally in charge of the hospital, had ordered him to bed soon after the arrival of the reinforcements.

Then Rachel was asleep while Luca woke up and returned to work, and it seemed as if their schedule would never allow them the time they needed together.

But apart from that frustration, which Rachel was too busy to let bother her, there was so much to be thankful for.

She was close to Luca for a start, and she could feel his love whenever he was near. On top of that, the baby was doing well, already off the ventilator, and surprisingly healthy in spite of lack of the personal care and attention he'd have received in a PICU. A young aide, following orders from Luca, was with him a lot of the time, nursing not only the post-op patient but other babies in the small ward.

Rachel learned her way around the single-storied building, built as a hollow square around a garden, spending time in Theatre when she was needed, helping out on the wards when no operations were under way. She learned a few words of the local language, and became friends with the local staff, finding them all gentle people, as bemused and distressed by what was happening in their country as people in any war-torn place must be.

Luca found her in the garden with the little boy who'd lost his legs, teaching him nursery rhymes from her own childhood. For a long time he just looked at her, taking in the dusty jeans and grubby T-shirt, the once shiny hair dulled by dust and lack of time to wash it, her face alight with pleasure as the little boy repeated words he didn't understand after her.

That she had come to find him still seemed unbelievable, and, though his initial reaction had been anger that she'd put herself in danger, now his heart was so full of happiness he didn't think he'd ever be able to express it.

He walked towards her, to tell her some news Martin had just imparted. The airfield had been cleared and more medical people were flying in the following day. They could fly out on the plane bringing in the relief later tomorrow.

He knew he must be frowning and tried to wipe the expression off his face, knowing Rachel would pick up on it.

'Luca!'

She looked up at him and breathed his name. Nothing more, just that, but the word was so full of love he thought his heart would burst.

'I love you,' he said, knowing the words had to be in English this time. Then he knelt beside her and took her hand. 'Always and for ever.'

She looked at him, her amber eyes as serious as he

had ever seen them, then a sad little smile tilted up the left side of her lips.

'That sounds a lot like the little speech you made back in the lounge at Jimmie's when I yelled at you and then you headed off to be captured by rebels in a foreign country.'

'I meant it then and I mean it now. Yes, I *had* thought of you coming to work for me, with me—of the two of us working together—but that was an added attraction quite apart from my love, because first and always it was you.'

Then his mouth dried up and no more words would come. She looked at him, eyes wide, the little boy on her knee also watching him.

'There's more, isn't there?' she whispered, the sad smile back in place.

He took her hands and nodded.

'A relief team is flying in tomorrow and the Red Cross has promised more medical staff to follow. Martin has suggested we fly out on tomorrow's plane when it leaves. He says we'll no longer be needed here.'

He hesitated, then said, 'I would like you on that plane. Away from this place.'

'But you said *we'll* no longer be needed—that means both of us, Luca.'

'I would go, but I cannot leave the baby. I know I haven't been able to spend much time with him, neither can I do anything any competent nurse couldn't do, but his drug regimen is still too important to his survival to leave him unsupervised.' He met her eyes and she knew he was begging her to understand.

'I can't leave so fragile a patient without specialist care.'

Rachel heard the words, and deep inside she felt them as well. This was part of what she loved about this man—his commitment to the infants he served.

Although…

'But he is one baby, Luca. Back in Italy there are dozens of babies who would benefit from your skills. Don't they need you, too?'

'There are other specialists back there,' he reminded her. 'And I don't intend staying for ever—just until we know the little boy is stable, and the hospital is operating efficiently enough for me to know he will get proper treatment. You understand?'

Understanding was one thing, but to leave this place without Luca?

It was unthinkable.

'We could take him with us,' Rachel suggested. 'He's off the ventilator, but even if he needed oxygen, there'd be some way we could hook him up to the plane's supply.'

'Take him with us?'

He looked so startled Rachel had to smile.

'Think about it, Luca. He'll need a second op before too long and, no matter how long you stay, you don't have the facilities to do it here. As things are, his parents aren't seeing him at all, but if we could visit them, or get a message to them, and suggest we do this, then, when things settle down here and they're free to travel—

'*If* they're free to travel!'

Rachel shrugged off the interruption.

'Whatever! They'll either be reunited with him or they won't, but at least the little boy will be OK. Don't you think they'd choose life for him no matter what their fate? They made that choice, travelling to Australia with him for the operation.'

Luca still looked bemused, though now he was frowning.

'But someone will have to care for him. He won't be in hospital for ever.'

'*I'll* care for him,' Rachel said quietly, hugging the little boy on her lap a little closer. 'I know he won't be mine but that won't stop me loving him, and I'll go into it knowing it's a foster-situation and one day I'll have to give him back. But I could do it, Luca. I *would* do it.'

She swallowed the lump in her throat and looked at him, not wanting to beg for his agreement but silently beseeching him to see her point. Then he smiled and she knew everything would be all right.

'*We* could do it,' he said softly, then he leaned forward and kissed her on the cheek. 'But you are sure? You would take on this child, knowing of his problems? Knowing you could grow to love him then lose him, one way or another?'

Rachel knew how important the question was, and she paused, thinking it through, before she answered.

'I'm sure, Luca.'

He must have heard the certainty in her voice for he nodded.

'I'll go and see who I can sweet-talk into letting me contact the parents.'

Rachel caught his hand.

'Go carefully,' she whispered. 'Don't put yourself in danger again.'

Luca touched his palm to her cheek.

'I won't do that—but I've built up some credibility

working here, and I think I know who to approach about this.'

Another kiss and he was gone, leaving Rachel half excited and half anxious. No matter how much work Luca had done for injured rebel soldiers in the hospital, if he was seen to be aligning himself with the old regime he could end up in trouble.

She didn't see him again until late that night. She was sitting by the baby's bed, wondering about his future, when she heard footsteps coming along the aisle between the beds.

Luca's footsteps, she was sure, though if she'd been asked if she could recognise them she'd have said no.

She turned to see him, and even in the muted light of the ward, she could see the smile on his face.

Behind him, two other figures moved, but it wasn't until Luca introduced them that Rachel realised his sweet-talking had achieved a miracle—the baby's parents had been released and would fly to Switzerland with the departing aid workers.

'So we shall all go,' Luca whispered, drawing Rachel away so the parents could touch their son.

Luca's arms closed around her and he held her for a minute, neither of them speaking—content just to be together.

'Come, I'll walk you to your room,' he whispered, and the huskiness in his voice told her just where that walk would lead. But much as she wanted to lie in Luca's arms and forget, for a little while, the horrors she had witnessed, she had to shake her head.

'One last night—I promised Martin I'd stay on duty. I can sleep when we're finally on the plane.'

Luca's arms tightened around her and he kissed the

top of her head—thank heavens she'd scrounged that bucket of water and washed her hair today!

'And I promised Martin I'd see some of the new patients that were brought in from some outlying district where fighting continues,' Luca admitted. 'But once we're home, my lovely Rachel, we will shut ourselves away in my apartment and make up for lost time.'

But Luca was wrong. Once home, he was claimed first by media people demanding interviews and information, then by government people demanding more information, then by his family, who clustered protectively around him, talking, hugging, touching him as if to make sure he was really there.

And through most of it, Rachel slept. They were staying at Paola's as the paparazzi were camped outside Luca's apartment building. Paola had taken one look at Rachel and led her to a bathroom, insisting she take as long as she like in the shower, handing her a towelling robe to put on after it, and showing her a bedroom near the bathroom where she could sleep.

'You are still sleeping?'

Luca's voice—the bed moving—Luca's body sliding in beside hers, smelling fresh and clean and so masculine Rachel felt excitement stir within her.

'Not now,' she whispered, but though he put his arms around her and drew her close, he was asleep before the kiss he brushed against her lips was finished.

So now he slept, while she watched over him, content to have him near while she explored all the wondrous feelings that were tied up in her love for Luca.

# EPILOGUE

THE summer sun beat down on the pavement, drawing up swirls of steamy heat.

'We could have called a cab,' Luca complained as he walked from the apartment to the hospital with his wife of three months.

'But that wouldn't have been the same,' Rachel told him, clinging to his arm and thinking of the other times they'd walked together along this pavement.

Luca had wanted to stay in a hotel in the city for this short trip back to Sydney, but Rachel had begged him to try to get his old apartment back, or another one in the same building.

'Not to relive the past,' she'd said, 'but for the fun of it.'

So here they were, walking the familiar street, Rachel excited at the prospect of seeing her friends again, though Kurt, Alex and Annie, and Phil and Maggie had all flown to Italy to celebrate Luca and Rachel's wedding.

As they reached the hospital gates, they saw Kurt standing there, while the other two couples were approaching from the opposite direction.

Kurt kissed Rachel on the cheek, shook hands with Luca, then put his arm around Rachel in his usual proprietorial way.

'That guy treating you OK?' he asked, and Luca saw colour sweep into Rachel's cheeks.

So often in this way she showed him her thoughts

of love, but this time, he suspected, the colour was due to other thoughts. Thoughts of the baby they had just learned she was carrying.

Maggie, too, was pregnant, and having discovered she had a luteal phase defect, which had caused her previous miscarriages, daily injections during her early pregnancy had ensured she would carry this baby to full term.

Luca wondered if Phil felt the same ridiculously overwhelming pride in Maggie's pregnancy that he himself was feeling in Rachel's. His sisters were constantly teasing him about the perpetual smile on his face, but why wouldn't he be smiling when he had so much to be happy about?

He looked at the woman who'd brought him this happiness. She was talking to Kurt, asking him about his life and his decision to remain in Australia when the rest of the team returned to the US.

Asking him even more personal questions, if the colour now rising in *Kurt's* cheeks was any indication.

Luca smiled to himself. Rachel had been certain her friend must finally have found someone he really loved, hence the decision to remain in Sydney as part of the new team at Jimmie's.

She was also hoping to meet this 'someone' during their few days in Sydney, and was no doubt pestering Kurt about where and when this meeting could take place.

Then the others reached them, and after a flurry of kisses, hugs and handshakes they walked as a group into the hospital grounds, where a big marquee had been set up for the official opening ceremony of the

St James's Children's Hospital Paediatric Cardiac Surgical Unit.

Becky was waiting for them inside, ready to usher them into their places in the front row of seats.

'And how's my favourite sexy Italian?' she whispered to Luca.

'Very well,' he told her formally, then nodded to where Ned hovered not far away. 'And how are you?' he teased, knowing an engagement between the couple was imminent.

'So happy I could shout it to the stars,' Becky said, and Luca knew exactly what she meant.

He put his arm around his wife and guided her to her seat, then, as he had done on the bus many months ago, he held her hand.

She was smiling, but he knew she was sad inside, for this was the real end of the team she, Kurt and Alex had been for many years. And this was the real goodbye to her friends, although Luca was sure they would all see each other whenever possible.

Then she leaned closer to him and whispered in his ear.

'I loved my work, but not nearly as much as I love you,' she reminded him, and he wondered when she'd begun to read his thoughts!

A dais had been erected in the front of the marquee, and above it the name of the new unit had been printed on a very long banner.

'At least no one will be able to make an acronym of it,' Kurt said. 'I mean, how would you pronounce SJCHPCSU?'

'Maybe they could call it Jimmie's kids' hearts' unit,' Maggie suggested.

'Or just,' Annie said quietly, "A Very Special Place". Wouldn't that describe it?'

And the people who'd worked to establish the unit, and save the lives of children who'd come through its doors, all nodded their agreement.

*A sneaky peek at next month…*

# By Request

**RELIVE THE ROMANCE WITH THE BEST OF THE BEST**

*My wish list for next month's titles…*

In stores from 17th May 2013:

❏ The Hudsons: Luc, Jack and Charlotte –
Leanne Banks, Emily McKay & Barbara Dunlop

❏ Bella Rosa Proposals – Jackie Braun,
Barbara McMahon & Barbara Hannay

*3 stories in each book - only £5.99!*

In stores from 7th June 2013:

❏ The Spaniard's Summer Seduction
– Kim Lawrence, Cathy Williams, Maggie Cox

Available at WHSmith, Tesco, Asda, Eason, Amazon and Apple

*Just can't wait?*

**Visit us Online**

You can buy our books online a month before
they hit the shops! **www.millsandboon.co.uk**

0513/05